A COTSWOLD INHERITANCE

Ella's Story

Ian Cullingham

Copyright © 2020 Ian Cullingham

All rights reserved, including the right to reproduce this book, or portions thereof in any form. No part of this text may be reproduced, transmitted, downloaded, decompiled, reverse engineered, or stored, in any form or introduced into any information storage and retrieval system, in any form or by any means, whether electronic or mechanical without the express written permission of the author.

This is a work of fiction. Names and characters are the product of the author's imagination and any resemblance to actual persons, living or dead, is entirely coincidental.

The views expressed in this work are solely those of the author and do not necessarily reflect the views of the publisher, and the publisher hereby disclaims any responsibility for them.

ISBN: 9798644316465

PublishNation
www.publishnation.co.uk

ACKNOWLEDGMENTS.

My love and thanks go to my wife Kath, who stopped me from throwing my computer into the bin on numerous occasions when things weren't going well. Also, to my daughters, Beth and Amy, the former for having the courage to tell me when I made mistakes (which was often) and the latter for checking and proof reading every stage.

CHAPTER 1.

CHADLINTON, OXON. 10th AUGUST 1944.

It is a fine summers morning, only a few weeks after the momentous D-DAY landings by The Allied Forces in France, which will lead eventually to the defeat and overthrow of Hitler's Germany in Europe. However, Ella Thornton remains completely oblivious to the factors that will change her life irrevocably and leave it in tatters on this very day. She is totally unaware of the reasons that will be the cause of what is about to happen, as she goes about her daily life in the exquisite village of Chadlington in The Cotswolds where she was born and still lives.

The sky is a clear blue dome above her head, while the only sounds to be heard are those of crickets gently chirruping and bees humming as they continue to pollenate. Apart from these, the only other interruptions to this idyllic bliss are from the occasional tractor as it wends its way through the narrow lanes of the village, virtually the only form of motorised transport in this rural agricultural area. All the houses are built of the local honey coloured stone which is prevalent to The Cotswolds and on a hot day like today when the sun strikes the stone it seems to sparkle and glow adding, in some strange way visually to the warmth.

The bearer of Ella's tragic news, Jimmy Dawson, the post office telegram delivery boy is now on his way from Chipping Norton some three miles away. He is very aware that the news he is carrying will have a devastating effect on its recipient because this is just the latest one of many that he has had to deliver in the last few weeks to various villages within a small circumference of Chipping Norton. Jimmy dreads delivering the messages and fears the reaction of those it addresses even more. To see their hopes and dreams evaporate in front of his eyes is a soul-destroying experience.

Eventually Jimmy reaches his destination and finding number four Bull Hill he hesitates momentarily before pulling himself together and advancing the three steps of the small front garden which brings him to the front door. The cottage is in the middle of a terrace of ten and before knocking Jimmy just has time to absorb the riot of flowers that enhance the appeal of this characterful property. The front door is surrounded by a heavy scented pink rose that continues on to circumnavigate the small front window. There is not much room between the front of the cottage and the stone wall that runs in front of the whole terrace, which is again built of the same honey colour stone. Purple and Blue Aubrietia festoon the wall, while the front garden contains a pure white mock orange, its sweet perfume pervading the whole area. The garden is completed with delphiniums standing tall at the back under the window. The whole effect is stunning, obviously the work of someone with creative abilities and no small knowledge of gardening.

Timidly Jimmy knocks on the door: there is silence for several seconds, until the sound of light running hurried footsteps can be heard approaching until it is suddenly flung open with a flourish, by a child of about five years of age. Surprisingly, the boy says nothing, but just looks at Jimmy. His complexion is fair, with pale blue eyes and his face is sprinkled with freckles across his cheeks and little snubbed nose, while his hair is an exuberant mop of flaming red.

"Is your mummy at home" asks Jimmy, but before the child can reply, a young woman joins him, smiling and saying "can I help you"?

"Are you Mrs Ella Thornton" questions Jimmy, which she acknowledges with a nod of her head. "Then this is for you" and saying such, he passes the telegram to her.

She is a woman, who Jimmy would guess to be in her mid-twenties, with auburn hair which falls just below her shoulders in long loose ringlets: her dark brown eyes appear almost jet black when she directs her gaze as she does now at Jimmy. She is about five feet eight inches tall, but the most prominent and obvious feature of her appearance is the fact that she is pregnant, her condition being accentuated by her clothing, which is a long yellow summer dress. This is covered by an apron, suggesting that she is in the process of cooking or baking, which is confirmed as Jimmy looks at her hands and notices them covered in flour which she hurriedly brushes off on to her apron before taking collection of the telegram. But the most striking thing about Ella Thornton is the sum of all her parts, which even Jimmy can appreciate at his tender age, exudes sheer beauty.

Ella pales visibly on the production of the telegram, while Jimmy waits as he has been told to, in case a reply is needed. For him the fact that he has to do this only prolongs the agony, because he knows that there will be no reply, but rather, only tears and desolation.

She hesitates before slowly opening the communication that is about to destroy her world, sensing it, but being unable to stop the inevitable. Jimmy sees the shock of horror flash across her countenance, which is quickly followed by a long-anguished wail, which seems to come from somewhere deep inside her and touches his very soul.

She sinks back against the hall wall for support, before sliding slowly down, paralysed by the mind-numbing shock that rages through her body, before tears quickly envelope her beautiful facial features: these are attended by deep racking sobs, her whole body shaking as if from a form of nervous ague.

During this time, the child has looked with growing concern at his mother and begins to wail in a lost voice "don't cry Mummy, please don't cry" and throws his small arms around her legs, burying his face in her lap, as if by so doing he can stop her pain.

Jimmy has experienced this reaction on a number of occasions recently, and realising that the mother is alone in the house, asks her quietly "Mrs Thornton, do you have a relative or friend locally that I can fetch to help you"?

Ella grabs at Jimmy's suggestion, like someone who has just seen a lifebelt floating past her as she treads water after abandoning a sinking ship. "Can you go to number twelve and fetch my parents please, and ask them to come? I don't think that I can make it there just at the moment".

But even before he can leave, Ella manages, after a series of manoeuvres to haul herself up to a standing position by using the small mahogany hall table which is next to where she has collapsed. However, the necessary effort required takes its toll as once she is upright the colour drains from her face and the pupils in her eyes seem to disappear under her eye lids, leaving the space where they have been a blank canvas. As Jimmy watches in horror Ella collapses again, but this time there is no cry of anguish from her lips, because she is unconscious even before she falls, her mind being unable to accept the dreadful news of the loss of her husband.

It is at this moment that Ella unknowingly experiences her second catastrophic incident of the day, of her life in fact, as she drops like a stone to the floor, first hitting her abdomen on the corner of the small mahogany table which collapses beneath her as she falls, causing further damage to the fragile foetus growing within her.

This has happened too quickly for Jimmy to react or intervene in any way, but he is faced with a dilemma; what should he do now. His knowledge of first aid is less than negligible and in addition there is now a child who is fraught with worry for his mother. Thinking quickly Jimmy scoops an objecting Daniel up in his arms and makes his way to number twelve to Ella's parents, where he knocks on the door. After several seconds an older woman opens the door. He quickly explains the situation to her, but before he can finish, she has already grasped the significance and uttering a "my poor girl" she takes a distraught Daniel from Jimmy's arms, before she goes into the back of the cottage and speaks to her husband. The two of them and Daniel, who is being comforted in his grandfather's arms, then rush past him and continue down the road to be with their daughter.

Jimmy's job is now done to the best of his ability, so he returns quietly to collect his cycle, before making his way back to Chipping Norton, or "Chippy" as the locals from miles around fondly call it.

Ella is still lying unconscious on the hall floor, so her mother quickly makes a cold compress which she places on her daughter's forehead while gently slapping her cheeks, all the while saying "come on, wake up Ella love".

After a few minutes her mother's ministrations become effective as Ella begins to murmur words that are not coherent but are never-the-less a good sign, while her arms move restlessly as though in protestation of where they find themselves.

Suddenly her eyes are open and as they come into focus Ella gives out a long shudder before saying "oh mum, my tummy hurts so much" and then remembering "Richard's dead, did you know".

Her mother replies "I know my love; I am so, so sorry, but we need to get you sorted and see what damage you've done. The telegram boy told us that you fainted and hit the table as you fell. Let's see if we can get you into the living room so that you can sit in the armchair".

Between them, Ella's parents manage to do this, but not without causing Ella severe pain as she repeats once more "oh my tummy hurts so much".

A slow dawning comes to her mother as she realises for the first time that there is a real possibility that her daughter might well lose her expected child.

Not wishing to worry or put her under any more pressure, her mother makes her as comfortable as she possibly can, before giving her aspirins to relieve the pain, and a hot water bottle as a comfort.

Ella's parents next console their daughter after they have read the perfunctory telegram telling of their son-in-law's demise. As she reads it, Ella's mother considers the nineteen short words that represent a life cut short. A life that means that the father will never see his children grow to adulthood, or the beautiful wife that he has loved who is now left alone to fend for herself: or the beauty of the clear blue summer sky, set in this idyllic Cotswold village setting. How can just nineteen trite words represent the short life and death on this mortal coil of someone who had meant so much to those he has left behind Elizabeth thinks?

"WAR OFFICE REGRETS TO INFORM YOU THAT YOUR HUSBAND CORPORAL RICHARD THORNTON IS REPORTED KILLED IN ACTION ON 12TH AUGUST".

Ella's mother's last thoughts before she tends to her daughter's needs are of the sheer inhumanity of those who have to send such messages, which are obviously prepared and sent on an "idiot list" basis. Thus, fill in the blanks for HUSBAND. WIFE, SON OR DAUGHTER, THEN FILL IN THE NAME FOLLOWED BY THE DATE CONCERNED.

All very clinical with no sense of sympathy or indeed gratitude for the sacrifice made.

Ella's parents, Elizabeth (Liz) and Alf Carter confer quietly out of her hearing. "Oh, Alf what a terrible thing to happen; Richard was the light of her life" and then as an afterthought "ours too, come to that. But in addition, I am very concerned for Ella's unborn child; she caused damage when she fainted, which may well mean that she has a miscarriage. I really hope that's not the case but it's a distinct possibility. I'm going to stay with her for as long as it takes. Meanwhile can you make a pot of tea: I think that might help Ella: she is very shocked. Once you have done that can you take Daniel out for a walk, I think that he would like that, wouldn't you little man" she adds as an aside to the child, who by now is looking totally bemused. "Why don't you take the dog as well: it would make some company for him, the poor little mite?"

Daniel's face comes alive at the thought of going for a walk with his Grandad and his dog, a beautiful black Labrador called Bonny, who Daniel loves to bits. In fact, the dog and the boy are of an age and have grown up together, during which time an inseparable bond has been forged between them. The two of them are completely content in each other's company and although the Labrador belongs to his grandfather, it spends a lot of its time at the boy's house. The dog seems to sense the time when Dan is due to return home from school and will go to the top of the road to wait for him, rushing to greet him as soon as he appears, its tail wagging furiously, while all the time giving a low whine of welcome.

Ella's dad, Alf, agrees readily at his wife's suggestion, not knowing what else he can do to help or support his daughter, but wanting to do anything he can to help ease the overwhelming pain of heartbreak and loss that she is experiencing. Before leaving, he first goes from the living room to the small kitchen at the back of the house to make tea for the two women.

Alf is now approaching his fiftieth year, but the nature of his work on the farm has taken its toll on him and he looks much older. His hair is now white, when it was once dark brown and his features are weathered and craggy from long hours spent out in all climates. He is tall, but heavy work has caused him to be stooped. Despite all this he has a ready smile and an infectious sense of humour.

Elizabeth is tall and willowy with auburn hair which she dyes occasionally, her one small concession to vanity. She is a similar age to her husband and they have known each other all their lives.

As he returns to the living room with cups of tea, Alf says to his wife, taking her to one side, out of the hearing of his distraught daughter "We really need to let Rachel know what has happened Liz". He is referring to their other daughter, Ella's sister, who lives at Charlbury, about two miles away.

"Yes, she will want to help, although I don't know what she can do" replies his wife, "but I'm sure that Ella will be glad to see her. They've always had a close affinity with one another: they're going to need it now, more than ever. It might be best then if you walk to Rachel's place and let her know. You can cut across the fields with Dan and Bonny: it will be a bit shorter that way".

"I had best let Mr Hobbs know what has happened, because I was due to plough several fields today, but I'm sure he will understand when I tell him" says Alf "come on then Dan my boy, let's get started".

Before he finally leaves, Alf crosses the room to his daughter and taking her face in his hands, says "I'm so very sorry for your loss my dear. Your mother and I both thought the world of Richard, and will miss him terribly too. There are no words that I can say to you that will ease your feelings of utter desolation, and I know that over the course of time the pain will never completely disappear, but he would have wanted you to be strong, for Dan and the new baby's sake." As he embraces her, Ella takes comfort from her father's strong calloused hands which gently brush away her tears, before he kisses her softly on her forehead, after which he finally stands and leaves the room with his grandson and Bonny.

Rachel arrives just before mid-day, having pedalled furiously on her bike all the way from Charlbury. Not bothering to dismount properly, she throws it against the wall in her haste, before hurrying down the passageway next to the house to get entry through the back door. As she comes into the living room she is met by her mother holding a finger to her lips, who says in a whisper "Hello my love, thank you for coming: let's go into the kitchen where we can talk, I gave her a water bottle and some aspirins, because she was shivering with shock about an hour ago".

As they move into the kitchen, they continue in hushed voices so that Ella cannot hear and Rachel replies "I know how she feels mum, I feel a bit like that too, what a dreadful thing to happen. Oh, I know that there's a war on, but you never think that it will happen to someone close to you, which is silly I realise, but if you think it might happen, you'd go crazy. What can we do to help her mum"?

"I don't really know Rachel there are no rules or guidelines for this sort of thing. My main concern at the moment is for the baby that she is expecting. As soon as she awoke from fainting, she complained of severe abdominal pains, which seem to be getting worse by the minute. I have put her on the armchair, but she is curled up in pain and I am worried that she may have a miscarriage due to the fall. She is about sixteen or seventeen weeks now and if she does lose it the birth will be almost as bad as going full term, the only difference being that she will not even have another baby to compensate for her loss of Richard. It's a cruel world at times like this Rachel.

All we can do is to be there for her, and hope that in the course of time she will come to terms with it sufficiently to enable her to live some sort of life. I'm worried about Dan, because he's too young to understand. Eventually the only person who can help Ella, is Ella, but how long that will take I just don't know".

Before they can finish their discussion, Ella screams out in agony from the next room. They hurriedly return to the living room only to find Ella thrashing around in the armchair while holding her stomach and crying "Oh, the pain is getting worse" before suddenly subsiding and saying "but I think that it's going off a bit now".

This is the pattern then of what seems to Liz and Rachel an eternity, and for Ella even longer, but which is in fact two days. After the first day Ella begins to experience light blood spotting which progresses to a heavier flow with some clots as time goes by. All three of them by now are certain that Ella's pregnancy is terminating prematurely. While all this is happening, she simultaneously experiences severe cramps and pain in her back and abdomen. Surprisingly she has no sickness or vomiting which has been such a feature of her pregnancy up until this point.

On the second day all their worst suspicions are confirmed as Ella's body rejects its foetus, which although minute and lifeless is still distinctive enough to recognise as female. Her overwhelming sense of failure and loss is now complete, leaving her too, dead inside. As she lies drenched in sweat and exhaustion from her long exertions, her only request to her mother is to ask in a voice trembling with emotion" was it a boy or girl"?

"A girl" says her mother quietly, knowing that both Ella and Richards preferred wish was for a sister for Daniel.

"Richard and I had agreed that if it was a girl, we would call her Lucy, and Martin if it was a boy" replies Ella before more tears come flooding down once again.

As she looks at her daughter, Liz is concerned for her very sanity and realises that she will need to stay with her for a period, until such time that Ella is more able to reconcile herself to Richard's death and the miscarriage of Lucy.

Once she is asleep, Liz and Rachel discuss Ella's situation and decide on practical things that they can do for her. They agree to be more of a presence in her life, although not too much, in case she feels swamped by their attention.

No, there is a balance that they must find, thinks her mother, but again that can only come ultimately from Ella herself. She will be the arbitrator in the course of time of how much she wants their company and how much time she can tolerate being on her own, but it's clear to both of them that her recovery is going to be a long one.

So ends the most traumatic day of Ella's young life, but as she drifts away into oblivion, she knows that the consequences of its events will live with her for the rest of her days.

* * *

The days and weeks that follow for Ella are relentless in their pain filled intensity. Unable to stop but not wanting to either, she constantly relives her life with Richard, being reminded of him everywhere she goes. In the village, where everyone knows one another she meets friends and people she has known all her life, who offer her their sympathy and condolences, which only adds to her pain. When she returns home, she is surrounded by his presence, the watercolour paintings on the living room walls a reminder of their life and love together. There are landscapes of the village, together with others of Oxford, the river Isis and some of the college buildings, all of which he has painted.

They would often go out for the day on weekends and Richard would take his sketch book with him. Finding a suitable place that he could sketch, the three of them would all find a grassy area, where Ella would spread a blanket and unpack the food hamper that she had prepared before leaving. They all loved these special occasions. Ella would play ball games or hide and seek with Daniel until Richard had completed enough of his sketching, after which he would join in playing games with his son.

But Ella's most poignant reminder is to be found each and every time she looks at their son. She finds this odd in a strange way, because while Richard was alive, she couldn't readily see any particular likeness. Oh, she could always see that their colourings were similar: the pale blue eyes and red hair, although this was not quite so pronounced in Richard, and she wonders idly if perhaps her husbands had been a stronger colour when he was young and if so, perhaps Daniels would tone down with age. But, with Richards's demise she begins to recognise more and more of Richards's characteristics in Daniel. The way he holds his head when he is listening, or the many ways he uses his hands to express and emphasise what he is trying to say: identical to his father, but comical in his son: or his radiant smile, which transforms his features and brings instant tears to Ella in her torment.

Each time she goes outside the back of the little house, she almost falls over Richards B.S.A motor bike, now covered with tarpaulin since the last time he left to serve his country. This is the machine that he used to get him to and from work to the garage in Oxford, or to take them both out at weekends before they had Daniel. But Richard didn't let the birth of his son stop them from going places: he merely bought a sidecar, in which Ella and Daniel used to travel in more comfort. They were the only family in this small parochial village that had their own mechanised transport, apart from The Lord of the Manor and one or two other local dignitaries.

Ella's emotions are at constant fever pitch at this time with reminders of him and also of her miscarried daughter Lucy everywhere, all of which she finds overwhelming. She and Richard had made so many plans for the arrival of their second child and the void that both their deaths have left leaves her unable to see her future.

Her mother becomes more and more concerned for her daughter, fearing a total mental breakdown. With this in mind she gets Doctor Gavin to call and prescribe sleeping tablets because Ella doesn't seem able to "turn off" or relax. Nights are the worst for her: lying in bed, the same thoughts constantly going around and round with no relief anywhere.

Elizabeth also sleeps in the house with her daughter; so that she can be at hand should any crisis arise. So, every night she goes along and spends the evening with her daughter, before settling down on the sofa to sleep after putting Ella to bed. But she doesn't forget her grandson, who has his own demons to fight and is grieving for his father as well. When Elizabeth comes every evening, she brings Bonny with her and Daniels life is transformed instantly. Not only does she join them but Bonny is also allowed to go to Daniel's bedroom when it is time for him to go to sleep. Here she sleeps in her bed, on the floor below Daniel's sleeping form, so that he can reach down and stroke her until he falls asleep. At least, that is how Elizabeth leaves the two of them, but quite often when she comes to wake him, she finds Bonny on top of the bed snuggled up to her young friend.

Rachel, too, visits often, sometimes with Fred her husband. When Richard was alive the four of them would sometimes go to the local pub, The Malt and Shovel, in the evening to play darts or Aunt Sally. They all enjoyed each other's company and Richard's death has shocked Fred deeply, his brother in law but also a close friend who he would sorely miss.

As time goes by, slowly almost imperceptibly, Ella begins to recover. It is Daniel who unwittingly contributes most to this transformation, however slight that it is. Once she has survived the initial shock of Richard's and Lucy's deaths, she begins to recognise the effect that it has had on Daniel. He has begun to become introverted, not able to talk about his father and not able to talk to her either. His only companion, who is able to console him in any way, is Bonny. He pours out his innermost secrets to this devoted animal, not being able to confide in any other person. It is only when she overhears him saying to Bonny one day "Daddy's not coming home anymore, which makes Mummy cry all the time" that Ella grasps just how much her son is suffering. This is a light bulb moment for Ella. When she hears this, the effect it has on her are twofold, guilt and sorrow in equal measure. From this moment on Ella realises that however much she misses Richard and Lucy, which she acknowledges she always will, she has no alternative, other than to give strength and guidance to their son.

She determines that her future must now be dedicated to his, that he might become the person that Richard would have wanted him to be and to be proud of, had he lived. Putting her own feelings of loss aside, Ella turns her attention to Daniel's welfare, spending more time with him, meeting him from school, which he had recently started, talking to him constantly, letting him see that she is always there for him. Slowly but surely the mother and sons' relationship grow and is re-established.

Bonny still remains a very important part of Daniel's life and they can often be found walking the fields surrounding the village on evenings and at weekends, but they are not always alone, Ella making sure that she finds time to accompany them when she can.

Elizabeth and Alf watch the transformation in silence and wonder, being grateful to whichever god has brought it to pass.

CHAPTER 2.

ELLA'S FAMILY.

Ella's parents, Alf and Elizabeth Carter were both born in Chadlington and their experience of the wider world has been limited to a large extent to its surrounding towns and villages, with an occasional day trip to Oxford to go to the cinema or to buy clothes. They were both born in Chadlington and the similarities in their ages have meant that they have grown up together, even before starting at the village school.

Their only social contacts have been those people locally in their own and surrounding villages. It is too such as these that they gravitate to when seeking to find partners, but even though they have only selected from this small pool their love for one another is unquestionable. Above all else they love their two daughters with a passion and do everything within their limited powers to help them whenever required.

Alf has always worked on the local farm, originally as a ploughman responsible for the shire horses. This entailed rising early each morning at five o'clock to first muck out the horses, before feeding them and making them ready for ploughing or whatever use they were to be put to. The days were long and arduous before he returned them to their stables, making sure that they were first fed and watered and had fresh bedding, before he returned home, which was often late evening.

As the twentieth century has progressed, mechanisation has gradually begun to replace both horses and agricultural labourers. Tractors, Lorries and other equipment have proved to be much more efficient, but fortunately for Alf, his employer, the farmer has always made sure that he was shown how to use and operate it, thus ensuring that he was not made redundant as so many who were less fortunate had been.

All the houses in the terrace are small, a living room and kitchen on the ground floor, with two small bedrooms upstairs. They are nearly two hundred years old, having originally been built by the local lord of the manor, to accommodate agricultural workers on his farms. The facilities are woefully basic with the only toilets being earth closets which are to be found in sheds at the end of each garden, while running tap water has only been installed within the last few years; the only form of heating being in the form of open coal fires. Most of the cottages are still occupied by agricultural workers, of which Alf is one, but some are now being rented out by the Lord of the Manor to villagers who do not work directly for their landlord.

Although life was tough for Ella and Rachel growing up in the wake of the First World War in Chadlington, it was by no means all work and no play. When they were both young, they would play endless games after school with the other children from the village. Although money was scarce, it cost nothing for them to play hop-scotch, or skipping, or hide and seek, or indeed any of the many other games that they quite often made up, making them all captives of their own imagination. They would play outside in the streets after their evening meal in the summer months until the sun went down, or until they were summoned home by their parents.

Being the eldest, Rachel almost always lead from the front, while Ella followed on behind. In fact, Rachel was very much a tomboy, giving everyone in the group grief if they didn't march to her drum, while Ella was content to follow in her elder sister's wake.

Rachel was born in 1916 and Ella followed two years later. Although Rachel was the more dominant sister, they both learned to be independent at an early age, mainly because their parents both worked on the land. Alf wore hats of many hues, driving the tractor to plough one day, then helping to milk the fifty strong herd of Friesian cows the next, or doing any of the many other jobs necessary to maintain the farm, sometimes cutting and shaping the field hedgerows, or rebuilding the Cotswold stone walls that needed repairing.

Elizabeth also worked on the land, planting cabbage and kale, or potatoes and other crops as well as helping the farmer's wife in the farmhouse. Later in the season she would then help to pull up the cabbages for market and the kale which was used to feed the cattle. When the potatoes were ready, she would follow on behind Alf in the tractor as it turned the soil so that they could be collected in sacks. This was all heavy back-breaking work which inevitably took its toll on the health of them both.

At harvest time all four members of the family were expected to work from morning to dusk in the fields, helping to gather the corn into sheaves ready for collection by tractor or lorry to go to the Mill to produce flour.

Rachel and Ella learned from a very early age to cook, clean, wash clothes and sew and do many of the other household functions necessary to save Elizabeth when she returned home from her labour-intensive days.

Sewing was a necessary basic requirement in any household: socks were repaired when holes appeared, shirts and dresses also, while alterations were made when clothes were passed from one person to another as "hand me downs". Money was tight and so new clothes were almost never bought, but rather purchased at large house sales, after bereavement of the owner, or the sale of the property because of bankruptcy. Additionally, knitting was something that most women learned to do at an early age, to make jumpers, cardigans and even socks.

Alf also grew vegetables in the small back garden of the house, as well as tending to an allotment further down the village. An area of the back garden was fenced off, where he kept a pig and half a dozen chickens. In this way the family became almost self- sufficient.

Both Rachel and Ella helped with the animals, feeding both the pig and the chickens and collecting the latter's eggs. But they didn't have to be coerced into doing any of this because they loved being involved and would give all of the animals' names and feed them individually. The pig was inexpensive to keep, rooting around in the back garden for food, which was topped up with scraps from the table and vegetables.

Nothing was wasted when a pig was killed. The carcase was cut up and then salted and hung, because the meat would keep for several months. The head, after the brains were extracted, would be boiled and eaten. The major organs would also go to feed the family, and even the offal was used. The intestines would be cut up, stuffed and cooked to make chitterlings. Even the trotters were cooked. The whole enterprise was a good investment to a humble farm worker and his family. Finally, the pig sticker would take his choice of a select couple of cuts of meat for his services, no money being available

Both Rachel and Ella loved Christmas. Alf would kill a chicken for the oven, which was a rare treat, and on Christmas Eve the girls would be sent to bed trembling with excitement, to await the arrival of Father Christmas. In the morning they would find one of Alf's socks each, filled with presents. Feverishly opening them they would find to their delight an orange and an apple, with perhaps a banana and a bag of boiled sweets. If their parents had managed to get a second hand toy from one of the other villagers whose children no longer needed them, they might also find a doll or a soft toy or a game, but whatever it was it would be a source of wonder and delight for them both.

Christmas Day was a time for the family. Elizabeth's widowed mother would arrive after morning service at the church, as well as her sister and her husband and children John and Edward. After dinner the fire would be stoked up with logs and they would all play games by the light of the fire until late.

It was at times like this that Ella displayed her impish sense of humour: one Christmas, when she was about ten years old, her elderly Aunt needed to visit the lavatory in the back garden. By this time, it was late in the evening and as soon as she stepped out of the back door she was enveloped by the darkness. Stumbling her way to the shed at the end of the garden she proceeded to take down her knickers and squat.

She had no sooner managed to get this far however, when the door was suddenly flung open and a white ethereal figure appeared, and began moaning in an unearthly way. The aunt, thinking that her time had come, gave out a scream, loud enough to wake the whole village, before rushing headlong back to the house. Perhaps rushing is an exaggeration, because she did not have time to adjust her clothes before leaving, and all that Ella could see as she took off the white bedsheet covering her, was her elderly aunt hopping away as fast as possible, allowing for the fact that her knickers were still around her ankles.

Ella, managing to slip back inside the house without being noticed, joined in the general commiseration being shown to her aunt by the rest of the family, none of whom obviously believing a word of her out of this world experience.

Even her father wasn't safe from Ella's sense of fun, when on another occasion Alf fell asleep in his chair one evening at about eight o'clock. Holding a finger to her lips to stop her mother or Rachel from talking, she managed to forward the time on his watch by several hours. Upon waking some few minutes later and looking at his timepiece he was stunned to see that it was now well after midnight. Now Alf never went to bed later than nine, because he always needed to get up by five the next morning to help with the milking or muck out the horse stables, so it was with a feeling of horror that he realised that he would only get a few hours' sleep. Rising swiftly from his chair he started to follow his usual nightly procedures, first winding up the wall clocks and making sure that the doors were locked.

The women watched him as all this took place, until suddenly Alf became conscious of their silence and looking at them, asked them why they too were not in bed. His reply was gales of laughter from all three of them, before Elizabeth told him what Ella had done.

Alf, being the good father that he was, joined in the fun, after wagging his finger at Ella, saying "You little minx, I'll get my own back for that, you just see if I don't", but there was a twinkle in his eye as he said it.

But where Rachel was serious in all things, Ella was irrepressible, sometimes making "apple pie beds" for her sister, so that when she got in it, the bedclothes would only cover her up to her waist, leaving her freezing cold. When this happened Rachel would let out a roar and crossing over to Ella's bed would proceed to hit her quivering form with a pillow. This would lead inevitably to the sisters having pillow fights,

Rachel eventually getting retribution for her younger sister's skittish behaviour.

Ella loved playing tricks on her elder sister, because she knew that Rachel would always take them in the spirit that they were intended. Just for fun. Rachel never knew when to expect Ella's next attack and what form it would take. There was the time when she was getting ready for bed and struggled for ages trying to put on her nightdress, before eventually realising that the neck had been sewn up so that it was impossible to put her head through, or on getting into bed she would find half a dozen small items, like brushes, or an iron or a picture, distributed under the covers.

Rachel, for all her protestations and assumed anger, secretly loved it when Ella made these things happen, particularly the day that Ella had positioned a magazine over their partially open bedroom door, on top of which she had delicately put some shredded pieces of paper. The intention was that as Rachel pushed open the door, the magazine would fall, together with the paper, like confetti all over her. The reason why Rachel liked this trick so much was because it wasn't she who entered the room first, but her mother, who having to take freshly ironed clothes to the girls room, pushed the door open, only to be deluged by shredded pieces of paper, which went into her hair and clothes, making her look as if she'd been out in a snowstorm. But she too, like Rachel, saw the funny side, and loved her youngest child even more for her zany sense of humour. These then were the conditions and environment that Rachel and Ella grew up in.

When she was fourteen, Rachel left school, but the only work available in the village was agriculture, and although she was used to being out in the fields, or working with animals, she could see by just looking at her parents, the toll that labouring had taken on their health. Having no other alternative, she looked outside the village to closer towns that were larger and had more different types of work that she could do. Although she had only received a basic education, she was proficient in Maths and English but, more importantly, she had a lot of common sense, which led to her eventually finding work in a shop in Charlbury that did dressmaking. This meant that they made their own bespoke dresses to order as well as others off the shelf. Rachel was delighted when the owner Mrs White offered her an apprenticeship to learn dressmaking.

Both Alf and Elizabeth were pleased for her, the only problem that they could see, being how she would get there. Charlbury was some two or three miles away, but Rachel was not deterred by the distance, and decided that she would walk until such time as she could afford a bicycle.

She took to dressmaking like a duck to water. The work room was separate at the rear of the shop, where two other elderly women worked as well. Mrs White, or Mary, as she insisted on being addressed, was a joy to work for, explaining the business of dressmaking to her at length and then sitting with her as she started her first projects. Not only that but Mary kept a close eye on her work, so that if it started to veer from the intended design, she could get Rachel to quickly correct it.

Within a few years, under Mary's expert guidance, Rachel was turning out work of a high quality and she was being requested by name as word of her reputation widened. Also, by this time, one of the other women dressmakers had retired, leaving just Rachel and one other, Jane, in the workshop. Mary could by now leave Rachel to her own devices, and it wasn't long before Rachel approached her with a portfolio of dress designs that she had produced in her spare time.

Mary was stunned when she saw the creativity and skill that Rachel had produced and quickly gave her autonomy over the designs, recognising that she herself was getting older and that her own designs were dated.

Rachel in return, recognised the opportunity that Mary had offered her and respected her even more. She had purchased a bicycle after the first few months of work, and apart from the few days when it rained or the weather was foul, she managed to get home within thirty minutes or so each day.

Both her parents watched her progress with pride and wonder, as did Ella, until it was her turn to leave school.

By comparison, on leaving school Ella had started to work at The Manor House, which was on the outskirts of the village, about half a mile away. She started in the position of maid in 1933, but quickly worked her way up the social ladder to Cook for the household. This was because The Lord of the Manor, Lord Anthony Stevens had inherited the Manor on the demise of his father, in the early nineteen thirties, but death duties had taken their toll. Lord Stevens had struggled financially ever since taking over the Manor, which meant that he could not afford the number of staff that he inherited, so consequently he had to dispense with a number of them fairly soon afterwards. The cook, Harriet Seamarks, was an elderly lady at this time, and she only had a couple of years to go before she could retire. Knowing this, Lord Stevens offered Ella the position of assistant cook, with the objective of getting Harriet to train her up for the time when she herself retired, because he realised that The Manor could be run with less staff in most other areas, but the position of cook would always be needed.

Ella took to cooking like a duck to water: here she found for the first time something that she could excel in. She absorbed everything that Harriet taught her, the latter, who was by this time feeling her advancing years, being only too pleased to step back and let Ella do most of the work. But Ella didn't mind in the slightest, because it meant that she could learn and develop her own menus and ideas for cooking. She wasn't afraid to try new combinations of food, in fact she positively flourished in such an environment, so much so, that when Harriet retired two years later, she was more than ready to not only step into her shoes, but couldn't wait to put some of her ideas into practice.

However, this was of no surprise to Lord Stevens, who had already tasted some of Ella's delicious culinary offerings, realising the obvious differences between Harriet's more mundane fare, and the more colourful, light, tasty efforts of her young apprentice.

By the time of the outbreak of the war in 1939, there was only Ella, one young assistant cook, two other young maids and two elderly part time gardeners left, compared to a staff of some thirty people who had been employed at the end of the First World War in 1918.

Both Ella and Rachel had always loved dancing from an early age. Dancing lessons were held every Wednesday in the village hall and were one of the most important ways to make social contact with people outside of the village. But the main reason that the sisters took to dancing was because they just loved it, taking them to a different world, away from their hum drum life styles to a world of glitter and promise of better things.

Dances were held in Chadlington village hall on a number of Saturdays throughout the year, something that all the villagers enjoyed. Additionally, The Lord of The Manor, as a gesture of goodwill to the villagers, would invite them to the grounds of his house a couple of times during the summer months. There would be a large marquee and here he would provide both food and drinks and there would be dancing to the village band. This would continue into the early hours and both Carter sisters could be guaranteed to be among the "last man standing", before wending their weary way home.

Additionally, some surrounding villages also held regular dances. Chipping Norton was often their destination, or sometimes it was Stow-on-the-Wold, or maybe Witney, and in all of these places' competitions were held for the best couple performing a particular dance, be it a waltz, quickstep, or a foxtrot or whatever else was decided. When they entered for any of these Rachel would take Fred Simmons to partner her, while Ella usually persuaded Bill Treacher, a young farmer who lived nearby, who she had known all her life, to accompany her. Not only did Rachel and Ella enjoy dancing, they were also very accomplished and over the years won a number of cups and cash prizes.

Rachel and Fred had courted for a number of years at this time, but Ella and Bill were just good friends who had grown up together and enjoyed dancing.

By their mid to late teens, both girls had developed into beautiful young women. Rachel's jet-black hair was in contrast to Ella's more auburn shade of reddish brown, but both of them had dark brown eyes, which look almost black when they became animated. Rachel was not as tall as Ella, but was also slender in build. Their facial features were similar, but Ella's were slightly more refined, whilst her height and tall slender neck gave her the edge over her older sister in beauty stakes. But the single most obvious thing that identified them both was their sense of fun and ready laughter, which transformed their already beautiful images, into something even more alluring.

As well as the surrounding local villages, dances were also held in Oxford City on a regular basis. The main attraction regarding those, was that the prizes were usually much better than those in the villages, particularly those where cash was involved, which appealed hugely to the girls.

Transport to all these places was a problem, but Bill very often managed to borrow his father's tractor and flatbed trailer and off they would go in style, dressed up in their ball gowns, sitting on bales of straw, both of them imagining that it was a golden carriage being driven by a Prince. Quite often they would pick up other wannabe dancers from the village and they would fill the trailer laughing and joking, while singing country songs as they progressed on their way, arriving eventually at the village hall, to be met by other tractors carrying contestants from other outlying villages.

If it was not possible for Bill to borrow the tractor, they would use their bicycles, but this was more inconvenient because it meant them carrying their dance dresses separately, in case they got them dirty, and then changing when they arrived.

This was perfectly acceptable for visiting the local villages, but when it came to the "big smoke" of Oxford, other methods had to be employed. This was usually in the form of the local bus service which was very infrequent and what was even worse, unreliable. The bus was based in Oxford and travelled round all the villages within a few miles' circumference. But by far the biggest drawback to this method of transportation, was that the last journey leaving Oxford was at ten thirty in the evening, which meant that Rachel and Ella had to leave the dance hall by just after ten o'clock, so that they could be in time to catch the bus, thus missing the last two hours of the dance.

CHAPTER 3.

RICHARD AND ELLA.

It is Rachel who inadvertently introduces Ella to Richard at a dance in Oxford, thus determining the path of her life that will become an all-consuming passion, but which will lead ultimately to loss, loneliness and despair.

"Hurry up lazy bones" cries Ella to Rachel, "we've only got ten minutes to get to the bus stop, and if we miss this one, we will have to wait another two hours before the next, which will mean that we'll be too late to enter the competition".

"All right, hold your hair on" replies Rachel irritably, who has only just got home from work, and hasn't had time to change into her evening clothes yet.

It is Saturday, the fourteenth day of February 1938, a date that will be forever etched on Ella's heart in the coming years. The four of them, Rachel, Ella, Fred and Bill, have arranged to meet in Oxford to compete in a dance contest which is to be held at The Lyceum Ballroom.

Fred and Bill have already left, travelling by bicycle, but the two women are going by bus, because they are having to carry their ball gowns in small suitcases, as well as the men's dancing suits

Eventually, Rachel and Ella get to the bus stop just in time to catch the bus, which is nearly full with people from the surrounding villages going to Oxford for various social events: some going to the pictures, to see the latest film with James Cagney, a few to eat out, (although there are not so many of these, the cost of restaurants being prohibitive) and some others, like the two sisters, to go to the dance. The bus is alive with the hum of excited chatter and laughter.

Meeting up with Fred and Bill, the four of them make their way to the Lyceum, and reach the dance floor where several hundred others are already circling to the music of the resident band. To compete in the dance competition, they have to formally enter their names for whichever type of dance that they wish to contend in.

As usual both couples enter for the waltz, the quickstep and the foxtrot, being very competent in all three dances.

Most of the people are just here with their partners to enjoy the evening, or are hoping to meet someone of the opposite sex, but a small number, perhaps twenty couples will compete.

The prize money for each type of dance is ten pounds for the winners, a huge amount for Rachel and Ella, who don't earn even half of that for a week's work. They recognise a lot of the other couples who are competing, and are quietly confident, because they have beaten most of them at other dances over the last couple of years. But neither of them is confident as to which one of them will win tonight if they reach the final, because they are both fiercely competitive, and the results of their recent previous competitions are that both couples have won and lost to each other.

Suddenly the announcer calls for those couples who have entered for the waltz to come forward, and wishing each other good luck they line up with the other contestants. The dance hall has appointed three judges who have vast experience in competition dancing, and indeed have won trophies at national level themselves.

The floor is cleared, all people other than those who are competing forming an audience all around the edges, before the process commences as five of the couples begin their performance, the judges marking their efforts on their cards, after which a second five couples perform and so on until all the couples have competed.

The judges then consult with each other and pick the three highest marked couples to dance in the final, to decide the winner. Both Rachel and Ella get through to the final dance off with one other couple who they know well from previous competitions. But this time the three couples have to perform individually after which the judges will announce the winner. Both girls wish each other good luck, as Ella and Bill take to the floor under the spotlight and the band begins to play "When they Begin the Beguine". Ella has spent a lot of time choreographing their routine, an artistic skill that she has a natural aptitude for. They have practised hard all week in the village hall and have introduced some new moves into their performance.

For some obscure reason that she cannot explain, even to herself, Ella is feeling elated tonight. She loves these evenings with a passion, enjoying the transformation from her hard, every day working life, to a world of glamour, colour and sophistication that she could not hope to experience anywhere else. Her dress, which has been designed and made by Rachel, is a beautiful green velvet ball gown, which has a plunging neck line, with three quarter length sleeves. It narrows at the waist, which emphasises Ella's slim figure, and then continues down until it reaches just above her ankles. She is wearing an underskirt of tulle which billows out every time her partner twirls her around, revealing her long slender legs. Her hair hangs long and straight down to just past her shoulders and swings in time to the rhythm, every time she moves her head.

Bill is wearing his dark dress suit coat and tails, as they move seamlessly through their routine under the spotlight. Ella is so immersed in her performance that she is totally unaware of the people standing around the floor at the periphery of her vision. The pair is in total symmetry with each other, gliding across the floor, their feet rising and falling in unison. They sweep around the floor effortlessly, using every inch of its huge proportions, drawing gusts of applause after each difficult move. Ella keeps her shoulders square, with her head thrown slightly to one side as she has been taught and tries to maintain her posture right through to the end of the dance. Although Bill and Ella have danced many times before, in this dance and on this evening, everything that they have worked towards comes to fruition in this spellbinding performance. They finish to tremendous applause from the audience, the light from the revolving glitter ball, which is suspended high up in the centre of the hall, reflecting in Ella's eyes, making them sparkle and glow.

Ella is particularly pleased that their performance has gone so well tonight because Bill has recently told her that he has started courting a girl from Witney, so that he will not have the time to be able to continue to partner her, meaning that she will have to find someone else.

Although this was a bitter blow when she first heard it, Ella is now reconciled to the news, and gives Bill her best wishes. They have performed together for so long, that she thinks that this is her last performance also, not wishing to go through the trauma of finding a new partner.

After Rachel and Fred and the third couple have performed, the judges have several minutes consultation, before announcing that Ella has won the competition, with Rachel second, their other rivals coming third.

The evening continues, with Rachel and Fred reversing the positions in the quickstep, while the third couple manage to win the foxtrot.

It has been a very good evening for the four of them, and the time is now nine thirty. Quickly changing from their dance clothes into their normal attire they make their way back to the ballroom to dance with the rest of the people there.

Ella enjoys this more informal dancing just as much as the competitive version, because she gets to meet other people, and although she gets trod on occasionally, she considers the pain well worth the trouble. This evening is no exception in this regard, as she is asked by several young men for a dance, and she is happy to oblige.

Like most dances there is a point in the proceedings late in the evening, when there is an influx of men and youths who have been in the local pubs drinking, purely for the purpose of gaining enough "Dutch

Courage", before moving on to the dance hall, so that they can ask girls for an "Excuse me". This is a well-known phenomenon, particularly for the girls, who understand the men only too well, because until this stage in the proceedings a large proportion of them have had to find other female dance partners, and are just waiting for this to happen.

This is the moment that Fred and Bill choose to say their farewells to Rachel and Ella, as they have to retrieve their cycles and ride back home to Chadlington, a journey that will take them in excess of an hour to complete.

They have only been gone for a few minutes, when suddenly Rachel who has been talking to a group of people that she apparently knows, comes rushing back across the congested ballroom to Ella, dragging a young man in tow, saying "look who I've found Ella".

Taking stock of the individual concerned, Ella says after a few seconds "well as I live and breathe, if it isn't Charlie Lainchbury: what are you doing here Charlie, I haven't seen you in the village for ages".

"Well, there wasn't much work in the village, so I left Chadlington a few weeks ago and got a job in a butcher's shop, here in Oxford. The money is good and so is the social life. I thought my mum, or someone who knew where I had gone would have told you".

This, as both girls know, is a long speech from Charlie, who is well known for his reticence in all matters vocal. He is slightly built, but fairly tall, and of fair complexion and hair, but he has ruddy cheeks, which give the false impression that he spends a good deal of his time outdoors.

The three of them begin to chatter at a fair rate of knots, catching up with each other's news, until suddenly Charlie realises that he is not on his own tonight and says "Oh, I am sorry, I almost forgot to introduce you to my very good friend Richard. Ella and Rachel, this is Richard Thornton; Richard, this is Rachel and Ella Carter, who both live in Chadlington and who I have known all our lives"

Turning, Charlie ushers Richard forward, and for Ella, time stands still in the moment. Neither of them can possibly know that their futures lie inextricably linked, but there is a sheer magnetic attraction that emanates from both of them, which seems to seal them in a vacuum, leaving them in isolation with each other, excluding the others completely. Rachel and Charlie are irrelevant, forgotten entirely in Richard and Ella's separate universe.

Ella experiences a shudder of mind-numbing excitement as she contemplates the young man before her. His pale blue eyes seem to dance with light in response to his open ready smile, one triggering the other. Hair of what can only be described as a light flaming-red hue covers his crown and falls to low on the nape of his neck. As with so many people of fair countenance, he has freckles on his nose, giving him a youthful air.

But he is quite tall, several inches taller than me, thinks Ella, assessing him; probably around six feet, but he has broad shoulders and matching build. As her gaze lowers, she notices his hands, which are large and careworn, obviously a working badge of office.

He is dressed in a navy blue, double breasted blazer, with grey bell-bottomed trousers with turn ups. A white shirt with pale blue stripes, together with polished black brogue shoes completes the look, which is the vogue currently in men's fashions. Ella registers all of this in a fraction of a second as she hears him say "It is a pleasure to meet you both, in fact I feel that I know you already, because Charlie has often spoken about you". Although he is addressing both of them, Richards eyes have not left Ella's face all the time he has been speaking.

Not wishing to break the spell existing between them, Richard goes quickly on to say "would you like to dance, I'm not very good, but I will try not to step on your toes. I saw you win the waltz competition earlier, so don't expect that standard".

Ella pauses for a second, not because she doesn't want to dance, but just to give herself long enough time to compose her reply; then "I would love to dance with you Richard, but don't worry about stepping on my toes, because there are so many people here that it's almost impossible not to".

Taking in her in his arms they step onto the floor and dance a slow waltz to the haunting melody of "I'll see you again". But this is not the gliding, sweeping experience that Ella had earlier in the competition, nor does she want it to be; rather she wants to be held close, to feel the warmth of this man who has just entered her life. They circle the floor, Richards's arms around her waist, with Ella's arms around his neck, her head nestled on his chest, immune to everyone and everything that is going on around them.

This is a totally new experience for Ella. She has had several boyfriends over the years, which were fun while she was growing up, but none of whom lasted more than a few months. However, she recognises that this is totally different, that somehow this man makes her whole.

Neither of them talks very much, both seeming to be content in each other's company as they slowly navigate the floor until the band finally finishes. Richard manages to avoid stepping on Ella's feet by hardly moving, rather just by revolving slowly on the same spot. They are both lost in each other, content to be close, dancing almost an irrelevance.

In the years to come they will always remember this particular melody as their tune.

As the band finishes, Rachel quickly crosses the floor to them saying "I think that we'd better go now Ella, if we want to catch the last bus".

Ella, who has been totally absorbed dancing with Richard, is distraught at the thought of leaving when they have only just met, but Richard, who obviously feels the same way, hurriedly interjects, saying "Can I see you again Ella?", to which she answers immediately "Oh, I would like that very much, but I don't know when, because I live in Chadlington and I don't often get time off work".

Richard looks disappointed for a moment, before suddenly saying, "Well that's O.K. because I could come and pick you up on my motor bike. Just let me know what day would suit you, and I will be there. We could go dancing, or for a drink, or just for a walk if you would prefer. What do you say"?

Ella's face beams at his reply, as she says "You've got a motorbike, wow that's swanky" and then her face drops as she continues "I am in service at the Manor House in the village, so I don't get much time off. My main duty is that of cook for the household, so I am needed most evenings, but I do get some Saturday evenings off, and sometimes another evening during the week, if the Lord is not entertaining"

Richard, not wishing to lose momentum, and fearing that he might never see this wonderful vision again, replies "well just tell me when your next day off will be, and I'll pick you up".

Ella, hurriedly finding a scrap of paper, scribbles out her address, saying "I'm not working next Thursday, so how about then"?

"That would be just fine, O.K. see you then, about seven "says Richard, as Rachel tugs at Ella's arm, saying "come on or we'll miss the bus".

Thinking it too soon to kiss her goodnight, and indeed not appropriate with Rachel in attendance, Richard pulls Ella to him in an embrace, before saying huskily "I have really enjoyed being with you this evening, and I can't wait already until next Thursday".

"Oh, me too" replies Ella, as she reluctantly pulls away from his embrace. "Don't be late, or I'll think that you're not coming".

"Wild horses couldn't stop me".

CHAPTER 4.

1950 TO 1956.
CHIPPING NORTON

Today is the 3rd July 1950, almost six years since Ella learned of Richard's tragic death, which has meant for her, six years of unremitting pain and loss, she waits alone in a mixture of trepidation and hope in her cottage, because this is the day that Daniel will find out if he has passed his eleven plus exam or not.

The school has informed the parents concerned that those children who have passed will be given a letter which they can take home to their parents. So, Ella waits, and waits, each minute seeming like an hour until Daniel can return home at dinner break, to discover if he has achieved his immediate ambition, knowing just how important it is to him. Daniel has grown into a thoughtful, serious child with a quick agile mind. All of that is rewarded today as he suddenly appears excitedly in the doorway waving the magic envelope, something that can possibly be a springboard for his future.

But before he even has time to discuss it with her, Ella rushes to him, hugging and congratulating him, knowing that he needs her over abundant adulation, to compensate for that which his father would have shown.

"Well done Daniel, I am so pleased for you and your father would have been so proud of you. It was his dearest wish that you should live your dreams and that the best way to do so was to get as far as you could with your education, because in that way you have options".

They are both soon in tears of happiness as they talk about which Grammar school Daniel can go to and all the things that attend such decisions. But they have only just begun when it is time for Daniel to return to school for the afternoon.

"We will talk about it tonight" Ella says, kissing him goodbye, and then "Oh I am so excited. Well done again son".

After Daniel has left to continue the rest of his day at school, Ella spends the rest of the afternoon contemplating the problems confronting her that she will need to be overcome to make Daniel's move to Grammar school possible. These are almost all of a financial nature. The first hurdle is which Grammar school would be not only suitable, but also more convenient. The choices available are, either, Chipping Norton, Witney,

Moreton-in-the Marsh, or Oxford, none of which is within walking distance, so he will require transport. The next hurdle that needs to be overcome is a new school uniform that has to be provided, consisting of a navy blazer and badge, grey trousers, white shirts and school tie, plus any other equipment, like cricket shirt and flannels that may occur.

These are all major obstacles for Ella, who only receives a small wage for her work at The Manor House, which was returned to The Lord of the Manor in 1946, by the Ministry of Defence.

Like many other large estates of this nature, death duties have taken their toll over the years, and consequently The Lord finds himself in an increasingly constrained financial situation. Ella is all too aware that her position at the Manor might be no longer viable at any time, leaving her with no option but to look somewhere else for employment. Her only other sources of income are those of barmaid at the village pub, The Malt Shovel, at those times when she has no other duties at The Manor House, and some farm work at harvest time, helping to reap and stack the corn.

But she does not mention any of this to Daniel, resolving that she has to make it happen, to ensure his future education.

Since Richard's death, Ella has managed to keep paying the rent on her little house, thanks to the occasional assistance from her parents, but even so, she is stretched financially most of the time. She also realises that when, rather than if her employment ceases at The Manor, she will have no alternative than to move back in with her parents, Elizabeth and Alf.

* * *

The next weekend, Ella gets together with her parents, and Rachel and Fred, where most of her fears regarding the cost for Daniel to go to Grammar School prove groundless.

"What are you worried about little sis" says Rachel, trying to allay Ella's fears, "I can make him a most of the clothes that he needs: blazer, shirts and trousers enough to get him started anyway. All you will need to buy him is a school tie".

"That's right" interjects Alf "and if you decide to send him to Chipping Norton, he can use my old bike that I still have in the shed. It only needs a little T.L.C. I can lower the seat, and if his feet don't reach the pedals, I can put blocks on them, and it will be right as rain. Anyway, you need to look into the times of the buses, because if they run at convenient times, you may be able to get a bus pass from the local authorities.

Ella is much relieved after hearing how supportive her family are, and tells them so, saying "Thank you so much, I don't know how I would manage without you", to which Alf replies "Oh my dear that's what we are here for".

After visiting the Chipping Norton grammar school on their open day, it is resolved that Daniel should start the next September. He is very excited at the prospect, although worried that he will not be seeing friends that he has grown up with, but Ella reassures him that he can still see them at weekends and holidays.

Life for Ella has stood still since Richard's death, the only time she goes out socially, is to a dance occasionally with Rachel and Fred. But nothing can fill the huge void in her life left by widowhood, something that she tries desperately to hide from her family and friends. Instead, she pours out all her love, energy and affection on her son, encouraging him to develop not only intellectually, but also as a person, someone who his father would have been proud of.

Her work at The Manor House leaves her very little time for leisure, her duties as cook to a large household, (albeit one that has been dwindling of late) means that she often has to prepare meals for evening dinner parties. Whenever this happens, she arranges for Daniel to stay with Alf and Elizabeth until she can get away.

As well as her parents, Rachel has always been there for her, visiting Ella whenever she can, and bringing her two boys, William and James to play with Daniel. They are of a similar age, William being one year older than Daniel and James two years younger, and the cousins get on famously with each other. On some occasional week ends the boys come to Ella's, to have sleep-overs.

Conversely, life for Rachel goes from strength to strength. After several years in Charlbury, her employer, Mrs White approaches her saying "Rachel, I am thinking of investing in another shop that I've seen in Witney. Things have been going so well here, thanks in no small measure to your wonderful designs, so I think that it is time to develop and expand the business further. But I don't want you to think that I've forgotten your input and effort, because I recognise that without it, things would have been very different. So what I am suggesting is that you become a full partner with me, and run the new shop in Witney, while I remain here in Charlbury. You would retain full autonomy over the designs for both shops. I propose that we both take a salary from the business, and for now that we pay you the same amount that I take, which will be a significant increase for you than at present. In addition, we will look at the profits that the business makes at the end of each year and pay ourselves a bonus, after allowing for some of it to be ploughed back for future developments: what do you say? We have always got on well and I think that we would make a very good team".

Rachel is stunned and overwhelmed for a few pregnant seconds, before replying "Oh Mary, what can I say. You've always treated me very fairly, so I would be delighted to be your partner. Thank you for giving me the opportunity".

"Nonsense Rachel, you deserve it because you've earned it, now let's shake hands on it, but before we do, I think I have a bottle of bubbly in the kitchen, so let's raise a toast to both of us and for our great future working relationship".

* * *

By contrast Ella's world falls apart in 1956 with the death of her employer Lord Anthony Stevens. His health has been deteriorating for some time, until finally he has a major stroke that leaves him paralysed on his left-hand side. This is followed within a few days by another, which is too much for his seriously weakened immune system to fight.

Lord Stevens of Leighton, to give him his full title, holds a hereditary title that one of his distant ancestors had earned from King Charles II back in the seventeenth century for his support in regaining his father's throne.

On his death, Lord Stevens's title is passed to a distant relative in Australia, because he has no children, or in fact any close kin. With his passing Death Duties become due, which threaten the existence of The Manor House, which he leaves to his wife, together with all his other worldly possessions.

Lady Stevens, who is by now Dowager Stevens of Leighton, is frail herself, is not able to continue living in the great rambling house, and at the same time is unable to pay the death duties demanded of her by The Inland Revenue. She has no option than to sell The Manor House, which will leave Ella without employment. Additionally, she has to sell the two remaining farms that are let out to tenant farmers.

This is probably the biggest crisis of Ella's still relatively young life. Daniel is now seventeen and in his sixth year at Grammar School, and doing well. Ella doesn't want to do anything that will jeopardise Daniels future, but however much she tries, she is unable to see a way forward.

Where does she go to from here? There is virtually no other work in the village and she has no savings to cushion her financially. She spends many sleepless nights, crying into her pillow, so that Daniel will not hear her. Her parents, simple country people that they are, try to keep her spirits up as best they can, but don't have the necessary tools or knowledge, to help her to find a job.

It is Rachel who once again rides to Ella's rescue when she finds herself in conversation with a client, Mr Souch, in the dressmaking shop in Witney. He is accompanying his wife, who is having an evening dress made and in passing, mentions that he had known Lord Anthony Stevens and how sorry he was to learn that The Manor House was being sold after his death. Rachel then explains that she knows all about it because her sister has worked there for many years as head cook, and will soon be without a job as a result of the poor man's death.

The client looks pensive for several minutes, before suddenly saying "well she must be a very good cook after being employed at The Manor House for so many years, so how might she feel about say, having her own shop, where she could bake and make cakes, or do teas, or something along those lines. The reason that I mention it is because I own a shop in The Market Place in Chipping Norton and the person who runs it and whose lease has just expired, is retiring, so I'm looking for a new tenant to take his place. The current lessee has run it as newsagents, but I don't see any reason why your sister shouldn't use her cookery skills and change it along the lines that I have suggested. I think that she will find the amount of rent and leasing terms to be agreeable, because I appreciate that anyone taking on such a project has to be able to make a living. What do you think? Why don't you talk it over with your sister, and, if she wants to pursue it further, tell her to come and see me", and he hands Rachel his business card.

Rachel is thrilled at this suggestion and makes a mental note to see Ella a soon as possible, and tell her

* * *

"So what do you think Ellie" says Rachel, using her pet name for her sister, "Mr Souch says that if you are interested all you have to do is to go and see him" and then pausing "I'll come with you if you like, he seems like a very nice man".

Ella, who has been listening to her sister with mounting excitement at the prospect of running her own shop, is suddenly hit by a dose of reality as she realises that she has no money or collateral to embark on such an adventure, and says "Oh Rachel, how can I possibly do something like that. It's not that I don't want to, in fact I would love the chance to be my own boss after working all my life for someone else, but I can't even afford the rent, let alone buy fixtures and fittings for a cake shop. And how am I supposed to be able to carry on living here as well".

Rachel, who can see and hear the disappointment in her sister's voice, and is determined to encourage and support her, says "Don't give up, we haven't even seen Mr Souch yet, he may have some ideas, and anyway, why give up when you don't know just what you're up against. I tell you what, let me get in touch with him and we'll both go and see him ".

After much persuasion over several days, Ella finally agrees and within a week finds herself dressed in her best dress (she only has two), together with Rachel standing outside Mr Souch's large detached house, which is situated in a wide leafy avenue just outside Chipping Norton. Ushering them in, Mr Souch, who is a large, stocky, jolly man, with blue twinkling eyes and a ready smile, says "I am so pleased that you have come to see me. I've been giving the matter a great deal of thought since Rachel mentioned you to me and I've come to the conclusion that the town could do with a tea shop. It already has a couple of shops that sell papers and that sort of thing, but it doesn't have anything like that which you have in mind. Tell me, have you given the matter any thoughts as to what you intend doing with it if you proceed any further"?

Ella, who is normally reticent when it comes to making speeches of any description, pauses for a moment, before she suddenly surprises herself, and says "well I have thought about it a great deal for the last few days. And ideally, what I would like to do is be able to run it as a café/tea shop.

It could be somewhere that I could make, bake and sell cakes and also if possible, make room for some tables and chairs where I could offer customers teas, with sandwiches. Not only that, but I would also like to be able to offer breakfasts to stall owners on market days, which are Tuesdays and Saturdays, I believe. Oh, one more thing, I think it would be nice, if, say, a couple of tables could be put outside the shop, on the pavement with chairs and parasols, so that when the weather is fine customers can relax and enjoy eating al-fresco". She then goes on to say "However I don't have any capital to invest in such an enterprise, so it all depends on how much the running costs will be, so I need to know how much rent etc., you intend charging".

As she has been talking, Ella's voice has gradually got louder and louder, as she expands upon her vision for the future. Rachel has not seen her sister so animated since before Richard's death, and vows to herself that she will do everything in her power to make Ella's dream a reality.

Mr Souch, who has stayed silent during Ella's epiphany, suddenly smiles and says "well, you certainly have given it some serious thought, and your ideas certainly make sense. Now I have no wish to make things more difficult for you than necessary, so I propose that you only have a one-year lease, instead of five, which I would normally insist upon, and would make it payable one month in advance, instead of three. Then at the end of your first year we can look at it again and if you are in profit, or only breaking even we can renew the lease for a further five years. Not only that but I can arrange that you keep the fittings that the previous owner used for his newsagents. Obviously, some of them will not be suitable for your needs, but I am sure that you will be able to adapt some of them to display your cakes, rolls, sandwiches, and so on. You will also need to open a business bank account and I can speak to my bank manager and arrange for you to see him and perhaps arrange a loan for you to get started. But before any of that, you will need a business plan, but I can help you with that too, if you like". He then goes on to mention the rent that he will charge for the next year, and finishes by saying "I think that the next thing we ought to do is to go and take a look at the shop, so that you can not only envisage if there's sufficient room for you to do what you've talked about, but also what equipment you may need to get you started".

Ella by now has been swept along by the excitement of it all and has no hesitation in agreeing to view the shop, so, leaving the house, the three of them take the ten-minute walk to The Market Place, just off the High street. Ignoring the decor which is quite dilapidated, the paintwork peeling in places, Ella concentrates on the proportions of the shop which is wide at the front with a glass door in the centre, with a glass window each side which extend from about three feet from the floor to the top of the first floor level, which allows the light to flood in from outside. The interior of the shop appears to be about twenty feet wide by fourteen feet deep. Plenty of room thinks Ella to put a counter at one end with a display of cakes and anything else that she decides to make or sell, leaving ample space for several tables where people could sit and have teas with cakes or sandwiches, or bacon rolls.

Giving Ella the keys to the shop, Mr Souch says "Here you are my dear, why don't you and your sister go and have a look around and I'll be here when you come back".

Trembling with excitement, Ella unlocks the door and steps inside the shop threshold. A rush of stale air greets her but she continues on in until she stands in the centre of the room. "It certainly needs decorating", she exclaims to Rachel, "I will need to get rid of this awful dark green paper and paint it a pale shade of cream or something, so that it reflects the light coming through the windows. But it's a really good size and easily big enough to sit some tables and chairs, don't you think".

Rachel nods her head in agreement, not wanting to stop Ella's creative flow, something that she has only just recognised for the first time, and wonders why she hasn't noticed it before.

"Oh! And look here" Ella continues, as she notices all the racks and counter that the previous owner has left, "I'm sure that some of these can be used. The counter is ideal: if I put it toward one end of the shop. I can put glass shelves on top of it, so that I can display my cakes and anything else that I decide on. It is also big enough to put a till on at one end, so everything is at hand, and if I do that, it looks as if the entry from the back of the shop will be just behind it. Job done: don't you think? That will leave all the rest of the space available for tables and chairs".

"That sounds excellent Ellie, but first let's have a look and see what space is available through that door, because you will need a fair amount for baking and stock".

Hurriedly making their way through the door they find themselves in a small kitchen area, which contains a sink, a gas cooker, refrigerator, with a plain wooden table in the centre of the room. There is also a standing cupboard, which has shelves behind wooden doors at the bottom, with a pull-down flap in the middle, which can be used to prepare food or make sandwiches. Finally, there are two smaller doors at the top, with shelves, in which condiments and sauces can go. In the far corner is a door, which to their surprise and delight, leads to a small sitting room, which has a fireplace at the far end, on which coal or wood can be burnt. The room is about twelve feet long by ten feet wide, not too big but large enough for two or three chairs and a small table where meals could be served. Once again, the room is dark and needs redecoration, with just one sash window at the right-hand side, which Ella recognises is at the rear of the property. "This is good place to come during lunch times when the shop is shut" she tells Rachel" only to hear her sister reply "You don't seem to have twigged yet Ella, that you'll be able to live here as well as running the shop. If we go upstairs, I'm sure that we will find at least one bedroom, if not two. If that's the case, you will be able to leave Chadlington, which will save you the money on the rent for the house".

Ella stands motionless for several seconds, before she says "How stupid am I, it had just never occurred to me" and then more excitedly "Wow, that means that Daniel won't have so far to travel to school. Come on, let's take a look upstairs".

Climbing the stairs, they reach a small landing area and turning left where there are two doors facing them. Opening the first door on the left there is a small bedroom with room enough for a single bed and a bedside cabinet. There is also room for a single wardrobe and perhaps a small desk, thinks Ella, where Daniel could sit and do his homework. The floor is covered by linoleum and is the only item in an otherwise, completely empty room. Again, the décor is dark and oppressive; something that Ella knows will have to be addressed sooner rather than later. Finally, there is a large sash window which overlooks the front of the shop and faces out onto the Market Place, which is a cobbled area thronged with people scurrying about doing their daily shopping. Ella knows that this is the same area where markets are held on Tuesdays and Thursdays each week. It is this knowledge that tells her that there is a ready market for breakfasts early on market days, followed later on in the mornings by teas and cakes

Leaving the room, the sisters then open the second door which leads to a passage taking them to the second bedroom which is larger than the first, because of not having room lost to a passage. Ella can see immediately what needs doing and how she would like the room to look.

There is room for her double bed that she has in Chadlington, which she has not wanted to change because of her memories of it when Richard was alive. It is almost as if, to her, that he's still with her while she retains it. Her double wardrobe and dressing table will also fit in here with space to spare. This room has more natural light than the first bedroom, mainly because it has two sash windows, which again both look over the front of the shop onto the Market Place. The décor is much better in this room, having been painted in a pale cream colour.

This is the sum total of the living area of the property, with no facility for a bath or wash sink, so Ella is resigned to having to use her old large zinc bath that she has always used, and to strip wash at the kitchen sink on those days when she doesn't have a bath..

By now she is beside herself with a mixture of excitement and trepidation and can contain her emotions no longer, as she says "Oh! Rachel, what do you think? The shop and accommodation need a lot of maintenance, mostly painting and decoration, but if I can make the shop pay its way, being here in "Chippy" would have so many advantages for Daniel and me. But how will I be able to afford to do all the things that need doing to get it up and running"?

"Wow, slow down, and let's not run before we can walk. As Mr Souch says, we need to establish just what we need in terms of redecoration and furniture needed for both the shop and the living areas. Some, in fact most, of your furniture at home can be moved here, so you won't have to buy very much, and what you do need can be bought at local house sales. However, you will need to get better cooking facilities in the kitchen to cook and bake enough to sell on a daily basis. You will also need glass cases in which you can display your cakes etcetera, so that they're kept away from flies, wasps and other nasties. As for decorations, I'm sure that Fred will do as much as he can, but we can all pitch in to help. Also, the signwriting will need someone who specialises".

"Well" replies Ella "I've been thinking about the kitchen and the oven in particular, because I am sure that Dowager Mrs Stevens will let me buy the double oven from The Manor House. The people offering to buy the house are a consortium of business men who want to convert it into a hotel. If that happens, they will need all new up to date equipment and will only be too glad if they can get rid of the existing stuff. There may also be other equipment and fixtures that Mrs Stevens will let me buy at a reasonable cost.

Anyway, I think that all our efforts should be concentrated on decorating and refurbishing the shop: the living accommodation must take second priority, and can be done afterwards, but I think that's about all we can do for the moment, so let's go and see Mr Souch and discuss it with him. What do you think?"

Before leaving, they go out through the back door in the kitchen, which leads to a small patio garden area. Here there is a large solid building, built of the local Cotswold stone.

Upon examination it is apparent that it has been used to hold stock, which Ella thinks she can probably use for a similar purpose, but will still leave sufficient room to do other things here, although at the moment she doesn't know quite what for. It has a window running the length of the building, which allows the light to penetrate even the darkest places, so she thinks that perhaps she can prepare food ready for baking or cooking.

Returning to the outside of the shop, the sisters are met by a beaming Mr Souch, who welcomes them saying "Well my dears, what do you think: will it be suitable for your vision".

Ella cannot withhold her excitement as she replies "Oh I think it's just ideal for what I would like to do, but it's all just a bit too much for me to absorb at the moment. My head is going around and round with it all".

Mr Souch looks at her and notes the excitement in her voice, before saying kindly "Well my dears, why don't we go back to my house where we can think about it while we have a cup of tea", which they both agree to do.

On returning and once they are ensconced Mr Souch opens the proceedings, saying "Look Ella, I'd like to help you in any way that I can for two reasons. The first is that I like you because you can obviously see the potential in working for yourself, even though you have no experience, but your cooking experience and your enthusiasm shines through and with a little guidance from perhaps myself or Rachel I am sure you will be fine. The second reason is that I think that a café/restaurant is just what is needed in Chippy: something that it doesn't have just at the moment.

On a practical note what I am prepared to do in addition to the other things that I have mentioned is to arrange for the façade of the shop to be painted and decorated ready for you to move in. However, any signwriting I will leave to you".

Before Ella can reply, Rachel interrupts, saying "Oh Mr Souch, you have been so generous, and both Ella and I appreciate your very kind offers, most of which I am sure that we would both like to take up, but when it comes to things like legal advice and banking, I have a number of contacts that I use for the business that Mrs White and I run. For both your and Ella's sakes I think it would be best if we used people who are independent of you.

I am also competent to sit down with Ella and draw up a profit forecast and projected cash flow forecast, which should tell us what sales she needs to achieve to make a profit".

Mr Souch is locked in his own thoughts for a few moments before his countenance clears and he suddenly smiles and says "well I can see why you would prefer to do that: neither of us wants to get into an impasse or a conflict of interests. I only offered because I thought that perhaps you didn't know how to begin the proceedings, but obviously you do" giving a nod to Rachel.

"O.K. then, if we're agreed I will issue instructions to my solicitor to start the ball rolling, so if you could let me have the details of who will be representing your interests in due course, I will pass the information on to them".

Having said this, he stands and says" I suggest we celebrate in the appropriate manner, so, what are your tipples ladies?"

Once they have celebrated, Ella and Rachel take their leave of Mr Souch , and as they reach the outside of his house, Ella says excitedly "come on Rachel, I can't wait to get home and tell Daniel all about it, I hope that he's as excited as me".

Before she goes any further, Rachel holds her arm saying, "Look, I haven't said anything before now Ellie, but Fred and I have talked things over and agreed that if the shop is something that you would like to do, we are prepared to help you out with an interest free loan to get you started", then seeing her sisters apprehensive look, goes on to explain "Oh don't worry, we can afford it because I'm doing very well now, and anyway it will really be a loan, and it may not be enough to get all that you need, but it should take some of the pressure off you right now. We would not be looking for you to repay any of it in the first year, but if you are doing well after that, you can start repayment then and spread the balance over several years. You will still need to get a business bank account and arrange an overdraft facility, but it shouldn't need to be very substantial".

Ella is overwhelmed as she listens to the sister that she adores and worships, the one person who has shown that it is possible to achieve things from very small beginnings, and tears are suddenly flowing unreservedly down her cheeks, as she says in a broken tear laden voice "Are you sure Rachel, you have already done so much for me: why on earth would you want to do this as well" before breaking down completely as Rachel takes her in her arms saying "isn't it obvious little sis. I love you, and after all the terrible things that have happened, you deserve a break. Cooking is your passion, as designing clothes is mine, and without Mary offering me a partnership, my life could have been without hope, just as yours has been so far. I know that you can make a success of this venture Ella, so let's get on with it".

In this way it is agreed, and Ella's future takes a huge lurch forward, from working as a chef for a large mansion to being the proprietor of her own establishment in charge of her own destiny.

CHAPTER 5.

1956: ELLA'S CAFÉ.

For Ella and Daniel, the next few weeks are both hectic and exciting as the café enterprise progresses. Much to Ella's delight, Daniel has reacted positively to the concept and is both encouraging and practical, making a number of suggestions to problems that she has not even recognised.

Rachel, true to her word has arranged for Ella to see the solicitor that she uses, to arrange the lease for the shop, which is done incredibly quickly, mainly due to the fact that Mr Souch is so accommodating to Ella's requests.

Once the lease has been signed, Ella, Daniel, Rachel and Fred descend on to the shop in a flurry of activity, which has been logistically choreographed in the period preceding, when the only thing they could do with their time was to plan the next stage.

It had been agreed that most of the decorating of the shop and some of the living accommodation should be where their efforts are first concentrated. Ella, and Daniel, who has now finished his school year, makes a start, moving everything out of the interior of the shop in readiness for decoration. The following weekend, Fred arrives and paints the ceiling white, after which Ella and Daniel paint the walls in a warm cream colour.

The work progresses at a pace over the next three weeks with Ella and Daniel making their way each day on their bikes from Chadlington, while Fred manages to get a couple of days in each week, together with a couple of evenings as well. Luckily it is mid-summer, with light evenings, so they can maximise the light available to them.

Meanwhile, Ella has tentatively approached The Dowager Lady Stevens with a view to buying the double gas oven from the Mansion House together with other kitchen utensils that will no longer be required.

But she has no need to feel apprehensive when the Dowager readily agrees to Ella's request, saying "Of course you can have them my dear, but I wouldn't dream of taking any payment from you. They will be no longer required by the new owners and if this is the only way that I can do anything to help you after so many years of dedicated service, then I am happy indeed. I only wish that things could have been different, but it was inevitable that I would have to sell the estate once Lord Stevens died. I wish you every success in your new venture my dear. Please do come and see me when you can: you know where I'm moving to. It would be nice if I could see you from time to time, but I know that you'll be very busy, at least to start with."

Before Ella arranges to move the oven, she is suddenly consumed by doubts as she realises that the double oven will not possibly fit into the small existing kitchen in the shop. Upon explaining her dilemma to Daniel, he has an epiphany moment when he says "well mum, why don't you put it into the outbuilding behind the shop. It's structurally sound, so if you can get the Gas Board to run a supply from the house you could do all your baking for the shop out there. Not only that, but the place is huge, so you could put a large table where you could prepare bread and cakes with cupboards in which you could keep cooking materials. I noticed the other day that there is a cold-water supply and sink in the far corner"

"What a brilliant idea Dan, now why didn't I think of that? I'll get onto The Gas Board right away: well done son".

* * *

After three weeks of hectic, concentrated, back breaking work they all agree that it is time for Ella and Daniel to move into the shop. She has already given notice to terminate her rent agreement on the cottage in Chadlington, so on the second week in August they are ready.

Alf comes up trumps when the time for moving arrives, borrowing the farms tractor and trailer. That morning everyone is available to lend a hand. Alf, Daniel and Fred move most of the heavy furniture on to the trailer while the women pack the smaller items. The last large item to go onto the trailer is Richard's motor bike which Ella cannot bear to part with, particularly because in the last two years Daniel has started to restore it to its original glory.

He is beginning to show a similar interest to Richard in all things mechanical and has already stripped the BSA 250cc machine down to its component parts, carefully rubbing down, cleaning and greasing the engine, replacing the sparking plugs and brake pads, before draining the old engine oil, replacing it with new.

When he was alive, Richard had kept a wealth of tools that he had used for a similar purpose in the outside shed, so it is these that Daniel uses to refurbish his father's motor bike. Finally, he manages to get replacement tyres from the garage that Richard had worked for in Oxford. The owner has always kept in touch with Ella, remembering Richard with a great deal of affection and so when Daniel approaches him to buy tyres for the motor bike, he not only lets him have them at cost, but also gives him advice on problems to look for and gives him a manufacturers' construction book to help him.

For the last eighteen months, Daniel has worked in the one small general store in the village, on Saturdays, which is situated at the end of Bull Hill. His job involved being a jack of all trades, putting out vegetables and filling shelves, cutting cheese into various sizes and delivering to customers locally, who were not fit or well enough to collect them. He had known the store owner all of his young life, and it just seemed inevitable that as the former got more elderly that he would ask Daniel to help him out with the heavier onerous tasks. The pay wasn't very much, but enough for Daniel to save up over a period to enable him to buy spare parts for the motor bike.

Ella has watched her son rebuilding his father's machine with a mixture of pride and emotional turmoil, as he works calmly, totally engrossed with what he is doing, but occasionally coming up against problems. Whenever this occurs, he refers to the manufacturer's book to determine what he needs to do to resolve the problem. His patience seems endless to Ella, before she remembers that Richard had the same methodical approach, and she is overwhelmed once again by the similarities between father and son

When he is finished, the machine looks every bit as good as it was in its heyday, its metal surfaces shining like burnished gold.

Although it has not been discussed, Daniel has every hope that he will be allowed to take his motor bike road test

* * *

Eventually they set off: Alf driving, with Ella, Rachel and Elizabeth on board the trailer, with Daniel and Fred leading the procession on cycles. As they leave and pass other houses in the village, their friends and neighbours come to their doorways wishing Ella and Daniel good luck.

Ella suddenly realises the enormity of what she is doing, and tears join her smiles of happiness at the thought of leaving all these wonderful people who she has known all her life. But she is comforted by the thought that she will see them all regularly again, because they all go into Chipping Norton to shop, it being their nearest town and they have all promised to visit her. Her other concern is how Daniel will adapt to the new circumstances. He still has several friends in the village, although he doesn't see them very often these days: he has had to spend so much more time on home work this year, because he has recently taken his G, C E's and is currently awaiting the results. He is expected to get good pass marks, which will mean that he will return to the Grammar School in September in the sixth form, in preparation to take his A level exams the following summer, which will be his final year.

However, he has not shown any signs of concern about moving, knowing Chippy very well by now and is comfortable when he thinks about it, although he knows that his life will change living in the Café, because his mother will need his help.

Ella is very proud of her son, who is the image of his father and, she thinks, has inherited also his placid temperament and thirst for knowledge. Where his journey may take him, she has no idea, but is determined that wherever it is, she will be there to encourage and support him.

As the trailer with its two outriders on bicycles wends its way towards Chippy, Ella suddenly makes them all laugh when she says to Elizabeth "Oh mum, we should have taken the table from your dining room" to which her mother mystified replies "Why is that then my lovely", only to hear Ella reply "because I left my purse on it, so we're going to have to go back".

Once they have all stopped laughing, Elizabeth says "you are a silly whatsit, how did you manage to forget that. I tell you what, we will get Daniel to go back and get it, rather than us returning with the tractor. He will be quicker than us".

Thus, Daniel is despatched to recover Ella's purse, but the episode has lifted their spirits and the journey continues in an increased aura of optimism.

Arriving at the shop they devote the rest of the day arranging Ella's furniture and equipment where she has already decided it should go. She is particularly pleased with her new cooking area in the outside building at the rear of the shop. The double oven has duly been delivered, installed and connected to the gas supply. Fred has managed to give the room a fresh lick of the warm cream paint that he has used in the shop. This has the effect of making the room look bigger and lighter than before. Additionally, Ella has managed to buy a large pine table, together with matching chairs, as well as a number of cupboards that she has placed around the room for storage of the equipment and materials that she will need for baking and cooking.

She is delighted with the effect that has been created and excited at the thought of beginning her new career here in this room.

Once they have finished for the day, they all look around to see just what has been done already and what else needs to be done before Ella can consider opening the shop.

Most of the decorating has now been accomplished, but the small kitchen still needs some attention. By contrast the shop is ready for trading, thinks Ella, as she allows her gaze to roam around the room.

Both bedrooms are finished and ready for occupation, which Ella Is particularly pleased with. Her own now has most of her furniture from Chadlington, but she has managed to buy a large wardrobe at a house sale and a small bedside lamp where she can read when she goes to bed, together with a radio so that she can listen to her favourite programmes. But it is Daniel's bedroom in which Ella takes the most pleasure. Although quite small, it is now a light bright cream colour, to which Rachel has added matching plain cream curtains. At the same house sale where she managed to buy her wardrobe, Ella has found a small bedside table, together with a small desk, at which Daniel can do his homework or for any other projects that he may need to do. The existing worn dark oppressive linoleum has been replaced by a new one in a warm caramel colour, with a small carpet of a similar colour at the side of the bed, so that Daniels feet will be warm at least as he steps out of bed. Other than two of Richard watercolour paintings which Ella has thoughtfully added, his small wardrobe completes the refurbishment, so that he can be constantly reminded of his father. Above everything else, Ella is happy because Daniel has been consulted at every stage and confesses himself delighted with the finished project.

Fred has spent a great deal of his available evenings amending the existing counter to suit Ella's requirements: making it shorter and decorating it to match the cream colour of the walls. The previous owners have left a till, which is placed at one end, with most of the rest of the space used for glass display shelves for bread and cakes. Rachel has also contributed by making pale green curtains which she hangs on poles the length of the shop window at head height when customers are seated at the set of seven tables and chairs that Ella has bought at house sales locally. Around the room Ella has placed low level shelves which have table lamps on to give it a relaxed feeling of ambience. Last but not least, the floor has also been given a covering of linoleum in a dark green colour.

As she completes her visual navigation of the room, Ella knows that it is now as ready as it will ever be. Oh, there are still things that she would like to do, but these will have to come, if and when she starts to make profits

Once they are all assembled together after their hard day's work, Ella says, in a voice trembling and full of emotion "Well I can't thank all of you enough: without your help none of this would have been possible, but looking around I think that I am now ready to start trading".

"Don't be silly love" says Elizabeth "we just wanted to help, and what's more, we will continue to do so as long as you need us".

"Well it's funny you should mention that mum" says Ella, laughing "I was just wondering if you would like to do a few hours a week helping me in the café, serving, or washing up. At the moment I have no idea how much work will be generated, but initially most of my time will be spent baking and cooking, which won't leave me much time for being in the café. It suddenly occurred to me that now you are retired it may be something that you would like to do. I will of course pay you. You could ride here on your bike. What do you think"?

For a moment Elizabeth is silent, then said "well, you have flummoxed me there my dear, but thinking about it, a few hours a week should be fine. If I don't want to ride my bike, I can catch the early bus, so let's give it a try".

Ella is now thirty-eight years old and is facing the biggest challenge of her life, not that anyone would know it. She has been gifted with a facial bone structure that defies the aging process, and although her crowning auburn glory is now showing a few grey hairs, she is still a woman of substance. Her figure has remained lithe and supple, again due in no small measure to her ancestral genes, but also because of her work lifestyle. She has always worked long unsociable hours, work that involved not only lifting, stretching and carrying but also standing for long periods.

No man has ever even come close to replacing her feelings for Richard in her heart and she is resigned to the fact: concentrating all her emotions and maternal feelings on Daniel, determining that he will have a successful future that his father would have been proud of, had he lived.

CHAPTER 6.

1938: ELLA AND RICHARD.

Luckily, Richard does not encounter any wild horses as he rides his motor bike to Chadlington, on this, the appointed Thursday evening in April for his first date with Ella. He has left himself plenty of time, being unsure how long it will take him. In retrospect this is an error on his part, because he arrives at a quarter past six, some forty-five minutes before his appointed time.

Finding Ella's house, he is too embarrassed to knock on her door until seven o'clock, so he rides aimlessly around and around this pretty small village, unknowingly drawing attention to himself to a number of villagers, who recognise him as an outsider and wonder where he is going and what he is looking for.

Unfortunately for Richard, Ella is one of them who are drawn to their front windows by the sound of his motor bike as it traverses up and down Bull Hill, passing her gaze several times until it is time for him to call for her. She has told her parents about him and they join her at the window and watch with amusement as Richard continues on his pilgrimage around the village.

Seven o'clock arrives eventually and Richard approaches Ella's parents' home with a feeling of trepidation, wondering if Ella will greet him favourably or regret agreeing to meet him and make an excuse not to see him.

But his fears are proved groundless as she meets him at the door before he can knock, saying guilefully, with a smile on her face and with lips that are trembling with suppressed laughter "Oh Hi Richard, so you managed to find this place without any problems. Have you just got here"?

Not wishing to admit the time that he had originally arrived, Richard replies evasively "Only a few minutes ago, but I did take a ride around the village just to get my bearings", only to see Ella suddenly unable to stop herself from bursting out with laughter, saying "I thought that I noticed you pass by the window once….or was it twice, or maybe several times".

For the very first time Richard experiences at first hand Ella's sense of mischief and humour and loves her immediately for it. As he gets to know her better, he will discover that her sense of fun allows her also to laugh at herself and to see comedy and fun in the most unlikely situations.

She is dressed in a pale blue short sleeved summer dress with a scooped neckline that maximises the effect of her slim figure. Almost flat heeled black shoes (sensible shoes, as her mother would say) with the pale blue of her dress emphasises her honey coloured complexion caused from her many days spent working outdoors on the land. Her auburn hair tumbles in ringlets down to her shoulders, the light wind just now blowing it across her face, which she automatically flics behind her ears. Her legs are bare, and indeed, stockings could not compete with her natural look. Neither does she wear make-up, just a light brushing of dark red lipstick being her only concession to its existence. Her dark brown eyes are almost black as she laughs together with Richard, but become softer, almost the colour of melting chocolate when she is more relaxed and contemplative.

As he looks at her properly for the first time tonight, Richard says "You look stunning Ella, that blue dress suits you perfectly", and before she can reply he continues "where would you like to go. I thought that we could perhaps either go to the pictures. There's a Marx Brothers film on, that's supposed to be very funny, or we could just go to the pub for a drink. It will be dark soon, so it's getting a bit late for a walk. What do you think: is there anything else you would prefer"?

Ella, happy just to be with this young man for whom she holds such strong feelings, smiles and says "let's go for a drink Richard: somewhere we can talk. I would like to find out more about you. But let's go outside of the village: I know everyone here so we wouldn't be on our own at the Malt and Shovel".

"That sounds great, then we can exchange notes, because I would like to find out about you too. I tell you what: there are some nice pubs in Oxford, so why don't we take a ride there on my motor bike. I think you might be cold on the back, so you will need a coat or a cardigan".

Once it is agreed, Ella goes back to get a coat and a headscarf that she can wear, before getting on and sitting behind Richard. This is a new experience for her and she begins to enjoy the excitement of speed, the wind rushing past her head, while her arms encircle Richards's waist, his male strength and riding skill comforting her as they speed down the narrow country roads that are overhung by trees on either side.

On reaching Oxford, they find a pub on a quiet street which is not one thronged by university students: one which Richard knows and has used before, which is evidenced by the welcome that the barman gives him.

They find a quiet table in the snug room, with drinks and bags of crisps to sustain them. Ella, her unfailing curiosity killing her, begins, saying "well tell me Richard, where do you live, what do you do for a living, where are your family and why were you at the dance last weekend with Charlie. I have never seen you there before, so what were you….."?

Before she can say anymore, Richard interrupts, laughing and saying "Whoa! Wait a minute, one question at a time. Well to begin with I don't come from Oxford and I have only been here a few months. The truth is that I am originally from near Birmingham. On leaving school I became an apprentice at a garage workshop learning how to be a motor mechanic. I completed it a few months ago, only to be told by my employer that they didn't have any vacancies for qualified mechanics. This left me in a difficult position because there were no jobs in the area in which I lived. I didn't know what to do until a close friend that I grew up with told me that his uncle owned and ran a garage here in Oxford, and that he was looking for a mechanic: so, I applied, and the rest, as they say, is history".

"Oh no, you don't get away with it as easily as that" retorts Ella "what did your family say when you told them you were leaving. They must have been devastated".

"Well I don't have much of a family to speak of: I am an only child and my father died many years ago when I was very young. My mother met another man after being widowed for several years, and although I get on with him reasonably well, I can't say that I was sorry when I had the opportunity to leave my family home. In fairness my stepfather makes my mother happy, so leaving was no big deal. As for why I was at the dance the other night, it's quite simple really: when I first came here, I spent several evenings a week drinking in pubs, not having anything else to do with my time, and one night I met Charlie and we hit it off from the get go. It was he who suggested the dance and I was only too happy to go with him, just as a way to see and meet new people. I live in a pokey flat over the garage where I work, which is not very salubrious, so I don't stay in very often in the evenings, but that's enough about me, now tell me about you"

As he finishes speaking, Ella, who has been entranced, listening to him, is suddenly aware of his intense gaze as he looks at her and is lost in the moment. Recovering her composure, she answers shakily "There is even less to tell about me. I have always lived in Chadlington with my parents and elder sister Rachel, who is getting married in August. My parents both work on the farm and I started work at The Manor House as soon as I left school when I was fourteen, staring as a maid and ending up as cook".

"As you know I enjoy dancing, and have won several competitions, not just in Oxford, but also at some of the other villages locally. I have been with my dance partner for several years now, but unfortunately, he told me that he is getting married soon, so our partnership has now finished. We were just friends who enjoyed dancing, but I will miss the excitement of the competitions, because it has been such a large part of my life" and then with a mischievous twinkle in her eye "How do you fancy joining me as my new partner Richard". Before he can even reply, she sees the look of horror on his face, and says laughing "Don't worry, I was only joking " and then in a softer tone filled with emotion "I love the way that you danced with me, it meant so much more than any formal dance that I usually do".

"It was good for me too" replies Richard as he revisits the occasion mentally, and then changing the subject hurriedly "So what time do you get off from work. I guess you work a lot of unsocial hours if you're the cook".

"Well I don't normally get a lot of time off, but I usually get one half day a week off and sometimes Lord and Lady Stevens will go out to eat at restaurants in the evenings, mostly in London but also locally. The trouble is that quite often I don't know until a day or so before when it's likely to happen. The amount of entertaining that is done at The Manor House has declined over recent years due to their financial situation, but occasionally I still have to prepare meals for up to twenty guests. But they are very kind and if they are on their own, they will quite often let me know and I can then prepare meals in advance, which can be served to them by the maid. It's just the way it is in this sort of employment and I don't know what else I could do if I didn't work there. When I first started working there, I lived in all the time, but as things have changed over the years, I only stay overnight if they have a large party for dinner: other than that, I go home to my parents' house. It only takes me a few minutes to walk to and from The Manor House. They don't have many guests that stay over these days, but if they do then I'm expected to be there".

The evening continues, both of them trying to find out as much as they can about each other, aware of their growing feelings. But eventually they can ignore the time no longer, and Richard takes her home to Chadlington. The adrenaline rushes that Ella experiences riding pillion is even more heightened than before as they travel home down narrow country lanes in the pitch-black dark of the late April evening, with only a small beam of light shining from Richards motor bike. The feeling of total isolation, that they are the only people for miles around as they travel without seeing another soul, excites and consoles Ella in equal measure. She loves the feeling that they are as one against the world and, taking comfort from Richard's shape in front of her, holds him ever more tightly.

Arriving just up the road from her home, because they want to say goodnight without Ella's parents interrupting them, Richard cups Ella's face in his hands and kisses her gently saying "I have really enjoyed being with you tonight Ella. Can I see you again?"

Her response is immediate as she pulls him to her and kisses him with an urgency that surprises both of them. "I would like that very much" she murmurs' as she folds herself around him, her body sending her messages that she has not experienced before.

They both stand entwined together like statues for several minutes, neither speaking, not wanting anything to disturb the moment, but both aware that the feelings they both have are so much more than either have had before with anyone else. They also realise subconsciously that sometime soon the feelings and needs that they both feel will need to be explored more fully.

Eventually, breaking apart they agree that Richard will pick her up the following Sunday evening. He watches her return home safely before making the long journey back to Oxford, which seems like a fleeting moment as he relives his evening with Ella.

The cottage is in darkness when Ella enters, her parents already having retired to bed, because there working day starts early the next morning. Making her way to the bedroom that she shares with Rachel, Ella is surprised to find her elder sister still awake and obviously awaiting her return.

"Well, what did you do and where did you go: was he nice: he's very good looking" begins Rachel "I've been waiting for ages for you to come home. Come on little Sis, tell me all about it".

Ella is flustered for one of the first times in her life, still living the evenings experience in her mind and not wanting to share it with anyone else. But she can see that Rachel is not in the mood to be denied, so she relates it to her, carefully editing out things of a personal nature between Richard and herself, finishing by saying "Oh Rachel, he's so very nice: a bit quiet, but very funny: I like him a lot".

The two sisters discuss Richard, much as they have discussed both of their various boyfriends over the years, although Ella is slightly more reticent on this occasion, realising that this one is different, more special.

Their conversation spent, they turn out the light, only for Ella to lie looking at the ceiling, reliving the evening in her mind again and again, until she falls fitfully to sleep.

CHAPTER 7.

RICHARD AND ELLA, THE COURTSHIP

Richard duly arrives to pick Ella up on Sunday evening as arranged, after spending the time since their last meeting in a fit of anguished anticipation. He has continued to relive every precious moment of it in his mind, so much so that is he has convinced himself that their next meeting cannot possibly go as well as the first.

But it does, as she is waiting at the door, ready for him in case he has trouble finding the cottage again. She has borrowed a navy skirt from Rachel, something that the two of them do occasionally, to give an impression that their wardrobes are more extensive than is in fact the case. To compliment the skirt Ella wears a thin cotton cream twin set with "sensible shoes" which she wears because they are the most suitable if she is going to ride pillion on Richards's motor bike.

Richard is stunned by the vision of beauty that greets him with a twinkle in her eye as she says "Oh, you found it then, I was just going to stand at the top of the road in case you got lost, so that I could stop you going round and round again. What shall we do: I quite fancy going to the pictures, how about you?"

"I am never going to hear the last of it am I", he replies laughing, before sweeping her to him and tickling her mercilessly, until she begs for mercy. "Come on then, let's get going if we are going to get there in time for the last show: don't forget your coat".

The effect of the banter between them has lightened the mood, leaving them more relaxed in each other's company. On reaching Oxford they manage to get in for the last showing of The Marx Brothers' film "Duck Soup", which has both of them laughing uncontrollably. After some half an hour Richard plucks up courage to put his arm around Ella's shoulders, which she responds to immediately by nestling her head on his chest. As the film ends, but before the lights go up Richard looks at her, lost in her beauty, and cupping her face, kisses her. The kiss not only lingers for a long time, but is repeated several times until they realise that the people around them are beginning to leave.

They leave the cinema, Richard with his arm around her waist and make their way slowly to where he has parked his motor bike, interrupting their journey regularly to take time for more hugs and kisses. They are by now completely lost in each other, not wanting the evening to end, but knowing that it must. Eventually they find the motor bike and find their way back to Chadlington.

Pulling up outside the cottage Ella is amazed to find that the lights are still on downstairs and before they can say goodnight to each other, the front door is opened and Alf appears saying "Why don't you come in Ella, and bring the young man with you. Your mother and I would like to meet him".

This is a first, thinks Ella saying "come on in Richard and meet my parents".

He hesitates for a split second, before saying "I would like that very much Mr Carter".

"Just call me Alf" says his future father-in-law, "come in and have a cup of tea".

Both Alf and Elizabeth like Richard instantly. Ella stands beside him, ready to defend Richard if necessary, but she doesn't need to worry as Alf asks him quietly where he comes from and what he does for a living.

Richard tells them about himself, in much the same way as he did to Ella a few nights previously. When he hears that Richard is a motor mechanic Alf becomes very interested and their discussion continues around the mechanical equipment that he has to operate on the farm. He has arrived at mechanised farm equipment late in life and consequently often has operating problems. The main piece of equipment which is the cause of most of his problems is not being able to start the tractor first thing in the mornings.

Richard, hearing Alf's exasperation in his voice, offers to take a look at it the next time he comes to visit Ella. "If it's anything to do with the combustion engine then I'm your man, but I cannot help you on anything to do with any of the other equipment, such as the ploughing or harvesting equipment. I just do not have the tools for anything like that. But your starting problem sounds as if there is a too rich mix of petrol and air, so it could be that the choke needs to be adjusted, or perhaps you're flooding the engine with petrol by putting your foot down too hard or too often when trying to start the engine. Either way it's easy to put right".

Alf's relief is visible and Richard goes up even more in his estimation, much to Ella's amusement, as she whispers in his ear "now look what you've done Richard: now I'm going to have to share what precious time I do have with you, with my father".

Richard laughs before replying "Well Princess, I thought that it would be more advantageous for both of us, for me to get in your father's good books, rather than upset him".

This is the very first time that Richard has called her "Princess", but in the years to come it will become his pet word for her, representing the way he feels about her.

As the evening draws to a close, and just as Richard starts to take his leave of them, Rachel returns home with Fred, who is now officially her fiancé.

They are both delighted to meet Richard for the second time. Fred is three years older than Rachel, but he and Rachel have known each other for several years, beginning when they started dancing together. To begin with their love was a slow burner, but once it began to blossom, it ignited like a forest fire. They have been engaged for two years and have set the date of their wedding as 21st August, some four months away.

After exchanging pleasantries for a few minutes Richard stands up to leave, but before he can say goodnight, Rachel says in a voice brimming with excitement "You won't believe this, but we got the keys to the house in Charlbury yesterday that we are renting, ready for when we are married. It needs some redecoration, but we have already got plans for what we are hoping to do, so why don't you and Ella come and see it, the next time you get together. I know Mum and Dad will want to see it before that but we would love to show it to you as well. Oh, I am so happy: I can't stop thinking about it".

Richard glances at Ella, who he can see is just as excited as her sister, but before he can say anything Ella runs to Rachel and embraces her sister saying "I am so pleased for you both, of course we would love to see the house" and turning to Richard "wouldn't we ".

Laughing, he replies "You bet - wild horses couldn't stop us".

In her most solemn voice, Ella replies "So there you are Rachel, Richard never lets wild horses stop him from doing anything, although they do seem to have an effect on his navigational skills, which makes him not be able to find his way to places. I will go further than that; they seem to stop him being able to find his way to this house in particular". She finishes by giggling and poking out her tongue at Richard, before both she and Rachel collapse laughing uncontrollably in a heap on the sofa.

Richard takes Ella's joke at his expense with a smile, loving her sense of humour and mischief, before saying "Well I really ought to be going, it was lovely meeting all of you". Then, directly to Alf "perhaps I could come one Saturday afternoon and have a look at your tractor. I have to usually work on Saturday mornings, but I get paid overtime so it's quite handy. Ella doesn't have to be here. That way I don't have to sacrifice time with her".

Nodding in agreement Alf says" Of course you can my boy; I would appreciate that very much".

Accompanying him to the outside of the front door, Ella says" I didn't intend that you should get so involved with my family. Are you sure that it's O.K? If it's any consolation I can tell you that they like you very much. In fact, not one of the boys that I have brought home previously was ever asked in".

"Don't be silly, of course I don't mind Princess. It was nice to almost feel part of the family. I haven't had that feeling in a long time. Now come here so that I can kiss you".

Ella feels her body melt to his as they say their farewells. Her lips part as he kisses and caresses her, feeling her warm body through her thin cotton blouse. They can both feel the sexual tension running like a river through them, until Richard eventually breaks away saying "I think it would be best for both of us if I go now, before I do something that we would both regret" only to hear Ella reply "Oh, I would never regret it Richard, because I feel the same way, but I think that we ought to take some precautions first, don't you"?

Richard nods in assent, but does not know what precautions she can mean. Ella can see the look of bafflement on his face and realises like her, that he too is a virgin.

"Ask Charlie Lainchbury, he will know what to get and where from" Ella whispers in his ear, not wanting to be heard by anyone in the cottage.

"You do know that I love you", Richard replies.

"Oh yes, of course I do my love" Ella confirms tenderly, "and if I didn't feel the same way I wouldn't have agreed, now get off home".

Ella's next time off is on Wednesday, and Richard agrees to come to her, after she says that she will speak to Rachel and Fred and arrange to see their house in Charlbury.

* * *

Several weeks pass, during which time Ella and Richard spend increasing amounts of time helping Rachel and Fred decorate their house and make arrangements for their forthcoming marriage. The relationship between the four of them has grown, so much so that after a few weeks, Fred asks Richard if he will be his best man, while Ella is to be one of Rachel's bridesmaids.

Although they enjoy Fred and Rachel's company, the fact that they have not had any time to be on their own with each other, has meant that their relationship hasn't been consummated, simply because they have not had the time or the opportunity. Taking Ella's suggestion to heart,

Richard looks for Charlie and mentions his problem to him, without telling him his source. Recognising Richard's reticence and naivety in such matters, Charlie laughs before saying conspiratorially "all you need to do when you go to next get your haircut is say yes when the barber finishes and asks "do you want anything for the weekend". This phrase is in fact code for, do you need any condoms: it's easy".

Richard's face is a picture of confusion and embarrassment as he says "blimey, I have often been asked that, but I have always said "no thank you", because I didn't know what it meant. I feel awful now, what must they have thought of me".

"Don't worry, we all have to find out sometime" says Charlie, "good luck".

Richard has had them in his possession for several weeks now, which adds even more tension between them. Every time they say goodbye, they are both very aware of their need to release their feelings in the most natural way. Eventually, after several frustrating weeks, as they are saying goodnight one evening and emotions are running high, as Richard caresses her, Ella responds, moaning softly, until she suddenly breaks away from his embrace.

"Oh, Richard this is sheer torture, we are going to have to have some time to ourselves, but where can we go so that we can be on our own"?

Richard, who has thought of nothing else each time he leaves her, says "I've tried to think of somewhere we can go my love, and the only place that I have come up with is my flat over the garage in Oxford. It's pretty horrible; there is only a bedroom, living room, small kitchen and a toilet, and it's dingy to say the least.

 I would rather that we could use a hotel, somewhere where we could have the luxury and comfort you deserve, but I don't think that I would have the courage, to sign us in as Mr and Mrs Smith.

But I want you so much, what do you think"?

"I am happy to go to your flat; it will give me the chance to see where you live as well as just being with you".

In this manner It is agreed and the next time they are due to see each other they tell Rachel and Fred that they are going to meet some friends of Richard's in Oxford; a little white lie, which they console themselves is necessary just this once.

On the appointed day Richard picks Ella up and they make their way back to his flat in Summertown. When they arrive outside the garage Richard seems hesitant, until Ella says "You don't seem very sure, what is the matter. Don't you want to do this after all; I will understand if you've changed your mind".

Looking very unhappy, Richard says "Of course I still want to my love, more than anything, but to tell you the truth I am apprehensive. This will be the first time for me and I love you so much, that I'm afraid you might be disappointed".

"Oh, is that all" replies Ella, laughing, "well, I will let you into a little secret; I am petrified. Don't forget, this is the first for me too, so I feel exactly the same way as you. The way you looked made me think that you didn't want me anymore".

The relief on Richard's face as she speaks tells her that she has no reason to fear that she will lose him.

"Come on then, it's this way" says Richard leading her round to the back of the garage where there is a door which leads to a small hall with stairs leading up to the flat.

Once upstairs the first door leads into the living room, which Richard has obviously tidied up, and contains a small two-piece sofa and an equally small table at which he uses to eat. Apart from a small coffee table and a sideboard the room is Spartan, but functional. However, the décor is dark, the original colour Ella guesses to have been a pale green when it was applied many years ago.

Not stopping, Richard continues to lead her into the next room, which is the bedroom. Once there they both become quiet until Richard takes her in his arms saying "This is silly, why are we worrying? After all there is nowhere else, I would rather be right at this moment" and bending his head he reaches down to kiss her ready parted lips. She responds as his tongue flickers in her mouth sending shivers through her body. Stepping back Richard reaches with trembling fingers to undo the buttons on her blouse, before running his hands over her back and hips. Then carefully he reaches behind her to undo her bra, which he finds difficult, until Ella helps him and then guides his hands to her breasts.

The rest of the undressing is carried out at breakneck speed until all their garments are spread around the room.

Their lovemaking is also carried out at the same pace, once Richard has managed to apply a condom. The delay, while this simple procedure is happening, just increases the intensity, and leads inevitably, prematurely on Richard's part.

He is mortified and apologetic, saying "Oh I am so sorry my love", but she comforts him saying "It doesn't matter, we just need to learn how to pace ourselves" and holding his head on her chest she caresses him until he is relaxed.

They talk, as lovers do, of their plans for the future, for some time, until suddenly she feels his hardness against her. This time she coaxes him with soft words of encouragement, until she feels that he is ready, before guiding him into her. She seems to know instinctively how to control him with a word or by holding herself back so that he slows down, making the whole experience much more satisfying for both of them. Eventually her best endeavours fail as she too is overwhelmed by her own pent up feelings, and both of them are suddenly uncontrollably lost in a welter of emotion and lust. Climaxing simultaneously, they part until they lay spooned together in a post coital haze, totally exhausted with Richard's arms around her, in complete harmony.

They sleep for a while until Richard gently shakes her awake, saying "I think that we ought to get back to yours Princess, the time is getting on".

Drowsily Ella rouses herself, before looking at him and smiling lazily "well that was wonderful my love, better than anything I could have wished for".

Sitting up she reaches for her clothes, only to see Richard looking transfixed unashamedly at her naked body. Then in a voice filled with emotion and awe "Oh Ella, you are so beautiful" and then reaching out to touch her "I just can't get enough of you, I want you again".

Ella laughing says" I thought you told me we ought to go," and then tenderly "you know that I love you. There will be lots more times when we can do this again, but you are right, we do need to leave now".

Hurriedly dressing they make ready to leave, but as they go through into the living room again Ella suddenly notices a pile of papers on the table. Glancing at them she can see what appear to be watercolour paintings. She looks at the top one and is amazed to see a head and shoulders painting of her own self.

Thinking she must be mistaken, and that it is just a coincidence she asks Richard "How did you get these, did somebody you know do these for you". And then she adds" is this one me, it's lovely, look she's even wearing the same clothes as I wore the other day".

Richard looks flustered and embarrassed for a moment, before replying "Yes that is you, do you like it, I did it from memory the other day".

"You did it"? Questioningly, then quickly perusing some of the other paintings, she says "These are really, really, lovely Richard, look here's one of Oxford city centre, oh, and here's another of the inside of the old market". Then accusatorily" I didn't know you could draw and paint like this, they are all very good. Why didn't you tell me"?

"Well there never seemed to be a right time. I have always loved doing watercolours. I had a very good teacher when I was at school that encouraged me and said that I should take it further, but I didn't know how. Anyway, I was going to give you the one of you as a present for your birthday, but I will get it framed and you can have it if you like".

"I certainly do like. It's beautiful, thank you so much" and then "You should get the rest of them framed, I'm sure you could sell them, especially the local views" and then, kissing him lingeringly" Let's go, before I change my mind about going back to bed".

So the new lovers make their way back to Chadlington, totally absorbed and besotted with each other, Ella thinking that she couldn't be more happy, while Richard makes a mental note to buy more than just one packet of condoms the next time he goes to the barbers, to avoid the necessity of having his haircut every week.

CHAPTER 8.

RACHEL'S WEDDING

Time for them both is a precious commodity and as the summer of 1938 moves on, so does Ella and Richards's relationship, their love deepening and growing. They manage to get to Richard's flat on a fairly regular basis, even though it's not enough to satisfy their growing need for each other. Each time that they manage to get there, to the place that they have come to regard as their refuge from the outside world, Ella adds her woman's touch; a vase of newly cut flowers, a frame with a photo of the two of them, even a cream bedspread that she has bought from the market in Oxford. She also cleans and tidies up, or tells Richard to, if she doesn't have much time. The flat still needs decorating, which will not happen, and it will never be as they want it, but it is the best option they have and they are both grateful for it.

They have never told any of Ella's family about their time together at the flat, usually just saying that they are going to Oxford for a dance or a show. Ella feels a little guilty about this, but consoles herself that she would feel worse if she didn't have the opportunity to be with Richard so that they can fully express their love for each other, remembering back to the frustration and need that they had felt previously.

Rachel and Fred have spent all their time so far this summer getting their house in order. Fred is a painter and decorator by trade, having served an apprenticeship with a company in Witney. About sixty guests have been invited to the wedding, which is due to be held in Chadlington Church, followed by the reception just across the road in the school hall.

Almost without anyone realising it, suddenly it is the 19th of August, just two days before Rachel and Fred's wedding and Rachel is showing signs of nerves, because she has designed and is making her own wedding dress.

The problem is that because she has had to spend so much time decorating and helping Fred at their house, she still hasn't quite finished her dress. Ella and Richard insist that they will go to the house this evening to help Fred with all the little finishing touches, which will release Rachel and give her time to finish the dress.

On the next night Richard has arranged to take Fred and Alf together with some of his friends out to the pub for his stag night, while Rachel,

Ella and their mother stay home talking weddings and going over the itinerary in case there is something that's been overlooked.

Knowing that beer will flow like lava down the side of a volcano, Richard decides that it is best if they go to the Malt and Shovel in the village, rather than go to a village further away, in order to avoid any transportation problems if they get drink too much, which will almost certainly be the case.

His supposition is proved correct and by closing time all of them are the worse for wear to say the least. The problem is that Fred is by now totally incapable of walking, but Richard thinking outside the box overcomes this, by returning to Alf's cottage and coming back with his barrow. Lifting Fred into it at a jaunty angle they all make their way to his parents' house where they deposit him unceremoniously and prop him up against the front door before ringing the bell and running off as fast as they can, laughing uncontrollably.

By the time Alf and Richard get back home to the cottage all the lights are out, Elizabeth and the two sisters taking advantage to have an early night, before Rachel's big day.

Alf makes his way upstairs while Richard goes to sleep on the sofa.

The morning of the wedding dawns bright with the sun hanging in a cloudless sky, illuminating the honey coloured Cotswold stone of the houses. Richard is the first to rise, wanting to be up before any of the others come down. It has been agreed that he should stay the night so that he doesn't need to make the journey from Oxford. He has brought his only suit and the other things he will need for the church service.

Just as he rises, he hears a light step on the stairs and Ella appears in the living room grinning from ear to ear. Knowing her and her zany ways, Richard says "come on, out with it, tell me, what you have done now".

"Well I couldn't let Rachel's last night sleep here, go without doing something that she will remember it by. I thought about it, and just before the two of us went up to bed last night I came up and put some itching powder in her nightie.

It didn't seem to work for a while, but once she settled down to sleep and turned over a couple of times, it worked a treat. She suddenly sat up in bed, scratching all over. I think that she thought that she was ill, that was until she looked across to me and saw that I could only stop myself from laughing by putting the corner of my bedsheet in my mouth.

The minute she saw that, she jumped straight out of bed and rushed over to me with her pillow, hitting me round the head and screaming, "I might have guessed that it was you, thank God I won't have to sleep here with you again" and then "I didn't mean that Ellie, in fact I will miss you like crazy"

"After changing her nightie, so that she stopped itching, the two of us sat up just talking about growing up and then how things were changing, but we both vowed that we would always be there for each other. I shall miss her Richard she has always been so kind and loving: the best sister anyone could ever have".

Taking her in his arms Richard remarks "You are going to get your comeuppance one of these days Princess, and if I have my way it's going to be me that give it to you. Now get on back upstairs before you parents find us with you in just your nightdress".

The morning disappears in a flurry of activity; most of it being duplicated by different people, in their panic to make sure everything is ready. The wedding is at twelve noon, so at just after eleven Richard and Elizabeth make their way to the Church, where they find Fred, who is looking pale and distracted, together with the ushers and some of the guests who have arrived early.

Arrangements for the bridesmaid's transport is by pony and trap, which leaves the cottage at half past eleven. Once it has arrived at the church, it turns around to pick up Alf and Rachel.

Arriving the almost prerequisite ten minutes late, Alf proudly walks his eldest daughter down the aisle to the sound of the organ playing "Here Comes the Bride".

Rachel's efforts in making her own wedding dress have been completely vindicated, as she moves slowly and gracefully down the church to meet her future husband. Made of satin with a high collar and three-quarter length sleeves, the dress then falls tightly to her waist, emphasising her trim figure, before flowing out to finish at mid-calf length, a daring, provocative length for this period. Her veil cannot completely conceal her wonderful smile as she reaches Fred, until, pushing it away from her face she reveals her serene countenance, her beauty for all to see. There is a tear in Alf's eye as he stands back, which runs softly, unashamedly down his face as he carries out his last official function for his daughter, although he suspects like all parents that there will be many more unofficial functions that he will be called upon to make over the coming years.

Vows completed, the congregation make their way outside to the front of the church for the obligatory photographs to be taken, before crossing the road to the school hall where the reception is to be held.

The world is only just recovering from the recession caused by The Wall Street crash of the late 1920's, so money is tight, most of their friends and relatives being low paid agricultural workers and others in service.

For this reason, Elizabeth, together with one or two others in the village, has made the food for the reception. It consists of vegetable soup to start, followed by a chicken and ham salad; then finishing with strawberries and cream; most of the ingredients coming from Alf's allotment and chicken run.

Alf, who is nervous and not used to making speeches, never the less has the guests in gales of laughter and tears in turn as he first relates Rachel's life growing up and then of his and Elizabeth's pride in the woman that she has become.

"She was always the leader when there were a group of children and she would take them on adventures over the fields, but here's the thing, she invariably got lost and Liz and I would soon have their parents' round to us at their wits end wondering where they were. But she always managed to find her way back eventually. I have always found her tenacity and determination to overcome obstacles one of her most endearing features as well as her sense of humour and fun. The other thing that she used to do was to invite her friends' round to our back garden and use my shed as her very own dress shop, using any of her and her mothers' cast-off materials, she would dress them up and very good they were too. As you can see Mary" continues Alf, addressing Rachel's employer who has been invited "she has always been interested in fashion and making clothes".

Richard, as best man makes a funny, emotive speech, recalling some occasions that the four of them have had, finishing by telling everyone about Fred's stag night and how he came to be propped up outside his parent's house.

Everyone who is here, with the exception of Rachel's employer Mary, has known her from the time when she was born, and their cries for her and Fred's best wishes follow them as they leave by pony and trap, to catch the train from Charlbury, for the start of their honeymoon.

Once the bride and groom have left, the guests start to say their farewells and drift away. Elizabeth. Ella, Richard and Alf, along with one or two others then clear up, before returning home, where Alf breaks out a bottle of sherry for Elizabeth and Ella and a bottle of whisky for Richard and himself.

Richard and Ella had talked about going in to Oxford once the wedding was over, but seeing that her parents are obviously missing Rachel, they stay and spend the evening with them. Alf and Elizabeth are in a reflective mood, recalling stories of Rachel and Ella growing up, which Richard in particular, listens to avidly, filling in some of the gaps in his knowledge of this close-knit family which he has come to know and love.

The next morning life returns to normal, Ella rising early and leaving to return to The Manor house to prepare breakfasts for Lord and Lady Stevens, while Richard spends time with Alf at the farm servicing the tractor.

* * *

Up to this point in their relationship, Ella and Richard have been content to let it develop gradually; both of them are completely assured of their love for one another, and although they have talked of marriage and their future together at some time, they have very little means to achieve this financially. Richard works as many hours as he can, which means that he can save something towards their future, but Ella's wage is meagre, because she lives partly at The Manor House, a factor which is taken into account as part of her wage.

However, Rachel and Fred's wedding is the catalyst, the defining moment in Ella and Richard's relationship that focuses and determines their future. It is as if by seeing that her sister can achieve this, then, by implication, so can they.

They optimise the little time they have together as much as possible, as summer turns to the autumn of 1938. As the last warm days gradually fade and the leaves on the trees change from green to their autumnal hues of red and gold, they explore the surrounding Cotswold villages and countryside, either on Richard's motorbike or sometimes on foot. Ella encourages Richard to take his sketch book with them, and finding a suitable place he makes rough draughts which he can develop into watercolours later. Meanwhile she sits close by reading a book or knitting, a skill that Elizabeth has taught her daughter, and which is almost a necessity, because of the cost of manufactured knitwear.

As the weather becomes colder, they either visit Rachel and Fred at their house, or return to Richard's accommodation in Oxford, because they have determined to save as much money as they can for their future. But every time she sees her sister at home in her own house it only makes Ella long for something similar for herself and Richard.

On the very few occasions that they manage to get to Richard's little flat, they welcome the opportunity to go to bed and make love. By now they know each other's needs and desires, the things that each of them likes to please one another; the positions that each prefers and most importantly, knowing when they are both ready, so their lovemaking can be immensely satisfying for both of them.

But these times are infrequent, so consequently they are both almost ravenous with desire for each other when the opportunity arises; so much so in fact, that on a particular day at the end of September, when they arrive at the flat and start to climb the stairs they both begin undressing each other in their haste. Not being able to wait until they reach Richards bed, they make love avidly on the floor of the living room. They lay prostrate on the floor murmuring words of endearment to each other for some time, before they go to the bedroom to continue exploring each other again.

Suddenly, as they are both aroused once more, Richard realises to his horror that he did not take any precautions on the first occasion. He is distraught with worry and hurriedly explains and apologises to Ella, who, to his surprise is relaxed, saying "Oh don't worry my love, we will have to be extremely unlucky for anything to happen; that was the first time and I know a lot of couples that have tried for years to get pregnant without success. Now forget all about it and let's make the most of this evening".

Similar incorrect assumptions have been made since the dawn of time as Ella eventually discovers after a few weeks, experiencing first that she has missed her period which have always been regular up until now, then the usual symptoms of pregnancy; the gradual swelling of her waist, the hardening of her nipples and growth of her breasts, followed by early morning sickness. She does not tell Richard that she has missed her period, but when the other symptoms appear, she has no other option.

After she has explained everything to him, Richard's expression is at first of shock and horror, the world at this time associating such situations as a sin and the women concerned, in particular, as no better than prostitutes. All this is running through Richard's mind as she tells him, but suddenly he sees the opportunity that this situation can give them and his demeanour lightens and he says smiling at her "well Princess, perhaps now is the time for us to get married. You must know that there is nothing in the world that I would rather do, so let's do it". Then looking at her worried expression, he hurriedly continues "you do want us to get married don't you"?

"You know I do my love, but I don't want you to think that I am trying somehow to trap you into it, because if we got wed under those circumstances, it would never work".

"Oh. Ella, how can you even think that? I love you more and more each day, and the reason that you are in this position is because of my carelessness, so marrying you solves both my and our problems".

"But what will my parents say; I expect they will want no more to do with me, bringing my shame upon them. They don't deserve it. Oh, Richard what are we going to do".

"Don't worry Princess; I'm sure your parents will do no such thing. They are the most loving attentive people, who, I am sure, want only the best for their children. Oh, they will be shocked I have no doubt, but that is understandable given the situation, and they will hold me responsible, as indeed I am, but ultimately, they will want that which is best for you, and hopefully us. But we have to tell them as soon as possible; not to do so will only make things so much worse. Once they can see that we love each other and want to get married, I am sure that any worries they have will disappear. In the meantime, I will ask my boss if we can live at the flat once we are married. He is a good man and I am certain that he will say yes. It won't be perfect, but it will at least be a start". Richard pauses before continuing "I think that we should tell your parents the next time that we see them, which will be next week; what do you think? Oh, once we have done that, I need to tell my mother; I have told her all about you of course, because I telephone her occasionally. Perhaps we could go and see her once we have seen your parents; she will be so happy to meet you Princess".

Ella nods, lost in contemplation, before replying "I would like to meet her very much and agree about everything else my love, providing you are sure that is what you want".

"I have never wanted anything more in my life than being with you Princess, so marriage will mean that we can be together all the time, instead of just a few fleeting moments now and then. Let's do it" and then "isn't everything both exciting and frightening at the same time. Would you believe it, I am going to be a father; I feel like dancing or singing. I want to tell the world".

Ella, listening to Richard, is caught up in his enthusiasm and says tenderly "I have a much better idea, why don't you take me back to bed".

CHAPTER 9.

ELLA'S WEDDING

Dreading the confrontation with Alf and Elizabeth, Richard duly arrives on the appointed evening. Ella greets him at the door and whispers "are you sure that you want to do this tonight" to which he replies "No, not really Princess, but I don't think we have any other option. Anyway, it will only become harder the longer we leave it". Then taking her in his arms they embrace briefly before going inside to meet their fate.

Alf greets Richard like a long-lost son as he usually does, until suddenly noticing Richard's strained look and grey pallor says "whatever is the matter son; you look as if you have just found a penny and lost a shilling; is there anything the matter".

Richard is almost glad in a strange sort of way that Alf has given him an opening to explain the situation. If Alf had not shown concern, then Richard would have had to interrupt the normal happy atmosphere of the house; but this way both Alf and Elizabeth are already half expecting to hear bad news, even though from their viewpoint it is much worse than they are thinking.

"Well there is something that Ella and I need to tell you" Richard says stumbling over his words, before pulling himself together "Ella and I have only known each other for a short time, but what you may not be aware of is that we both love each other very much and have always planned to get married since soon after we met". At this point, as Alf begins to respond Richard holds up his hand and says "Sorry Alf, just let me finish while I have the courage. Well the truth of the matter is that Ella is now pregnant with our child, which, although we obviously didn't plan for it to happen at this stage of our relationship, has made us both so happy.

At this point Ella moves closer to Richard and takes his hand in hers to support him as he continues "although we are both deliriously happy about it, we realise what an awkward situation this puts you in, so will understand completely if you want nothing more to do with us; but we both desperately hope that you will find it in your hearts to support us"

As he finishes speaking there is a deafening silence which is suddenly broken by Elizabeth as she moves to Ella and embraces her saying "Oh my dear child, you must be worried to death. How can you think that we wouldn't support you; we love both of you so much" and then more sombrely "of course we would have preferred that you got married in your own time, only because it would give you more choices. But hey, we get very few choices in this life, so in the grand scheme of things I guess it's more important that you love one another, because whatever the future may bring you can face your adversities together.

The disadvantages of having a child before marriage is that you don't have time to plan for it, so you are constantly at a disadvantage; for example have you thought where you'll live or how you'll manage once you have to finish work at the Manor House. I'm sure that you could live here with us for a while, but with only two bedrooms things will be cramped. So, you see, you have to think of the next stage of your relationship, because your new life begins now".

As she finishes, Richard replies "We agree that the circumstances are not ideal, but the first thing that we need to do is to get married. Oh I know that people will still count back on their fingers once the baby is born to the day we got married, but they have been doing that since the beginning of time; there is nothing we can do about that, other than to say that it was born early when the time comes, so the sooner we get married the more plausible it will be.

Our main reason to do this soon is for your sakes. The fact that Ella is pregnant is our fault, or mine actually, but we don't want it to reflect on you, because you have always been considerate and caring to me as I know you have to Ella.

Obviously, it would be better if we got married discretely, in say the Registry Office in Oxford, rather than Chadlington church, which will save you a lot of embarrassment.

As regards where we will live, I have already approached my boss at the garage, who has agreed that we can both occupy the flat that I'm living in at the moment. When he first started the garage, he lived in it with his family until the business picked up, after which he moved a few miles out into the countryside to a larger property.

It's not ideal; there's only one bedroom, a small living room and a kitchen, but it will at least be something until we can find an alternative. The major advantage is that my boss doesn't charge me anything for it, mainly because he knows that it is a huge factor when he wants to employ someone, to be able to offer the facility. It also comforts him to know that there is always someone on the premises most of the time as a deterrent to stop the garage being vandalised.

With regard to Ella's work, we have agreed that she will work as long as possible at the Manor House. That is about as far as we have come regarding what we'll do, so what do you think"?

For a few seconds there is total silence as Alf contemplates Richard's remarks,, before saying in a husky voice filled with emotion "well you've obviously given the matter a lot of thought, which is to your credit" and then, giving Elizabeth a sidelong glance he continues, "As for your wedding, I am sure that your mother and I both want you to be married here in Chadlington. I hear what you say about trying to save our embarrassment, but you have no need to worry on that score because nearly every family in the village has had a similar experience over the years. I know of at least one occasion where two daughters of one family had to make premature trips to the altar; so, you see most people will understand because it's invariably happened to them as well".

Before he can be interrupted, Alf continues, a smile breaking through his up until now serious countenance "Anyway your news has just been the icing on the cake for your mother and me, because Rachel and Fred dropped in last weekend to tell us that they are expecting a baby in May of next year. Can you believe it - we are going to be Grandparents to both of you within a few short weeks of each other"? And then "hang about, this deserves celebrating, I'll go and get some of that beetroot wine that I made back in the summer, so that we can do the job properly.

The relief that Ella and Richard both feel as they realise that her parents understand and support their situation is palpable. But the news of Rachel's pregnancy is fantastic, not only because it means that the two sisters will be able to share the experience together, but also because its news has disarmed to a large extent, the possibility of any hostile attitude her parents may have adopted toward them.

As they drink Alf's beetroot wine, they continue to discuss Ella and Richard's wedding, with Alf and Elizabeth insisting that it is a white one, carried out in the traditional manner in Chadlington church, with the date set for 17th December.

Richard, continues to offer the Registry Office as an alternative venue, not completely convinced that Alf's explanation that everybody in the village will understand their situation, until after mentioning the subject for a third or fourth time, Alf looks across to his wife and says "well Liz shall we tell them"?

Ella's mother with a sparkle in her eye replies "Oh. I think that we have to, they are not going to understand unless we do".

Ella and Richard are completely mystified with her parent's obviously private conversation, until Alf says "where to start? Well you have left us no alternative, the truth of the matter is that your mother and I also had to get married all those years ago, when she fell pregnant with Rachel, so you see we understand perfectly how you're feeling. In fact, you seem to have more answers to the problem than we did, because our only option was to live with your mother's parents until we could afford or find somewhere where we could live. So now you see why we want you to be married in Chadlington church. Not only that, but I have no doubt that more than half of the women in the village who have been married there were already pregnant by the time they walked up the aisle".

"Oh, I know that they and we have committed sin in the eyes of God, but I am sure that he forgives those whose only sin is to love one another and who show it by cementing their union in his house".

Ella and Richard are stunned as Alf's tale unfolds, but the atmosphere in the room is lifted now it has been told, and the four of them begin to plan in more detail the arrangements for the forthcoming wedding which, they all agree will be held in Chadlington Church.

Having only just a couple of months previously funded Rachel's marriage, Alf and Elizabeth's finances are not in a good place, or as he will admit, they are skint.

But they are resourceful and experienced in making silk purses out of sow's ears. The first thing to be recognised is that the numbers of guests to be invited to the wedding will be small, but taking a leaf out of Rachel's wedding they can still do a buffet using vegetables from Alf's allotment and drinks from his home made wine, although they could probably afford to buy sparkling wine for the toasts. Richard tries to insist upon contributing towards some of the costs from his savings, but Alf and Elizabeth are resistant.

The evening ends on a high note, something that Ella and Richard would not have believed possible when he first arrived.

For his part Richard, who already respects his future in-laws immensely, holds them even higher in his estimation now.

As he leaves Ella he says "Well that went better than I expected Princess; I think that the next thing I'd like to do is for us to visit my mother and tell her that we are getting married, but I think it's best if we don't mention that you are pregnant".

After further discussion, it is agreed that he should telephone her and arrange a suitable day that they can visit her.

* * *

On the appointed day Richard, with Ella on pillion, rides to Solihull on his motorbike to see his mother. This is the area of Birmingham where his mother lives. As they get near, he points various places which have meant something to him over the years. They reach Uffington Avenue after two hours, a street of terraced houses, all very similar in appearance.

The avenue has plane trees running down each side of the road and this somewhat softens the austere symmetry of the houses.

Reaching number 85, they dismount and approach the front door, which is opened before they can get there by a grey haired woman of diminutive height who rushes out to greet her son and, hugging him, says "Oh Richard, it's so lovely to see you after all this time", and turning to embrace Ella "come in my dear you are most welcome. I can't wait to hear all about you; Richard can't stop talking about you".

On entering the house Ella discovers that it is quite small, the front door leading directly into the living room at the front. From this room there is a door that leads through into a small kitchen at the rear of the property. Richard has already explained that there are only two bedrooms upstairs, neither of them being very big

Richard's mother (call me Deidre, she asks Ella) appears to be about sixty years of age, thinks Ella, which if it so, means that she would have had Richard late in life, which confirms what he has already told her.

Her face is lined, indicating a life of hardship and worry, although it is alive with excitement and expectation at this moment, softening her features considerably.

"Come and sit over here" says Deidre, indicating two small sofa's, one each side of the open hearth coal fire which is burning brightly, throwing out flames, their silhouettes flickering on the walls of the dark room "I will just go and get Stephen, I think he's out in the garden. Then I'll get us all a cup of tea and some biscuits".

As she leaves the room Richard and Ella look at each other, before he says "Stephen is my step father" and then "just keep to the story that we agreed; that we are getting married mainly because the owner of the garage has agreed that we can have the flat to live in. It will serve no good purpose for them to know that we are expecting a child. Not that I am ashamed or anything like that, but just because mum, being mum, will only worry herself sick about us".

As he finishes speaking his mother and stepfather appear and introductions are made again. Stephen is slightly built with pale blue watery eyes and thinning sandy hair, but he has a ready smile and welcomes them profusely. He too looks aged, probably before his time thinks Ella, knowing that he is only in his early sixties.

Once cups of tea and biscuits have been produced, Deidre opens the conversation "Come on now both of you tell me all about Oxford and your work and how you met each other".

Not wanting to prolong telling his mother the main reason for their visit, Richard begins "well mum, we have some news which we hope that you will like" and then taking a deep breath "you see Ella and I are getting married on 17TH December and apart from her parents, you are the next people to know".

He then goes on to explain how Ella and he met, and how they feel about one another, before explaining that his boss, knowing that they are thinking of getting wed, has offered them the flat, so that they can have somewhere to live. To reinforce this, he tells Deidre that Ella's parents have given their consent to the union, which is necessary, because Ella is not yet twenty-one. This is not something that applies to Richard, because being born in 1917 he is already of age.

" That is such fantastic news son, we're so pleased for you, aren't we Stephen". "You bet we are; I think, so much so, that it deserves a celebration. Now let me see if I can find that bottle of Sherry my dear", after which he begins to rummage around in the sideboard on his hands and knees, appearing triumphantly after a few minutes holding the said bottle aloft.

The afternoon continues with a question and answer session, Richard and Ella fielding all Deirdre's potentially lethal verbal queries as best they can, without committing any obvious faux pas that will give away the fact that Ella is pregnant.

Once this has been overcome, the conversation turns to the more prosaic, with Deidre and Stephen getting Richard up to date with the happenings in their life, until it is time for them to go, because Ella has to be back at The Manor House that evening.

* * *

It is only after much discussion that it is agreed that the wedding should take place on 17th December; the major disadvantage being that it will be very close to Christmas, but they all feel that if they are to play "the premature birth card", with the baby's expected birth date to be the middle of June the following year, it will be more credible. Richard and Ella have by this time told Rachel and Fred their news and congratulated them on theirs.

Rachel is ecstatic when she learns of her little sister's pregnancy and the two of them spend many hours comparing notes as time progresses. But she is also a tower of strength in helping Ella with her wedding arrangements.

With little money being available, Rachel decides that Ella can have the dress that she was married in only two months previously. When she first tells Ella, her sister is slightly alarmed, thinking that everyone will recognise it, but Rachel reassures her that she will alter it, so that it will look not only different, but also as new.

She is as good as her word and Ella is left once again in awe of her sister's prodigious talent, as she tries the dress on for the first time. Gone is the high satin collar only to be replaced by a rounded neckline that shows off Ella's long elongated neck to perfection. The waist has been slightly let out to accommodate Ella's burgeoning baby bump, which she feels conscious of, but which Richard feels is a figment of her imagination.

Rachel has left the skirt length to mid-calf, but has added a train at the waist which flows around the skirt and reaches almost to the floor. When Ella walks, the train gives the impression that, rather than walking, she is flowing effortlessly.

"Rachel it's perfect" cries Ella "I can hardly believe that it's the same dress; thank you, thank you, thank you a thousand times my wonderful sister, how can I ever repay you?"

Laughing, Rachel replies "The look on your face is all the payment I need. Now what is next on your wedding agenda"?

"Well, dad and mum have booked the church and the school hall for the reception; oh, and the invitations have been sent out, although there are only about forty people invited; still I am very grateful, because it's better than just four or five guests at the registry office. The only problem with the service being at this time of year is that I will have to work at The Manor House all over Christmas and the New Year, because Lord and Lady Stevens hold several banquets during this period, which means that we cannot have a honeymoon or even see much of each other until early January. Not that we could afford to go away, but if I didn't have to work, we could at least spend time together at the flat".

* * *

The seventeenth of December dawns with a widespread white frost covering the village and surrounding area like a mantle. As the morning progresses the frost continues to hold.

Rather than make the journey from Oxford and being told in no uncertain manner by all the women of Ella's household that it is unlucky to see the bride on the day before the wedding, Richard stays over at Rachel and Fred's home in Charlbury.

On his stag night, the previous evening, Fred had wreaked his revenge on the bridegroom-to-be. Gathering much the same crowd of friends that had attended on his stag night, they all adjourned to The Ragged Staff pub in the village, where Fred plies Richard with a cocktail of drinks, to which he succumbs amazingly quickly to everyone's amazement. In fact, by shortly after nine o'clock, Richard is slumped asleep in a chair in a corner of the bar, totally dead to the world.

The rest of the party continue the night of conviviality completely unconcerned, each one of them in turn saying something as they pass the recumbent figure slumped in the chair, who is also snoring loudly at this juncture; things like "We are leaving now, but don't bother to get up Richard" or "it's your round Richard, mines a pint of bitter" .

Despite all the ribaldry Richard continues to take no further part in the evening's proceedings, even when the rest of the them start to sing slightly risqué songs, that let it be said, relate to farming and animal husbandry in an obscene way.

Eventually closing time arrives and the Landlord ushers them out with a smile, saying "go on home now and look after yon lad; he needs to be fit for his wedding tomorrow".

The temperature has dropped to near freezing as they make their way home to Fred's place, six of them in turn carrying the lifeless figure of Richard aloft while continuing to sing their ribald songs.

Rachel is aghast as they carry Richard into her sitting room and place him comatose on the sofa, but eventually she sees the funny side of the situation. Rather than try to wake him, which is an impossible task anyway, Fred and Rachel decide to leave him where he is and make their way to bed.

In the morning Richard wakes with the daddy of all hangovers and after the fug has lifted in his head a little, he is appalled and not a little surprised to see how easily the demon drink has brought him low. That is until Fred descends the stairs and after gently ribbing him, tells him how much his drinks had been spiked with shots of whiskey and rum the previous evening.

Deciding that he can't attend his own wedding looking like death, he eats the cooked breakfast that Rachel has prepared for him, before wrapping up in a heavy coat and going for a long walk.

The frost and freezing weather play their part in his recovery as he walks as swiftly as his hangover will let him, but gradually his faculties return and he finds that his head is clearing from the fug that has enveloped him. The wedding is due to start at two o'clock and one hour before, a horse and trap, which Fred has arranged with one of his farmer friends, arrives to take Richard, Rachel and Fred, (who is best man) to the church.

On arrival, Richard is delighted to see his mother and stepfather deep in conversation with Elizabeth. Ella and he have already told Alf and Liz of their visit to his mother and the fact that they have not informed her of their expectant baby, so they aware not to let it slip when they meet.

Richard's mother greets him with a hug, while holding out an envelope to him at the same time, saying as she does so" here is a small gift from Stephen and me for you to buy whatever you want for your new home".

"Thank you, Mum" Richard replies, who then suddenly realises that he doesn't know how his parents have managed to get to the church. "Did you come down by coach from Solihull".

"Oh no son, we caught the train to Oxford and then the bus to Chadlington this morning; we haven't been here very long, but there was no way that I was going to miss my son's wedding".

As he looks at his mother Richards realises that he has not treated her as well as he should since he stopped living with her. Although he justifies this to himself as because at the time, he felt that he wasn't a very big part of her and Stephen's life anymore, he can see that he was wrong and that they both have always loved him unconditionally.

Wanting to try and make amends he tells her "Look Mum, once we have sorted out the flat why don't you come and stay with us for a few days. It's not possible just now but once we have got it how we want it, I'll let you know. There isn't a lot of room but I'm sure that we can sort it out for a short time. What do you say?"

Deidre's face lights up at his suggestion and Richard realises that he has done the right thing which gives him a warm feeling as she replies "oh that would be lovely, now you go and enjoy your day with your lovely bride".

Gradually the church fills up, which surprises Richard, until Elizabeth explains that the village always supports its own, so that even though only a few of them have been invited to the reception they still come to witness the woman who has grown up in their midst and who they have known since her birth.

Ella arrives in a pony and trap with Alf alongside her. She is the expected few minutes late and although Richard knows that she loves him, he still experiences the feeling that she might possibly have changed her mind as he waits for, what seems to him, to be an eternity.

As she steps from the trap with Alf helping her to get out without damaging her dress there is an audible gasp from the few people still waiting outside the church as they see her beautiful dress and train which two of the bridesmaids pick up, to stop it trailing and getting mud on it. Ella herself looks radiant, her veil up over her head until she reaches the church entrance, where she lowers it before walking down the aisle with Alf.

The service and reception are a blur to both Ella and Richard because they are both completely lost in each other. Photographs are taken and speeches made, Fred taking the opportunity to generate laughs at their expense as he tells the guests how, on the first time he came to pick Ella up, Richard went round and round the village looking for Alf and Liz's house and then tried to make out that he had found it straight away, despite the fact that Ella had stood at the window as he slowly went pass a number of times.

Alf makes an emotional speech, this the second of his daughters to wed in such a short space of time. For someone who is not used to speaking or long words he still has the capacity to make his audience laugh when he explains "I look upon today slightly differently perhaps than other father-in-law's when I tell you that I am not only gaining a son-in-law but also my own private mechanic". As laughter fills the hall, all the villagers being aware of Alf's limited knowledge of farm machinery, he finishes, smiling at Ella "in fact I consider that I have got an even better deal than Ella".

Liz, together with one or two other women of the village, has worked her magic on the reception breakfast in a similar fashion to Rachel's a few months earlier

All of this is of no matter as the world around them almost ceases to exist; but at five o'clock on this freezing December evening Richard and Ella take their leave of their guests, with everyone's good wishes ringing in their ears. It has been a day to treasure for the newlyweds, which Ella has cause to remember with poignancy some five years later when she reflects on the death of her husband.

Once the Bride and Groom have left the reception the guests begin to drift away. This is the moment when Elizabeth and Alf, along with one or two others start to clear up so that the hall can be left in the same state as they found it in, before returning home.

Because Ella has to go to work early the next morning at The Manor House, she and Richard are staying with her parents overnight, which is not what they would have wanted had they been given the choice, but in order for her to get to work at six o'clock the next morning in time to prepare breakfasts and start preparations for a dinner party, they would have had to leave the flat in Oxford at about half past four.

But they have promised each other that the next break of two days that Ella gets from The Manor House; they will go away somewhere overnight.

They have not been at Ella's parents very long before Alf and Elizabeth return, together with Rachel and Fred after they had finished their cleaning duties at the Hall.

The evening is spent reliving the day's events, each of them relishing every magic moment, but the time comes when Rachel and Fred take their leave, but before they do, Rachel remembers that she has left a book that she left in her room before she was married, and hurries upstairs to reclaim it. After what seems an age, she returns downstairs with the book tucked under her arm and quickly hugging everyone, she and Fred take their leave.

As Rachel and Ella stand outside the front door saying their goodbyes, Rachel suddenly says "well Ellie I suppose the next significant events in our lives is the birth of our babies; mine in March and yours in June. I just can't wait, can you sis"?

Ella starts to reply enthusiastically saying "Oh me too Rach, it's going to be wonderful" before breaking off, pausing and holding her head to one side in an inquisitive manner "did you mean what you just said, that your baby is due in March".

A huge smile spreads slowly across Rachel's face as she replies "Oh completely"

"But that means that you must have been pregnant on the day that you were married"

"Oh Ella, don't look so horrified, you of all people know just how easily these things happen".

"But mum and dad never said anything to me" complains Ella grumpily.

"That's because we didn't tell them, silly" retorts Rachel "now give me a hug and go back in and enjoy the rest of your day".

Rachel's revelation has thrown Ella's mind into total confusion and she can't wait to go to bed so that she can tell Richard. At half past nine the two of them say goodnight to Alf and Elizabeth and make their way upstairs to bed; her parents looking at each other knowingly, and no doubt making the wrong conclusion for their early departure

As soon as they reach their room, Ella tells Richard of her conversation with Rachel. For a few seconds he is speechless, before breaking into uncontrollable laughter and saying "they are a crafty pair that Rachel and Fred. There are the two of us worrying ourselves silly about telling your parents and all the other repercussions that it entails, while they, who are in exactly the same situation, just ignore it and tell no one. I think that there's a lesson here for us, don't you"?

"Of course, I do, but when she told me, it only made me love them even more" replies Ella. "What a brave thing to do; what a fantastic sister I have, she does so much for me I don't know why I deserve her".

They both prepare for bed, undressing each other in feverish haste, but even while this is happening, Ella is still reminiscing on Rachel's revelation, and the warm feelings that she holds for her elder sister. However, all such thoughts are brought to an abrupt end, as on getting into bed and putting her head on the pillow she feels a sharp pain from a lumpy object within the pillow, while at the same time Richard is having a similar experience.

Sitting up they both take off their pillowcases, only to find several items hidden within; a number of books as well as a couple of china dolls which have been taken from their usual places on shelving units.

Looking at each other they both come to the same conclusion at the same time. "Rachel" they cry in unison, and then Ella "I thought that she was a long time getting her book" before breaking into laughter. "She said that she would get her own back one day, well now she has".

Richards's amorous thoughts have been severely dented by now, but things are only to get worse, as they lay down together and pulling up the sheets, they discover that they only reach to their ankles, because Rachel has made them an apple pie bed.

Sisterly love is under severe pressure by now as Ella leaps from the bed before stripping it down and remaking it.

As she strips the bedclothes off, she comes across a note, in what she immediately recognises as Rachel's writing.

Picking it up she reads "I hope I haven't dampened your ardour too much, but after all the times that you tricked me, I just couldn't resist the opportunity. Have a lovely time and I look forward to watching our children grow up together over the coming years. Much love, Rachel".

After she has read the note, Ella cannot possibly hold a grudge for her sister, who means so much to her, but promises herself that she will get her own back.

Amazingly once all these interruptions have been dealt with and they are once more in bed, their amorous feelings return and they are able to consummate their official union in a most satisfying and tender loving manner.

As they fall to sleep with Ella's head upon Richard's chest, his arm around her shoulders, she tries to envisage their future together, little knowing of the train of events that have already begun across the Channel in Europe, which will ultimately destroy her hopes and dreams. The Genie is already out of the box and it will take millions of lives and another six years to put it back in again.

CHAPTER 10.

1956.
ELLA'S CAFE

The opening day for Ella's Cafe finally arrives on Monday 29th August. She rises from her bed at 4 o'clock in order to bake bread and buns ready for opening time. Once the mixture of flour and yeast together with a little salt has been made, it is left to rise. Using her experienced eye, Ella then puts it into pans, together with mixture for bread rolls into the double oven that she has used for years, for baking. Once this stage in the process has been reached, Ella can start preparing other things ready for opening time. She has already made a Victoria Cream Sandwich and a Carrot Cake the previous day. These she places in the glass display cabinets on the counter in the shop.

The next item in her busy schedule is to make soup that once made can be kept in a large container and left on a simmering heat. She has made tomato soup today, made with tomatoes from Alf's allotments.

The one single thing that she can't know, for all her cooking experience, is what demand she will get, and she knows that she needs to get the volumes right as soon as possible. If she makes too much, she will have to throw good food away, but if she doesn't make sufficient there is a good chance that she will lose potential customers. She knows just how critical it is if the business is to prosper that she gets to grips with this aspect as quickly as possible.

Elizabeth arrives shortly before opening time at eight o'clock. She has agreed that she will come every day for the first few weeks to help Ella with the initial opening period, after which she will reduce her working mornings to three or four.

There is an air of anticipation between them as the opening time of eight o'clock arrives. Ella has placed an advertisement in the local paper the previous week announcing the opening. She has also designed a uniform for both of them to wear, born from her years of being in service. These consist of a white frilly blouse and black skirt. In addition, Rachel has made aprons of green and white stripes, with "Ella's Café" embroidered across the front; colours which Ella wants to establish as those to identify her establishment.

Daniel comes downstairs at just after seven and after getting breakfast for the three of them, goes outside with Ella to help in the bakery. Until he has to start back at Grammar School in a few days' time, he has offered to help Ella in whatever capacity he is needed; despite her protests he insists and she reluctantly agrees, mentally thinking that she needs to pay him. Once the day starts Ella is quickly made aware just how useful Daniel is to her enterprise. Once he reached his teens, he had assumed a more senior role in the household, as if making up for the fact that because his father was no longer there, it befell him to fill his shoes. Ella has noticed this phenomenon with pride and a little sadness, realising that his father's death meant that Daniel had lost to a large extent, his childhood.

But now Daniel does many of the little chores that nobody notices in the Café, but without which the operation will come to a grinding halt. He prepares a list of things that Ella needs, like flour, yeast, sugar and cleaning materials for her to approve, so that he can order them. He has also agreed to clean the shop at the end of each day, wiping down the surfaces and mopping the floors, as well as adding up the day's takings and banking them in the overnight safe at the bank.

Business is slow until about ten o'clock, apart from several men who are working just up the road, digging it up to lay cables for an electricity supply. They are working men, dressed in blue overalls and heavy working boots. They joke and chide with Ella and her mother in a manner which men so often do, and which both of the women are used to. Because they work in the open air, the men's appetites are huge and they consume large quantities of chunky bacon sandwiches which they wash down with large steaming mugs of tea. They leave, promising to return the next day at about the same time.

Once they are gone Ella says to her mother "I'm so glad that I allowed for a varied type of customer. Allocating those two tables for working men at the other end of the room means that they won't make the floor dirty with their muddy boots. It wouldn't have been any good giving them china cups and thin bread sandwiches would it"?

"No, you had best save them for the mothers and children who hopefully will come in for their elevenses tea and cakes.

Elizabeth is proved right as those people, mostly women, who have come in to Chippie by bus and are shopping, eventually finding their way to Ella's Café, before they either continue to go on to shop or return home.

To Ella's delight a number of these customers are from Chadlington, who as they have promised, have come to support her. "This is such a good idea Ella: I wonder why someone didn't think of it before" seems to be the thing that most of them are saying. "Always before, we have just come in to shop and then caught the next bus home; but now we can take our time and have a break. You can be sure that we will make it a regular stop off. Well done, we love it".

Elizabeth experiences a feeling of motherly pride as one by one her friends and neighbours from the village congratulate her daughter on her new enterprise.

As lunch hour approaches a number of customers appear who are obviously looking for something more that tea and cakes. For this reason and anticipating that this may be the case, Ella has prepared soup and bread rolls as an option, with a choice of sandwiches as an alternative. This proves very successful but Ella can see that there is another opportunity to be had if she were to make hot food available. Nothing elaborate, perhaps shepherd's pie which she could make in a large dish and cut up into portions as and when requested, or steak and kidney pie, in much the same manner. If these were served with just peas or carrots with mashed potatoes, work could be kept to a minimum. More importantly, they can be made the previous day; it is not something for just now, but rather a possibility for the future.

There is a lull after two o'clock until just after three, when a number of young married women come in with their children, who they have just picked up from school. They all know each other and have obviously decided to use the café to have a conflab in comfort, rather than stand outside the school in all weathers.

Another group of what can only be described as older women of substance also find their way in to partake of tea and cakes.

These are wives of prominent people in the local community, some of whom Ella has met in her previous life as cook at The Manor House, when they attended as guests.

Apart from one or two other stragglers, the activity for the day is finished and Ella puts the closed sign up at five o'clock and after Elizabeth leaves, she returns inside to the kitchen to prepare an evening meal, while Daniel cleans the Cafe. As she begins to cook, the thought occurs to her that if she were to make hot food for lunch times for the cafe, she would then have hot food that she could use for her and Daniel's evening meal, which would save her time, money and above all much effort at the end of the day.

In the evening Daniel adds up the days takings which Ella is agreeably pleased with when he tells her it amounts to just over fourteen pounds, a sum well in line with her projected forecast.

They both go to bed early, exhausted by the efforts of their day, but Ella lies awake for several hours, her mind going over the events of the day as she questions herself how she can improve the food and service that she is offering customers. Eventually she falls into a shallow sleep until, as it seems to her, only minutes have passed before her alarm clock is ringing out its shrill message, telling her another day has begun.

Tuesdays and Saturdays in Chipping Norton are market days and Ella is hoping that extra trade can be picked up from both stall holders and the increase in the volume of people coming to town for bargains. Her problem is, by just how much, which she soon finds out, as before Elizabeth has arrived for opening at eight o'clock, there are several stall holders waiting outside ready for breakfasts.

As she opens the door Ella makes a mental note that she will need to open earlier on market days to make sure that she captures this readily available source of income.

All of the stall holders are friendly and well behaved, some expressing their pleasure that there is now somewhere they can go to, once they have set up their stalls and before the public arrive. There is much laughter and gentle ribbing each other, as they discuss their experiences. It appears that most of them travel from place to place, almost daily, some from long distances. Inevitably this means that they mostly go to the same places regularly and consequently know each other very well.

In her earlier life Ella as cook at The Manor House has bought meat and poultry, cleaning products and other items from some of them, who recognise her now and congratulate her on her new venture.

The rest of the day passes in a flurry of activity, very much busier than the previous one, as people who had been shopping in the market make their way to Ella's for sustenance and as a place to sit and rest.

As her food and cakes start to disappear at an alarming rate, Ella makes another mental note to increase both the choice and volume available on Market days. But she just about makes it through the day as the market stallholders start to take down their stalls about three o'clock in the afternoon.

Liz has once again proved herself invaluable, waiting on customers and resolving issues as they arise, while Ella is out in the bakery making sandwiches, rolls and soup, while Daniel serves at the counter distributing cakes and taking payment which, he rings up in the till.

At five o'clock the day finishes leaving Ella with a number of questions for which she will need to find answers if the Café is to grow and improve, but these are things that she has learned to deal with in her previous working life, so she has no doubts or worries that she can overcome them.

* * *

Wednesday in Chipping Norton is half-day closing for all the shops, so although she still needs to get up early to bake bread, the volumes that she needs to make are a lot less. The working men still come in early for their cooked breakfasts, and the school mothers for their teas and cakes, but the shop closes at one o'clock, giving Ella time to relax or even go to visit her mother or Rachel in the afternoon.

Thursday and Friday are similar to Monday, except that word has got around locally, of her customers positive culinary experience in Ella's café, so, Liz and Daniel and she are kept busier as more new faces come to try the place for themselves.

The extra numbers put Ella's baking capacity under pressure and she finds that she needs to bake larger volumes of bread as well as cakes. The latter can be overcome fairly easily, Ella just having to make more cakes in the evening, but to bake more bread she will have to make it in two processes, because her oven space is already up to capacity.

This is a huge problem for her and she is at her wits end and decides to talk the problem over with Liz and Daniel. It is her son who once again demonstrates his aptitude for problem solving, when he explains that he has noticed that The Co-op shop in The High Street has just begun to sell loaves of white bread, which is a new process and invention. Bread up until now has only been brown or wholemeal, which is more labour intensive to make, meaning that it can only be made in relatively small volumes.

As he continues to explain, Ella can see the benefits of just buying white bread to make sandwiches, leaving her to make a smaller selection of wholemeal bread and rolls for those customers who prefer it. She becomes very animated as Daniel explains, saying "that sounds like the perfect solution Dan, if we just buy white bread. Of course, I will continue to make some bread, but not as much as I do now, which should save me a lot of time".

But Daniel hasn't finished his explanation as he continues with a twinkle in his eye "Oh, it's much better than that mum, because it is also made in an already sliced version, which should save you even more time. Why don't I just go and buy a couple of loaves right now and try it out"?

Ella's relief is visible, as she becomes aware of the potential that white bread can mean for her to develop and increase the Café's volume, realising once again that it is her son who has solved her problem, in much the same way in fact, that he resolves his own, by looking one or two stages ahead. It is not something that he is aware of, but rather a gift of genealogy that has been handed down to him.

Returning with two white sliced loaves, Daniel and Liz prepare sandwiches for the day, some of which they put in glass covers for customers to select as they come in, but others which they wrap in grease proof paper, before writing on them a description of the contents. This is yet another of Daniels ideas, which he explains can be used for those people who are probably working locally and don't have time to come in and sit, but can just come in during their lunch hour to buy from the selection of readymade sandwiches, which they can then either take back to work to eat, or alternatively, if they have shopping to do, which they can eat as they walk.

All of this works brilliantly, customers welcoming the choice of white and brown bread, meaning much less work for Ella in the future. However, sales of readymade sandwiches are slow, with a few being left over, but as Daniel explains "Give it time mum, until people are aware of it. I think that we should mention them when we place the next advert in the local paper, but I'm sure that existing customers will tell their friends that we're making take away sandwiches, and sales will hopefully pick up from word of mouth".

By now, Ella needs no convincing that Daniel is right in his assessment of the situation, and acquiesces with a nod of her head.

On Friday evening Ella makes an even larger selection of cakes and homemade soup, ready for the following day, being aware that it could be the busiest day of the week for the Café. She has also bought in extra eggs, bacon, sausages, black pudding and tomatoes in readiness for an invasion of market stall holders first thing in the morning.

Her suspicions and preparations prove to be well founded. Waking at four to begin her bread and roll baking, she becomes aware of murmured voices and occasional laughter in the market square and the High Street at about six o'clock, together with the clatter of steel poles which form the frames of the Market Stalls.

By half past seven there is a queue of ravenous stall holders forming outside the Café as Ella experiences her first Saturday 's trading.

All her preparations could not have prepared her for this day as Daniel, Liz and she are inundated, at first by market stall holders, who mostly want cooked breakfasts to sustain them through the day, followed by people who have come into town looking for bargains at the market.

There is a lull in proceedings after this, until eleven o'clock, which gives them time to clear tables and put more food out, but the relentless pace is then renewed as people who are still arriving into the town and others who have already been around the market come in to find somewhere to sit and relax with tea and cakes.

Just before mid-day people begin to come in looking for an early lunch. This continues until two o'clock when there is again a short lull until nearly three, when people who have now finished their market shopping return for tea and cakes before catching their buses home.

Surprisingly after half past four the Café is almost empty, the stalls already beginning to pack up for the day and Ella is able to shut the shop. But it has been an exhausting, gruelling day for her and her small band of helpers, although financially a very rewarding one.

Afterwards, as the three of them sit and relax, mentally and physically drained, and before Liz has to make her way home to Chadlington, Ella is suddenly aware how precarious and vulnerable the whole Café operation is. The next Monday Daniel is due to return to school to take his A level exams. This will mean that he will only be available to help her in the evenings and on Saturdays. She also realises just how great his contribution has been in this first week and wonders how she will manage without it.

Her other major concern is Liz, who has been invaluable to her, but looking at her mother for the first time this week, Ella can see just how much the effort has taken out of her.

"Oh! Mum, I don't know how to thank you enough for all your help this week; I just couldn't have managed without you. But at least we've learned two things in that time. The first is that there is more than enough demand here to make the Café financially viable, and the second is that I will need more staff unless we are going to very quickly run ourselves into the ground".

Liz is silent for a heartbeat, before she replies "well I must admit that I never thought for one moment that it would be as busy as it has turned out to be, but I think that you're right when you say that you will need more staff. None of us can keep this pace up for long and with the level of business you're getting you will be able to afford more staff".

"Look my love; there are one or two girls in the village, who left school in the summer, who are looking for work, but before we approach them why don't you try to advertise locally first. To start with you could put a notice in the shop window, which will cost you nothing, or advertise, in the local paper. Either way will give you a good chance of getting someone who lives near-by. However, the first thing that you need to decide is just who you are looking for and what you need them to do. For example, do you just need someone to wait on tables, or do you want them to learn to cook meals and bake bread and cakes, because at the moment you are the only person capable of doing it"

Recognising the truth in her mother's words, Liz replies "You are right mum and I will give it some thought, but ideally I would like someone who could work full time waitressing and another who could do part time helping me to cook and bake. Once I can find a full-time waitress, you will be able to work less hours, only coming in perhaps three mornings a week as we originally envisaged".

"The waitress could either be a school leaver, or even an older, more experienced person. A school leaver would need to be thoroughly trained before I could let her loose to serve customers, and I'm not convinced that either of us will have the time to train anyone. As you know mum, some customers can be difficult, to say the least, and that is when experience is the most valuable commodity. For example, I watched you on a number of occasions this week dealing with one or two customers who thought that they had waited too long to be served, or felt that some other customers were served out of turn and who were all starting to raise their voices in complaint. You dealt with them beautifully, calming them down and making them relaxed, thus avoiding any unnecessary fuss in front of the rest of the customers".

"I'm not sure that a young person will be able to deal with these situations in quite the same manner; it's something that only comes with age and experience. The person that I would need to help me with cooking and baking could also be hard to find, although I do have contacts from my time at The Manor House but we'll see".

"Well, I'd best be off my love" declares Liz. "I tell you what, why don't you and Daniel come to Sunday lunch tomorrow. You're not working, so you can both have a lie in. Rachel has promised to come after lunch, so we can all be together"

"Oh that would be lovely mum, I think that we'd both like that" and then, after her mother had left, "Hey Daniel, do you fancy going to the pictures tonight; there's a good one on in Oxford, David Niven in "Around the World in Eighty Days". It's supposed to be very good". Daniel nods his agreement, as a huge grin lights up his face. Ella continues "Come on then let's get something to eat and then get changed so that we can catch the six o'clock bus".

The sudden realisation that she doesn't have to get up early the next day, together with the fact that she has completed her first week as proprietor of her own business rolls over her like a warm blanket as she reprises it in her mind and additionally that her first week has also been very successful, both in terms of volume and financially.

True, Daniel will be commencing his A level year next week, but he is predicted very good results in the four subjects that he will be taking; Maths, English, History and Science. She doesn't know where that will take him, but he has already talked about getting into journalism and eventually using it to see the World.

Ella knows that he has an extremely inquisitive mind which is always seeking information, be it politics, (although he does not have or share any affiliations to one particular party or group) or world events, always listening closely to the wireless whenever he can. He just wants to know why and how things occur and why people behave the way they do. Whatever he decides to do when the time comes, Ella is determined that she will support him as much as she can.

CHAPTER 11.

1939.
RETURN TO CHADLINGTON

Life for the newlyweds at first is difficult, but only in terms of logistics. Ella's position at The Manor House means that she either stays at her parents' home or at her employers once she has finished work for the day.

Richard does manage to pick her up when she has a half or a whole day off, which isn't very often. When this occurs, they go to their flat in Oxford and live the life of a normal married couple, for a few precious hours at least.

Sometimes they go out to the cinema, or shopping at the indoor market which they both love doing, but their preference is to stay indoors, where Ella makes them sumptuous meals, before sitting in front of a roaring log fire listening to the wireless, maybe In Town Tonight, or Paul Temple, special agent.

Inevitably as the evenings wear on, at a point simultaneous to both of them, they suddenly gaze at one another, which is the unspoken catalyst for them to go to bed, where they consume each other avidly, making up for the nights that they cannot be together. As her pregnancy develops this becomes less frequent, but when it happens it is more tender and satisfying, but the need for each other is still strong.

Ella eventually tells her employer of her condition, before it becomes noticeable and before anyone in The Manor House becomes suspicious. She fully expects Lord Stevens to terminate her employment, but to her amazement he is distraught at the thought of losing her, and after a few days he calls her to his study and tells her he is sorry to be losing her, but hopes that she will continue as long as possible before her due date. To her increasing surprise he goes on to tell her that both Lady Stevens and he will like it very much if, in due course, she can take up her position as cook once again.

Before she can reply, a host of objections and queries springing to mind, he holds up his hand like a policeman stopping traffic, saying "Of course Lady Stevens and I have given this a good deal of consideration and we are agreed that you will obviously need quite some time off to look after the baby, but maybe it would be possible for you to come in and help when we entertain occasionally some evenings. We will ensure that most of the preparation is done beforehand, leaving you to do what you do best, i.e. cook".

"As you know it doesn't happen very often, but our guests always compliment us, and by that, I mean you, on, the quality of the meals that you provide. But we would rather do that than lose you Ella. You are our rock upon which we depend, so what do you say? Hopefully once the baby is older you could return again in your full-time existing role".

Then, almost as an afterthought he continues" Oh by the way, one of the tenants in Bull Hill, old Mrs Bird has given notice, because she is getting on in years and finding it difficult to look after herself, so she's going to live with her daughter in Stroud. What that means, of course, is that I am now looking for a tenant to replace her and I was wondering if perhaps you and your husband would like to take it on. I would, of course let, you have it for a very reasonable rent. Am I correct when I say that she only lives a few doors from your parents?"

Ella stands completely stunned in front of her employer who has always treated her with such consideration and affection, not knowing initially how to reply, before saying emotionally "Thank you My Lord, I don't know what I have done to deserve such an offer, but before I give you an answer I need to discuss the matter with my husband. As far as I'm concerned, I have always loved working here for you both, and to live in Chadlington again would be wonderful. I will speak to Richard and get back to you in a couple of days, if that's acceptable Sir"?

His lordship said "We will wait and hope that everything is agreeable to you both Ella",

* * *

At first Richard is hesitant when Ella tells him her news, but she explains that it means that they will not only see each other more, but also that they can live in a larger place with two bedrooms instead of one, in which they can put their eagerly awaited firstborn. Another big plus is that they will be living only a few doors away from Ella's parents, which even Richard agrees is a good thing, having great respect for Liz and Alf.

Richard's main concern is that they will be paying rent, however small, compared to the flat, which is rent free. But after taken everything that Ella has said into consideration, he concedes that having an extra bedroom and being able to see his wife most days, far outweighs the extra costs, even though it means that he will have to travel daily to work in Oxford.

Taking her in his arms, Richard brushes a lock of her hair that has fallen across her eyes, saying "O.K. Princess, you win; I just hope that

Lord Stevens will only charge us a small rent. Now where's that bottle of port, because I think that this calls for a celebration".

"I'll ask him what rent he's thinking of charging before we say yes" replies Ella, already excited at the prospect of returning to live in the village of her birth.

* * *

The next day Ella sees his Lordship and says to him "I talked to my husband last night about your very kind offer my Lord, and we agreed that we would very much like to move into Mrs Bird's cottage. Our main problem is the amount of rent which would be the deciding factor, because you see at present, we are living in a rent free, one bedroom flat in Oxford, so that is a big consideration".

Lord Stevens looks pensive for a few seconds, before smiling "Well my dear, I think that I can put your mind at rest on that score, how does five shillings a week sound. I want you to be able to live locally for two reasons, in the first instance from a personal, selfish view point, so that you are close to us here at The Manor House and, secondly, because I know that you'll be happier living here with all your family support around you".

Ella is unable to stem the trickle of tears that run down her face, realising just how much she adores working for this elite family, with their lifestyle, which is already almost an outmoded way of life. She is aware that this way of life is coming to an end; in fact, it has lasted longer than most large houses that attract so much in death duties when the owner dies. A way of life that's demise began after the end of The First World War.

* * *

Once Ella and Richard have agreed with Lord Stevens offer, things move on at a pace. By now it is late April 1939 and Ella's baby is due in the middle of June, (although nearly everyone else assumes that it will be in early August).

Lord Stevens kindly offers the use of an open backed lorry which they can use to collect their few bits and pieces of furniture and other goods from the flat in Oxford.

Due to her extreme age, the previous tenant of their new home, Mrs Bird has not been able to decorate the cottage for many years. Although they are unable to afford to decorate all of the rooms straight away, Ella and Richard both agree that they should paint the living room and kitchen as a matter of urgency. So once again they rope in Fred, who comes to their rescue, and with Richard to help, the two of them working mostly in the evenings and at weekends get the job done.

At this stage Ella comes into her own, adding artistic little touches that transform Mrs Bird's run-down cottage, into a warm welcoming home. Several of Richard's paintings are hung in the living room, while his portrait of Ella is framed and stands on her bedside cabinet. Fresh flowers, which grow in abundance in the garden and in the surrounding fields, give the rooms a warm feeling of light and space.

Rachel has made several chintzes throws for their well-worn sofa and chairs, giving them a bright, airy look. Meanwhile, Alf has already started on the garden, turning the soil and planting early potatoes, leeks, beans and onions. He has left a small patch of lawn close up to the back of the house, saying to Ella "once the warmer weather arrives, you can sit outside with the new bairn".

By now it is early spring, a time when and the lovely village of Chadlington is at its very best. Daffodils are out in profusion on the green banks beside the narrow roads, their blooms looking like trumpets, blaring out their message of hope and renewal.

The newlyweds have determined, in the face of an uncertain world, to live life to the full, going for long walks whenever possible, or going into Oxford to the pictures, or just shop gazing. But their activities begin to slow as Ella's pregnancy progresses. She continues to work at The Manor House, determined to continue as long as she can to help both Lord Stevens on the one hand and her own finances on the other.

But nature is a fickle companion, who often has the last say in such matters, which is demonstrated in the evening of 12th June. Ella has been on her feet all day preparing meals for a number of invited guests to The Manor House. Suddenly, without warning, her waters break and she begins to feel contractions.

Lord Stevens, on being informed by the staff, hurriedly arranges for Ella to be taken back to her cottage in his car, where she can get help from the local midwife.

When she arrives home Richard hurriedly goes to get Mrs Amy Collins, the midwife, who quickly grabs her bag and they return together. By now it is late evening and Ella is experiencing contractions which are still several minutes apart.

"She won't be giving birth yet for several hours" the midwife, a woman of middle age declares, after giving her a quick examination.

"Is there anything that I can do" asks Richard tentatively, more than slightly in awe of this dominant female, who has dealt with situations like this hundreds of times before.

"No, waiting is the only thing that any of us can do for the present, the baby is presenting itself in the right position, so it's just a matter of time. Perhaps in the meantime you can get us all a cup of tea".

Ella, although in severe discomfort, is resigned to the situation and seeing that Richard is becoming worried for her, even taking on similar symptoms to her as he complains of stomach pains and a headache, she does her best to reassure and comfort him.

This eventful night continues in much the same fashion until nearly five o'clock, just as dawn is breaking, when Ella's contractions begin to come more often, until they are almost continuous. These are the signs that the midwife has been waiting for, so she quickly ushers Richard from the bedroom and sends him downstairs to await developments.

But it is a further hour before Richard hears to his joy, the sound of his baby's cry of indignation as it enters the world. Taking the stairs two at a time he halts almost reverently at the bedroom door, not knowing whether he should enter, or knock first. The decision is taken from him as without warning as the midwife throws open the door and seeing him, says with a smile "well you had best come on in and meet your new son. Ella is doing fine, but she is just exhausted, so try not to excite her too much".

"My son, wow that's great, but is Ella O.K." exclaims Richard as he makes his way to join Ella and baby on the bed. Ella smiles weakly at her husband saying "come and have a look at our new family member, he looks just like his father" as she peels back the shawl that she is holding.

Gently kissing his wife first, Richard is overwhelmed as he sees his son for the first time, a miniscule living object, swarthy in appearance, looking almost indignant to be here. But Richard also sees the faint fuzz of red hair and pale blue eyes which identifies this bundle of humanity as inescapably his.

"Well my son, what do you think of your new world" he whispers, before gently taking him from Ella and holding him for the first time, and then to his wife "oh my Princess isn't he just perfect, now we are a family".

After several minutes the midwife interrupts saying "well, I think that's enough for now, your wife needs to rest. Let's leave her to try and get some sleep. We can leave baby in the cot, he seems settled for now, anyway, but if he wakes, we will come and get him".

Richard wastes no time in going downstairs, and along to Alf and Elizabeth to give them the good news. They return immediately with him and wait impatiently in the living room until Ella is rested enough to see them. Eventually they get to see their new grandson; their second in the course of a few short weeks, because Rachel has, as expected, already given birth to her son George.

The next few weeks are a hectic flurry of activity in which Richard and Ella experience a steep learning curve. After much debate on boy's names, they have settled on Daniel for no other reason than there is no such other in either of their families. He is an even-tempered child, only objecting to life quite vociferously when he is hungry, tired, has wind, or in need of changing.

Ella is breast feeding him, which means that she is inevitably woken for the night feed and suffers from lack of sleep as a consequence. But after several weeks she begins to express milk into a bottle for just such a purpose, so that Richard can share this burden.

But the pleasure that their son gives them far outweighs all such inconveniences, and they are lost in wonder when he offers them the slightest of smiles, or gurgles incoherently at them. Sometimes, during the week, Ella goes to Rachel's and spends the day, the two sisters and their children enjoying the summer together. On one such occasion they agree to have both babies christened in Chadlington on the same day in August.

With the prospect of war an ever increasing threat, with Germany threatening to invade Poland after the Anschluss, the union of Germany and Austria, followed by the invasion of Czechoslovakia, Richard and Ella determine to make the most of whatever time they have available, knowing that Richard could be called up for active duty if events continue as they are.

Most weekends they take rides on the motor bike, to which Richard has added a sidecar, and with Ella and Daniel sitting in comfort they go wherever their fancy takes them. Ella first makes picnics before they set off on their adventures to see the places which have for so long just been names on a map.

It is a curious fact thinks Ella, that neither she nor Richard have ever been to anywhere on the coast, or seen the sea, and vows to herself that they will one day make the pilgrimage.

There excursions follow a similar pattern as they first visit Gloucester, the county town of Gloucestershire, at the centre of the Cotswolds. After finding somewhere to park, they then browse the streets, in which there are still many medieval and Tudor period gabled and timbered buildings. Gloucester Cathedral is next on their list and while Ella wanders around the interior with Daniel strapped to her chest by a large sling made from an old sheet, Richard remains outside, sketching the exterior which he will work up as a watercolour when they get home.

The Museum of Gloucester is next on their unofficial itinerary, but they are only there several minutes before Daniel becomes fractious, demanding to be fed. Seeking somewhere suitable, they find their way down to the Docks, which is the most inland port in the country. From the Docks, The Gloucester and Sharpness Canal continues up until it reaches The Severn Estuary.

Finding seating alongside the Canal, Ella hurriedly feeds Daniel before they have their picnic, after which Richard makes a number of sketches of the Dock and Canal area, with its rich tapestry of cargo carrying boats and yachts of every description.

Suitably fed and watered they leave the city and make their way back to Burford, a beautiful market town deep in the heart of the Cotswolds, before heading north to return home. Stopping in an area of outstanding beauty they find a quiet field which has a stream running through it with a wooded area at one end. Spreading a blanket under some shade, Ella and Richard sit Daniel between them and watch the wonder in his face as he feels the sun and sees the surrounding landscape spread out before him. His contentment and happiness are expressed by chuckles and laughter.

Soon Ella finds herself nodding off, the sheer beauty of her surroundings inducing feelings in her of completeness, as if all her life up until now has led her to this point.

She lies down, her long auburn hair spread eagled like an exotic fan beneath her. Richard watches her for a while thinking that she has never looked more beautiful. Motherhood has added to her already striking looks. Her skin is soft and clear, a slight tan lightening her countenance, while her figure has returned to its pre maternity shape, no doubt due in no small part to the amount of walking and exercise she now has to do.

As he watches her sleep, Richard feels a well of emotion which threatens to overwhelm him, realising once again how much he loves his bewitching Princess and just how lucky he has been to find her.

Eventually Daniel becomes bored, or maybe hungry, but for whatever the reason they both decide that it is time to return home. So reluctantly they pack up and make their way back. They both love these stolen days when they can be together as a family, their pleasure being heightened because of the fear of the possible alternative threat to their way of life, emanating from a troubled Europe.

As the summer progresses, they continue to make the most of such opportunities, making pilgrimages to other places. To Cheltenham, Cirencester or Evesham: wherever it is they find somewhere suitable to picnic, after which they lie on down on a blanket and one of them dozes off while the other spends time playing with Daniel and generally obeying his every whim.

Once or twice they manage to visit Richard's parents in Solihull, each time much to Deidre's surprise and delight.

She is also delighted to observe the likeness of her son to her grandchild, his flaming red hair and steel blue eyes becoming more pronounced daily.

* * *

On a hot Sunday in late August both sisters and their families gather at Chadlington Church for the christenings of their first born. All the grandparents are present giving the day more relevance, while, what seems like all of the inhabitants of the village of Chadlington have come to wish them well.

After the service everyone make their way back to the back garden of Alf and Elizabeth's cottage where a spread has been laid out to celebrate the occasion.

As she looks at her friends and family present, Ella can wish for nothing more, she has everything that she could want or need and hopes that nothing will change that might disrupt it.

Within days her and everyone's world is not only disrupted, but completely blown apart as Germany invades Poland on the first of September. This action is followed by an ultimatum given by Great Britain and France to the aggressors, that if they do not withdraw by the third of September then a State of War will be declared between them.

The family gather together in the living room at Alf and Elizabeth's cottage at midday on the third, all clustered round their wireless set, waiting to hear what their Prime Minister, Neville Chamberlain has to tell them. Only a year previously he had returned from Berlin waving a piece of paper and declaring "peace in our time", after meeting with Adolf Hitler.

His message today however is of the worst possible nature as he declares that Germany have continued to invade Poland and that consequently Great Britain has no alternative than to declare war on Germany.

There is an audible silence as he finishes speaking, the older members in the room revisiting the horrors of The First World War, which had killed and maimed so many millions of people, both in Europe and throughout the World only some twenty short years previously.

When they do begin to speak, everyone tries to at the same time, their fears and concerns to the fore, but also realising that events are beyond their own personal feelings and that they have no alternative than to wait in trepidation, to see what their country will require of all of them in the coming days and months.

Within a few short weeks, Parliament passes The National Service (Armed Forces Act) conscripting men between the ages of 18 to 41. Only those who hold jobs which are exemptions, such as farmers and those in the manufacture of armaments are excluded.

Time passes without Richard receiving his call up papers and their fears are allayed in the coming months as the rest of this momentous year continues as if nothing has happened. Apart from commencement of the critical Battle of the Atlantic between German U boats and British Naval convoys.

Western Europe is quiet during this "phoney war". Preparations for war continue, but there are few signs of conflict and civilians who have been evacuated from London in the first month's drift back into the city. Gas masks are distributed, and everybody waits for the proper war to begin.

In Chadlington life carries on much as before and, although both Ella and Richard wait fearfully, he does not hear or receive his call up papers, but they both know that it is just a matter of time.

As summer turns to autumn, Ella and Richard continue to explore the countryside around them, even on one occasion managing to reach the beautiful Georgian city of Bath, which has some of its Roman remains still intact. Ella has been taught all about the Roman Baths at school, but never for one moment has she ever thought that she would see them, but here she is with her handsome lover and husband, and their even more handsome son, exploring its glorious Georgian streets, the buildings of which are constructed of local golden coloured stone.

But the place above all that they would both like to see, is somewhere on the coast. Their curiosity is tempered by the thought of the imminent war still to come, but they realise that if they don't do it now, it may not ever be possible. The major problem is that the return journey cannot be made in one day, so they would need to take two or more days, meaning that they will need accommodation at a B and B, which will escalate the costs.

Fred comes to their rescue after they tell him and Rachel their problem. "Well, we have a tent that you can borrow mate, which you are welcome too. You would need to buy meals of course, but we have a primus stove and other cooking equipment, so I suppose that Ella could buy food and do the cooking which would keep costs to a minimum, so what do you say"?

The answer is of course a resounding "yes, thank you", so the next decision is where? After much deliberation and poring over maps they both decide that they would like to visit Lyme Regis in Dorset, Ella remembering conversations of a number of guests who were invited to The Manor House over the years and who spoke of it with enthusiasm and fervour.

Not wanting to leave it too late in the year, they set off one Saturday in late September, Richard taking his time, and being unwilling to disturb his wife and child in the side car. But he has no need to worry, because the sound and rhythm of the motor bike had a soporific effect on them both, and they were soon fast asleep, Daniel cradled in Ella's arms.

After three hours they stopped for refreshments which Ella had prepared, and after feeding and changing Daniel they continued until they were just outside Lyme Regis. Ella has already had her first glimpse of the sea from the A35 as they travel from Dorchester to Bridport which takes her breath away. Hurriedly tapping at the window of the sidecar she beckons Richard to pull over so she can take a better look.

Reaching the grass verge, they stand transfixed looking down and across to Lyme Bay in the distance. It is a bright sunny day, the early morning mist having burnt off, and they can see for miles, the vista constantly changing as the sun bursts through small cumulus clouds, their shadows hurrying away like a thief in the night, leaving the sea shimmering and glistening below them. On Its almost blinding surface a number of small boats are bobbing up and down in the bay, the local fisherman laying crab and lobster pots ready for collection and harvesting the next morning. Further out in The Channel a large merchant ship moves slowly across the horizon.

The Jurassic cliffs for which this area is renowned can be seen in the distance, its highest promontory, Golden Cap standing distinctively just the other side of West Bay.

Ella is blown away with the sheer grandeur and spectacle before her and an involuntary "wow" escapes her lips, followed by a deep satisfying sigh as she says "This is even more impressive than anything that I could have imagined my love. I don't think that I have ever seen anything quite so beautiful in my life".

Richard agrees saying "Well Princess, I'm so glad we came, I can understand now what people mean when they talk about the lure of the sea".

After standing for several minutes they reluctantly move on and reach Lyme Regis by mid-afternoon, but they do not stop in this pretty little town, but rather continue on up through the steep High Street until they find their campsite near Up-Lyme.

They are by now completely relaxed, experiencing a sense of achievement even, to have got this far. But they are brought down to earth with a bump when they try to erect the tent that Fred has lent them. He had explained how to do it before they left, but his instructions do not seem to relate to any of the debris laid out before them.

They try for nearly an hour, but with little success, at first getting short tempered with each other, but eventually as time goes by, they begin to see just how ridiculous their efforts are. By now Ella is trying to hold up the whole canvas while Richard attempts to fix guy ropes. Suddenly she is unable to hold it any longer, and it subsides over and around her, driving her to her knees. All that Richard can now see of his wife is what appears to be a green mound which is now gently shaking as Ella sees the humour in their situation and begins laughing uncontrollably.

Her laughter is contagious leaving Richard gasping for air, and after he manages to lift the canvas from her, they stand together holding one another until it subsides momentarily, only for it to start again.

The process is repeated again and again until eventually Ella, beginning to worry about the plight that they are in, says" Oh my love, what are we going to do, we just have to get this tent up somehow".

Their prayers are answered and their blushes saved, from an unexpected direction, as the man in the tent which is next to theirs suddenly appears smiling, saying "I couldn't help but see your predicament; would you like it if I showed you how to put the tent up. I know it's not easy if you haven't done it before, I used to have the same problem".

They are delighted to accept Matthew's (for that turns out to be his name) kind offer and are amazed how easy the operation is once you they have been shown.

Thanking him profusely, they invite him and his wife to join them later in the evening. Ella then retrieves Daniel, who has lain in the sidecar, thankfully asleep, oblivious to all that is happening around him all this time.

Wanting to make the most of the time available to them, they quickly sort out the bedding and food which they have brought with them, and leaving it all inside the tent, make their way back down the steep High Street to the quay. From here they walk along the esplanade on the front of the beach until they reach an area which is sandy and where a number of families are playing with their children.

Richard, who has been carrying Daniel in a sling strapped to his chest, lays him down on the sand where he kicks and shakes his hands with delight, happy to be in this strange new warm environment with his parents. Ella and Richard take it in turns to walk down to the water's edge and taking off their shoes, paddle gingerly out into the surf. They are amazed at how refreshing this simple activity makes them feel, until suddenly Ella walks out too far and a large wave drenches her to the waist. Gasping at the shock she beats a hurried retreat back to the beach, where once again she sees the funny side of her predicament and begins laughing convulsively once more.

Richard is delighted to see his lovely wife enjoying this new experience and looks at her anew, watching her standing at the water's edge, her long auburn hair blown by the gusts of wind blowing off the sea. Her dress, wet from the waist down, follows the contours of her lithe body which he knows so well. As she sees him looking, Ella knows immediately the effect she is having on him and reaching him whispers "I wonder what it's like making love in a tent: we'll find out tonight shall we"? Richard not wanting to spoil the moment nods enthusiastically, before laughing and saying "well we'd better make a start back then, my curiosity's killing me".

As they leave, they buy some freshly caught mackerel from a wet fish shop on the beach and when they get back to the tent Ella starts to prepare a meal for them. Although her equipment is very limited, a small primus stove and a few pots and pans, her cooking experience stands her in good stead and the two of them are soon eating the mackerel from tin plates, accompanied by thick chunks of bread and butter, washed down with steaming mugs of tea. Finding some kindling Richard manages to light a fire which the two of them sit around.

Feeding and changing Daniel they spend some time playing with him before settling him down in a sleeping bag that Ella has made for just such a situation. She places him first on a pillow which serves as a readymade cot, which they then put in the tent. To their joy and amazement, he falls asleep almost immediately, so they return to the outside the tent and sit on a blanket as they enjoy the evening, before Richard goes to find Matthew and his wife Joan next door.

Wishing to thank Matthew again for his timely help, Richard produces a bottle of cider which they consume with alacrity, during which they tell each other their reasons for being here at this time.

It transpires that the main reason they are all here is because of the impending war with Germany, and from that the need to experience as much of their beautiful country as they can, because there may not be the opportunity in the future. This is not stated in so many words, but an observer reading between the lines would have no difficulty drawing this conclusion.

Matthew and Joan are from Taunton in Somerset, so their journey has not taken them as long. He is a head cowman on a farm while Joan works part time in a shop in town. They do not have any children, and as a couple they are several years older than Richard and Ella, but they all get on as if they have known each other forever.

They sit as the evening sun goes down, with just the light from a couple of torches and the fire, which flame flickers and dances, its reflection lighting up their profiles as they talk animatedly together.

By now it is late evening and Ella begins to nod off, the effects of good food, warmth and good company taking its toll, despite her desperate efforts to stay awake. Richard noticing this makes his apologies for both of them, saying they need to get to bed in case Daniel has a restless night, so Matthew and Joan take their leave, but not before promising to repeat the experience the next evening.

They tumble into bed, which is in the form of a thin mattress and despite all of Ella's promises of a night of love and lust, she falls asleep instantly, the effects of sun sea and sand taking their toll, much to Richard's chagrin.

But his luck changes as the sun begins to rise the next morning and before Daniel wakes, they enjoy each other once more as they experience sex in a tent for the first time.

"That was wonderful my love" Ella whispers in Richards ear as they climax. "I think that it's probably because it feels that somehow we shouldn't be doing it; you know, as if we're not married and have come away for a dirty weekend". Richard laughs as Daniel wakes crying, reminding them that they are not alone.

"I know what you mean, but I think that it's because we are away from our usual environment and routines and we are more relaxed. But whatever the reason Princess I want you to know that I love you and always will, whatever happens in the future".

Ella is to remember these prophetic words on that sad day some five years later.

By now fully awake Ella feeds Daniel before joining Richard outside who is preparing a cooked breakfast, before finding out where they can wash and do their ablutions.

The camp site is not very big with only enough room for a dozen or so tents. Facilities are very basic with only one toilet and a couple of showers. But the site is at the top of a hill and looking over the hedge the sea can be seen shimmering in the distance.

They spend this warm Sunday morning lazing around the camp site while Daniel has his morning nap. Once he is awake, they decide to go to the beach again while the weather holds. On arrival they do much the same things as the previous day, but this time they have put their swimming costumes on underneath their clothes, so each of them takes it in turns to watch Daniel while the other swims. As is the fashion, Ella's costume covers most of her body, just leaving her arms and legs to be seen. This is the most that women of her generation dare to expose.

Her costume is navy blue and her final touch is a white bathing cap, under which she tucks her long auburn tresses.

Richard's costume also covers him from neck to knee, the top being a vest like arrangement, with separate trunks.

Daniel lies contentedly on the sand under a parasol to stop the sun from burning him, while his parents change and feed him at regular intervals.

So the afternoon passes in this idyllic fashion, the only sign that things are not as normal being workmen erecting large rolls of barbed wire at the top of the beach, while lower down at the water's edge heavy pieces of metal in the shape of triangles are being put in place, all pointing out to sea, to act as deterrents for invading forces. This is a chilling reminder to them that their time here is transitory and spurs them on to enjoy every last second while they can.

Leaving the beach at last, Richard drives up and out of Lyme Regis which takes them along the coast road which leads to Seaton and then to Sidmouth, a continuation of Lyme Bay which they can see on their left, the sea lying smooth and still, taking its luminous smooth blue translucence from the reflection of the clear blue sky above.

Ella is mesmerised as she sits in the sidecar, the canvas cover pushed down so that the wind is rushing over her head, her beautiful long hair splaying out behind her, making her feel more alive than she can ever remember. Daniel is safely tucked up behind her asleep, the movement of the sidecar having a soporific effect on him.

Ella feels euphoric, the combination of sea and wind, combining with being with the two people she loves working their magic on her. Whatever happens she knows for certain that this short period has been the most amazing experience of her life.

They stop in Sidmouth and examine its quaint shops and white painted thatched cottages, before finding a teashop, where they experience Devon cream teas for the first time. Ella loves the combination of scones, and strawberry jam, together with Devon clotted cream, which she tucks away in her memory bank to be resurrected at some time in the future.

Returning back to the camp site, they spend their last evening together with Matthew and Joan, who invite them to their tent, and sit talking and drinking late into the night, before saying their farewells after exchanging addresses', and promising to keep in touch.

They are up early on Monday morning, not wanting to make their way back home, but knowing that they must. Ella is surprised when she wakes to see how much the sun has burned her face, which Richard thinks makes her look even more beautiful and poised.

Taking their time, they return home following the same route in reverse, stopping off in Blandford Forum to feed and change Daniel and get refreshments in a tea shop in the High Street. This is their last stop and, taking their time, they arrive back in Chadlington at five o'clock, treasuring their memories of this wonderful weekend.

As the year draws to its conclusion, Ella and Richard experience their first Christmas together as a family, as they welcome her parents on Christmas Day and then Rachel, Fred and baby George on Boxing Day. Presents are few, with money being tight, but nothing else matters as they celebrate. All thoughts of War put firmly from their minds.

But fate has one more unexpectedly cruel trick to play on them, when Richard's call-up papers drops through their door on the last day of 1939.

CHAPTER 12.

1956 –1957.
ELLA AND DANIEL

Ella's café continues to go from strength to strength as 1956 proves to be an immense success for her. On the week following her first week as proprietor of her café she places a notice in the window for a vacancy for a person who can help her with both cooking and baking and another for a waitress to help to serve customers.

She strikes gold almost immediately when Fiona Betteridge applies for the kitchen assistant position. Fiona is a woman of about the same age as herself, perhaps a year or so older and she has held a position similar to that of Ella in a large country house in Great Tew, just north of Chipping Norton. Also, like Ella, she too has been made redundant when the owner had died leaving those who had inherited the estate a huge sum for death duties. This had happened some two years previously and Fiona had been unable to find alternative employment ever since.

Luckily, she and her husband have managed to find accommodation, thanks to an aunt who lives in Chipping Norton where Fiona now resides. Although she has found a number of short-term jobs doing cleaning at large houses in the surrounding area, or serving in bars of pubs locally, she has been unable to secure a full-time position or one where she can use her cooking skills.

Ella likes her at first sight, being able to reconcile Fiona's situation with that of her own, but is careful to ask if she had any references, before going on to ask further about her cooking skills and is delighted with her response, as she appears to have even more experience than her own. Like Ella, Fiona too has a child, a daughter named Naomi who is grown up and living and working in London.

Taking a deep breath, Ella offers Fiona a full-time position on a three-month trial basis, but is careful to ensure that her hours include some early starts to help with the preparation of meals and bread baking. Fiona assures her that this is not a problem, having been used, as indeed Ella has, to working a good deal of unsocial hours.

The deal is struck and in the years that follow Ella never has any reason to doubt her new appointment. In the years that follow their friendship will develop and blossom, confirming Ella's decision to employ Fiona, something that she will never have any reason to regret.

The position of waitress is a little more problematic. Using the same method Ella puts a card in the Café window advertising for the position for a part time waitress and receives a number of applicants, from which she chooses an older person, who turns out to be very suitable and competent, but who only stays a short while before giving in her notice, because standing for long periods causes her problems with the circulation in her legs.

Thinking that it might be better to get someone younger Ella offers the position to a school leaver, but the amount of training that is needed proves to be too much for Elizabeth and Ella and they have to let her go.

By a series of elimination, the third person Ella appoints, after discussing the matter with both Elizabeth and Fiona, is a young woman in her mid-twenties, who is married with a young child, and is living in town with her parents and husband.

Catherine, for that is her name, fits in with the rest of them like a well-oiled machine, completing Ella's team, which, although she doesn't know it yet, is to remain constant for many years. Fiona has a more serious nature, but Catherine brings with her a sense of fun and laughter, a useful tool to defuse situations with difficult customers, or to raise staff morale when they are feeling low.

Daniel returns to Grammar School this same week, for his last year, at the end of which he is due to take his A level G.C.E.'s.

Christmas 1956 arrives in a flurry of activity for Ella, the Café by now being a place for people to meet either before or during their shopping and consequently Ella and her staff are kept busy right through this period. Closing early on Christmas Eve, Ella and Daniel make their way by bus to Chadlington to her parents who have invited them and Rachel and Fred and her family for the Christmas period.

On a cold and crisp Christmas Eve, they all attend the midnight service at Chadlington Church, before returning to Alf and Liz's, where a roaring log fire greets them, which they all huddle round rubbing their cold hands and feet back to life. Mince pies and sherry are the order of the day, before they go to sleep, some on the floor, others on sofas and chairs.

The next morning Ella and Rachel help Liz prepare the Christmas dinner, making sure that there are a liberal number of threepenny pieces in the Christmas pudding for the grandchildren to find, while Alf and Fred go to the Malt Shovel to work up an appetite.

Meanwhile the grandchildren, Daniel, George and his brother Harry, who is two years younger, go for a walk around the village and catch up with the events in each other's lives. Now that Daniel is living in Chipping Norton, the three of them don't get together very often, but when they do, it's like they have never been apart, something that both Ella and Rachel take great comfort in.

After dinner they all sit round the fire as they have done for many years to listen to the Queen's speech. This year it is particularly sombre, reminding them of the events that have occurred during the year, in particular the invasion of Egypt by Great Britain, France and Israel, to regain control of the Suez Canal, which had been seized by Colonel Nasser. Despite the fact that this had been achieved, The United States of America would not support the enterprise, insisting that all the invading countries leave Egypt. It had been a traumatic period, reviving memories of the Second World War and Korea, with all the hardships and heartaches that they had caused.

As the Queen finishes her speech, Ella is lost in thought, but Alf who is watching her for just such an eventuality, says "well who's for playing charades; here you go first Ella, you're good at it ".

In this way the year comes to an end, a year which has been life changing for Ella and Daniel, but the following year is to be even more eventful.

As 1957 progresses, Ella's café and team become more productive and efficient as they get to know each other better. Ella makes sure to encourage and reward them with little things, like letting them go early if the business is quiet, or occasionally taking them out to Oxford to a pub for a drink and a meal.

Now that she knows her market, Ella changes the choice of food periodically that the café offers, ensuring that it does not become too boring, and looks for other things that will attract new customers. She knows that the largest part of her business comes from existing customers, but she also knows that providing that they are happy, her business will continue to grow from word of mouth, as they tell their friends of their experience.

Daniel is now under extreme pressure because of preparations for his exams which are due in July, but he still finds time to help out in the Café when he can, although Ella discourages him, knowing just how much pressure he is under from school. But the two of them have a very close relationship, born out of the adversity from Richard's death, so she comforts and encourages her wonderful son.

Both their efforts are rewarded in late July when the results of his A level exams are announced. To her absolute joy and pride Daniel achieves A. grade passes in all four subjects. But even this achievement is surpassed when Daniel hears that he has been offered a "free" entry to Exeter University to read English Literature.

For Ella and all her family as they all begin to slowly digest and savour this information there is a sense of overwhelming joy in Daniel's success, because he will be the first of any of them to go to University.

Ella realises that although he has gained a free entry, which will cover his tuition fees, there will still be other costs, for lodgings, reference books and materials, as well as money for food, but is determined that none of this will stand in her son's way, so she must find the money somehow.

Before Daniel leaves to begin his first year in October, Ella throws a celebration party in Chadlington Village Hall, where most of the residents attend to congratulate and wish Daniel well. Ella and Fiona have prepared a feast fit for the occasion and the celebrations go long into the night.

As she looks around at all the happy faces, Ella is reminded of the last occasion that she was here, her wedding, and thinks nostalgically, with a lump in her throat, how proud Richard would have been to be here to witness their son's success.

The day in October eventually arrives for Daniel to leave. Ella has fussed around him, helping him pack and preparing food for him to take for the journey. Her final task is to ask him to make sure that he writes to her regularly and tell her how he is getting on, and if there is anything he might need.

Mr Souch has kindly offered to drive Daniel to Gloucester where he can catch a train to Exeter. As they leave Ella stands, waving until the car disappears from sight, at which point she returns inside the café before collapsing into uncontrollable tears, feeling almost as if she has been widowed for a second time. In her heart she knows that this day is inevitable; if not now then on another, sometime in the future, and that she has to be strong for her son's sake.

Work is her salvation, as it has been so many times in the past. She throws all her energy and efforts into the café, working long hours to ensure that she is tired enough to sleep when she goes to bed, to stop her thoughts dwelling on Daniel. It doesn't always work, but the result of all her efforts means that the Café goes from strength to strength.

She is constantly refining the Café's offering, putting a number of tables under large parasols outside on the pavement where customers can drink tea and eat cakes in the sun, or selling ice creams and lollies for passing customers and their children.

Daniel is as good as his word and writes to her regularly, telling of his progress and how much he is enjoying University life. He doesn't make the journey home during term time; being only too aware of the drain it would be on Ella's finances, although she often asks him too. He finds the course work totally absorbing and for the first few weeks confines himself to his studies, using the University library for research, which also sells used reference books that he needs very cheaply.

Always aware how much his course is costing Ella financially, he finds a part time job behind a bar in Exeter for several evenings each week and some weekends. Wanting to be involved as much as possible with university life he begins to play rugby for the second team, which inevitably leads to drinking sessions in the clubhouse after games. Although he is not a heavy consumer, he discovers very early on that if he drinks too much, he is either violently ill or tends to fall asleep, much to his teammates' amusement. All these activities, combined with his work load leaves him very little time for other social activities, although he does get dragged down against his will to the University bar by a couple of friends occasionally.

He manages to return home at the end of the Christmas and Easter terms where his mother makes a great fuss of him. Here he recharges his batteries, catching up with friends and family, making the journey to Chadlington to visit his grandparents, who proudly welcome him with open arms.

Christmas particularly is a great event, as Rachel and Fred and their two children, and Ella and Daniel spend the day with Alf and Elizabeth, the first time that they have all been together for some time.

Daniel's fresher year passes like snow on a summer's day, as he tries unsuccessfully to hold back time to enable him to do all the things that he wants to do. All too soon the year is over and it is time for him to return home to his mother's welcoming arms.

He spends his vacation helping in his Ella's Café, (although she insists that it is not necessary) before returning to Exeter for the start of his second year.

Daniel's second year is more relaxed, although his course work is more intense. He has come to love Exeter and its surrounding area, its ancient buildings and Cathedral and friendly inhabitants. He is no longer a fresher and consequently has no fear of not knowing where things are, or to have feelings of isolation because he now has friends and feels in some small way part of the fabric of this ancient institution and this gives him the confidence he needs.

He has become firm friends with Martin Bird and James Cleverly, both of whom are reading English Literature. There are also two females that he gets on very well with, although his relationship with both Barbara and Melanie is that of just good friends. But they all offer great comfort and encouragement to each other in times of adversity, for which Daniel has reason to be grateful. They invariably all meet from time to time in the University bar to discuss the highs and lows of their lives, be they personal or academic.

Daniel loves the challenge of the work, the research and investigative aspect of which he thinks might be useful if he were to take up journalism or something similar once he graduates.

He continues to play rugby in the winter months and in the summer offers his services to the University cricket team, a game that he has always enjoyed. In between, to his great delight (and hers) Ella journeys down by train to see him for several days. Daniel takes great pride in showing her the beauties of Exeter, the University and the surrounding countryside, making several bus journeys to do so. Ella is happy as she realises that her son is content and settled and she is proud of the man that he has become.

She updates him with the progress of the Café and tells him of her next venture to expand the business. "I have just begun driving lessons" she tells him to his amazement "and, when I have my driving licence, I want to get a small van which I can use to collect provisions for the shop or to deliver food to catering venues. I am convinced there is a good market for it, because I am constantly being asked to do catering for weddings, fetes and special events. What do you think Daniel, I remember that you mentioned it as a future possibility some time ago" she finishes, reverting to their old method of discussing the development of the business?

Once he has got over her announcement Daniel agrees "Good for you Mum, I'm sure you're right. It's something that I would have got around to suggesting to you eventually, so we're both on the same wavelength".

Before she returns home, Ella takes her son out to a restaurant in Exeter where she feeds him, before visiting the local supermarket to buy provisions to stock him up before she returns home. She still misses him desperately, but now that she has reliable staff she can leave in charge in her absence, she feels that she can now see him occasionally without worrying how things are once she has left the café.

Time, the winner of all circumstances, seems to accelerate, or that is how it feels to Daniel, and the end of his second year is upon him as he tries to cram his course work as well as all the other activities that he enjoys so much.

Saying farewell to his friends he makes his way home once again, feeling somewhat bereft at leaving them, the University and City, which is by now so much a part of his life. He wonders with a mixture of trepidation and exhilaration what his final year will bring.

CHAPTER 13.

1958/1959.
DANIEL AT EXETER

Daniel commences his third and final year, his objectives and determination to achieve them enough to justify both his own efforts and the deep need that he feels to repay his mother for all the sacrifices that she has made for him. He knows that all she has ever wanted for him is that he has the opportunity to achieve whatever he wants, and that she has delivered her part of the bargain without ever mentioning it.

He still works at the bar in Exeter some nights and sometimes his friends visit so that they can discuss matters of no consequence whatsoever and he is pleased when this happens, delighting in their company. It is during one of these uneventful evenings that Martin mentions that there is going to be a dance in the University hall on the next Saturday and insists that they should all go. Daniel is reluctant at first, but after a lot of pressure from the four of them, Martin, James, Barbara and Melanie, he begins to waiver.

"You have got to come, it's going to be a great night" says Martin, and then in a conspiratorial voice "The beer's cheap and there will be loads of girls all gagging for it" which he assumes will be the clincher and to which both Melanie and Barbara reply "In your dreams". Not to be put off, Martin continues "Yes and there's a great band, so forget work just for one night, so what do you say?"

Not wanting to always refuse their offers, Daniel reluctantly agrees, and duly finds himself in the hall at eight o'clock, where to his amazement he finds that the combination of the music and cheap booze has an uplifting effect on his mood. As the evening wears on some students begin dancing, or rather a number of females do, which is the usual scenario at these dances, until such time that the males have had enough beer or are smashed out of their skulls and get enough courage to join them.

Up until this point in his life Daniel has had very little contact with members of the opposite sex in any way other than just good friends. Chipping Norton Grammar school was for boys only, so he rarely met females in a social environment, and his work load meant that he didn't have time anyway.

But his lack of experience even talking to girls becomes obvious as he watches several of his friends happily asking girls to dance, while he stands rooted to the spot in terror at the prospect. To make matters worse he has been observing a group of five or six girls who are all talking excitedly and animatedly to each other, one of who he finds extremely attractive. In no way could he ever consider her a girl, she's definitely a young woman, of medium height with black glossy hair of shoulder length, which accentuates her pale complexion, in which her startling vibrant clear green eyes are illuminated, her long dark lashes emphasising and drawing his attention, transfixing him with her gaze. She is dressed in the almost mandatory student gear of a tight grey and white top with short sleeves, her curvaceous figure leaving little to Daniel's imagination. She wears tight blue jeans, which have numerous design patches and which show her long legs to their best advantage. High heeled shoes complete the vision.

As he continues to stare at her she becomes aware of his gaze and returns it with one of her own, until he becomes embarrassed and looks away blushing violently.

Unfortunately for Daniel, Martin and James have noticed the incident and, when they return from dancing with their partners, they begin baiting him to ask her for a dance. After some time of continual harassment Daniel feels that he has no other option than to ask the vision of loveliness for a dance, so, waiting until there is another surge of people getting up to dance, he walks apprehensively across the floor to her, but his timing is not good because just before he reaches her another student appears from nowhere and beats Daniel to it.

As she begins to move onto the floor with her partner, she suddenly notices Daniel whose intentions cannot be disguised from her, and she smiles gently at him, recognising his actions. For his part Daniel wishes that the floor would open up and devour him and returns dejectedly to his friends who give him even more stick.

"Wait until the next dance and go back to her" says Martin. "You can't give up now" says James. But Daniel is distraught, the feeling of rejection uppermost in his mind, so he prevaricates, wanting to delay the inevitable, but the situation continues to be out of his hands as Daniel's rival and the vision stay on the floor for several more dances, until she obviously decides that she has had enough and returns to her friends.

Suddenly the last dance is announced and Daniel is almost physically forced onto the floor by his friends who almost carry him in her direction, until he shakes them off and again makes his way to her. His mouth is dry and he is almost shaking as he reaches her and whispers hoarsely "May I have this dance please"?

For her part she looks at him quizzically before dazzling him again with her smile which makes the rest of her come alive.

"Of course, I would like that: I only hope that you can dance a bit better than that last oaf. He kept treading on my feet and kicking my shins to pieces".

Although he is petrified about asking her to dance, he has no inhibitions about his dancing abilities, because Ella has, over the years, taught and instilled in him her talent.

Taking her in hold he says "I will do my best, I haven't crippled anybody for ages" which makes her laugh, a deeply satisfying sound to Daniel's ears. The dance is a waltz and Daniel whisks her expertly round the floor much to his partner's amazement, who has suffered several times this night at various drunken students hands, or feet rather. As she considers the situation, she realises that she has never moved so smoothly and silkily like this on a dance floor before and her perception of her partner begins to become a little more appreciative. No words pass between them until the music slows considerably and couples all over the floor go into a slow tempo, holding each other close and no longer moving round the floor, but rather in small circles, lost completely in each other.

Daniel is now out of his comfort zone, not knowing whether to put his arms around his partner, not wanting her to think that he is assuming that he can, or to return her to her friends. But before he can do anything, she closes the gap between them saying "Well you didn't maim me after all, so I'm grateful for that. How did you learn to dance like that"? As she finishes speaking, she smiles and puts her arms around his neck.

They are now standing together and he puts his arms around her waist pulling her to him as they too move slowly in a small circle. He can smell her fragrance, a combination of perfume and musky woman as he holds her feeling her body moving next to his, and he wants this moment to last forever.

"Well my mother was a very good dancer when she was young, so she taught me" and then plucking up courage "I'm Daniel, but my friends call me Dan and I'm in my final year reading English, how about you, what's your name? I can't keep thinking of you as THAT BEAUTIFUL GIRL IN THE CORNER".

Laughing, she says "Wow, you don't say much, but when you do its mind blowing. Well to answer your question, it's April and this is my third year too, studying Medieval History".

The floodgates are now open as they try to find out more about each other. Daniel tells her about himself, where her lives and explains about his mother's Café, but says nothing of his father, because after living just with his mother for so long, it does not enter his vocabulary any more. Of course, he still thinks of him constantly, but doesn't necessarily want to share those memories with new people.

April begins "I live in Taunton in Somerset which isn't too far away. My father is an engineer for British Gas and my mother runs a nursery for under five-year olds in town. I have two brothers, both of whom are older than me, so I'm the young spoilt brat of the family. That's what my brothers keep telling me anyway".

As they continue talking, they are suddenly aware that the music has stopped and that most of the couples have moved off the floor. They are still holding each other, talking ten to the dozen before April steps back saying "well I'd better go and join my friends: it looks like the evening is over".

For several seconds Daniel panics as he realizes that he doesn't want the evening to finish and says clumsily "Can I see you again April, perhaps we could go to the pictures or for a walk somewhere?"

April's friends are now beckoning her to join them and she pauses for a moment before saying "Oh Dan, I don't think that would be a good idea because I have a boyfriend at home who I've known for several months and we have both said that we would be true to one another" and then more conciliatory " that doesn't mean that you and I can't see each other as long as we are part of a group, similar to tonight, but I don't think it would be a good idea to go on a date together on our own. I'm sorry but I just don't want you to think that our relationship can be anything other than good friends".

Daniel is once again completely out of his depth, feeling both hurt and humiliated, but determines not to let his feelings show, before saying "I'm sorry too, but perhaps it's for the best, because I need to work to get my degree which won't leave much time for socializing, but thank you for being honest with me. I've enjoyed your company very much and will no doubt see you around from time to time. Please accept my apologies for presuming too much. Goodnight April".

He returns to Martin and James and several other friends, before going up to the bar for last orders, intending to get smashed, but however much his friends rib him, nothing seems to rekindle the spark that April has so briefly lit and he leaves to return to his room in misery.

The evening has been a wakeup call for him and from this point on, until the end of the term leading up to Christmas, so Daniel devotes all his time to learning his subject and does not get involved in any social events or meetings. He moves from his tutorages to his room, or sometimes goes for walks on his own. His encounter with April has hurt him so much, that he has no wish to repeat the process with her or anyone else, so he keeps himself to himself where no one else can hurt him.

He has seen April several time from a distance and has avoided her when it looked as if their paths might cross. His friends keep him up to date without him wanting them to. They tell him that she has occasionally gone to the bar and to the dance, but that she hasn't been seen there after the first few weeks.

Daniel knows that the way he feels is ridiculous, unreasonable even, but he cannot seem to think about it any other way. The truth is that he has been smitten for the very first time. "This is silly", he keeps repeating to himself when he is alone. "It's not her fault that I misread her feelings, I should not have gone in like a bull in a china shop". But deep down, he knows that his feelings for April run deep. His friends keep telling him that there are plenty more fish in the sea, but that is no consolation to him.

* * *

The Christmas break arrives and he is only too ready to return home to Chipping Norton and Ella. Stepping from Mr. Souch's car, Ella rushes from the shop to welcome him as always with open arms.

The period between the two semesters is both busy and happy for Daniel as he helps his mother in the Café and in between times spends Christmas with all his family, seeing his Grandparents, Rachel and Fred and his two cousins. But when he is on his own, his mind returns to THAT BEAUTIFUL GIRL IN THE CORNER, and he wonders what April is doing right at this moment. Is she with her boyfriend and if this is the case, has he been true to her?

Ella senses that there is something troubling her son, but although she has tried to discover what it might be, Daniel insists that there is nothing wrong. His mother suspects that it may be the result of a lost love and fears for her son, knowing that if so, it will be his first experience of the kind and accordingly, a rejection will have had a strong effect on him. But she also knows that there is nothing she can do or say that will help him, and is concerned that it may affect his studies.

Being away from Exeter, Daniel feels refreshed and ready to return when the time comes in mid-January. He has had time to analyze his feelings about April and student life generally, and resolves that this term he will become more involved with student functions, and not be so withdrawn.

He still cannot face the thought of seeing April, but as the term progresses there are a number of activities that the students have arranged, one of which, a trek across Dartmoor over a four-day weekend, appeals to him very much. Martin and James and one or two others have expressed an interest and a small ten-seater coach has been booked to get them there.

On the last weekend in March, the nine brave candidates gather at the front of the campus waiting to be collected for their adventure to begin. They intend camping for the three nights and are carrying between them four tents. These will be distributed between them, one for the three hardy female students, a second for three males and a third slightly larger version which is big enough to accommodate the three remaining males and the cooking equipment and food supplies.

Some navigational skills are necessary, so Daniel carries a compass, which he knows how to use, having spent many excursions with his cousins and the scout group over the years. By the time that the cooking utensils are packed, as well as two small paraffin stoves and basic food supplies, each person is carrying a substantial load. The bus drops them at the small village of Bovey Tracey at the eastern periphery of the park.

Objectives are not as important to the group as the need to test themselves against the elements, so survival is the criteria rather than finding a particular place, although they do obviously need to know where they are at any given moment.

They have discussed previously the main areas that they wish to get to, which are all basically as far from human habitation as possible. Starting at Bovey Tracey they begin to trek across The Moor heading across Haytor Vale, bypassing Widdecombe in the Moor and continuing west to reach the small hamlet of Postbridge. This takes them several hours and it is now mid-afternoon, so they determine to head on out into the wilds of The Moor for another hour, before bivouacking for the night.

The conversation, which is at first excited and animated between them, has by now been reduced to the occasional word of complaint, usually in the form of an expletive, as they all become tired.

At four o'clock they decide to set up the tents before they lose the last of the daylight. They select a site just under a Tor on the eastward side to avoid the westerly wind. The temperature is dropping rapidly and a mist is settling over The Moors eerie landscape. Some of them struggle to erect their tents but the more experienced among them come to their aid. All of them are now ravenously hungry and the stoves are lit and tins of soup are put in a large tin basin and heated up. This is consumed rapidly with large chunks of bread, followed by tinned ham and salad, washed down with steaming cups of tea.

Two of the more experienced among them dig a small pit and after gathering whatever pieces of wood and twigs that they can find, light a fire which they all huddle around as the temperature drops. Their spirits are high, now having achieved what some of them secretly never thought possible. Jokes are told and much banter ensues as the light from the fire flickers, throwing impenetrable shadows across the bleak landscape.

Quantities of beer and cider are produced and consumed which relaxes the atmosphere as they all get to know each other better. After a while, it becomes obvious to Daniel that his friends, Martin and James, know two of the females in the group very well, a fact that they have not mentioned to him before.

The two women, Sandra and Caroline, are in their second year and a third woman Theresa is in her final year. The first two spend most of their time snuggled up to Martin and James, while Theresa, who has all the rest of the males' attention, joins in the conversation, chatting easily but always offering her own opinion on any subjects raised. Daniel is drawn to her like a moth to a flame; he has never come across someone who knows their own mind so strongly and yet is so open and ready to listen to others arguments. Looking at her, for what seems to him for the first time, Daniel sees an attractive brunette, with hair cut short into a bob fashion. She has dark brown eyes and a short snub nose, but her most attractive features for him are her broad effervescent smile and infectious laughter, which she uses a lot. She is tall, standing about five feet eight inches or so Daniel estimates, with a slim elegant figure to match.

He is slightly in awe of her as she holds sway over the rest of the company, recognizing in her a woman confident in herself and her abilities.

The evening passes with camp fire songs, mostly from the males with dubious lyrics, which Theresa joins in with, seeming to know all the appropriate, inappropriate words. Eventually the efforts of the day take their toll and one by one they slip quietly off to their tents and to their warm sleeping bags. Martin, James and Daniel get ensconced but as soon all the rest of the group have settled for the night his two friends suddenly get up and Martin says to him "Well we are off to the girls' tent now Daniel, I hope you don't mind, but we're on a promise".

Daniel is stunned to say the least, not previously having been given any inkling that this might happen, but just as he settles down again to sleep there is a rustling on the outside of the tent and a dark figure enters stumbling over the detritus of clothes and sleeping bags laying around. There is a muffled "shit" as Theresa stubs her toe, thus introducing her entry, followed by "Are you there Daniel, your two friends have thrown me out, so the only place that I could think of was here" and then "come on, budge over, there's room enough in your sleeping bag for both of us".

Daniel is almost transfixed with fear as she wastes no time getting in with him in his bag. This is something outside his experience and he does not know how to react, but Theresa snuggles up to him as if it were the most normal thing in the world. The feel of her warm body against his soon produces his natural reactions and to his shame and embarrassment his body betrays him. Feeling his erection Theresa surprises him by saying "Oh good I thought that I'd failed" and then stripping off her nightgown "come on Dan, get your kit off; have you got any protection". Before he can reply she carries on "Oh don't worry, I have some here, because I daren't rely on you blokes".

Helping him out of his clothes she suddenly becomes aware of his reticence and says knowingly with a gentle smile playing on her lips "This is your first time Dan isn't it" and then "Don't worry, I'll show you; we all have to start sometime".

Daniel's initiation to the world of sex is a revelation as Theresa guides him in an exploration of her body, emphasizing her erotic zones and where his hands and mouth excite her the most. By this time, he is at fever pitch and noticing, Theresa says "slow down Dan, you need to put this condom on before we go further" and then seeing his look of perplexity, adds "Oh come here, let me do it". But all the excitement is just a step to far for Daniel as he loses control prematurely and the moment is lost. He starts stuttering his apologies but Theresa stops him saying "Oh Dan it doesn't matter, these things happen, we'll wait a few minutes and try again, but the next time we we'll take things more slowly" and she snuggles him to her, his head against her breasts.

Sure enough, Dan experiences the same feelings of desire and need within a few minutes, and Theresa sitting astride him, leads him slowly through the process once again, pacing both their needs until they can wait no longer. Theresa is kissing him open mouthed, her tongue reaching inside his, (increasing his excitement, if that were at all possible). This time they climax as one, Theresa collapsing exhaustedly across him, while Daniel lays quietly beneath her, marveling at this wonderful experience, the most exciting event of his young life.

They fall asleep totally spent, but, to the amazement of both of them, they wake again twice during the night and make love, each time better than the last.

As dawn is breaking Theresa says "I'd better get back to my tent and kick your friends out before the rest of the campers wake up". Kissing him she makes to leave, but Daniel doesn't want her to leave, saying "please don't go just yet, tell me a little about you, the only thing that I know about you is your name".

Theresa is silent for a moment, before she smiles and says "Look Dan, I like you a lot, but I'm not ready for a full-time relationship now, or at least until I have finished University and got my degree. That's my priority and must come first. But if you want to, I'm happy to see you occasionally when I'm not under pressure from my work load". Then noticing the look of disappointment on his face, she continues hurriedly "Please don't be sad Dan, I'm sure that you too will find that you won't have sufficient time for social events as your course progresses. There's no other man in my life, although there was for a couple of years up until I started at University. But that was a bridge too far for him and he ended it, which was devastating for me at the time, because I loved him, or thought I did anyway.

Then on a lighter note she continues "I live in Nailsea, which is a small village in Somerset. My father works in Bristol which is about ten miles west, as the Manager of a shipping office. My Mum works in Clevedon at Hales Cakes. I have a brother, who is two years older than me and a sister who is five years younger. I'm studying law and hope to take a Master's degree after graduating or alternatively I might join the police. Now tell me about you Dan".

Not knowing where to start he begins hesitatingly to tell her about himself, explaining that his father was killed in the war and that his mother runs her own Café in Chipping Norton. Theresa, listening, can hear the sense of both loss and pride in his voice.

"She sounds an amazingly strong woman Dan. It must have taken a lot of courage for her to get out of her comfort zone and start a new venture at that stage of her life, with all the challenges that it presented".

While Daniel is very proud of his mother and what she has achieved, he has never quite recognized just how difficult it must have been for her, until Theresa has at this moment pointed out. He finishes by telling her that he is taking English Literature as his subject and although he is not sure what he will do after graduation one avenue that he might pursue is journalism.

As they finish talking, Theresa makes to leave again saying "I really must go now Dan, it's getting quite light". To which he replies hurriedly "when can I see you again? Oh, I don't mean now, but when we get back next week. I understand and accept what you are saying about needing to get your degree, but how will I know when you have time available so that I can see you "?

Laughing Theresa replies "Let's just wait and see Dan, I don't know, is the answer, but I promise that when the time comes, I'll let you know". And then "anyway there's still two more nights left on this trip that we can see each other, if you want to".

Daniel is consoled with her last few words as she slips silently out of the tent and crosses back to her own.

* * *

The next two days are both the most exciting and depressing of Daniels life. During the day after they take down the tents and prepare to move on, he tries to remain close to Theresa, but this is not always possible. What is worse he realizes suddenly is that the other males in the party are beginning to show her attention, realizing that Sandra and Caroline are effectively spoken for, but also not yet aware of Theresa's night visit to Daniel.

This makes her the only female available in their eyes and they act accordingly, joking and laughing with her and generally trying to draw her attention to them. To Daniel's amazement and disappointment Theresa responds in a like manner, laughing at their jokes, (which Daniel doesn't think are at all funny) and pulling their legs in return. To make matters worse every time Theresa needs help, either carrying equipment or assistance overcoming obstacles, be it a small running stream that needs to be crossed or a Tor that needs to be climbed, one or other of the three males makes sure that one or other of them is there, leaving Daniel fuming silently in their wake.

For her part Theresa seems not to be aware of their efforts, but rather accepts their help as if it is the most natural thing in the world, thanking them and promising to make it up to them by cooking meals or washing up dishes when they stop for the night.

All this makes Daniel unsure how to proceed. He feels isolated, unable to get close to Theresa and although she includes him in her conversation, any contribution that he tries to make is usually unheard because of one or the others loud interruptions, negating anything that he might say.

They head north and reach Fernworthy Reservoir at midday where they collapse and stop for lunch, intending to continue on to an area known as Buttern Hill. Again, as they all lay around on an area of grass overlooking the reservoir, Daniel tries to get close to Theresa, but to no avail as she is quickly surrounded by the three men, and although she beckons him over, there is nowhere that he can find, so after trying, he stays where he is.

The afternoon continues in a similar vein until they stop for the night, totally exhausted by the terrain which is a mixture of either boggy marsh or rocky outcrops. The evening follows a similar pattern to that of the one before, first making a campfire and then heating tins of Irish stew and potatoes together with salad, followed by tinned custard and fruit.

As they relax more banter ensues, much of it aimed at Theresa, who holds her own, giving even more in return. Then as before they begin to sing folk songs until the temperature begins to drop, making them all head for their beds, but not before one of the three men sitting next to Theresa whispers something to her, to which she smiles and shakes her head in a negative way. Daniel wonders what has been said, feeling pretty sure that it was personal and making him even more depressed.

But to his delight and amazement once his friends have left him once again to see Sandra and Caroline, it is only a few minutes before Theresa appears in his tent saying "are you there Dan, I can't see a bloody thing in here" before she once again stubs her toe and lets out a cry of "bollocks, that bloody hurt".

Daniel can't stop himself from laughing, despite all the mental suffering that he has endured all day, until she says, stopping him short in his tracks "If you're going to laugh at me then I'm going to William's tent like he suggested".

Seeing his haunted look, caused by the remark, which has highlighted the cause of his concern all day, she regrets it, and says "I'm so sorry Dan, but I was only joking, I wouldn't give those three chancers the time of day, especially William".

"He did ask you then, I thought that is what it must be when he whispered to you".

She replies, "Yes, but I told him no, and anyway I wanted to be with you" and then questioningly "I hope you don't think that I would sleep with just anyone Daniel, because if you do then I'll go back to my tent right now".

"Of course, I don't think that, but I have had a terrible day wanting to be close to you, but not being able to because of those three guys who seem to want to monopolies you all the time".

Cuddling up close to him Theresa murmurs "but what else would you have me do Dan. I can't just ignore them; we're all supposed to be together on this trek. Anyway, I said no because I wanted to be with you. As for the sex, I can tell you that you are the only person that I have had it with, since the boyfriend who dumped me; and he was the first"

Completely consoled and feeling guilty of doubting her, Daniel envelopes her in his arms, content to just hold her and let their body warmth lift the temperature in the tent. Just as the previous night however his body soon begins to betray him and with a long sigh he reaches for her once again, only to feel her immediate response as they both continue their experiences where they left off.

The last day of their journey is both exhilarating and exciting for Daniel as Theresa stays close to him, although still talking to the rest of the company gregariously, as is her nature: but she recognizes the hurt that she caused him unknowingly the previous day and makes every effort to include him as much as possible.

Setting out from their site near Chagford they head south, needing to be within striking distance of Bovey Tracey by the end of the day, in order to be picked up by their transport at ten p.m. the next morning.

For once the Sun is high in the heavens casting its light over the dramatic landscape and lifting their spirits simultaneously, heightening Daniel's feeling of euphoria. They make good progress reaching the small village of North Bovey by midday where they restock supplies of food and drinks, before finding a local pub to have lunch.

They find it difficult to motivate themselves once they have finished eating and sit for some time playing cards, but eventually they set out on their final leg of their trip, talking vociferously and laughing, each of them quietly pleased with the achievements of the last three days.

They cross the small river Bovey and carry on south, coming across an area where settlements of Iron Age people have lived over two thousand years before, only a few stones lying around, leaving evidence of their previous existence.

Reaching a suitable place to stop just outside Bovey Tracey, they set up their tents for the last time, and after lighting a fire they gather round discussing the highlights of their journey, all of them concluding that it has been an unqualified success and vowing to do something similar at some unspecified time in the future. Their mood understandably is relaxed as after making their last evening meal they all chat excitedly, before the mood turns to singing songs, mostly of dubious origins. The drink flows in copious quantities and Daniel soon becomes drowsy, unused to such volumes, until he falls asleep, unable to stay awake any longer.

By comparison Theresa, boosted by ever increasing quantities of alcohol, which have been surreptitiously administered by William, is becoming louder and more vociferous by the second, her body swaying to the songs that they are all singing. She is not even aware that Daniel has collapsed and is lying comatose only a few feet away from her.

The situation suits William's evil plan to bed her, come hell or high water this night, so he continues to ply her with drinks, filling her glass with Vodka and tonic until after a further hour she suddenly succumbs and without a sound collapses slowly to the grass, like a rag doll that has had its stuffing taken out.

This is the moment that William has been waiting for as he winks at his two companions saying "look, get Dan into his tent and put him into his sleeping bag. Meanwhile this young lady and I are going to get it together, whether she likes it or not; now help me get her into our tent and leave the rest to me. I presume you two don't mind sleeping in Dan's tent in Martin and James' sleeping bags"?

William's two compatriots, Brian and Norman are loath to disobey his instructions, knowing from experience that if they defy him, he has a volatile temper and is capable of attacking them or making their lives a misery. The result is that they comply with his instructions, lifting Daniels unresponsive form and putting him to bed fully clothed into his sleeping bag, before joining him in theirs.

Meanwhile William has struggled to get Theresa's unconscious body into his tent by a mixture of dragging and carrying her. Once he deposits her limp body onto his sleeping bag, she lies inert and unresponsive both to him and her surroundings.

* * *

Daniel awakes slowly, his head pounding and with a feeling of nausea threatening to engulf him. Hurriedly exiting his tent, he gets away as far as he can from the campsite before throwing up.

Returning, he is surprised to find Brian and Norman occupying his two friend's sleeping bags, and wonders for the first time where Theresa can be.

Violently shaking them he asks them if they know where she is, only to be met by surreptitious glances between the two of them. The reason for their reticence regarding Theresa's disappearance suddenly becomes blindingly obvious to Daniel, who lets out a great roar of anger and emotion before rushing outside and crossing the few yards to William's tent.

His worst fears are realized as he roughly pulls the entry to the tent open and enters. There before him he can see William and Theresa lying together in one sleeping bag and the pain and hurt that he experiences at the sight of the woman who he trusts so much and has such strong feelings for engenders in him anger of unequalled magnitude that he has never felt in his short life to date.

His presence in the tent has had no visible effect on the occupants so far, despite the noise he is making and his cries of pain. As he looks around him, he can see Theresa's clothes strewn around the tent as if the result of her hurriedly undressing, which only increases his distress.

Wanting to confront her, Daniel reaches down and pulls the sleeping bag open where she lays. Peeling it back, to his despair Theresa's body is revealed, naked to the waist and can only assume that she is completely nude in the lower half. She is lying with her head turned away from William, who Daniel can see, has his arm casually around her shoulders.

But to Daniel's amazement despite the noise that he is making and the disruption caused to her sleeping arrangements, Theresa does not respond and shows no sign that she is aware of his presence: she remains completely comatose, as indeed does William beside her.

Daniel can contain himself no longer and begins to shake her awake, crying all the while "so this is what you mean by not sleeping with <u>just anyone</u>. I should have known you meant with <u>just everyone</u>. God what a fool I have been".

As he continues to shake her, he is aware that her eyes are suddenly open, although not focused, as she tries to concentrate and discover where she is and why Daniel is shouting at her. Looking closely at him she can see that he is crying and upset, then looking down to one side she notices William next to her and Dan's reasons are immediately apparent. Her embarrassment and shame are complete as she realizes that she is naked, the only interpretation being that she is here voluntarily for the purpose of sleeping with William.

But she has no recollection of any of this happening, although she is aware that Daniel is unlikely to believe anything that she says, if only in mitigation: but there is no mitigation, she does not want to make excuses for her behavior, rather she wants to remember how she came to be here in bed with a man that she has no respect for, instead of being with Daniel who she should have been with.

As she tries to explain the unexplainable to Daniel, William wakes and seeing Daniel says "What are you doing in here, you had your chance and now it's mine, so piss off, she doesn't want to be with you".

To Daniel, the fact that she is here with William is the unassailable truth, but although Brian and Norman have to acquiesce to William's demands, Daniel is in no mood to do the same. "She may not want to be with me anymore, but I think the treacherous method that you both used to get rid of me is disgusting". As he finishes speaking, he hauls William to his feet and hits him with a satisfying thud in the face.

To his amazement William cowers away from him, blood spurting between his fingers which are held to his face, obviously not prepared to retaliate in any way, as is often the case with bullies.

Daniel looks down to Theresa and says "I hope you both rot in hell, you deserve each other" and begins to make his way out of the tent.

Theresa, still looking utterly perplexed grabs him by the arm "But Daniel, I don't know what happened. The first I knew of anything was when you woke me a few minutes ago. I told you the truth when I said that I would never sleep with William; I don't even like him. Please believe me: I think that there is something special between you and me".

"You expect me to believe that, after I find you in bed together. I'm sorry but just thinking about it hurts too much. I suggest we go our own ways in future and forget that the two of us ever happened".

Theresa continues to implore him to change his mind, but Daniel is adamant and leaves the tent to nurse his pain and suffering on his own.

After breakfast, the remainder of the journey continues in total silence as far as Daniel and Theresa are concerned. They travel apart, separately, on their own, bearing their individual pain until they reach the bus at the pick-up point.

Most of the others are buoyant and excited, William bragging to his mates of his conquest, while Martin and James and their partners, Sandra and Caroline talk excitedly of the future.

The return journey for Dan and Theresa is a miserable experience for both of them until finally it is time for them to disembark. As they inevitably come face to face as they collect their back packs Theresa tries one last time "Can't we please talk about this Dan, I have already explained that I can't remember anything that happened last night".

As he looks at her tear stained, beautiful face, he is torn by the strength of his feelings for her, until the memory of the events of last night come flooding back and he stiffens his resolve before saying "How very convenient; well unfortunately I can remember all too well what happened when I found you this morning. I don't want to ever go through that again".

Picking up his luggage he walks quickly away, before he can change his mind, leaving Theresa distraught on the pavement.

CHAPTER 14.

1959.
DANIEL, THERESA AND APRIL.

Daniel is now in his final term before graduating and after the shock of losing Theresa he decides to concentrate on his work, not being able to face the outside world, or even his friends, who he is convinced are laughing at him behind his back. This isn't true, of course, because both Martin and James have made efforts on a number of occasions to get him to go out, realizing that by dealing with his emotions by cutting off all contact with everyone, only makes his pain harder to bear and take longer to overcome.

But Daniel is adamant in his pursuit of a good degree and although he does join his two friends occasionally, he does not flinch in his desire for excellence.

The early summer disappears like footprints in the sand, once the tide comes in, and Daniel feels as though his protagonist, time, is winning the contest between him and his achievements. But such thoughts are a myth and he manages to complete his thesis with time to spare.

However, his hopes of forgetting Theresa have proved futile and although he has not seen her since, his mind returns time and again to the wonderful moments they had before the disastrous last night on Dartmoor.

Although he has looked for her, if only to avoid direct contact, neither Daniel nor any of his friends have seen her either, which makes him wonder what has become of her.

As their time ends, the third-year students arrange for a final dinner and dance before graduation. Martin and James insist on Daniel joining them, saying "You can't miss the last celebration of Uni, the climax of three years of our lives". So reluctantly Daniel acquiesces, even joining them to arrange for the hire of formal dress suits and bow ties for the occasion.

The evening arrives in a blaze of summer glory as all the third-year students' throng excitedly. As they sit for dinner a number of speeches are made by tutors wishing them well for their futures, before the tables are cleared and the student union band is set up at one end of the hall and the dancing begins.

Up until this point Daniel has coped quite well because his friends have surrounded him, but once the dancing starts, he begins to feel like a fish out of water as first Martin and Sandra begin to dance, followed soon after by James and Caroline. Noticing this, Sandra asks him to dance and which he accepts, rather than ignore her kind request but he feels at the same time that he is spoiling his friends' evening.

As the music dies and they return to their friends, Sandra compliments Dan on his dancing skills, saying "Oh that was great Dan; I wish that Martin could dance like that. I'll have to get you to teach him ".

As the dancing continues Daniel makes his way outside the hall to an area of lawn where a number of others are taking a break, enjoying the late evening sun. Sitting on a bench he is suddenly aware of another person doing the same thing, but before he can look and see who it is he hears a female voice say "Hi Dan, I thought that it was you leaving the dance, so I hope you don't mind if I join you".

As he turns to see who it is, he is astonished to find that it is April, the woman who first rejected his advances, and he is struck once again by her ethereal beauty. Before he can even reply, she goes on to say "Where have you been since the night we danced, I have looked for you but you seem to have vanished completely".

He said, "Well you made it quite clear that you had a serious relationship already and that you didn't want to jeopardize it, so I kept out of your way".

"But I never meant that I didn't want to see you again, just not on your own, and anyway my so-called serious relationship finished several months ago, after I found out from friends at home that he was seeing someone else. I'm so sorry Dan if you misunderstood me" and then, smiling, "let's go and have a dance, it will be a pleasant change to dance with someone who isn't going to kick great lumps out of me".

Daniel's mood takes an upward swing as she finishes speaking, which she notices and starts laughing, saying, "come on, it's our last night here, so let's make the most of it".

As she stands and holds out her hand for his, he is reminded just how beautiful she is. She wears a long flowing full-length dress of pale blue material that accentuates her tall elegant figure. The top is scooped low cut with sleeves reaching to half way down her arms and is tight at the waist. Once again, he is mesmerized by her stunning beauty, her green eyes dancing and flickering in the reflection of the lights strung around the outside of the hall.

Daniel cannot hold back "You look stunning April".

"You don't look half so bad yourself" she replies "That dinner jacket and bow tie make you look positively elegant. I think that you scrub up very well".

Once inside they take to the floor and April is once again entranced as they float almost without effort, gliding around other couples who do not share Daniel's skill.

They remain together on the dance floor for the rest of this magical evening, neither of them wanting it to end. Towards the end the music slows, and so do they as they hold each other close, hardly moving, shuffling almost on the same spot. Daniel is intoxicated once again by April's musky smell, a mixture of woman and perfume and as he nuzzles his mouth to the warmth of her neck he can feel her sigh deeply and satisfyingly before she responds by putting her arms round his neck and saying "would you like to come back to my room Dan, before Wendy, who I share with, returns".

April's offer, the meaning of which is completely unambiguous and crystal clear to Daniel, comes as a complete surprise. "Are you sure that's what you want April"?

Laughing, a deep husky sound, she says "Oh yes Dan, I'm sure: now come on let's hurry while we have time".

Together they begin to flee the dance hall, making their apologies to friends as they go. By now they are both almost feverish at the promise of things to come as they climb the two sets of stairs to April's room. The student's accommodation is in a block built on two floors, for females, with two students to each room, the presence of males being strictly prohibited at all times, although ensuring that this is adhered to is almost possible to administer. Male students have their own block built some distance away.

Opening the door with her key they stumble inside, clawing at each other's clothes in their haste to undress. As he looks around, Daniel can see that it is in complete chaos, with clothes, books, and other detritus spread everywhere. Noticing him looking April explains "Oh, sorry about the mess, but we are in the process of packing up because our parents are picking us up tomorrow".

The next few minutes are a flurry of activity as they try to both disrobe each other while enjoying the discovery of each other's bodies simultaneously.

Daniel quietly contemplates that he is grateful that he has now had some sexual experience, because it is obvious that April is no novice in the bedroom. This time he is able to be more controlled, first bringing her almost to a climax, then slowing the pace before repeating the procedure, until she hoarsely cries "Do it now Dan, before you drive me mad".

The results are deeply satisfying for both of them as they lay expended on the bed, before making love again, this time more slowly and leisurely, while at the same time both of them very conscious that April's flat mate Wendy may return at any moment.

Daniel eventually dresses and kisses her goodnight while she remains naked sprawled across the bed. As he begins to leave, he says "I had best go before Wendy returns: will I see you again before we leave tomorrow"? The thought of not seeing her again after this wonderful evening is not to be contemplated, although he doesn't know how easy or difficult that will be from now on, and curses his luck inwardly that circumstances have meant that they didn't get together again before now.

"Oh, I hope so Dan, I'd like to think that we can see each other again sometime, although I don't quite know how that will work. Tonight, was special for me and I'm so glad we managed to get together, even though it was at the last knockings. Anyway, what are your plans for the future?"

"Well I have no definite plans, although I would like to get into journalism. I have enjoyed very much, the research and investigative aspect for my thesis and am very interested in people and events, so I think I might contact some of the London National papers and see how it goes. What about you"?

"Quite honestly I haven't given the matter much thought up until now, but a couple of possibilities spring to mind, either working in a library, perhaps in a University, or in a museum, to hopefully work my way up to be a curator eventually".

As they continue talking Daniel is hit by the sudden revelation that although he has had a fantastic evening with this woman, the first that he was attracted to, and although she is stunningly beautiful and great company, he still has a strong haunting overwhelming memory of Theresa, the girl who cheated on him, but who he still cannot quite forget.

The thought is so disturbing, that its memory for him begins to affect how he feels about April, feelings which have been all that he could want or hope for up until now. But every time he looks at April now, he compares her to Theresa, whose uproarious laughter, sense of fun and companionship and above all her beauty make him realize that although this evening has been magical, wonderful even, his feelings for April are not the same for him as those for Theresa.

He also realizes that to continue a relationship with April will be a mistake, because even though it he can never renew his experience with Theresa, he should at least want to meet someone who can make him forget her. This is something that April obviously cannot do.

After hurriedly exchanging address details, Daniel kisses April for the last time, thinking that it is unlikely that their relationship will survive them leaving University.

"I'll try and see you before we leave tomorrow, but I expect it will be chaotic. In any event we will hopefully be back for the Graduation ceremony in September".

"Of course, Dan, but try and write or telephone before then, because I would like to keep in touch".

In this manner, this most wonderful evening ends, leaving Daniel with more questions than answers. Although he has no regrets, how could he, he knows that any relationship with April cannot survive unless he can at least forget Theresa.

Leaving April's room, Daniel begins to make his way back to his own accommodation. As he reaches the bottom of the stairs a number of women enter the building, Wendy probably among them and he realizes that the dance has now finished.

As he stands for a moment outside the doors of the block, he sees a solitary female also making her way back and as she comes into focus, to his dismay he sees that it is Theresa and for a few moments he is stuck like a rabbit in the headlights of a car. As the gap between them closes, Theresa notices him for the first time, which she quickly follows by noting the place that he has come from, the reason for which there can be only one conclusion.

Daniel would be happy if she chose to continue on her way and ignore him completely: in fact that is what he thinks she will do, but it is not to be as she reaches him and looking up at him says" "Well Dan I see that you have had a productive last night. I had hoped to see you after we got back from Dartmoor and explain that as far as I am aware nothing untoward happened that last night, and if it did, I was not aware of it and furthermore, what is even more important, I never gave my consent to anything".

"I know that you don't believe me, but there's nothing that I can do about that" and then resignedly, looking at the females' student block from which Daniel has just left, "but I can see that it's too late to convince you and even if I did it's too late for the two of us. Good luck for the future and if you ever think of me, try to remember what I have just said. Good bye Dan".

This time it is Daniel's turn to be wrong footed and he stands not knowing what to say, being both embarrassed because of the place where Theresa has found him, but more importantly that, if for nothing else, this evening has taught him that his feelings for Theresa are as strong as ever.

But before he can even respond, she is gone, leaving him feeling guilty as hell about his evening with April and although he wants desperately to believe Theresa's version of events regarding the last night on Dartmoor, he still has difficulty reconciling it with the evidence of his own eyes.

"What a bloody mess" he mutters to himself as he makes his way back to his room for the very last time.

* * *

The morning breaks to a flurry of activity throughout the Campus as everyone hurriedly packs their belongings and bid their farewells to friends and tutors.

Daniel, like most third-year students has accumulated mountains of books and equipment, most of which he cannot possibly hope to take back to Chipping Norton with him on the train, so he has to be selective in his choices. All the bits and pieces of furniture that he has bought second hand he leaves for the next occupant. His bicycle which has seen an enormous amount of service, ferrying him to his bartender job and around town, he sells to a second-year student, which just leaves his books and manuscripts. Some of these he sells and the rest which have been such an integral part of his student experience he boxes up to take home.

His packing chores completed, he makes his way to say his farewells to Martin and James. Embracing and slapping each other on the back, they vow to keep in touch, which Daniel knows only too well is often something that never happens. But he is comforted that the three of them have been there for each other during the last three years and feels that theirs is a special relationship that will stand the test of time.

Exchanging address and telephone details they part, vowing to meet again in September at their graduation day.

Looking at his watch he notes that the time is now half past ten, and he knows that the train that he has to catch leaves Exeter at twelve thirty. He realises that he still has time to say goodbye to April, so he makes his way to her room. But after seeing Teresa last night, his doubts about any future relationship with April have grown, but he has promised to see her if he can before they leave and feels that it is the least that he can do in the circumstances.

The door to her room is open and as he enters, he sees a perspiring April fighting to close a large suitcase which lies on her bed. As she sees him, she says "Oh am I glad to see you Dan, help me close this suitcase, I have been trying for ages, only my parents will be here shortly and I still have loads to do". As the two of them wrestle to close the suitcase Daniel asks where Wendy is.

"She has packed and gone, her parents were here at nine o'clock with their car, because they have a long journey in front of them; they come from Chester".

Not wanting to prolong his goodbye Daniel says "I just popped in to say goodbye and wish you all the best for the future. No doubt I'll see you again at Graduation". Somewhat to his dismay he hears her say "Of course Dan, but I hope that we can see each other again before then, so please keep in touch".

Mumbling his acknowledgement Daniel bends to give her a quick peck on the cheek, but April has other ideas and turns their brief goodbye unto a long lingering kiss, to which despite himself Daniel eventually responds.

Pulling himself away Daniel leaves, his senses reeling, with April's parting words ringing in his ears as he makes his way back to his room for the last time. "Come and see me soon Dan, I am missing you already".

His journey home is uneventful, except for the fact that every student from the University seems to want to catch the same train that he does. Every seat is taken and people are standing in the corridors making it almost impossible to get to the toilet or the buffet bar. There is a cacophony of noise of excited students releasing their pent-up emotions, having completed another University year.

The train eventually arrives on time at Gloucester Station and Daniel staggers off dragging his heavy luggage with him, an achievement of no small measure considering the obstacles he is faced with as he runs the gauntlet of students, some of whom he knows and some who he cannot remember ever having met.

Steam from the train fills the station, its odour reminding Daniel of egg sandwiches. As he makes his way to the station approach, to his surprise and delight he is met by Ella who, rushes over to him and envelopes him in a bear hug, crying "welcome back son, now let's get you home so we can catch up on what you have been doing, while I fill you in with all the local gossip".

Daniel thinks, as if seeing his mother for the first time, that she is still an attractive looking woman, who still turns men's heads as they make their way out of the station. She is dressed in a short sleeved blue top, with navy slacks, (a relatively new addition to women's fashion, brought on no doubt from the result of land girls and female forces use of trousers during the war) which emphasizes her tall figure and long slim legs. Her complexion is flawless, her dark brown eyes now twinkling as she is reunited with her son.

"Where are we going mum, where has Mr. Souch parked his car"? Ella looks at her son for a moment before they continue to the next corner, where rounding it she says "Mr. Souch sends his apologies but says that as I can now drive, it would be more appropriate if I picked you up". As she finishes speaking, they draw level with a small Morris Minor van, where she stops and holding both arms aloft in homage continues "da dah".

Looking closely, Daniel notices to his amazement that the cream coloured van has large black lettering on it which reads "Ella's Bakery and Catering services".

Turning to his obviously delighted mother he says "I knew that you were taking driving lessons but you never told me you'd passed your test".

"Well it was only two weeks ago so I thought that I would surprise you by picking you up today. I only bought the van just after I got my license, after which I had to get the lettering put on, so I have only been able to drive it for a couple of days. Come on, get in slowcoach".

Their journey home is spent exchanging news, Daniel telling his mother all about his last year at University while carefully sanitizing his experiences with April and Theresa, while she tells him excitedly about the café and just how much the catering side of her business has developed.

While they have been travelling Ella recognizes a change in her son, something that has obviously been brought about by Daniel's experiences with the two women, of which she has only just been made aware, but she surmises correctly that they were much more intense affairs than her son is admitting. But she can also see that he is more mature now and that he has an air of confidence about him, something that was lacking before he left for University.

"You seem to have had a busy and exciting year" she tells Daniel "when will you know if you have your degree and what grade it will be"?

"Well my tutor thinks that I should attain at least a 2.1 with an outside chance of a first: I should know by sometime in August. When and if that happens will you come with me to the Graduation ceremony in September"?

"Of course, I would be the proudest mother in the world to be there Daniel: you just try and stop me. Have you thought about what career you might pursue once that's all over"?

"I've thought for some time that I would like to be a journalist. My tutor asked me the same question and, when I told him, he was most supportive and even said that he knew a couple of sub editors on two National papers in Fleet Street and that he would contact them on my behalf, so I'll just have to wait and see. But for the moment Mum I just want to get back and help you in the Café. Tell me, how it's doing"?

Our conversation seems to be all questions and answers, thinks Ella, before realizing that it is inevitable, as they haven't seen each other for some time. She says "It's doing fantastically well, in fact so much so that I was able to pay your Aunt Rachel back the loan that she gave me when I first started. I have been very fortunate with staff, both Fiona and Catherine are treasures and we all work together as a team which great, because they take their share of responsibilities, which means that I don't have to be looking over their shoulders all the time. Grandma Liz still comes in occasionally if one of the others want a few days holiday, but I only ask her if I absolutely have too, because her health isn't so good lately. But the new success, really, is catering, which has taken off in quite a big way. I do everything from Wedding Receptions to Funerals, with Business Training Conferences, Fetes and Village Fun Days in between. Obviously, I have to hire in temporary waitress staff when this happens, but I have got a few regulars that I can call on now, several from Chadlington who are not able to work full time but are happy for the occasional days' work".

"I can see that you won't need me at all" laughs Daniel, genuinely pleased for his mother and her achievements.

"Of course I will" responds Ella "but I think your strengths have always been in examining new areas of development as well as where to purchase products at the best price for the business, so if you have any time, those are the things that I would like you to look at. Anyway, If I remember correctly it was you who suggested Catering as a logical progression for the Café".

"That's right, but first I may have to go to London if I get an interview with a newspaper" he replies.

"Of course, Daniel, there is no pressure, so if you don't want to do anything then that's good too. Anyway, to change the subject, when everyone heard that you were finishing at University, they all wanted to see you and get together, so I have arranged for your Aunt Rachel, Fred and the two boys, together with your Grandparents to come to us on Sunday. The Café will be shut, so I thought that we could have a slap-up meal in there. I will select one from my catering list and get Fiona to help me cook and Catherine can serve".

Seeing Daniel, Ella continues "don't worry I'll pay them, but if we do it that way then we can all have more time to be together: what do you think?"

"It sounds as if it's a done deal" laughs Daniel "but that would be fantastic. I can't wait to see them all again".

* * *

The appointed Sunday duly arrives and all the relatives start to assemble in the shop at midday, Daniel excitedly welcoming them in, realizing just how much he has missed them all.

"Hello Grandad, it's lovely to see you again. Mum tells me that you've retired: what do you do with yourself?" and then suddenly looking more closely Daniel can see that his Grandfather, who he has worshipped and who has been like a surrogate father to him since his own father died, is looking far from well. His pallor, which is usually the colour of mahogany from the time that he has always spent in the open air, subject to all its vagaries and extremes, is now grey, while his features are pinched and drawn. Additionally, his once upright stance has become stooped, his shoulders rounded, while his chest has become concave, his walk slow and measured, almost as if he is reminding himself to put one foot in front of the other. Daniel is shocked by his appearance and vows to talk to his mother about it as soon as they can speak on their own.

His grandfather, not being aware of Daniel's concerns regarding his health replies "that's right Dan, I retired last year and for a while I kept getting under your Grandmother's feet. That was until I got a dog, another black Labrador, Charlie, who has been a great companion. I take him for walks every day, which gets me out of your Grandma's hair, so it's all good".

Daniel is immediately transported back to his childhood and to Bonny, the first black Labrador, who had been such a source of comfort to him when his father died.

"That's great, when can I see him grandad. I tell you what, why don't I come over one day this week and we can take him for a walk, if Mum can manage without me, which I'm sure she can, cos she's managed perfectly well without me the last three years".

Liz, listening to the conversation says "yes, why don't you do that Daniel, then you can stay for lunch, can't he Alf", to which the latter nods his head in agreement.

Daniel greets the rest of his relatives enthusiastically, his Aunt Rachel hugging him and congratulating him on his graduation, while Fred slaps him on the back saying "well done son, we are all so proud of you"

His cousins, George and Harry are next to welcome Daniel home before they all start talking nineteen to the dozen, while laughing and joking at the same time. Daniel reflects quietly to himself of the sheer "ordinariness" of both of them, a virtue for which he is immensely grateful, recognizing that if he ever thought too much of himself, they would soon bring him back to reality. George has joined his father in his decorating business, while Harry is in the last year of an apprenticeship to become an electrician.

Eventually dinner is served and as promised, is from a selection of Ella's catering menus. She and Fiona have worked on it since early morning, Ella wanting to get everything just right for her family. All her menus are the result of her vast experience of cooking at The Manor House, something for which she is more and more grateful. Once they are all seated Catherine begins to serve their starter course of Salmon Gravadlax with beetroot and orange.

It is almost an hour before the main course is served because everyone is still talking nonstop, catching up with all the local gossip. Daniel of course is the main recipient of their attention as he tries to explain how University life works.

Ella has selected one of her own favorites for main course, pork belly with crackling, dauphinoise potatoes with tender stem broccoli and pork gravy. This is followed by a selection of ice creams or a blackberry and apple crumble for the pudding course.

As the meal has progressed, they have become more lethargic and conversation has dwindled quite considerably. They sit for cheese and biscuits and Ella stands and delivers a short speech congratulating Daniel on completing his time at Exeter University, telling all of them how proud that she is of her son, to which they all applaud in unison.

Daniel acknowledges their good wishes and congratulations, before standing himself to reply.

"I thank you all for your support and I can honestly say that your contribution and being there for me not only for the last three years, but for all my life has been invaluable to me. The number of times particularly in the first year when I was struggling to come to terms with living away from home, only to return back here to the comfort and support of you all is something that I will always remember. But I am sure that you understand that I need to pay tribute and recognize the contribution and sacrifices my mum has made on this journey of mine. She has been my rock and safe harbour, my source of comfort and joy. Nothing has ever been impossible but rather a short interlude while she navigates her way around it before moving forward again:

Thank you, Mum, for all the sacrifices you have made to get me this far. I will try and justify the faith that you have shown to me".

As he finishes speaking the rest of his family begin clapping and saying things like "well said Daniel" and "quite right". Looking across the table to his mother he sees that she is softly crying. Seeing him looking concerned she whispers "thank you Daniel, I just wish your father could be here: he would be so proud of you".

CHAPTER 15.

1940.
DUNKIRK.

Richard duly presents himself at Oxford for registration to the armed forces on the 1st February 1940, proving to be fit A1. He enrolls in the Royal Army Service Corp (R.A.S.C.), which is responsible for the distribution of supplies to units in the front line. "Supplies" include transporting ammunition from Base Ordinance Depots to forward ammunition points, as well as Petrol, Oil and Lubricants.

Additionally, they are responsible for supplying food and water to keep the Army personnel and animals fed and watered.

His mechanical work experience means that his services are of interest to the Royal Army Ordnance Corps as well, but at this moment in time it is felt that this Corp is up to strength.

The next phase of Richard's new life is when he presents himself at Aldershot Barracks in Hampshire, where he goes through the initial six weeks' training, learning to march and use weapons. Like almost everybody else he finds the experience excruciating and soul destroying, both mental and physically. The N.C.O's operates a brutal regime, the only purpose of which as far as Richard can see, is to humiliate and degrade anyone who defies it, even if it is by errors of omission. Richard doesn't come to understand the reasons for the use of these methods until much later on when he enters combat zones and discovers the need to respond immediately to the methods that he has been taught in training, which are necessary so that each member knows what is required of them in moments of adversity .

Having completed his initial training Richard returns home to the comfort of his family on a seventy-two-hour pass.

Here, Richard, Ella and Daniel's live lives that are compressed into three days of extreme moods, from depression to euphoria. They go for walks, pushing their much loved son in his pram in the late winter days, as if trying to absorb the sight and sounds of the people and places they know best, so that they can recreate them from their memory larders at some point in the future when they can be released again to sustain them in a time of need.

Each night, once they have put Daniel to bed and made sure that he has gone to sleep, they too go to bed to make love copiously with appetites that seem never to be slated, both of them fighting their own demons of the future.

"You will come back to me my love, won't you?" Ella whispers as they lay spent in a post coital haze.

"Always, so don't worry" replies Richard, trying to allay her fears "anyway, only the good die young".

"That is what I am afraid of" she says!

They lie awake for hours talking of their hopes for a future that will see them united as a family once again but the doubts that this may ever happen are just below the surface of their consciousness.

As he wakes and looks across to his sleeping wife, Richard marvels at his good fortune to have found such a beautiful, caring soulmate. Kissing her briefly he goes downstairs to make her a cup of tea, before taking it back up to her with buttered toast. Hearing a noise coming from his son's bedroom, he peers round the bedroom door to watch him lying gurgling in his cot, smiling at the brightly coloured mobile revolving slowly above his head. Suddenly seeing his father, he raises his small arms invitingly asking to be picked up.

Richard is unable to resist such a silent request so eloquently given, so picks his son up and cuddles him, welcoming the opportunity to offer comfort and reassurance to this small part of himself. Taking him back to their bedroom he places him next to Ella saying "He was awake so I thought that we might as well be all together. I was thinking that perhaps we could go for a walk this morning. We can put Daniel in the pram and perhaps take Bonny too if that's O.K. with your dad. Daniel seems to like being with him, in fact I think that the feeling is mutual: the first person that Bonny makes for is Daniel. I found him lying quite happily next to Daniel's cot the other day, as if he was standing guard over him.

In this way the three days pass, both of them wanting and needing to spend every waking moment together before Richard has to leave. On the third morning, Richard wakes early before hurriedly dressing and getting ready to leave. They have spent the whole night alternatively making love or just lying embraced, savouring each second as if it were their last. When he leaves, Richard looks in to his son's bedroom and says his farewell, before returning downstairs where Ella joins him at the front door.

"Take care my love" whispers Ella "and come home safely to me", before watching him walk swiftly away down the still dark street, the only light coming from a waning moon sinking slowly in the west, as he moves swiftly to catch the first bus into Oxford. She continues to watch long after he has disappeared into the distance, until tears blur her vision.

* * *

It is now nearly the end of March and the country has so far only experienced a "phony" war. But on the European Continent things are gathering momentum. Britain have already sent The British Expeditionary Force to aid in the defence of France in 1939, and it is to here that Richard is transported on returning to his unit at Aldershot.

On arrival, Richard's R.A.S.C corps, is ordered to join the British Expeditionary Force on the Belgian border, where they will be able to engage the German Army, should it decide to avoid The Maginot Line, a series of fortifications built by France along their border with Germany. The French High Command have discounted all assumptions of a German attack against the heavily fortified Maginot Line because the Area to the north of this line is covered by the heavily wooded Ardennes region, which they think is impenetrable, believing that any enemy emerging from the forest would be vulnerable to a pincer attack and be destroyed.

Based upon this false assumption the area is left lightly defended.

Working with the BEF are the Belgian Army and the French First, Seventh, and Ninth Armies.

In Britain, there is no awareness that a war is being fought, and even Richard wonders what all the fuss is about, spending most of his free time fretting about not being with his family, for no good reason as far as he can see. Everything changes, however, on the 10th May when Germany attacks Belgium and The Netherlands using their "Blitzkrieg" or total war tactics.

The BEF is then ordered to advance from the Belgian border to positions along the River Dyle within Belgium, where they fight elements of Army Group B.

But they are soon ordered to begin a fighting withdrawal to the Scheldt River on the 14th May when the Belgian and French positions on their flanks fail to hold.

Of course, neither Richard, nor any of his colleagues know how the bigger pictures is being played out, but are only concerned with the small part that they are now heavily involved in.

His experience of fighting is not like anything that he could possibly imagine, as first the Germans unleash their bomber and fighter aircraft against the BEF defensive positions, softening up the Allies underbelly. Without air power to respond in a similar fashion they take heavy casualties and loss of artillery, tanks and other equipment and are ordered to withdraw to the River Dyle where they regroup and entrench once more.

Up close and personal, Richard sees many of his comrades cut down in swathes by machine gun fire from German fighter aircraft and blown to smithereens by bombs from German Stuka bombers, which dive vertically at tremendous speed, resulting in an ear-piercing sound that its enemies come to recognize and fear. When it is only very close to the ground does it release its bombs, before the pilot pulls heavily back on the stick and with its payload released the bomber is able to climb steeply away.

This form of bombing is devastating and very accurate and causes huge destruction, wiping out many of the BEF'S tanks, vehicles and equipment, or rending them inoperable. However, by far the most damage that this form of warfare causes is to morale, with the constant nagging at men's fears and doubts.

The BEF and indeed its Belgian and French Allies either side it is being pounded mercilessly by a ruthless and efficient foe and the only retaliation that they can make is by the use anti-aircraft fire.

Richard has never experienced seeing men killed before, and to see it on such a scale, including losing friends and comrades, has an emotional effect on him of mind-numbing proportions, so much so that he awaits his own similar fate in a lethargic haze.

Meanwhile Germany has attacked through the South Ardennes region using three Panzer Corps and then drive directly for The English Channel with a view to cutting off the Allied Armies in Belgium and France.

To make matters worse, because France has relied upon the fact that Germany will not attack through the Maginot Line, it has only left meagre resources to defend it, instead putting all their strengths into defending their border with Belgium. The result is that the three Panzer corps cut through to the Channel like a knife through butter, leaving the BEF, French and Belgian troops caught in a pincer movement. By 24th May the Germans have captured the port of Boulogne and are surrounding Calais.

The British realize that their only option to avoid being destroyed or captured is to withdraw to Dunkirk the closest and in fact only location with good port facilities. Surrounded by marshes, Dunkirk boasts old fortifications and the longest sand beach in Europe, where large groups can assemble.

The British begin planning on 20th May for Operation Dynamo, the evacuation of the BEF. Ships begin gathering at Dover for the evacuation while in France sluice gates have been opened, flooding the marshy area around Dunkirk, making the progress of the German Panzer Corps almost impossible to advance.

The evacuation is undertaken amid chaotic conditions, with abandoned vehicles blocking the roads and a flood of refugees heading in the opposite direction.

For his part, Richard's Corps are ordered to retreat to Dunkirk, but to ensure that all vehicles are disabled and rendered useless before leaving them. Also, all paperwork that may be of use to the enemy is burned.

As Richard's Corps retreat, they suffer constant harassment by German fighter aircraft and bombing by their feared Stukas', resulting in many deaths and the splitting up of men from their companies and regiments, so much so in fact that by 23rd May Richard and his corps, which is by now broken down into small groups, neither know where they are or how to get to Dunkirk.

The roads to the coast are by now impassable, clogged with abandoned and broken down army vehicles of every description and demoralized troops, so Richard and two others, Bert Williams and Roger Phillips who have been left together take to the fields and follow the road north to the North Coast of France as best they can. Their other major problem is that they have no supplies of food or water, the system that supplies the army under normal conditions being destroyed.

Things become so bad that they have no alternative but to steal from local farms as they make their way. Eggs are taken from chicken runs and potatoes and vegetables are purloined from where they have been stored in barns or clamps. The latter are mostly eaten raw, but meat is almost impossible to obtain, that is until Bert manages to shoot a rabbit in a field, which they strip and cook over a fire made from pieces of wood or tree branches found lying around and lit by use of their cigarette lighters.

Food has never tasted so good, but it doesn't sustain them for very long.

On the third day they notice German vehicles containing troops and artillery also moving down the road that they are shadowing. By good fortune they are able to find cover behind hedges to avoid being spotted. They are all aware of the Geneva Convention which states that providing they are wearing uniforms and do not resist arrest they will be treated as prisoners of war, although rumours which have spread like wildfire, suggest that this may not always be true, the Nazis not always respecting conventions.

For this reason, they decide to continue wearing uniform although this makes them very conspicuous. It is at this moment that Richard suggests that they find cover and rest by day, and only move on once darkness falls. He is only too aware that the Germans will put pressure on the French locals, some of whom will betray British soldiers, if only to save themselves from the wrath of the invaders. On the other hand, Richard is also aware that a good many local people will hide and protect them, the problem is how to know which are which.

Exhausted as they have now become, they have no other option but to continue north towards Dunkirk. As they do so they come across small groups of British soldiers taking the same avoiding action as them, but there is no suggestion that they should all move forward together because bigger groups will find it much more difficult to become invisible to the enemy. But each group has its own horror stories to tell of German brutality, of the relentless bombing of both the fleeing Armies and civilians, the latter of which travel in their thousands either carrying all their possessions on a cart pulled by a horse, or, more often than not, pulling their carts themselves.

This travelling sea of humanity is extremely vulnerable from air attacks for two reasons, the first because they are so numerous, the second because people can only move as fast as the slowest in the queue. On seeing the approach of enemy aircraft, the only avoiding action that can be taken is for them to leave their carts and barrows containing the only things that they have left in the world and throw themselves from the road into the ditches on either side. But there is never enough time for all of them to do this, leaving the rest at the mercy of the German M E 109's machine guns, or their Stuka bombers.

Listening and witnessing these stories of horror, Richard and his two friends decide to push on faster, fearing that if they don't get to Dunkirk in time for the evacuation, they will be left stranded, without any other option other than to give themselves up to the conquering German Army.

Totally spent, they eventually reach the Canal system surrounding the Dunkirk area on 29th May, from where they make their way into the town and beach. Passing through a series of constructed defensive works which have been hurriedly erected by British troops they are met by a truly amazing site, one that Richard knows will indelibly burned into his brain forever. The beaches and harbour are inundated by hundreds of thousands of troops, mostly British, but also Canadian and some French and Belgian.

As some of them who have radios listen to the BBC, they are aware that just before 7 pm on 26th May Winston Churchill had ordered Operation Dynamo (the evacuation of Dunkirk) to begin.

Richard and his comrades know that many of the troops are able to embark from the harbour's protective mole onto British destroyers and other large ships, while others have to wade out from the beaches, sometimes waiting for hours in shoulder deep water. Some are ferried from the beaches to the larger ships by what becomes known as the little ships of Dunkirk, a flotilla of hundreds of merchant marine boats, fishing boats, pleasure craft and lifeboats called into service for this emergency. While this is happening, the troops on the beach and the boats ferrying them are being constantly strafed and bombed by the German Luftwaffe, causing thousands of death and injuries.

The evacuation starts slowly, but with gathering momentum as the days pass and the little boats arrive in ever increasing numbers from their England ports. They come from everywhere, fishing boats from Cornwall to Norfolk, pleasure craft from the Thames and hundreds of other self-owned small cabin cruisers, as well as speedboats, car ferries and the most useful of all, the motor lifeboats, which have reasonably good capacity and speed.

Richard, Bert and Roger try to stay together on the beach, because they are not able to get anywhere near the mole. They are strafed many times, taking avoiding action by moving to the top of the beach, hiding in the marram grass as best they can as soon as they see enemy aircraft approaching. But even this is difficult because of the sheer numbers of troops of many nationalities on the beach. There are so many, that when German aircraft are seen approaching, most of them are unable to take avoiding action because of the overwhelming volume of troops and equipment.

In his mind Richard compares the situation to a cinema in which there are perhaps two thousand people, when the fire alarm goes off. Despite there being three exits it is completely impossible to get them all to safety within the time envisaged, for a number of reasons. The two major problems being that the exits are too narrow and restrict the numbers and secondly people can only exit as fast as the slowest of them and if they try to go faster the result is the weakest and most vulnerable are trodden and crushed in the stampede to escape.

This then is how it is here on the beach at Dunkirk. Men cannot move quickly enough to get off the beach to the marram grass which has at least some cover, albeit very limited. Inevitably, they die in their thousands by bullet, bomb and shrapnel and helpless to defend themselves or each other.

By now Richard and his two comrades have been stranded on the beach for three days without food and very little water, the latter which they manage to obtain from locals in the town.

Realizing that neither Bert nor Roger are capable of making a decision about what to do next, Richard decides, on the 2nd June that, if they are going to get back to England, they need to move as quickly as possible, by the only means available left to them: by wading out to sea in the hope of getting aboard one of the small boats that can then ferry them to one of the destroyers.

There are several reasons why Richard has decided that the right time is now; the first is because thousands of additional troops are still finding their way into the town and down to the beaches after long journeys by foot to get here. Secondly the three of them are becoming weaker by the hour, not having received sustenance of any kind since they arrived, and finally because the docks in the harbor have finally been rendered unusable by German bombing, meaning that the only place that the large destroyers can get close enough to pick up troops is at two long stone and concrete breakwaters, called the East and West mole, the latter of which stretches nearly a mile out to sea.

Entering the sea at low tide in the hope of getting picked up quickly, the three of them are to be disappointed for hours as troops even further out, standing up to their shoulders are the first to get onboard the brave little armada. Even as these are clambering aboard the small boats, enemy aircraft continue to machine gun them in the water, causing not only an intense hatred for the enemy, but also has them crying out in despair "where's the bloody RAF when we need them".

They were not to know until months later that the RAF had, in fact, flown some 3500 sorties engaging the Luftwaffe deep into enemy territory to stop them getting as far as Dunkirk, losing some 145 aircraft, of which at least 42 were Spitfires. But these aircraft aren't visible to the tired and demoralized troops on the beach, who naturally think that the RAF have done nothing to help them in their hour of need.

After several hours in the water on a rising tide which by now comes up to their shoulders, a small boat which in a previous life had been used to collect and sew lobster pots at Lyme Regis in Dorset, began rescuing them ready to transfer them to a destroyer further out in the bay. The boat is small, only having a cabin from where the captain and possibly one other can be accommodated. Downstairs there is room for two other crew members, while at the rear there is a hold where catches of fish and lobster pots are normally stored. Richard considers how far this sturdy little vessel has come to rescue them and thinks that the fact that it is here is a miracle in itself. The only crew on board is a father and his son: the latter only appearing to be in his mid- teens.

Holding their rifles over their heads to stop the sea water damaging them, they proceed to climb aboard with the aid of the crew. Richard and Bert have just managed to roll into the scuppers, but before Roger can get onboard there is the menacing sound of a German fighter plane travelling at great speed at low altitude across the bay, its target, for once, not those troops on the beach, but in fact the boats and ships presently loading their human cargo.

The first that Richard or anyone else is aware that things aren't as they should be is when they hear Roger give a muffled grunt as if the wind has been knocked out of him. To their consternation he makes no further sound before slipping below the surface of the water, a red stain spreading slowly giving the only indication of where he had been. Richard is mortified to lose his friend who has come so far with him on this terrible journey, when it seems as if they have overcome the worst of their travails. But this thought is immediately stifled as he hears the skipper of the boat wailing with a heart-rending cry "my son has been hit, please help him".

Turning, Richard sees the young teenager slumped against the davits with blood pouring from machine gun wounds. With all the sights that he has seen in the last few days, he recognizes at once that it is already too late to save this man, who is only a child and who has shown such courage to be here. Consoling the father in his agonizing grief, Richard wonders where when and how this bloody war will end.

The journey to the destroyer is uneventful, apart from the fact that, during the skirmish, the small boat had also sustained significant damage and is slowly sinking from holes received from the German Aircraft. After being helped aboard by the British crew, Richard, Bert and the Captain of the small boat spend another two hours waiting for other small ships to pick up further troops and ferry them to it. Eventually the anchor is raised and the journey back to England begins.

The troops lie on deck, fearing that if they go below and the ship is to be sunk by enemy action or mines, (something that had happened numerous times already to other unfortunate ships) they will have a better chance of survival.

Nor is the voyage home without its dangers, sailing north out- of Dunkirk and heading towards the North Goodwin Lightship before heading south around the Goodwin Sands to Dover. The route is the safest from surface attacks, but the nearby minefields and sandbanks mean that to use it at night could be very dangerous.

On arrival in Dover the boats are welcomed home by thousands of the public wishing their heroes well. There are also Army and Hospital medical teams to deal with the wounded as well as army personnel whose duty it is to debrief those who have been rescued, who might be able to contribute anything that might be construed as useful knowledge regarding the happenings in France.

The public are overwhelmingly supportive of their returning troops, but the mood amongst the exhausted that have been saved from the jaws of hell is quite different. Quite simply they feel humiliated by what has happened in France, leaving them depressed and lethargic, unable to understand the publics' euphoria over their deliverance.

* * *

The whole nation read in their daily newspapers of the speech that their Prime Minister Winston Churchill makes in The House of Commons on 4th June in which he reminds his country that "we must be very careful not to assign to this deliverance the attributes of a victory. Wars are not won by evacuations".

He then goes on to call the events in France "a colossal military disaster" then adding further, saying" The whole root and core and brain of the British Army had been stranded at Dunkirk and seemed about to perish or be captured". In his "We shall fight them on the beaches" speech he hails their rescue as a "miracle of deliverance" and informs the House that some three hundred and twenty eight thousand troops, of which one hundred and ninety thousand were of British and Canadian origin, while the rest were Allied troops of which there were over one hundred thousand French personnel, were rescued before the fall of Dunkirk.

* * *

Like all the rest Richard is given a medical examination and found to be suffering from hypothermia and malnutrition and is sent to a field hospital for seven days, after which he returns to Aldershot to join his RASC Corps once again.

He has to wait a further two weeks before he can return home to Ella. Although he has managed to write to her several times assuring her that he is safe and well and has not suffered any injuries, her mood is frantic until the time she can welcome him home, fearing that he has been injured or maimed or something worse and that he is frightened to tell her. It is true that Richard does not bear any visible scars as witness to his experience in France, but he carries horrendous memories and a deep feeling of shame and failure since he left home that he is unable to talk or discuss with anyone, and in this aspect only, he fears meeting Ella.

She has received only scant information, gleaned mainly from gossip and hearsay since Richard left. This is due to wartime censorship and the desire to keep up British morale, so the full extent to the unfolding disaster at Dunkirk is not initially publicized. However, on 26th May a National Day of Prayer is declared. The Archbishop of Canterbury leading prayers for "our soldiers in dire peril in France" while similar prayers are offered in churches the same day, confirming to the public their suspicion of the desperate plight of the troops. Because of these Ella is aware of some terrible event that has occurred, which makes her all the more distraught about what may have happened to her husband.

On a day in late June, Richard arrives home, where Ella welcomes him and after embracing for several minutes she holds their son out to him, excitedly saying "Oh my love I have missed you so much" and then noticing his withdrawn expression "Are you feeling OK, you look pale: would you like something to eat, or a beer perhaps".

"No, I am just tired. I would like to sit quietly with you and Daniel and catch up with all your news. Although a cup of rosy lea would be nice".

* * *

Ella finds the first few days difficult to deal with after Richard's return home. His experience in France has obviously taken its toll more than she has realized. It is not helped by the fact that he cannot or will not talk to her of his experiences. She knows that if she cannot get him to tell her just what occurred in France, it may well have a detrimental effect on their relationship.

Although she has had only limited schooling, intuitively she knows that she has to make Richard tell her everything, knowing that if he doesn't unburden his feelings, he will become even more introverted and depressed. She also realizes that a major part of his condition is caused by a sense of failure and guilt, so this is where she begins after a few days, once he has had time to adjust.

As she walks together with him through the village on a beautiful sunlit afternoon, she approaches the subject. Speaking in her soft Oxfordshire accent she says" Now Richard, I think that it is time to tell me what happened to you in France. I know from the radio and the newspapers that the operation to stop the Germans invading France was disastrous, and I also know that you feel somehow that you were part of that failure, but don't you see My Love, that you were not responsible for other people's, both politicians' and senior army personnel's', decisions. So, you must stop feeling that you bear responsibility for that."

Richard listens contemplatively as Ella continues to try to reassure him that he should not bottle up all his feelings, that if he can talk about them, he will feel much better. She talks in a low soft voice in much the same vein for another thirty minutes, gently persuading him that she doesn't feel that he has failed her or anyone, until eventually he replies in a voice cracking with emotion "Oh my love, thank you for trying to help: I know that you are doing it with the best intentions to help me. As you say, I do have a feeling of guilt, and failure as well I suppose, but what you say makes sense".

Suddenly his mood changes as he continues to speak "But by far the worse things that happened, that keeps me awake every night, are the visions of people being killed: no let me rephrase it, slaughtered in their hundreds and thousands, by bullets, grenades and bombs. Not just comrades who I lived each day with, although there were, but civilians as well, as they tried to escape from the ruthless and relentless enemy".

He tries to continue, but words fail him and tears begin to fall, slowly at first, but rapidly in a torrent as he relives the scenario again in his mind.

Seeing his distress, Ella enfolds him in her arms and knowing that he is now prepared to talk to her, encourages him to continue. He is sobbing uncontrollably now as he describes in detail the things that he has seen and experienced. He tells her of those friends and comrades that he has known being blown to pieces by bombs and grenades: of men next to him being shot and of trying to help them as they cried out for their mothers or wives for help.

He then tells her of the retreat, when demoralized men had to find their own way back to Dunkirk, not in formation in a proud and orderly fashion, but by stealth and in small groups, half the time not knowing where they were. He goes on to tell of the civilians killed in droves by German aircraft, and finally of the beach and its horrors.

Ella continues to embrace him as Richard empties himself emotionally, hoping that by so doing he can come to terms with himself.

Eventually she says "Do you feel better now my love", to which he slowly nods in acknowledgment. "Come on then, let's go home and have dinner. Dad managed to shoot a couple of rabbits last night, so I've made a casserole. Now that everything has been rationed, I think I'll have to start keeping some more chickens to help out".

Richard smiles gently at his wife's practical approach to life. That night they make love with both passion and tenderness, after which Richard sleeps deeply and soundly for the first time in many weeks.

The days that follow do show a small measure of improvement in Richard's depressed condition. He is obviously still severely traumatized but has occasional lighter moments when he can smile at his son's antics, or when Ella makes him laugh, or even more importantly he can laugh at himself when Ella gently chides him that he should lighten up.

* * *

The mood in the country is sombre, fearful even, after Dunkirk. The common feeling between the Government and the public is that Germany will invade Britain now that she is at her weakest. However, nothing happens for several weeks, until July in fact, when the German Luftwaffe launches an all-out air assault. So begins the period that is soon recognized as "The Battle of Britain".

Meanwhile Richard has received instructions to return to his unit at Aldershot.

When the day arrives Ella sheds many tears, fearful of what will happen in the coming months. Richard does his best to reassure her that everything will be alright. "Don't cry Princess, bad luck never strikes twice" Anyway I can't see anywhere that I will be shipped to abroad; it's much more likely that I will be sent to somewhere on the south coast, in case Herr Hitler decides to invade, in which case I'll write to you every day. How's that? I hope that you'll write to me too and tell me how you and Daniel are".

"You know I will my love" she says "I just wish that this war was over so that we can get back to things being as they were" and then smiling "come home soon".

The day arrives and Richard leaves on a warm summer's day in early July, his polished army shod boots with their studded soles making the sound of that similar to a machine gun as he walks swiftly away up the street, bringing friends and neighbours to their doors in curiosity. Ella watches him go with sadness in her heart, only to cheer up as she switches on the radio to hear Vera Lynn singing "We'll Meet Again".

Returning to Aldershot Richard and his unit are transferred to the south coast at Newhaven in Sussex. Here they help Army sappers and engineers build defenses in readiness to repel a German invasion if and when it should occur. In fact, the whole length of the south coast and much of south east Kent is strengthened with troops and fortifications for just such an eventuality. However, Hitler decides that rather than cross the English Channel with an armada, it will be easier if his Luftwaffe can soften up major British ports and cities first and the first actions the German Luftwaffe take in this regard is to attack Coastal Traffic and British Shipping in The English Channel.

Everybody who has a radio listens in avidly to the BBC as it broadcasts daily the number of attacks carried out, although even these are censored by the Air Ministry to keep up morale in the country. The Luftwaffe begins its main offensive on 13th August, moving inland to concentrate on airfields and communication centres. During the last week of August and the first week of September in what is the critical phase of the battle, the Germans intensify their efforts to destroy Fighter

Command, and some of those particularly in the South East are significantly damaged but most remain operational. However, at the beginning of September the Germans stiffen the weight of their attacks away from the RAF targets and onto London and other large cities and ports.

Richard of course witnesses many of these attacks from his viewpoint close to the English Channel, watching small numbers of British Fighters, Hurricanes and Spitfires engaging far superior numbers of German fighters and bombers.

The trails of their exploits are written clearly in the sky above their heads as they struggle magnificently to destroy as many of the foe before they can get through to release their bombs on their targets. It is not always possible to stop the bombers getting through, but the RAFs' brilliant, courageous fighter pilots, mostly young men, some still in their teens, give the Hun a bloody nose day after day, inflicting severe losses that are becoming increasingly unsustainable for the Germans.

For her part, Ella is a lot less aware of the conflict until the Luftwaffe switches their attacks to the larger cities and ports. Oxford City is attacked, as are other Midland towns of Birmingham and Coventry, as are also the Ports of Liverpool and Bristol. Sometimes when this happens the Luftwaffe's route takes it over her small village of Chadlington. Although the village is never attacked, the sound of the German bombers distinctive low drone overhead, as they go over in their hundreds is one that she fears and dreads in equal measure, being only too aware of the damage and lives that they destroy.

There is a moment of light relief however on one occasion when a German bomber who has been unable to find its target and turning for home the pilot has lost its bearings. Needing to get rid of its bombload it jettisons several two hundred and fifty pounders, thus enabling the aircraft to become lighter so that it has enough fuel to return to its base. The result of this is that when the village of Chadlington awakes the following morning, a couple of inhabitants are amazed to see three cows in a field lying stone dead on their backs with all their legs pointing straight up in the air. The reason for this becomes obvious when a crater from one of the bombs is discovered only some hundred yards away. The conclusion drawn is that the shock of the bombs exploding has killed them. An examination of the carcasses reveals that there does not appear to be a mark of any description on them.

The farmer reports the deaths of the cows as total destruction with no part of the animals being fit for consumption. When the Ministry of Agriculture arrives to examine what remains of the cows, they can only find parts of the animals which are distributed over a large area.

From the remains they cannot establish how many have been killed, although they realize that there are only two heads and not enough legs for three cows, but they are unable to pursue the matter any further, because the farmer insists that one of the cows took a direct hit and was blown to smithereens.

The Ministry has no alternative than to make restitution to the farmer, while meanwhile, hardly able to believe their good fortune, the villagers dine on beef of every description for weeks.

The bombing continues for several more weeks, by which time it has become clear that the Luftwaffe has failed to secure the air superiority that it needs for an invasion by land. By October Hitler decides to indefinitely postpone "Operation Sea Lion".

However, The Defence Chiefs of Staff are unaware of Hitler's decision and are still expecting an invasion by sea from France, but as time goes by the threat begins to recede and by Christmas 1940 some of the units are told to stand down and return to their bases.

On Christmas Eve 1940 Ella is busy baking bread and cooking one of her chickens ready for the next day when on hearing a knock at the front door, she is overwhelmed to find a beaming Richard in his uniform holding a posy of flowers, standing in front of her. He said, "Hello my beautiful Princess, see, I told you there was nothing to worry about, now come here and give me a kiss, I have missed you and Daniel so much".

Enveloped in his arms Ella replies "Oh Richard what a lovely surprise. This is the best Christmas present that I could ever wish for" and then "how long have you got"?

"I have a three-day pass so I don't need to go back until the day after Boxing Day".

"This is going to be the best Christmas ever my love, now come and see your son, he has grown so much since you went away"

CHAPTER 16.

1959
DANIELS JOB OFFER

For the first few weeks after he has returned home from University, Daniel is busy catching up with friends and family. His first visit is to see his Grandfather, Alf, because of his concern for his health. The day after his welcome home party Daniel speaks to Ella who confirms that she too is worried about him.

Ella says "I keep telling your Grandmother to get him to see the doctor and she tries, but he is such a stubborn old man and refuses to go. Things became so bad last week that she insisted on taking him. When the doctor examined him, he said that he couldn't tell what was causing all his symptoms, but that he would make arrangements for him to have x-rays taken and, once he got the results, he would see where to go from there. He has an appointment at The Radcliffe Hospital this week. I must admit that I am really worried about him; he has smoked forty roll up cigarettes a day all his life, which can't have done him any good, but we shall just have to wait and see."

Daniel has resurrected his father's motorbike from the back shed of the shop, cleaning and checking the engine since returning home. He has also insured it and has paid for the road fund for it, and has obtained a provisional driving licence in his own name.

Once this has all been done Daniel climbs aboard his late father's motor bike for the first time and sets off for Chadlington to see his Grandfather. On arrival, to his surprise, he finds Alf sitting on a bench outside his cottage. He is holding a pipe which is giving off smoke signals as he puffs at it intermittently, his eyes gently watering as the smoke occasionally blow the wrong way. At his side lying prostrate beside him on the floor is the most beautiful black Labrador, who looks up at Daniel, his soft brown eyes following him while his head remains firmly on the floor. Daniel can see that Charlie is not fully grown and estimates that he can only be a few months old.

"Hello Charlie, come here boy" Daniel commands, only to find that Charlie completely ignores him.

"You will have to give him a little time Dan" says Alf "but he'll come to you when he's ready. Here take this lead and take him for a walk and he'll soon be your best friend".

"I will Grandad but don't you want to come too?"

"Not just now Dan boy, I'm not feeling up to it just at the present, but when you get back you can have a bit of dinner with me and your Grandmother and we can catch up on all your adventures at University. I would like to hear all about them".

Daniel finds himself recreating the scenes of his younger self, as he walks a now excited Charlie, retracing some of the walks that he and Bonny had walked years before.

His Grandfather's words become reality as Charlie and Dan follow the grass paths across the fields, Charlie running ahead, barking at butterflies as he disturbs them, before returning to Daniel, his tail wagging furiously as if to say "isn't this fun, come on keep up".

Master and pupil hit an instant rapport after a shaky start and Daniel is suddenly overcome with emotion as he remembers previous times with Bonny; times that eased his pain after his father was killed, but then he is brought back to the present as Charlie returns to him hurriedly after being chased by a Yorkshire Terrier, only a fraction of his size.

Completing his walk, Daniel returns to Alf and Liz's cottage which has a climbing rose which covers the façade, while blue and pink hydrangeas fill the small front garden. Daniel does all the talking as they three of them sit down to eat, telling them about his life and experiences at University, carefully air-brushing out some of the more personal ones involving Theresa and April.

Alf and Liz interrupt him from time to time when he tells them of things that are outside their experience, asking him to explain, which he does, showing a great deal of patience to these two people who have always meant so much to him. He finishes by telling them about the graduation ceremony in September and the career he hopes to pursue in journalism.

He spends the remainder of the afternoon with them, sitting in their back garden and catching up with all their village news. His concern for his Grandfathers health has increased steadily as he observes just how breathless he is, even though he is just sitting still, but he makes no mention of it to them, firstly knowing that his Grandfather is seeing the appropriate people to help him and secondly not wanting to add his concerns to them both. Promising to see them very soon Daniel takes his leave and gets on his motorbike. Charlie is distraught at the thought of his new pal leaving him and whines pitifully as the bike roars away up the road.

About a week after Daniel's return home from University he receives a letter from April in Taunton, asking how he is and telling him how much she is missing him and asking if he can visit her soon. She then goes on to say that she has been offered a position in Bristol University Library and that perhaps they could meet there once she has found accommodation which will be in several weeks' time.

This is the one thing that Daniel has been dreading and he is consumed with guilt because she obviously has very strong feelings for him, which he feels unable to reciprocate. He has deliberately avoided getting in touch with April, hoping that the problem will go away and that her feelings for him will have changed once she is away from the University environment.

He prevaricates when he replies to her, not knowing what to say, but deciding eventually that if he intends telling her that there is no future in their relationship, then he should tell her face to face, however difficult that might prove. His decision being made, he replies to her letter, agreeing to meet up with her in Bristol once she is established. He is still haunted by her beauty and the evening they spent together, but still can't quite forget Theresa, even though she cheated on him.

Three weeks later Daniel receives a letter from The Daily Compass in Fleet Street, asking him to attend an interview for the position of junior reporter on the following Wednesday at eleven o'clock, and to ask for Sub Editor Graham Morton. Daniel is delirious with joy and rushes to tell his mother, who reads the letter in awe, wondering how she can have raised her son to such prodigious heights. "Oh well done Daniel, I know that this is what you want more than anything, so let's hope they offer it to you" and then proudly "I'm sure they will".

The next few days pass in a mixture of emotions for Daniel, part of him wanting the day to come, while another part wanting to put it off, fearing failure, primarily because it is so important to him, knowing that this is what he wants to do with his life.

His mother, in her infinite wisdom, understands perfectly both the doubts and the hopes that her son is going through and wisely says very little, apart from an occasional word of encouragement or a hug. The one thing that she never does is to question him or his abilities, but concentrates mainly on the positives.

Wanting time to find his bearings when he gets there, Daniel leaves home early on the next Wednesday and eventually arrives at Paddington Station at half past nine. Not knowing London very well he decides to get a taxi to The Daily Compass and arrives there in time to get a cup of tea from a café just a few doors away.

At two minutes to eleven he presents himself at the reception and asks for Graham Morton, explaining that he has an appointment. The receptionist speaks to someone on an extension and within a minute a young lad who can only just be in his teens appears and asks Daniel to follow him. Daniel follows the youth through a maze of corridors until they arrive eventually at a nondescript looking door that has no obvious markings on it. Not waiting to knock, the youth enters with Daniel following closely behind.

He is met immediately with a raucous cacophony of sounds which are coming from a number of sources. The room is huge and contains several rows of tables at which people are sitting, most of them speaking loudly on the telephone. Daniel can see that the reason for this is that if they don't, then the person on the other end that they are talking to will not hear them over the extreme babble that everybody else is making. The noise has its own viable entity within these four walls, its presence controlling everyone's response, a self-sustaining screeching volatile blast that encompasses everyone in the room.

To add to this mayhem, people seem to be constantly rushing around with sheaves of paper which they leave at the appropriate desks, or at least that is what Daniel presumes. Typewriters too, make their contribution to the noise level and everywhere staff, journalists or secretaries are smoking cigarettes at an alarming rate, a layer of smoke hanging in the air, contributing its own toxic mix to an already lethal cocktail.

Still following the youth Daniel finally arrives at the furthest end of the office where he sees a door marked Graham Morton and, beneath this worthy's name, the position of Sub Editor is displayed.

As he knocks on the door, he can hear someone, obviously of authority, who he can only assume is Graham Morton, talking another individual to task. "Why the fuck didn't you go and see the witness to the attack" he thunders "It's not enough just attending the scene, any old reporter can do that, but The Daily Compass demands more. It can only survive if we get the extra ingredient that other dailies fail to find. Now the witness saw the two men attack the third defenseless elderly male with crowbars, so if another paper interviews this witness, we have lost the initiative. But if they haven't then we will be the only ones to print a description of the assailants, apart from the police that is, but they won't be giving that information out just yet, so get your arse back down there and find the witness."

There is a sudden silence as the sub editor notices Daniel standing in the doorway, until he speaks again "yes young man, can I help you?"

Daniel, who has listened to the one sided conversation with trepidation, replies in a confident voice, instinctively knowing that anything less will make him fodder for a similar verbal blast "I've come for an interview with you at eleven o'clock today as requested by you, so here I am".

As he is speaking, he evaluates Graham Morton who is standing behind a desk, facing another man at the other side. He notes that he is a short stocky individual with thinning hair and dark piercing eyes that seem to assess every minute detail it observes in a glance. Daniel assumes that this is because of the job that he does. He is wearing a grubby white shirt with the sleeves rolled up. It is unbuttoned at the top with a tie hanging loosely below. At this moment he is holding a sheet of paper in one hand, which is no doubt the cause of his outburst aimed at the other man in the room. In his other hand he holds a cigar which has ash hanging from it, which he occasionally taps onto an ash tray on the desk before him. His pallor is sallow and he wears a beard growth several days old. Red rims surround his eyes, no doubt caused by the conditions of working long hours in badly ventilated offices.

"O God, I completely forgot, I thought it was tomorrow" replies Graham. There is a silence in the room for several seconds as he considers the situation before adding "look, I won't lie to you, I'm very busy just at the moment: a number of things have come up that need to be sorted before we go to press tonight, but they should all be resolved within a couple of hours, so I could see you then. In the meantime, why don't you go with Harry here, to see the witness to the assault on the old man; it will give you an insight into the sort of thing that a reporter does. Then when you get back, we can have a chat".

This is not something that Daniel has expected; in fact it is totally outside his experience to date, but the thought of doing the thing that he wants more than anything else sways his decision as he says "Thank you, I would like that very much sir."

As they both prepare to leave, Daniel takes stock of his companion Harry, who is obviously a senior staff reporter with the newspaper. He sees an angular man who stands well over six feet tall. He is of dark complexion and is showing several days growth of beard. His facial features are sharp with chiseled eye brows under which his dark brown eyes are focused on Daniel. His apparel is unconventional to say the least: a scruffy dark green sweater covers his torso with no shirt that Daniel can see, with a pair of denim jeans and a pair of soft loafer shoes completing the picture.

But when he smiles, as he does now, beckoning Daniel to follow him, his face lights up, showing a handsome man of somewhere in his late fifties, possibly early sixties years of age.

Daniel follows Harry from the offices out to the front of the building, where the latter hails a taxi to take them to Marylebone police station. When Daniel asks why, Harry tells him that is where the police have taken the witness after the assault, no doubt to get her statement. "All we have to do is wait for her to leave the station and then we can question her. There's a café opposite so we can get a cuppa and keep an eye on the station at the same time. But first I'll just contact a policeman I know to see if she's still there".

Finding a phone box Harry rings his contact who confirms that the lady in question is nearly ready to leave, having finished giving her statement.

Before she arrives, Harry takes Daniel to one side and in a low voice says "Now Dan here's an opportunity for you to gain some interviewing techniques. When she arrives, I want you to question her about the attack that happened this morning. The major things to bear in mind to establish the facts are, what when, how and, finally and probably the most important, why. I will assist you if I think you need assistance, but I would like to see what sort of a fist you can make of it.

Within a few minutes the witness appears on the steps outside the station and Harry and Daniel hurry across the road and introduce themselves to her, Harry showing her his reporter's badge as authenticity. She is a young woman in her early twenties, Daniel assumes, with peroxide blond hair and she wears heavy make-up. She is wearing a white blouse top and a black slim line skirt under a beige mackintosh which is not buttoned up. Although relatively young she wears a tired worn look of someone a good deal older.

Harry tells her why they are there and invites her to join them in the café for refreshments, where they can talk.

Looking flustered, she eventually agrees to go with them and after they have ordered drinks and food Daniel begins by saying "Well, its Brenda isn't it, can you just tell us what you saw this morning".

"I will, but first promise me that my name and address won't appear in the paper. I don't want those thugs coming looking for me"

Harry knowing that Daniel does not have the authority to answer replies "I think that we can promise you that, but I have to say that your details will soon be available to everyone. Either the police or someone who recognizes you from the T.V. news is bound to see you, so I will promise not to divulge your details, at least until they become common knowledge. So now tell me just what you saw this morning".

"Well I was on my way to work this morning and I took my usual short cut through Huntsworth Mews which takes me up to Gloucester Place from Marylebone Road. It was about eight o'clock and was very quiet as I reached there, nobody yet being at work in any of the offices. As I entered Huntsworth Mews there was an elderly gentleman walking in the same direction, about fifty yards ahead of me and as I looked two men appeared in front of him coming towards both of us. The whole thing must have been prearranged because as the two men drew level with the old man, they both took out metal crowbars from underneath their long coats and without a word of warning began attacking him. After just two blows the old man was on the floor begging for mercy, and all the time the men kept repeating to him "give us the money and we'll stop, if not we'll carry on until you do."

A further flurry of blows were landed, during which time the old man protested that he didn't have any money on him, but it was of no avail, because suddenly one of the men started searching him and within seconds uttered a triumphant shout to his companion, saying "here it is" while holding up a cloth bag, after which he kicked the old man several times before saying to his companion "come on let's go".

"The whole incident was all over in less than thirty seconds" exclaims Brenda. "In fact, I just stood still with the shock of it all until the two men had gone. I don't think that they even noticed me; they were so busy hurting the old man. As soon as they had gone, I went to help him, because he was obviously in agony. I helped him as best I could and told him to lie still before I went to Gloucester Place, where I found a telephone box and rang for an ambulance, after which I returned to the old man again".

Harry and Daniel listen to Brenda's story attentively and when she had finished Daniel said "so did you manage to talk to the old man and if so, what did he tell you."

Suddenly a strange look crosses Brenda's face as if she realizes for the first time that she has information that might have a monetary value.

"What's it worth" she says, almost defiantly.

Harry sits back in his chair, with a look of distain on his face. "Well I'm sure that the paper could contribute something for what you know, so how does one hundred pounds sound"?

Brenda is silent for a heartbeat before her face takes on a crafty, furtive look, before saying "I think it's worth more than that".

It is Harry's turn to consider his next move as he says "well I think that the offer is fair under the circumstances, Brenda, bearing in mind that we could reveal your personal details in print if we choose."

Brenda's shoulders slump as she realizes that she has gone as far as she can negotiating a fee and reluctantly says "when I got back to him, I asked the old man who he was and what the two thugs wanted. He was in a good deal of pain and it was difficult for him to answer, but between periods he told me that his name was Aaron Gold and that he was a Diamond dealer from Hatton Garden. The cloth bag he was carrying contained twenty diamonds that his company had just polished from their uncut condition and he was on his way to a famous retail jeweler in The Burlington Arcade to deliver them."

As she finishes, Daniel says "so it wasn't just a few quid that was stolen this morning. In fact, the value must have been substantial. Now tell me Brenda did you get a good look at the attackers and if so, would you recognize them again?"

"The police asked me the same question and made me look through their rogues' gallery but I couldn't identify either of them. I never saw their faces because they both had scarves covering the lower half and anyway, I was still about forty yards away from them. All I can say is that they both wore long black coats, no doubt to hide the fact that they were carrying crowbars, and that one of them was tall, over six feet I would say and bulky with it. The second man was a lot smaller and lighter by comparison, but I think that he was the leader if you like, because he was the one giving the orders."

Daniel interrupts Brenda at this juncture saying "You say that they didn't hesitate to use force rather than just confronting the man and demanding money with menaces, but rather saw force as the more immediate method to get what they were looking for, which suggests that this is something that they have done before."

"Oh yes they were quite ruthless once they reached the man".

"Did you notice what type of footwear they were wearing"?

"Yes, they both wore heavy industrial type shoes with steel toe-caps, no doubt to inflict pain as quickly as possible."

"Which direction did they take when they left their victim?"

"Well luckily for me they didn't try to go past me, but retraced their steps back towards Gloucester Place, but where they went after that is anyone's guess."

Daniel questions Brenda for a few more minutes but it is quite apparent that she has told them everything that she knows, so reluctantly he asks Harry if there is anything else that he has missed.

"No you have been pretty thorough Dan, the only thing we need to do is to get Brenda's personal details so that we contact her if we need to" after saying which he takes a tight roll of bank notes out of his pocket and proceeds to peel some off until the agreed sum of one hundred pounds is reached, which he then passes to Brenda.

She takes the money and stuffs it into her bra much to Harry and Daniel's amazement, before proceeding to give them her name and address and hurriedly leaving.

Now the two of them are left on their own again, Harry addresses Daniel "What do you make of that then Dan, do you think that she was telling the truth?"

"I think so, but I don't think that she saw very much, not in the time that the robbery took place. One thing that I did think was strange was that the men that attacked the victim at first demanded money, but were not surprised when they found diamonds instead. The only conclusion that I can draw from that is that they knew who he was, and why he was where he was at that particular time. Now I imagine that the movement of diamonds from his offices is a tightly guarded secret, so the question that springs to mind is how did the two attackers know? The only answer that I can come up with is that someone in a trusted position at the offices in Hatton Garden betrayed the old man, or alternatively someone in the jewelers at The Burlington Arcade told a third party, either accidentally or deliberately that he would be delivering the diamonds at that particular time. Either way I think that we should question both him and the jewelers at Burlington Arcade to see what we can discover."

Harry is contemplative for a few moments before saying "well I hadn't thought of that and I'll follow it up; but first I had best get you back to Graham for your interview. He's a great bloke by the way, whatever conclusions you came to when you first arrived. I have the greatest respect for him; he knows the industry inside out and providing you work hard he will support you and make sure that you get opportunities as they arise."

Having completed their task as far as possible, they return to The Daily Compass office once more and make their way to Graham Morton's office.

Harry tentatively knocks on the door and enters upon the command "come" with Daniel following hard on his heels.

Daniel is brought to an abrupt halt as once inside he sees Graham standing behind his desk with a smiling Brenda standing alongside him. Gone is her worried, flustered look and in its place is a pretty, good looking woman with an air of authority.

"Welcome back Daniel" begins Graham "as you can see things are not always as they appear. Instead of a conventional interview I thought that it would be more useful to us if we could see how you would react if you were faced with a situation similar to that you might face any day if you were to be a reporter. Brenda here, who is one of our most accomplished administrators, has spoken very highly of the questions that you asked her and how you conducted yourself."

At this point Harry interjects "I was very impressed also Graham" and he continues to explain Daniels hypothesis regarding the fictional robbery and assault.

"Well that's good enough for me "exclaims Graham" the job of junior reporter is yours if you want it. We will talk salary and conditions in a moment, but the first thing that you need to know is that you must learn journalist short hand. It is similar to Pitman's shorthand as used by secretaries the world over, except that it's quicker. It normally takes about six months to pick it up, but you need it when taking notes at a meeting say, or when interviewing a witness."

"So that's what you were doing Harry, when I was interviewing Brenda. I saw you but I just thought that you were taking notes. I should have realized that you couldn't possibly have written them out longhand in the time that you had" says Daniel.

"That's right "confirms Harry, it's quite easy once you have mastered it."

At this point Graham turns to Brenda and Harry and says "well thank you for your help, but I would appreciate it if you'd leave us now so that I can talk to Dan in private."

After the two have left Graham explains to Daniel the role of a junior reporter and what salary he can expect, and then goes on to say "One of your biggest problems will be to find accommodation in London at a price that you can afford. It will probably mean that you have to share a flat with others, but I can get someone in our Personnel Department to help you with that. They are used to it, because it comes up all the time."

They discuss the job further until Graham says "well I'll take you to see the Personnel Department now, unless you have any more questions."

Daniel thinks for a moment before saying "Thank you, but when would you want me to start, because I have a number of commitments up until the middle of September, but I would be happy to start then, or earlier if it is imperative."

Graham smiles slowly, altering his stern look to one of relaxed pleasure. "The middle of September will be fine Dan; it will give me time to find somewhere to put you. So welcome to The Daily Compass, and if there is anything that you need to know before then just speak to Personnel. I'll write and confirm the details as we discussed."

After showing him round and introducing him to Sandra, a lady in her mid- fifties, Graham leaves him. Sandra has years of experience dealing with the sort of problems that Daniel has and after researching through her records, she finds a number of Flats which have rooms and accommodation to share, which are fairly local.

"Try some of these first and if you don't have any luck get back to me Dan, in the meantime good luck and we look forward to you joining us in the near future."

Daniel is in seventh heaven as he leaves The Daily Compass offices, his head in a whirl. Not knowing what his next step is, he finds a tea shop where he can consider his options. As he sits and contemplates, his first thought is that there is little point trying to find somewhere to live now because he will incur costs immediately in terms of rent and a possible deposit, even though he will not be moving in for several weeks.

This problem resolved, or at least parked to one side, he decides to buy a London A to Z, after which he decides that he will have a look around the area of Fleet Street before making his way home to Chipping Norton.

As he travels back on the train, he goes over again the events of the day and is filled with a warm sense of accomplishment.

Ella is waiting for him and greets him with a hug, before saying "did it all go well then Daniel, did you get the job and if so, do you think that you will take it"?

He explains all that has happened and as he finishes, Ella interrupts "well that all sounds fantastic" and then another barrage of questions are fired at him like bullets from a machine gun "will you have to live in London and if so will you be able to afford it? When do you have to start? Will you be able to get home occasionally and ......"?

"Whoa, whoa, Mum," laughs Daniel, excited by his mother's obvious delight and interest "Yes I will have to live in London, and the paper have given me a list of possible places to rent, but I will probably have to share. I am due to start about the middle of September, but they are going to write to me and confirm it all.

I hope that I will be able to afford living there, but it all depends how much rent I will have to pay, but it should be doable. On the way back on the train I had an epiphany moment which was that I could use the motor bike to get to and from London, which should save a shed load of money in train fares. Not only that but It would be even more useful getting around in London, because the nature of the job will mean getting out and about visiting places of news interest".

All the while they have been talking, Ella has had one hand behind her back, which she now brings forward and Daniel can see that it is a holding a letter.

"I thought it best that we talked about your interview first before you saw this" she says smiling. "It's from Exeter University". Then seeing the look of excitement and apprehension on her son's face, she continues "go on, open it, it won't bite you".

Daniel takes the letter hesitatingly from his mother and slowly opens it, before reading it through in a rush, a huge smile enveloping his nervous face; a shout of joy escapes his lips as he tells his mother "I got a first mum", before reading it again more slowly this time, as if he doubted it the first time.

"Oh well done Daniel, I am so proud of you" and then "I just wish you father could be here today, then my world would be complete".

There is silence for a moment as the import of her words sink in, Daniel sensing that this special moment is emotionally charged for her.

Wanting to break the spell before Ella breaks down, he continues "The Graduation Ceremony is on the eleventh of September mum; I hope that you are coming".

"You just try and stop me" and then giving the matter more thought "I tell you what, why don't we go the day before and stay overnight before the ceremony. It will be a bit of a rush if we try and do it all on the same day, would you prefer it if we did that? Then you can show me around the University and I would also like to see Exeter Cathedral".

"That sounds a great idea. I know one or two places where students can get discount, so why don't we try one of them"?

*　*　*

The following morning Daniel receives a letter from April. Opening it with trepidation he reads,

Dearest Dan,

Since we last spoke, I have managed to find accommodation in Bristol. It is a flat and I will be sharing it with two other female students. The best part is that I will be living just off Park Street, which is only a few hundred yards from Bristol University. The flat has three bedrooms and I have one with a single bed. The living room and kitchen we share, but I am sure that it won't be a problem. It's a bit like living in University again really.

I am so excited and looking forward to seeing you again and showing you around this beautiful city.

At present I have a job working several evenings and lunch times in a bar locally, until I start full time working at the University.

Please let me know when you can come, and if you can, make it for at least two days. You can stay over with me at the flat, so you won't need to find accommodation.

Oh, one other thing, we have a telephone at the flat (we have agreed to share the costs) so you can ring me and we can sort out when would be most suitable.

Make it soon, because I have been missing you.

Love,
April.

P.S. I nearly forgot: the telephone number is Bristol 27941.
P.P.S. See you soon. Did I tell you that I am so excited?
P.P.P.S. Another thing, I got a 2.1. How about you?

Daniel is both pleased and slightly disturbed as he reads Aprils letter. Pleased, because she has achieved good grade in her studies, but disturbed because he now has to confront his feelings about her again and decide what to do about their relationship.

He realises that he can no longer put off seeing her again, so he picks up the phone and dials the Bristol number shown in her letter.

After several rings there is a female's voice which he doesn't recognize, who says after he has enquired for April "Oh, she is just in her room, I will call her".

After another short delay, during which time Daniel is beginning to become stressed, he hears April's voice, and as he replies to her, he is almost deafened when she shouts down the line deliriously "Oh fantastic, you rang. Tell me how are you, what have you been doing, when can you come to see me? There are so many things that I want to show you".

Surprising himself, Daniel is caught up in April's enthusiasm and replies, telling her about his job offer and his degree result before saying "When is the best time for me to come to see you in Bristol. You say in your letter that you are working some lunch times and evenings, so which days do you have when you are free? I guess that weekends are out of the question, because they are probably the busiest days"

After discussing the matter, they decide that the best time is on the Monday and Tuesday of the following week and that Daniel will travel there on his motorbike.

Still not knowing how he really feels about April, although he has been caught up in her excitement, he is surprised when he discovers that he is looking forward to seeing her again.

It is with some apprehension that he explains to Ella about April, not even having mentioned anything about her previously and finishes by telling her that he is going to see her the next week.

For her part Ella is both delighted and surprised that her son has formed a relationship with someone, thinking that his work at University had consumed all his attention, leaving no room for social discourse of any sort.

"Well I think that you had better tell me a little about her Daniel, because this is the first that I have heard. For example, how did you meet, how long have you known her, what is she like, where does she live" ….

"Wait a minute mum, it is for just these reasons that I have never told you until now. We are just good friends, nothing more or less" replies Daniel, hoping that his mother cannot distinguish between his truths and half-truths, her intense interest frightening him.

"We only met a couple of times while we were at University, both times at a dance. She has just got a job as a librarian at Bristol University and she wants me to go and see her so that she can show me around the city.

I think that she is a bit lonely there and she needs someone familiar to spend some time with until she becomes more acquainted with her new surroundings. That's all it is mum".

Ella does not believe her son for even one second, remembering her own early courtship days, but not wanting to embarrass him she says "I think that is an excellent idea. It will do you good to get out and relax before you have to start work in London", while all the whole time she is smiling inwardly to herself, thinking how transparent her son's feelings and emotions are. "Have a good time son".

CHAPTER 17.

APRIL AND BRISTOL.

On the appointed day, Monday 22nd August, Daniel mounts his trusty motorbike and heads south. It is a bright and crisp morning, a heavy shower the previous night freshening up the myriad hues of green of the fields, hedgerows and trees.

Passing through Burford, one of the Cotswold towns that he considers among the most beautiful of the area, he is enthralled to see the honey coloured stone cottages and shops, some of them covered in wisteria, while others are clad in Ivy. The next town he passes through is Cirencester, before continuing down to Chipping Sodbury, after which he heads West to join the conurbation on the outskirts of Bristol.

Knowing that he is still on the East side of the city and that he needs to get to the west where Bristol University is based, he decides to go through the centre, but the sign posts leave him confused and frustrated. Eventually he stops and asks an old man who is carrying a paper, who he assumes must be a local.

The old man is only too pleased to be asked and Daniel thinks that his request is probably the highlight of his week. What Daniel has not considered, or indeed is even aware of, is that people born in Bristol talk with a dialect all their own. However, after much repeating of where he needs to be, and with much gesticulation and hand signals, with the old man interspersing occasionally with an" ooh" or" ah" Daniel thinks that he now knows the route.

Setting off once more it is a further three old men that he stops and asks before he eventually finds himself at the bottom of Park Street and it is only a few minutes afterwards that he finds himself outside Aprils flat.

She has obviously been looking out for him, because as soon as he draws up, she comes running out to greet him.

Flinging her arms around him she embraces him and as they briefly kiss, she cries "Oh it's so good to see you Dan, now come on in and I will show you round the flat. I expect you are tired, so let me make you a cup of tea to ease your weary body".

She is dressed simply in a blue, tight, low cut short sleeved top, with dark blue three-quarter length denim jeans that seem to be moulded to her, leaving very little to Daniels imagination.

He is stunned once again at her sheer beauty and surprised that he has obviously forgotten just how attractive she is.

As they go inside to the upstairs flat, Daniel disrobes from his motor bike leathers, helmet and goggles as April goes into the kitchen to make tea.

Returning to the living room she says laughing" drink this first, then I will show you round the flat. It will probably take all of ten seconds".

They talk again of everything that has happened to them since they last met, April showing her concern when they discuss Daniels job in London.

"But we will still be able to see each other once you go there, won't we? I hate the thought of only seeing you once in a blue moon Dan".

For a moment Daniel is lost for an answer, eventually replying "I'm sorry, the truth is I don't know just what hours I will need to work, because if a story comes up at any time during the day, then if I am assigned to it, I will have to go, no matter what".

"I understand that, but if you can't get down here then perhaps, I could come to you in London. There is a great train service to Paddington, so that shouldn't be much of a problem".

"Let's wait and see" replies Daniel, not wanting to commit himself without first deciding if he wishes to continue their relationship, although he is already wavering now that he has seen her again, becoming entranced once more by this beautiful woman who first weaved her spell on him all those months ago.

"Anyway, let me show you the rest of the flat" says April leading him first to the small kitchen, before showing him the two other double bedrooms which the two other girls occupy. Finally, she throws open the door of the third bedroom, declaring "this is my room; it's only a single because I was the last person to join, but the upside is that I pay less for that reason".

As he enters the room Daniel is surprised just how small it is, but is impressed when he sees how organized April has made it.

It contains a single bed with a bedside cabinet on one side, on which there are what Daniel assumes to be several family photographs. A comfortable small armchair is placed on the opposite side to the bedside cupboard, while a mirror is placed on the wall at the end of the bed. There is stand-alone bookshelf which reaches almost to the ceiling, which is crammed full with books of every description. Next to it is a small wardrobe, which completes the items of furniture. The walls are decorated in warm cream emulsion paint and April has put her own stamp on the room with a pale blue and white bedspread with matching curtains, together with several small porcelain items which she tells him she has purchased from several house sales or from some of the very many shops that sell collectables locally. The sum of all this gives the small room an impression of space and light, but even more than that, it has an overall feeling of comfort.

Daniel stands transfixed, gazing at the effect that April has achieved with the small room. "It looks lovely April; you have a wonderful talent for interior design".

"Thank you, Dan, I'm glad you like it".

Daniel is suddenly very aware how close he is to her, and as he looks, she lifts her head to meet his gaze, revealing her mesmeric green eyes that seem to almost hypnotize him. With one automatic, inevitable movement, she is in his arms, any doubts that he has been harbouring regarding his feelings for her resolved. How could he possibly ever have doubted them?

Daniels body's automatic response as he kisses and caresses her, leaves her in no doubt of the effect that she is having on him and she giggles delightedly "so soon Dan, I thought that we could go out for a meal first" and then as he pulls away thinking that he has somehow offended her, she continues softly" don't be silly Dan, I want it just as much as you do".

As if to prove it, she stands away from him and slowly begins to take off her clothes. He looks with wonder and awe as she reveals her slim body, her firm breasts and long slender legs that seem to go on forever, and for a moment it is enough for him just to look at this wonder of nature, until she suddenly giggles with embarrassment saying "come on Dan, I have shown you mine, now it's your turn" and begins to undress him, saying softly "Come on Dan, I want you now".

He moans as she reaches for him, before he responds running his hands slowly over her body, until she shudders with anticipation. He continues to explore her until she can wait no longer and pulls him onto the bed.

"It has got to be now Dan. I have been waiting such a long time for this".

Their lovemaking this time is even better than before and is repeated a second time. Afterwards they both lay replete, entwined in each other's arms, murmuring endearments, both drowsy and on the verge of sleep. Daniel thinks that he has never felt this happy before as he brushes away the dark glossy hair from her face and gently kisses the long bewitching eye lashes that now flutter open in response to reveal her intense pure green eyes, which crinkle at the edges revealing her infectious smile.

"What are you thinking" April asks, her smile now spreading to lighten up all her beautiful features, eyes, mouth and even her nose seems to wrinkle as if in agreement with the rest of them.

"Oh well if you must know, I was thinking that at this moment there is nowhere else that I would rather be" replies Daniel truthfully, while his conscience reminds him in no uncertain fashion, that before he arrived, he was considering if he should break off their relationship.

"Oh, I am so glad, because I feel like that as well. I was frightened that you thought of our last evening at University as a one off, and that you would not want to continue to see me. It's funny really when you think of it, because I sort of gave you the cold shoulder when we first met at the dance. The problem was that I liked you a lot, but I didn't want to be the one to break up my existing relationship, because we had been together for some time. Everyone said that it would not survive us both living apart, but I didn't want it to be me that walked away. You can understand then that I was hurt when my partner did the dirty on me despite all his promises to the contrary".

"Well it's his loss and my gain" replies Daniel as he kisses her while caressing her body with a touch as light as a whisper.

Though not intending it, the result is that similar to a lightning strike for both of them as his body responds to that of nature's most common demands.

Daniel suddenly becomes aware of his surroundings and says" Where are the other two girls, it would be embarrassing if they were to walk in on us right now".

April giggling says "Have you only just thought of that. Well you need not worry because Sally has gone home to Birmingham until the new term starts in September, while Andrea has gone out to her boyfriend's parents for the rest of the week.

Andrea's own parents live in Canada, so she rarely goes back because of the expense. I think actually that she decided to go out knowing that you were coming today. Very thoughtful, don't you think"?

"Very" replies Daniel, before continuing where he has left off.

"Don't worry; they bring their men friends back sometimes. It all works very well. As you can tell, they owe me big time".

They lay together until early evening when Daniel suddenly becomes aware that he is hungry and says," come on let's go somewhere for a meal and then you can show me some of the Bristol high-lights".

April protests at first, saying "I wanted to make a meal just for the two of us" but Daniel doesn't want to put her to the trouble, especially after their exertions of the afternoon.

Leaving, they find an Italian restaurant where they consume large plates of steaming Spaghetti Bolognese which they wash down with Chianti. As they finish April says "right, let's go for a walk now. I would like to show you where the University is among other things".

Leaving the restaurant, they stroll slowly, holding hands up Park Street until they reach the top. Continuing on they reach the university Campus which is closed and silent.

"This is where I will be Dan, the place where you can imagine I am when you think of me".

"Oh, I will think of you in a much better place than this" he replies smiling broadly.

"Yes, I suppose your right" says April, in a soft small voice, the image of the two of them in her bedroom uppermost in her thoughts.

Moving on, they pass The Bristol Zoo and reach The Bristol Suspension Bridge, one of Isambard Kingdom Brunel's engineering masterpieces, built in the 1850's, the bridge spans the Avon gorge and is several hundred feet above the Avon River flowing like a silver strand several hundred feet below.

As they stand looking down April is reminded of a true story that she has heard and says "many people over the years have committed suicide by jumping from here, but there was one famous occasion when a women in the late nineteenth century jumped, but was amazingly uninjured, because the dress and petticoats that she was wearing ballooned out as she fell and acted like a parachute, setting her down at the bottom of the gorge as if she were a feather".

As they wend their way back to Aprils' flat she says "tomorrow if you like we can have a look at the shops, or we could go to The Bristol Hippodrome in the afternoon. I think that there is a comedy play on at the moment. Or I could show you some of the older places of interest, because Bristol has a long history. Or whatever else you would like to do".

"Let's see how we feel in the morning because we could also go somewhere on my motor bike, perhaps Weston Super Mare or Gloucester".

In the event, they don't wake until eleven o'clock the next morning, having continued where they left off the previous afternoon. The single bed is a challenge to say the least, but as Daniel points out "At least you can't get away from me" only to hear April reply "why would I want to"?

As they shower together, a novel and exciting experience for both of them, some considerable time passes, which neither of them begrudges, delaying them even further. April eventually reluctantly extricates herself from Daniels clutches and makes breakfast for them both, after which they decide to explore Bristol.

Walking down to the centre of the city they look round the shops before finding their way to the covered in market and explore its many stalls each with their own blend of intoxicating sights and smells. Just off Queen Square they find The Landogger Trow, the oldest Inn in Bristol, where they consume bacon sandwiches and beer, all the while laughing and talking nonstop.

Daniel tells her the story of an old woman in Chadlington who had glaucoma in both eyes, the vision of which was marginally better in one, more than the other. On one particular day she wanted to see if her vision had deteriorated any further, so she stood in front of the wall on which there was a picture and holding her hand over the eye with the least vision she peered myopically to see how much she could still see.

To her utter disappointment she saw nothing at all, but thinking that she would see more in the eye that wasn't so damaged she repeated the exercise. and holding her hand over her bad eye she looked once more, only to find to her horror that she could not see anything of the picture with that one either.

Sitting down with a thump, her brain telling her that the day had arrived when she had finally gone blind, she was in torment, until she suddenly looked up and noticed an outline of the place where her picture had once hung, and remembered with relief that she had taken it down to clean a few days earlier.

April laughs until her side's ache, which reminds her suddenly just how much she enjoys his company and that he will have to leave at some time later that day, so she appeals to him as she tries desperately to prolong his stay.

"Can't you stay one more night Dan, it seems as if you have only just arrived and I was looking forward to us going out dancing tonight. I don't have to start work in the bar until tomorrow night, so you could stay for breakfast and then leave for home".

Daniel considers what April has said, knowing beyond all doubt that he would rather spend time with her than return home to Chipping Norton. His mother will be expecting him back by this evening, but other than that he has no other commitments. She can cope very well without him, her staff being very able and proficient.

"I would like that very much, but are you sure that you want me around for another day"?

"Of course, I wouldn't ask you if I didn't, would I".

"That's O.K. then I will telephone my mother and let her know not to expect me back until tomorrow".

Ella is not the least surprised when Daniel telephones her, rather she is pleased, knowing that her son's relationship with April is deeper than he himself realizes.

Returning to April's flat they spend the afternoon making love and talking ten to the dozen about their hopes and fears for the future, both of them leaving some questions of their future together unspoken. Eventually she gets up and throws on her skimpy nightdress, which leaves little to Daniels imagination, which is still at fever pitch, and goes into the kitchen, insisting on making them both a meal.

Daniel falls asleep after his strenuous afternoon's activities, until April wakes him gently. "Dinner is served my Lord" she whispers, skipping away as he makes a grab for her and fails.

Wanting to impress him with her culinary skills April has prepared lasagna with a salad, all washed down with red wine to accompany it, which Daniel wolfs down ravenously, before leaning back and declaring "that was superb my love, well done".

April notes the "my love" and is pleased, while at the same time acknowledging to herself that it might be meant only as an expression of pleasure rather than endearment.

"Well thank you sir, at least I know now how to give you an appetite" she replies, her eyes twinkling again in the manner that Daniel has just begun to recognize as the tool that she uses to make him laugh. Continuing, she says "look, I thought that it would be nice if we go to the bar where I work first, before we go to the night club. I think that you will like it; it's a nice bar which also serves food, so it is very busy. Not only that but you can also see where I work".

"Sure, that sounds fun".

Their evening is spent in a leisurely fashion beginning at the bar where April works, Daniel consuming beer while April drinks cocktails. Finding a pool table Daniel challenges April to a game and much to his surprise she proves to be very competent, beating him comprehensively. "Where did you learn to play like that" asks Daniel in exasperation as April makes a circumference of the room holding her cue above her head, all the while dancing and laughing excitedly.

"Well, what I didn't tell you was that my dad is passionate about pool and he had a table installed in our garage several years ago, so I used to play regularly" she says, coming to a full stop at last.

Looking at her beautiful smiling face, Daniel cannot but do the same. "You little minx, you must have been laughing quietly to yourself when I challenged you. You caught me right and proper". Before he can say anymore April embraces him and kisses him passionately, her tongue flickering between his open lips, reducing his mood of irritability to one of need.

"Come on, let's go to the nightclub that I was telling you about" she whispers in his ear as she pulls away from their embrace.

"I would rather we went back to yours".

"We will I promise" she says, "But just let's go dancing first. You know how much I love dancing with you. We won't be late, because I want to be alone with you too".

On the dance floor April is once again captivated by Daniel's skills as he holds her close, their bodies moving as one, making her feel as light as a feather. But the floor is crowded, meaning that they move slowly, locked together. Her arms are around the back of his head, while his lips nuzzle her long swan like alabaster neck. They dance like this forever, until eventually Daniel is so aroused that he whispers "can we go now, or I may get arrested for rape", only to hear her reply "you can only be arrested if the other party is not consenting, so you are O.K, but I think it's time that we went".

Their last night is a sex fest, as each of them try to extract memories of this night that they will be able to remember, until the next time that they meet.

The thought that it may be some time before they can see each other again drives them to the point of exhaustion as they explore each other's needs. Eventually they fall asleep as the sun begins to rise, spooned together, only waking at mid-day as they hear the milkman delivering downstairs. Lying together April raises the thought uppermost in both of their minds. "When will we see each other again Dan. The thought that it may be weeks is unbearable".

"I feel the same way too, but I could possibly make it again next week for a couple of days, and the week after that is Graduation, so I will see you then, although we will be with our parents, which will mean that we will not be able to do this again, which will drive me mad. The week after Graduation I start work in London, which will make things even more difficult, but I am sure that you could come to see me there once I have found somewhere to live, perhaps on a weekend. As I explained I don't yet know what hours I am expected to work, but I am sure that if an incident happens even when I am not working, then I will be expected to be there. I will know more once I have begun. What do you think"?

"Of course, I will come to see you in London, I would like that very much, but the thought of seeing you at Graduation and not being able to do anything more than speak to you is terrible. Can we not get a room for just one night and tell our parents that there are a lot of us getting together so that they don't suspect anything untoward"?

"That has definite possibilities" replies Daniel. "Let me think about it. The last thing that I want to do is upset our parents, so we will have to be very careful what we tell them. Let's leave it there for now and we can discuss it more when I see you next week. Is that O.K"?

"Next week sounds fantastic".

A reluctant Daniel leaves April after a prolonged good bye, to return home to Chipping Norton, where his mother waits excitedly with a list of questions waiting for him, although she knows that she will not get many answers.

"Well how did you get on with April, where did you go, what did you do and when will you go again..................".

Daniel fends off Ella's barrage of questions as best he can, while not wanting to deceive her in any way. "It was really good Mum; Bristol is a beautiful vibrant City and April showed me lots of it, including the University where she will be working. We went out to eat a couple of times and we got on together like a house on fire, so much so that I am going to see her again next week for a couple of days". He conveniently neglects to expand any further on how their personal relationship has developed or indeed of the fact that April and he had the sole occupancy of the flat for the whole of the period.

But Ella remembers very well her own first tentative relationship with Daniel's father, the heady intoxicating feeling that battered and swept their emotions, always leaving them wanting more. She recognizes these symptoms in her son as he stands before her and is glad, but she also recognizes that his story is also selective in its content. "I am really pleased for you Daniel" and then as the thought occurs to her for the first time "I know that you are just friends, but what will happen if it continues after you begin working in London. Will you still be able to see each other"?

Daniel air brushes her question with a brief "Oh we will just have to wait and see how it goes" and then "April says that there is a fast train service from Bristol to Paddington if that happens".

His answer tells Ella all she needs to know; that their intentions are to continue seeing each other as much as possible after he begins work in London. The realization both pleases her beyond measure, while a still small voice in her head tells her that any relationship will be under extreme pressure under these circumstances. Changing the subject Ella says "Your Grandfather went to see the doctor to get the results of his x-rays the other day and thank god they were clear. However, the doctor went on to say that he had emphysema and that if he didn't give up smoking, he wouldn't see his next birthday. It frightened the life out of him, which I think was what the doctor intended, but he is now like a bear with a headache, and grumpy with it".

"Poor old grandad; I will go and see him soon and try and cheer him up".

I'm sure that he would like that" says Ella," he doesn't get enough company, but be careful what you say, he seems to take offence at the slightest thing these days".

* * *

Wanting something to take his thoughts away from April, which he is finding almost impossible to do, Daniel decides to use the next few days catching up with his family. Mounting his, or rather what used to be his father's trusty motor bike, he first makes his way in trepidation to Chadlington, to see Alf and Liz.

To his surprise his grandfather greets him with a warm welcome, giving him a hug before saying "It's so nice to see you Daniel" while Liz kisses him saying "I'll just put the kettle on so we can have a brew up. Your mother told us that you have been to Bristol to see a friend. Come and tell us all about it".

Daniel spends the next two hours telling them both about April and his visit to Bristol, a carefully edited sanitized version, because he does not want to offend their moral code (a false assumption on his part).

Why do the young think that they are the first to experience love, sex and infidelity thinks Alf as his Grandson relates his story? How do they think that they got here in the first place? But he keeps his counsel to himself, until his grandson begins to tell them about Bristol.

Alf's curiosity is aroused because he has lived all his life in Chadlington, in fact the furthest place that he has been his whole life is to Oxford a handful of times and annually most summers to Blenheim Palace, when The Duke of Marlborough invites residents from the surrounding villages to tea in the grounds. His limited experience of travel and life in general makes him keen to hear all about Bristol, (even more than about April thinks Daniel), questioning his grandson about Bristol Suspension Bridge and other places on interest of which he has only heard.

Charlie, the Labrador has been outside in the garden up until now, but hearing Daniel's voice he begins barking, wanting to come in and greet him. To Daniel's joy the dog welcomes him excitedly, tail wagging, a low sound of pleasure emitting from his mouth, before proceeding to lick his new young friend voraciously.

To Daniel's surprise Alf says "do you fancy walking the dog with me Daniel. It's a lovely day and it will do us all good".

"I would like that very much" and then hesitatingly "are you sure that you are well enough, mum tells me that you haven't been too good".

"It will be O.K. if I don't go too far. When I have had enough, I will come back and the two of you can carry on ".

So they set off, the old man slowly making his way across the fields that he has tended all his life, while Daniel slows his pace to match, leaving Charlie to explore the hedgerows, snuffling through accumulated rotting dead leaves until he suddenly is confronted by a hedgehog, at which he barks in surprise before nudging it with his nose. Charlie's pain is obvious for all to see as his tender muzzle makes contact with the hedgehog's prickles. Emitting a noise somewhere between a low growl and a whine of pain he leaps backwards almost suspended mid-air for a split second before returning to his master's side for comfort.

Grandfather and Grandson fall about laughing at Charlie's antics, until both of them ruffle his coat to console him.

The harvest has just been gathered in and all the wheat fields are alive with stubble which will be burnt off in the next few days.

As they continue to walk Daniel ventures to ask his grandfather if he has given up smoking cigarettes.

"Well I'm trying very hard, but I am finding it difficult because I have been doing it since I was about ten years old. I know that I have got to, but the craving gets me, particularly first thing in the morning and after meals. But I will get there, your grandmother will see to that". As he finishes speaking, he is caught with a wracking cough which seems to go on forever. "I'm sorry son but I think that I will call it a day and go back home, but you carry on".

Worried about his grandfather Daniel returns with him to his cottage, explaining that he ought to be getting home anyway.

* * *

The next week as promised, Daniel returns to Bristol to spend as much time with April as he can before he has to start work in London. She has remained uppermost in his thoughts since he saw her last, but they have spoken most days on the telephone, which has made it almost impossible to forget her, not that he wants to. As he leaves Chipping Norton, Ella says "Why don't you ask April to come here sometime Daniel, I spoke to her the other day when she rang and she sounds lovely. I would very much like to meet her"

Stunned for a moment Daniel replies "I will ask her, but I don't know what her commitments are, and anyway you will get to meet her at graduation".

April has been looking out for him and running out she welcomes him on the pavement as he arrives. As they embrace, she says "Isn't this wonderful Dan, I am so glad you came. Before we go in, I have to tell you that Andrea is back here now, although she will be going out to see her boyfriend, but he will probably stay here over tonight, he does most nights when they see each other".

April is dressed in a baggy pale blue sleeveless top, and skintight jeans that follow every minute contour of her long slender legs. She does not wear make-up, a fact that emphasizes the sheer beauty of her natural features. Her long black hair is tied up into a pony tail, highlighting her classic high cheek bones which are at other times partially obscured by her long flowing hair in its usual form. The whole effect leaves Daniel breathless, mesmerized almost.

Any concerns that he has in regard to Andrea are proved to be groundless as he is introduced to her. She is a typical twenty-year-old student, attractive, blonde, tall and beautiful. Her natural manner puts Daniel at ease as they discuss and laugh at each other's experiences of University life and work. Eventually Andrea leaves to meet her boyfriend, having arranged to meet him for lunch.

As the door to the flat shuts behind Andrea, April takes Daniel by the hand and leads him into her bedroom. He needs no persuading as she says "Come on let's make the most of it, before Andrea and Mike return. Oh, by the way I have booked tickets at the Bristol Hippodrome Theatre for tonight: there is an up and coming Irish comedian on called Dave Allen who is supposed to be very funny". And then questioningly "you don't mind do you"?

Daniel is putty in her hands as she weaves her sexual magic on him, replying "That sounds like a great thing to do, but it's not a patch on this" as he reaches out for her again.

Their time together follows a similar pattern to the week before. They go out to the theatre, which they love, and go sightseeing and for meals, and make love as often as possible, trying to satisfy their insatiable feelings for each other, their concerns for the future uppermost in both their minds.

Andrea and her boyfriend Bill prove to be great company and they all stay in for the evening together. Chinese take-away is the order of the day and they are held enthralled as Bill, who is in the Merchant Navy, relates some of his experiences in far flung countries. They drink copious quantities of beer and white wine, their sound levels being raised proportionately as they laugh and enjoy each other's company, until eventually they fall asleep one by one.

Andrea wakes just long enough to wake the others and at half past one they go to bed exhausted. That is until a few hours later Daniel is woken by the recognizable sounds of Andrea and Bill making love.

This in turn wakes April who, seeing that Daniel is already awake and listening, begins to laugh, saying "Do you think that we sound like that Dan" to which he replies "I suppose that we must" and then "but I love to hear you moaning", a brief second before Aprils pillow hits him in the head. "But if we do it now, they won't be able to hear us over their own noise" says Daniel.

April's unspoken reply is all that he needs, as she reaches for him, her clear green eyes alive with agreement and anticipation.

Their time together finishes all too soon and Daniel leaves, after a prolonged goodbye, but not before he arranges to see her at their Graduation in a few days' time. "But what are we going to do after that" whispers April as she stands in his embrace.

"We will just have to take every opportunity that we can. Either you can come to me in London, or I will try and come to you here. You must know how I feel about you by now my love".

His words only make things worse as April begins to cry saying "Oh you must know that I feel the same way too ", causing him to console her until she is calm, before he sets off on his journey home.

CHAPTER 18.

1959 GRADUATION.

The morning of 10th September dawns warm and sunny as Ella drives the two of them in her van to Gloucester railway station in readiness for Daniel's Graduation Ceremony the following day.

The Cotswolds' are showing in all their early autumn glory, as they pass through exquisite villages. each one slumbering peacefully, only occasionally to be woken with a start as a tractor makes its way from a farmhouse to a field a couple of miles away, or by the postman's tuneless whistle as he wends his way from cottage to cottage, delivering messages of hope and despair in equal measure: but Ella loves this small part of England, never ceasing to wonder at its beauty and tranquility.

Catching the mid-day train, they arrive in Exeter at three o'clock in the afternoon, before getting a taxi which takes them to the small guest house which Ella has booked for the night and which is within a stone's throw of the University. Once they have put their luggage in their respective rooms, they make their way into the centre of Exeter and to The Cathedral.

Daniel takes great pleasure in showing his mother round the Cathedral which has more than a thousand years of history, parts of the original dating back to the Saxons. As they come outside Ella can see ancient houses, built in a semi-circle, some dating back to medieval times on the road facing the entrance to the Cathedral grounds. One such is now a café and she seizes the opportunity for the two of them to have tea and cakes before venturing any further.

They then continue to explore Exeter which is still a beautiful old city, but which unfortunately had been damaged quite badly by German bombing in the Second World War. Some reparations have been made, but there are many gaping holes between buildings, filled with rubble give an indication of much more work still to do.

By now Ella is thoroughly but pleasantly tired, so they return to their accommodation where they have booked dinner for half past six. As they eat Ella analyses every aspect of the guest house presentation, menu and methods of delivery. This is something that she has subconsciously developed over the years, comparing them to her own operation to see if there is anything that she can do to improve her offering.

Daniel has already told her that there is a gathering of students at the campus hall at eight o'clock and that all parents are welcome. There will be a band playing and the student bar will be open for the evening. It is one last opportunity for them to all get together before they go their separate ways.

"That sounds lovely" says Ella "I would like that very much" and then "will April be there"?

"Yes, and she is looking forward to meeting you".

In this way the die is cast, not without some apprehension on Daniel's part.

They arrive at the hall at half past eight, to find April waiting at the door to meet them. Daniel makes the introduction as Ella finds herself looking at this woman who has made such an impact on her son's life. His reasons become obvious to her as she sees a beautiful young woman dressed in a full length, sleeveless off the shoulder cream ball gown. She is quite tall but her most compelling features are her intense green eyes and high chiseled cheek bones, which are surrounded and softened by a mane of lustrous glossy black hair.

Finally, Ella notes, she has a figure to die for.

April breaks the momentary silence as she says "It's lovely to meet you. I have been waiting such a long time to meet the person who taught Dan to dance so beautifully. I can assure you that it is a rare attribute in this day and age. Later on, I would like you to tell me about your own dance career, Dan has told me a little, but I am sure that he missed out quite a lot". Then beckoning to both of them she goes on to say "My parents are just over the other side of the room, please come and meet them".

Crossing the room, they find April's parents Malcolm and Audrey who, Ella is pleased to see, are looking just a little out of their depth, something in fact that she is herself. Malcolm is tall, and heavily built, with balding hair and a windblown complexion that speaks volumes to Ella of a life spent largely outdoors in all elements of weather. His wife appears to be in her early fifties and is an older version of her daughter. She has the same intense green eyes and high cheek bones, which are even more pronounced by her long dark glossy hair. These features Ella thinks will always ensure that her looks will defy time, even if other parts of her anatomy deteriorate eventually, but there is no indication of this either at the moment, as she stands tall and slender next to her husband.

Once that the Introductions have been made, Ella Audrey and Malcolm, move to one side talking animatedly. Their discussion is totally dominated by April and Daniel's relationship, which they rapidly realise is something that any of them have very little knowledge.

"Daniel only told me about a couple of weeks ago and I think that he wouldn't have even then, only because he had to tell me that he was going to see April in Bristol" says Ella. "Then to cap it all he told me that they were just friends".

As she finishes speaking the three parents look over to April and Daniel who have joined some friends at the other side of the hall.

"I ask you, do you think that they are just friends" continues Ella as they observe Daniel who now has his arm around April's waist, while she leans into him, her head on his shoulder.

Malcolm replies "In fairness, she did mention Daniel briefly to us when she finished at University; how they had met and so on, but we have heard nothing further since. I suppose we have to just let them get on with it, only time will tell if they are right for each other; but I hope that they are".

Ella agrees wholeheartedly saying "they certainly look right together and Daniel seems much happier when they are together". Then changing the subject, she says "How about we get drinks from the bar and find a table where we can talk, because our children seemed to have joined a lot of their friends, so we are not likely to see them for some time".

Across the room April and Daniel have found a number of their close friends although both groups are not together, so April leaves to join hers, while Daniel does likewise to his, joining Martin, James and one or two others. The first few minutes are spent catching up with what has happened to each of them since their last days together. Daniel has just finished telling them all about his job offer as a journalist in London, when he is interrupted by Martin saying "well you are a dark horse, we had no idea that April and you were an item; when and how did that happen"?

Daniels reply is lost as the rest of them all clamour, wanting to know every last detail of the relationship. Not wanting to divulge too much, Daniel gives them a potted version, being careful only to mention the briefest details. As he looks across to April who is deep in conversation with her friends, she suddenly looks up and sees him and gives him a warm engaging smile, before rolling her eyes up to the heavens. It is obvious to Daniel that she is going through a similar situation to him, having to explain to her friends about the two of them.

In the meantime, Ella is already exchanging telephone numbers and addresses with Malcolm and Audrey, before saying "you know that you are welcome to visit us anytime"

"Oh, we would love to that, wouldn't we Malcolm" exclaims Audrey.

"Wait a minute, I have a better idea" continues Ella "when you come why don't you bring April as well. I am sure that Daniel would like that.

He can show her around the local villages". April's parents nod their heads in agreement that on a future date, still to be confirmed, they will visit Ella and Daniel at Chipping Norton.

As Daniel and his friends are catching up with each other's news, Martin suddenly pulls his friend to one side, saying "have you got a minute Dan, there is something that I need to tell you; something that I think you ought to know".

Daniel, who is by now intrigued, agrees and they make their way to the outside of the hall. "What is it Martin, you have my undivided attention. It must be something mind blowing if you can't say it in front of the others".

"Well the reason that I didn't mention it to them was because it is personal to you" and then he continues "you see I saw Norman and Brian, those friends of that bastard William who we went to Dartmoor with, and your name came up in conversation".

"What did they say" demands Daniel grimly, hurtful memories of that last night coming flooding back into his mind.

"Quite frankly I was amazed, because after we had been talking together for a few minutes I told them that you and April were an item, so to speak, then without any warning they told me that on the night that you got drunk, William spiked Theresa's drinks until she was paralytic and then got her into his tent".

"William did manage to get her clothes off, but he told both Norman and Brian afterwards that was as far as he got, because Theresa was completely unconscious and did not respond at all. Furthermore, William was furious with her because she ruined his reputation as someone who always got what he wanted. His fury was so strong that he was unable to keep it secret from his two friends, telling them of his rage at not being able to have sex with her".

"But why did the two of them decide to tell you now after all this time" demands Daniel.

"For two reasons I think; one because they saw you and April together, which reminded them of that night and secondly because after Dartmoor they were both disgusted by William and the way he operated, that they stopped being friends. They also felt bad that he had ruined your relationship with Theresa and wanted you to know the truth".

Daniel's mind is by now reeling with this revelation as he revisits the events of that night and how he reacted to Theresa. As he remembers he recalls how he felt about her and the wonderful time they had together and he feels ashamed. Finally, her words of innocence come back to him, which are swiftly followed by his uncompromising, unbelieving response to them.

But he is with April now and they have a fantastic relationship and he thinks that he is in love with her. But if that is the case, why can't he forget Theresa? He thought that he had, but Martin's revelation has bought her once again to the forefront of his mind and he cannot quite shake off the image of her laughing and joking with him during those few days and then their love making together at night in the tent.

"Thank you for telling me Martin, I appreciate it, I really do. If I see her before I go home, I will apologize, but I doubt very much that she will accept it".

Returning to the hall, Daniel is pleased to see April talking animatedly to her group of friends, her beauty and happiness obvious to those around her, making his doubts about Theresa recede for a while, only to discover that after a short period they have resurfaced as he recalls once again his feelings for her on Dartmoor.

As the evening draws to a close April joins him again and says" do you remember what I said about finding a room for tonight? Well as luck would have it, I had an extra key cut for my room last term in case Wendy or I lost the only other one that we had, which means that the room is still unoccupied until the new term starts next week. Several of my friends have got the same problem as us, which they have resolved in a similar fashion. Sandra and Caroline have a key to their old room which they intend to use for Martin and James to join them. As you can see there are a number of them who are going to do the same thing and we have all agreed that we tell our parents that we are going out to a night club in Exeter, so what do you say".

Although the thought of not telling Ella the truth appalls Daniel, the chance of one last night with April has an even stronger pull, so he readily agrees.

"I will have to take my mother back to the Guest House, so I will tell her on the way back, after which I will come back here for you".

Ella, not having been born the previous day, is not taken in by Daniels story of going on to a night club with his friends, but remembers the times when she and Richard wanted to be alone to express their feelings and needs with each other, so merely says "well don't leave it too late, because we will need to be away by eleven o'clock in the morning so that we can get to the graduation ceremony at midday" and then smiling "have a good time".

Daniel returns hurriedly to the hall to find April, virtually on her own, all the other couples already having departed to their rooms.

They are already half undressed as they reach Aprils old room, being totally unable to keep their hands off each other, their hunger at fever pitch. Their love making is intense, each trying to satisfy the other, until they lie totally expended together, Daniel's arm encompassing April, as if claiming his rights as her alpha male.

But strangely, now is the time that the doubts about their future come to the surface as April whispers tentatively "you are sure that you want us to continue to see each other in the future, despite the difficulties of not being together very often".

"Of course, you must know that by now" declares Daniel, brushing away mind visions of Theresa which have kept intruding since Martin told him the true version of what occurred on Dartmoor.

But April needs the comfort and security that the distance between them will not be a problem and replies "you must know how I feel about you, but the thing that I dread most is a repeat of that which happened when I left home to start university. My then boyfriend and I agreed that we would be faithful to each other, and I was, as you know, because I wouldn't go out with you for that very reason. I couldn't bear the thought of the same thing happening again with you".

"You have no reason to worry about that my love, because I feel the same way about you. I don't know how easy or difficult it will be, or how often, because I have no idea of the commitments that my new job will demand. I guess that sometimes I will have to work weekends as and when the occasion arises, but we will just have to see. The only thing that I will say is that if it is humanly possible, we will be together at weekends at least, maybe more, once your university semesters finish in Bristol".

This precious night continues as their conversation alternates with their love making, as they first try to solve the unknowable, and when no satisfactory answers are available, they resort to the one overwhelming thing that they hope will be enough to weld them together over the difficult times to come. They consume each other as their lovemaking becomes even more intense, reaching new heights as they seek to satisfy the other's needs, and after they climax, a more measured and tender period follows as they continue to touch and hold each other.

They both dread the thought that they will soon have to return to their respective guest houses before sunrise, but the time is rapidly approaching, so Daniel takes her one last time, exploring her very being as she moans softly in response.

They can no longer delay, so they dress hurriedly and say their goodbyes before leaving.

Daniel creeps back to his room at the guest house just as the sun is rising and he realizes that he will not get much sleep before he has to go down to breakfast to meet his mother.

* * *

Ella sits in the hall as each graduate's name is called, waiting, for what, to her seems forever, for her sons to be announced.

Tears run unrestrained down her face as he is eventually called onto the stage to receive his diploma. She is mesmerized as he stands in his traditional robe and hat, looking the image of his father at the same age, smiling broadly as he looks for her in the audience and finds her.

Once all the graduates have received their diplomas, they and their families all spill outside onto the grass where photographs are taken and the traditional hat throwing into the air takes place. While this is happening, Ella is busy taking as many pictures as she can with a new camera which she has bought just for this occasion. It is while she is doing this that she captures, completely accidentally a most significant image of Daniel as a female student passes by behind her, who he can see, but Ella can't. His face takes on a different expression as this occurs, one of a mixture of sadness and loss which is so obvious that Ella cannot possibly mistake it.

She continues to click the shutter, but is surprised as Daniel calls out to the person behind her "Hey Theresa, hold on a minute, I would just like a quick word" and as she stands and waits Ella swings round to see who it can be that is having such a dramatic effect on her son.

As Daniel reaches Theresa, Ella can see that she is a brunette whose hair is cut short and shaped into a bob fashion with a fringe at the front with tendrils extending down over her ears and sweeping across her cheeks. She has dark brown eyes which appear to be almost jet black when she frowns as she does now. Quite tall, her height is emphasized by her slim figure.

Ella waits as Daniel reaches Theresa and they stand talking together and she suddenly realizes that her son is embarrassed and is trying to apologize for some unknown reason. She catches the odd word or two as he humbles himself to her. "I should have believed you………can you please forgive me……" This continues for a few seconds, during which Theresa makes no reply until she suddenly says abruptly as she sees another man approaching "Oh don't worry about that, I forgot about it a long time ago" and then "Daniel let me introduce you to my boyfriend Peter" indicating the new arrival.

Ella sees a tall, six-foot, broad shouldered man who appears to be in his mid-twenties of dark complexion, with long jet-black unruly hair that hangs loosely over his forehead, which he brushes back with his hands at regular intervals. As Theresa speaks Ella sees her features transformed by her ready smile which lights up her face.

By comparison, Daniels features convey a look of complete and utter shock as he hears this news, managing only to mumble a curt "pleased to meet you Peter" before making his own apologies and returning to Ella, who to her credit, has continued to take photographs of the whole episode. She doesn't pursue the matter with him, realizing that he is embarrassed and does not wish to add to his discomfort, but does question in her own mind just what it is that can have caused him so much obvious pain. She and Daniel then go to find April and her parents to take more photographs before saying goodbye.

Malcolm and Audrey again extend their offer for Ella to visit them, which she acquiesces to, saying "Thank you for your very kind offer. I would love that but as I explained my Cafe keeps me very busy and my parents are getting more elderly now, so it may be sometime before I can manage it. But similarly, you are most welcome to visit me anytime".

The subject it is left at that, but Ella is concerned when she reflects on the meeting of Daniel and Theresa earlier and wonders where his true affections really lie: as indeed does Daniel himself, if she only knew it.

On Daniel's part, seeing Theresa has been a wake-up call, which has made him realise much too late of his true feelings for her. He finds it impossible to reconcile his feelings for both April and Theresa, the former for which he has a very strong relationship, loving her company and laughter, while recognizing also that their sexual relationship is a major factor. On the other hand he knows that every time he sees Theresa that he is drawn inexorably to her, but this morning's apology has been swept aside as if of no consequence, with the introduction of her boyfriend being the final coupe-de –gras, and he wonders what might have been if the bastard William had not tried to take advantage of her on Dartmoor. His misery is compounded every time he remembers this morning's encounter and knows that it will take a long time for the scars to heal.

CHAPTER 19.

1959.
LONDON AND BRISTOL.

Daniel decides to leave for London several days before he is due to start work at The Daily Compass in order to find accommodation and acclimatize himself with his surroundings. He travels by train because he is not able to take his belongings with him on the motor bike, but vows to return and collect it as soon as possible. On arrival his first priority is to try to find somewhere to live from the list that the personnel department of the paper has provided.

To his utter surprise and delight he finds a flat on his first attempt in Southwark, only a few minutes' walk from Blackfriars Bridge to the Victoria Embankment, which in turn is a short walk to Fleet Street.

After knocking on the door several times at this address, a man answers saying irritably "Yes, what do you want, can't you read the notice. It is there for a purpose, because I work nights at the printers setting up the paper for the next day, so I only get to bed at seven in the morning".

As Daniel looks to where the man is pointing on the front door, he is mortified to see the said notice and apologizes. "I am so sorry to wake you; I didn't see the notice. The reason I am here is to see if you have a spare room; I was given your address by The Daily Compass who said that you may have one".

The man, who Daniel can now see is in his mid-twenties, has fair tousled hair and complexion. His eyes are red rimmed and deep sunken (due no doubt to the fact that he has been woken from a deep sleep). He is tall and lean and has stubble of several days' growth which gives him a wild unkempt appearance.

As Daniel explains the reason for his visit, the man's eyes light up and he says" oh, in that case I am glad you woke me, I have been looking for someone to share for a while now. Come on in and I will show you round; my name is Charles by the way, but everyone calls me Chas".

Entering, Daniel replies "well my name is Daniel, but my friends call me Dan".

Chas shows Daniel round the two bedrooms flat which is over a shop selling green groceries. The décor has seen much better days, but is clean and tidy. There is a reasonably sized living room which has a black and white television in one corner with two unmatched settees spaced appropriately to enable occupants to see it while still being able to sit in front of the electric fire if necessary. There is a small kitchen which has a cooker, sink and a number of cupboards, together with a small fridge. Finally, In the middle of the room there is a small table with two chairs. Chas finishes his tour by showing Daniel the bathroom and toilet. "Well, what do you think Dan" says Chas naming a price for the rent, adding, "Costs for electricity and heating we share, so how does that sound"?

Daniel is pleased and shocked simultaneously. Pleased because he has found somewhere to live, but shocked at the cost, although he knows from looking at a number of agencies that it is by no means extortionate for London.

"Is there anywhere that I can park my motor bike and how do I get my laundry done" are the only two things that Daniel can think to ask Chas, who replies "There is a small courtyard at the back which is not big enough to swing a chicken (though why would you want to anyway I don't know), so you can use that: as for washing, I take my stuff to the launderette up the road once a week or so".

As they continue to discuss the matter, Daniel begins to warm to Chas who is funny and very down to earth. Carefully Daniel broaches the subject of April visiting him some weekends and is pleased when Chas replies "Oh that won't be a problem Dan, my girlfriend often stays here and the beds are both doubles as you saw. I expect you will go home to Chipping Norton sometimes, as I do to Maidstone".

Chas makes tea as they sit and talk and he explains that he has worked in London for several years after taking an apprenticeship in printing. All costs having been agreed, Daniel pays Chas two weeks rent, of which one week is in advance.

"I am so pleased that you coming here "says Chas "I have been looking for someone for several weeks, but I have not found anyone suitable. The right person must be considerate and be prepared, with me, to keep the place clean and tidy. I don't need anyone who is likely to give me trouble with the landlord. Luckily you seem to fit the criteria like a glove".

"Well thanks for that Chas; look what I would like to do now is to leave my suitcase and belongings in my room, so that I can return home to Chipping Norton to get my motor bike, which I will probably ride back here tomorrow".

* * *

From the very first Daniel is intoxicated with London. It is as if it is the last piece of a jigsaw that he has been searching for all his life. His first few days at work are spent being taught the journalists shorthand, which will be so fundamental to his progression in the industry. He has a short period every day with a tutor who shows him the subject and sets him a task for the following day. After that he has a small desk in the main office which has a typewriter and a notebook. As news stories break, he invariably joins a senior journalist, (usually Harry) in the field to get some experience.

Little does Daniel know it but the sixties are to be the defining decade of the century. The forties and fifties were beset by rebuilding and the last of the food rationing after the Second World War, but all of these were swept away as the Swinging Sixties progressed, and the centre of the world during this period is London.

Harry is an invaluable mentor and advisor to Daniel, specializing in crime, while others have their own area of expertise, be it The Royal Family or politics as they attend places where news is breaking, be it a society wedding, a car crash or the scene of a violent assault; very occasionally it might be where a murder has occurred. When any of these happen, it is always the senior journalist's name that appears, but Daniel doesn't mind, being grateful just to gain experience.

Harry shows Daniel how and what to ask witnesses, small time crooks or police when it is necessary. Over the years he has built up a retinue of informers, mostly small-time crooks who are prepared to betray fellow criminals for small amounts of money, just enough usually to keep them in beer for a few days. Marcus, another senior journalist who specializes in articles on The Royal Family has built up a list of people in Royal circles who will keep him informed of any juicy tittle tattle emanating from them, while Arnold has a number of members of parliament from both sides of the house who will tell him of anything that they know about any proposals or legislation that the Government is considering, which is against their own wishes and prejudice. By releasing such information, they are hoping that if it is brought into the public domain that it will prove too difficult for Government to introduce. Sometimes even, the Member of Parliament will introduce him to a member of The Cabinet.

Harry never meets his contacts while Daniel is present, saying "I am sorry Dan but the reason that you can't come is because my relationship with them is sacrosanct. They trust me not to betray their confidences because if I ever did it would place their safety, lives even, in serious jeopardy. I would not even reveal my sources if It meant that I would go to jail because of it. So, you see that even though some of them are of the criminal fraternity, trust between them and me is paramount.

* * *

For the first few weeks April is unable to visit Daniel for one reason or another. He is busy learning the journalist's shorthand, while April's commitments to her work and family are proving more than she expected. Fortunately, they are able to contact each other by phone from their respective employers, but they also write to each other regularly if this is not possible. Eventually at the end of October they finally manage to arrange for April to come to London for the week-end, so on the appointed Friday evening Daniel meets her from the train at Paddington. Their embrace is prolonged and passionate until eventually Daniel pulls away saying "come on, I have booked us a table at an Italian restaurant in Chelsea. I have not been there before but someone at work recommended it. After that I have booked seats for us to see West Side Story at the London Paladium. Does that sound O.K"?

The evening passes in a blur, both being wrapped up in each other. They enjoy the meal and theatre, but in all truth both of them cannot wait to get back to Daniels flat where they can be on their own.

Their love making is frantic and hurried the first time, as if they are trying to catch up for all the time that they have been apart. But as time passes, they take things more slowly, exploring each other's needs, until they climax simultaneously, totally consumed.

They are woken the next morning by Chas, returning from his night shift at the printers. Daniel shakes April awake and they go into the kitchen, where Chas is just making his breakfast before going to bed.

After introductions have been made Chas suddenly says "Look, my girlfriend is coming tonight and we are going to the pub for a pint and something to eat. Why don't you join us; it's good fun; they will have a singer or group so it gets noisy".

Both Daniel and April look at one another, before he says "That sounds good Chas, I think that we would both like that".

"What are you doing today then"?

"Well I thought that I could show April some tourist attractions. She has not been to London before, so it is a good opportunity for me to show her some of the sites".

Once Chas goes to bed, they leave the flat, not wanting to disturb his sleep.

Their tour starts by Daniel showing her where The Daily Compass is in Fleet Street, before catching the tube to Marble Arch where they disembark so that they can walk up Oxford Street.

April is amazed and stunned as they make their way, at the variety of goods on offer, before stopping to visit all the department stores, where she does some retail therapy, buying some clothes and a small picture for her flat.

Daniel wants to show her as much as he can in the short time that they have, so they take the tube again to Victoria and walk up to Westminster to arrive at The Houses of Parliament where April takes photographs, before they go into Westminster Abbey. Daniel has not been here before either and they spend an hour taking in the magnificent building with its thousand-year history, its statues, relics and burial places of the many famous people buried in Poets Corner. Next, they walk along the Embankment, past Big Ben where they stop for a sandwich and cups of tea and talk of what they have seen. Looking at his watch Daniel is surprised to discover that it is nearly five o'clock, so they decide that they have done enough for the day and make their way back to Daniels flat.

On arrival they find Chas is now awake and he introduces them to his girlfriend Fay, who has obviously been there for some time, because as Daniel and April walk in, there is a hurried sound of the rustle of clothes of people getting dressed.

To Daniels surprise Fay is not at all the type of girl that he imagined from the description that Chas had given. She is blond, tall and beautiful, but not in a delicate sort of way. Rather she is a confident, funny and in your face sort of woman, who obviously dominates Chas.

The evening at the pub is a great success, with great basic food, things like pie and mash, fish and chips, steaming plates of muscles or a selection of roast dinners, all washed down with beer or cider. They sit talking and laughing as the local resident folk band begins to play, enjoying each other's company. The evening passes until Fay suddenly begins laughing for no apparent reason. On being asked by Chas why, she says "I was just thinking of something my mother told me the other day about one of our neighbours who was heavily pregnant and due at any time. Well the day came when she had to go into hospital, because according to my mum, she had to be "seduced. I couldn't make head or tail of this, until I was visiting the lady in hospital a couple of days later, and she mentioned in passing that her doctor had got her into hospital, because she had been in labour so long at home, that he thought it best that she be admitted so that she could be induced".

As she finishes the four of them burst into laughter, until Daniel says "did you tell the women" only to hear Fay say "not likely, if my mum found out she wouldn't ever forgive me".

As "last orders" are called, they make their way drunkenly home, wasting no time when they get there to go to bed, both couples taking the maximum opportunity of the time available to them.

* * *

April's weekends in London become more and more infrequent as the year progresses. Although there is nowhere else that she would rather be, the toll of travel and expense, coupled with the fact that she never has any time for herself and other friends begins to erode her very soul.

Daniel does manage to travel to Bristol once or twice, but they both know instinctively that none of it is enough to sustain their relationship.

The overriding problem is that they both enjoy their jobs, which are becoming ever more demanding of them, something which neither of them is prepared to compromise on.

Christmas comes and Daniel manages to get home to see his mother for the day, before travelling to Bristol to see April on Boxing Day. For her part April sees her parents in Somerset on Christmas Day before returning to Bristol to be with Daniel when he arrives.

In reality it is the last throw of the dice, the straw that breaks the proverbial camel's back. Neither of them admit their feelings, but instinctively both know how the other feels, but it takes a further six months of death by a thousand cuts before April reluctantly calls it a day, by writing to Daniel and explaining that although she still loves him she does not want to continue their relationship in the way that it is at present. She knows that his life and work is in London which will not change, while hers is in Bristol which she doesn't want to change either.

When he receives her letter, Daniel rings April and they spend hours discussing their situation both crying inconsolably into the receiver, both knowing in their heart of hearts that this is the end of things between them, but both recognizing just how much they have been to each other.

"We can at least still be friends can't we, even though we won't be together? I would still like to think that we can still be there to support each other" says Daniel once the point of no return has been reached.

"I would like that very much, but not just yet, because I am feeling a little bruised and need some time to heal"

"Me too, but I still need to hear your voice occasionally, so I will keep in touch".

* * *

Ella is sad when Daniel tells her of his break up with April, but she retains a vivid memory of Daniel's Graduation Day in her mind, when the appearance of Theresa caused him such anguish, and thinks perhaps that his and April's decision was inevitable at some stage.

CHAPTER 20.

1960.
THE DAILY COMPASS.

Daniel's progress in journalism and the amount of time and effort that it requires, anaesthetizes to some extent his loss of April, leaving him very little time to reflect on his feelings, his work being all consuming.

He is writing his own bye lines now, on society weddings, putting his own spin on events, his dry wit pointing out things or circumstances in a non-offensive way that are funny or sad, but which would not have been noticed unless his powers of observation had not picked them up. This enables him to see little details that others miss, while his use of words draw pictures of such clarity in readers minds, which are so strong, that they can envisage themselves perhaps standing in the Church, listening to the service, or being outside waiting for their photographs to be taken next to the bride.

It is a knack, a way of seeing things and converting them from a visual image into the written word, something which will give him recognition to readers throughout his working life. His preparation for these events is the major factor that makes his writing interesting, charming and full of both pathos and laughter. He spends as much time as he can before the event researching the major players involved, for that one-minute snippet about any of them that will give his feature a difference over his competitor newspapers, however small.

It is this aspect of his work that will ensure that his progress in the industry is ensured, although to Daniel it is just something that comes naturally to his insatiable thirst for information; something that is within him that comes out when he communicates with the public. He is by now extremely proficient in the use of journalist shorthand which enables him to take notes on things that he has seen, or to write down interviews as they are being conducted. Once a ceremony is finished Daniel returns to his office to write up his notes, which together with photographs is to be included in that day's paper.

After some twelve months at the paper, he is called in to Graham Morton's office and after asking Daniel to sit down, begins "I have asked you here today to discuss your future role in the paper. I have been very impressed with your reports and Harry is always full of praise of you. I think that it is now time that you moved on to something more demanding. After mulling it over I would like it if you could follow up on stories from local newspapers that are sent in to us. You know the sort of thing "man saves cat from a tree" or "local soldier is awarded medal for gallantry in Northern Ireland". This is potentially a huge project, of which at the moment we are only scratching the surface. A lot of local newspapers will contact us if they have a juicy story that they think has something to offer on a national basis, which we pay for of course, but we don't get them all. What I need you to do Daniel is to be proactive, by building up a dossier of local newspapers and keeping in touch with them regularly, so that we can maximize their potential. Too often other daily papers beat us to the punch in these areas and we lose out, because it's no good reporting these items after another daily has printed them".

"Moving on from there what I would like to see in addition is for you to perhaps follow up some of the more newsworthy items, to dig around for other details that the local paper has missed, that would give the story more impetus. Your style of writing is ready made for this; your observation, analysis and writing critique is excellent and doing this well will be a big move forward for your future in journalism, so what do you say?"

Daniel is at a loss for a few moments, until he at last says "Thank you Mr. Morton, I appreciate the opportunity very much, but where do I start"?

"Well at the moment if a paper or individual contact us with information, the person who receives it deals with it individually. However, you can see that by doing it this way we have no cohesive file or list of who they are. What is needed is for you to compile a record of these contacts, along with the very many others which we do not have at present, so that we can be in the driving seat so to speak. We need to get to the position where we can contact these people to see if they have something newsworthy before they take it to the opposition. Does that make sense"?

"Yes sir, I understand perfectly".

"Good, then I will make arrangements for you to be allocated an office, not a very big one though, but somewhere you can build up a catalogue of contacts for the purpose. I will also inform all staff that when such items are received that they are forwarded to you to be dealt with".

* * *

If Daniel thought that his life had been busy up to this point, he is soon made aware that it has been as nothing compared to his new role. But he takes great pleasure in it, knowing that if he does it well, it will give him the tools to speed his progress in journalism.

Initially he works seven days a week, speaking to those members of staff who have contacts with local newspapers, so that he can begin building a dossier, before he can move on to make his own contacts. The small list that other staff provides for him is indicative of why Graham Morton wants Daniel to do this function.

He begins adding to his list as he makes contacts with larger regional newspapers at first, before drilling down to smaller provincial ones. This involves giving them his name as the contact when they have stories that may be of interest to The Daily Compass. Obviously, the newspapers want either a monetary reward or a mention as the source of the report.

He makes good progress for a while until suddenly the hard work that he has made begins to reap rewards, as stories begin to come in to him from the contacts that he has made. At first when this happens, he has very little time to verify the content, other than preliminary checks with the newspaper or person from where the story has originated, but he knows that at some stage it will be necessary to investigate further, to establish if there is further information to be gleaned. This begins to happen eventually and he sometimes has to make a pilgrimage to the place from where the story originates, to interview either witnesses to the event or the people concerned. In this way he is often able to obtain the additional nugget of information that, together with his small observations which he brings to it, makes the story much more interesting.

As this begins to happen more and more, Graham Morton begins to see how right he was to get a contact list made, while also realizing that his appointment of Daniel to do it was a stroke of pure genius.

From a position of hardly ever being the first national daily to print these local stories of interest, The Daily Compass is now nearly always the first, or in contention to print them.

Daniels main problem now is that his success threatens the development of the contact list, as he finds that he has less and less time to work on it, because he is too busy following up leads from local papers.

After several months Graham Morton holds a progress meeting with Daniel and congratulates the latter saying "Well Daniel I just wanted to catch up with you and thank you for all your hard work. Some of the stories that you have managed to get from local sources have been fantastic. Not only that but you have managed to get them before the opposition. I just wanted to see you, to ask how things are from your perspective, because I only see the results of your labour and not the problems you experience getting it. Is there anything else that you need to continue this excellent work"?

"Thank you for your support," replies Daniel "My major problem now is that I have very little time to build the contact list because I am verifying stories that are coming in, either on the phone, or alternatively, out in the field on location. It would help me enormously if I could have a part time secretary to assist me taking and making calls, or if not, a student just joining who, could be a "go-for" while I am out".

"Leave it with me Dan; I will see what I can do. In the meantime, keep managing as best you can, but you are right, if you have to choose between getting a story or building the contact list, the story must always come first. You are doing a great job Dan; I think that you have a great future in this industry".

Within a few days Daniel has the facility of a pool secretary for five mornings per week. This creates minor space problems of where she sits and works, but these are overcome to a large extent, because Dan is very often not in the office, so they compromise as best they can. Pamela is an older woman who has worked for the company for many years, so Daniel is appreciative of her experience and knowledge of who people are, and the departments they work for. This means that he can tell her what needs doing and if he has to go out, he can leave her to it, safe in the knowledge that she will carry out his wishes, or if not, leave it until he returns so that she can ask him later.

By now Daniel's social life is effectively defunct, apart from an occasional visit from his mother Ella, who realizes right from the beginning that his new position is totally demanding and all consuming. This means that if she is to see him at all she will have to go to him in London, but she thinks it worth the effort, taking him little luxuries that she knows he will never buy for himself. If she can see him on a Saturday, she tries to book tickets for the cinema or a theatre, just to get him away from his job for a short period, after which they go for a meal, before Daniel accompanies her to Paddington in time for her return to Chipping Norton.

Daniel continues to keep in touch with April, telephoning her weekly, but now that the fire has gone out between them, there is very little that they have to say to one another. Then after several months April shocks him to the core when she announces that she is seeing someone else. Obviously, Daniel knows that this is inevitable, but she is one of the last links that he has with his University life and he knows that he will miss speaking to her dreadfully. He even questions his feelings for her, wondering if he should have fought harder to keep her, but knowing deep inside that their time has come and gone, so he congratulates her and wishes only the best for her. By the time that they disconnect the call they are both in floods of tears, but both of them also realise that their worlds have moved on, taking them to different places.

When he is told that Daniel and April's relationship is finished, his flat mate Chas surprises him with his concern "I thought that you two were joined at the hip for life" he exclaims when Daniel tells him. "Never mind Dan, I tell you what, why don't you come out to the pub with Fay and me on Saturday; we can have a few pints and a laugh and it will take you out of yourself. No wait, better still, I will see if Fay has got a friend that she can bring to keep you company".

Daniel laughs when he hears Chas's offer, before saying "no, it's O.K. I think that April and I had just about run our course, although it was a bit of a jolt when it happened, but thanks for your offer. I won't come with you this time but I would like that very much some other time". As he finishes Daniel is suddenly aware of just how far his relationship with Chas has come. From co-inhabitants, and although they only see each other fleetingly, Daniel now looks upon Chas as a friend. The thought gives him a warm glow and some comfort in the wake of breaking up with April.

But Daniel's main focus now is on his work as he spends hours looking at the many items that come into his office from local newspapers each week. Some are considered good enough to be included for publication, some are discarded as having insufficient interest on a national level, and the remainder is those that attract Daniel's attention as having a good story line, but also the have the possibility with further investigation of being of even more interest to the public. It is these that Daniel pursues personally, by visiting the area from where the item has originated and talking first to the people concerned, before looking further into the incident to find that missing ingredient that will transform the story from a good one into a great one.

On one occasion Daniel had received an item from a paper in a little village in Dorset about a man who had rescued a young boy of eight years of age who had been with a friend trying to skate on a frozen pond. The ice was not thick enough in the middle to support them and it suddenly cracked and one of the boys fell into the freezing water. Luckily the second boy made his way to the edge of the pond screaming for help. As luck would have it a young man was passing by and witnessed the incident. He quickly realized that if he tried to reach the lad in the water, the ice would probably give way again, so he went onto the ice as far as he was able before taking off his jacket and lying flat to spread his weight as much as possible. Then he threw his jacket for the young boy to reach, while retaining hold of it himself. In this manner, the boy eventually managed to pull himself out of the water and onto the ice, the young man talking to him and encouraging him all the while.

Backing off slowly the two off them managed to get to dry land.

The incident was reported by the local paper and the young man was recommended for an award, but Daniel while thinking it was a worthy story for a national paper to carry, thought that there just might be something more, so he caught the train down to Weymouth and made his way to the village where the incident had occurred.

He began by interviewing the two boys that had been involved, but despite all his efforts he was unable to extract any further information, other than the fact that both sets of parents insisted on telling him how grateful they were to the man who saved their children and wanted it put on record that he deserved a commendation for what he had done.

Feeling that he had achieved very little so far, Daniel decided to talk to Frank Dugdale, the person who had performed the dangerous rescue.

This time he hits gold dust, after talking through the incident again with Frank, an open, unassuming man of about twenty years of age, who brushes away Daniels plaudits before replying apologetically" I am not trying to say that it was nothing, because I was quite scared, but what else could I do, I would not have been able to live with myself if I had done nothing and the boy had drowned, that would have been terrible".

Daniel is full of admiration as he listens to this incredibly brave man, who doesn't even recognize how brave he is, someone who weighed up the risk of this particular situation and went ahead with the rescue despite his fears and the very real risk for his own safety. But after talking to him further Daniel discovers the missing ingredient that makes this story have even more appeal to readers when he asks Frank what he had been doing at this place on this particular day; was it the way he would normally go to work for example, or was it for some other reason.

"Well that was the strangest thing about it really because I don't usually go that way at all, but I was on my way to an interview for a job in town, so I took a shortcut to get there".

"You mean that it was sheer coincidence and that you wouldn't normally have been there" says Daniel, and then as another thought strikes him "how did you get on with the interview anyway".

Looking despondent for the first time Frank continues "Unfortunately I was unable to attend because the whole thing made me too late, and anyway my clothes were pretty much ruined, so I didn't get there".

"You mean that you lost a job opportunity because you took the time to save a child from drowning. What job was it and why were you going to an interview anyway" says Daniel, sensing a story.

"I have been out of work for several months after being made redundant at an advertising agency and the interview was with a large conglomerate, working in the marketing department".

Here then was Daniel's story and after talking it through in greater depth with Frank he finishes by saying "well I think that is tragic Frank, but what I can do is to include it in my story for The Daily Compass. You never know the company may read it and invite you back again for an interview".

Taking his leave Daniel returns to London, but not before telephoning the company that Frank had been due to attend an interview for on that fateful day. After getting put through to the person concerned that Frank had been due to see, Daniel explains in great detail why he had been unable to attend and then goes on to say that The Daily Compass will be printing the story that day.

"Come to think of it, I did see that story in the local paper, but I didn't associate the person who saved the child as being one and the same person that didn't turn up for the interview. Thank you for telling me, we have not made a decision as yet regarding the vacancy, so I will get in touch with him and arrange another interview. I can't of course guarantee that he will get the position, but he at least deserves a chance".

"Of course, but I thought that you should know before I print the story, so that you can do something about it".

Daniel duly prints the story in that day's edition which causes a huge amount of public interest. A few days later he gets a call from Frank thanking him and saying that he has had an interview with the Company and has been offered a different position in their advertising department.

"I'm so pleased, but it's not finished yet Frank" says Daniel "I hear on the grapevine that your name has been put forward for a gallantry award".

These then are the type of stories that Daniel is searching for; where he can sense that there is another dimension that has been missed that will make the story even more appealing to The Daily Compass readers.

CHAPTER 21.

THE PINES.

For her part Ella's life has burgeoned since Daniel left for London, although she misses him terribly at first, feeling almost that she has been widowed for a second time. But he always makes time to return home when he can and she is grateful for that.

The Café has continued to grow and she has come to realize that there is a need for a more formal restaurant that people can go to for lunch and evening meals in addition to the facilities that she already offers. She speaks to Rachel, her sister and mentor about such an enterprise, who encourages her to look for suitable premises because it will be a totally different operation from the Café and suggests that she speak to Mr Souch.

"You do realize that it will take much more of your time Ella. Not only that but it will be more unsociable hours".

"I know that but I love the type of work and anyway it's become my life now: what else am I going to do with myself".

Rachel is made aware once again that her sister is still mourning for her husband even after so many years, and that work is the only antidote that stops the process, at least while she is occupied.

"Fiona can run the café pretty much without me now, so if I make her Manager and find someone else to take her place it will give me time to take on another project. I will still keep my eye on the Café of course, but Fiona and Catherine have proved to be very capable from time to time in my absence. The only condition from my point of view is that if I am to do this then the location must be in Chipping Norton, because I don't want to be far away from everything that I know".

* * *

On approaching Mr Souch she finds to her delight that he agrees with her about opening a restaurant.

"There is a need now in the town; people are becoming more affluent and at present their only option is to travel into Oxford if they want to eat out in the evening. In fact, if you don't do it Ella, someone else very soon will. I don't have any suitable premises available at the moment, but I know another landlord who does and will jump at the opportunity. The place he has is in a really central position in the town and is just the right size for your needs. The shop has been unoccupied for some time now, since it closed as a furniture shop, so you are in a strong position to negotiate a favourable rent. I tell you what, I will speak to him and arrange a get together and if you like I will sit in the meeting with you to help protect your interests".

Sure enough Mr. Souch is as good as his word and Ella manages to get a five-year lease on the property concerned at a very good rent, which is fixed for two years and can only be increased by a maximum of two and a half percent per year after that.

Ella is stimulated once again and concentrates all her energy into the new project, after appointing Fiona as Manager of the Café with Catherine as her number two. When she tells her, Fiona breaks down in tears until Ella consoles her saying "Look, you both deserve this, because without you I couldn't possibly have been so successful. Anyway, you are both more than just people who work for me now, because I look on you both as friends. I tell you what, why don't we go out and celebrate this evening; you can bring your husbands? I will pay of course".

* * *

The Restaurant, which Ella names "The Pines" in tribute to these trees that grow all along the road which runs outside the premises, needs considerable investment to convert it to its change of use. This time however Ella is able to get a bank loan on the strength of the Cafe's performance, because they welcome her back with open arms. Rachel helps her with the design and layout, and it takes two months for the transformation to take place. The look that Ella wants to achieve is that one that where people can go to in an environment that is relaxed and welcoming. To achieve this end the restaurant walls are painted a pale muted cream colour, while there is a profusion of expensive lined drapes hanging from floor to ceiling along the wall which had previously been the shop window. A heavy duty Axminster carpet covers the floor, which has room for fifteen tables, each are able to sit between two, four and six people. Lamps are distributed throughout the room, some of which are on tables, while other light is provided by uplighters on the walls, all of which are subdued. The whole ambience that Ella is trying to create is one of quiet opulence where people can relax with food and drink of the highest quality.

For people arriving she has arranged a small area just inside the entrance door, where there are two sofas and a couple of winged chairs.

It is here her clients can sit and have drinks and order from the menu, before going to their tables.

Ella has spared no expense because she knows from her previous life at The Manor House, beautiful surroundings, together with good food and drink at a reasonable price will encourage people to return again and again.

The other major area that Ella turns her attention to is the kitchen which is at the back of the premises. This time she doesn't compromise on second hand equipment, but with a blank canvas before her, designs a room with all aluminum surfaces that can be easily wiped down, during and after use. The "Best Of" theme is replicated in the purchase of ovens, equipment and utensils, because she is determined to provide the very best produce for her customers, in both a clean and sterile environment.

Once these areas have been tackled Ella turns her thoughts to who she should have in the kitchen to help her provide the quality products that a place of this stature demands. After much consideration she decides that initially she will be the Head Chef, but will in addition take on a senior Sous Chef who can work under her, but will also be capable of taking charge temporarily when she is not there, or even permanently at some time in the future if she so chooses.

The Pines is duly opened in late September and is an immediate success, Ella having managing to find a Sous Chef just in time, as well as two waitresses who have been vetted by Catherine.

For the first few weeks Ella is in control of all the cooking and the choice of menus, because she needs to discover for herself just how efficient the kitchen that she has designed is, so that any faults can be ironed out as they arise. She quickly finds that the amount of work that she has taken on is extremely onerous, leaving her little time for the Café or even worse, the catering business which she has overlooked somewhat in the excitement of her new enterprise.

Tony, her new Sous Chef is soon proving to be a great addition to her team and after a few weeks she finds that she can leave him to run the kitchen, initially on the odd occasion, but increasingly for longer periods as time goes by. Eventually, taking the bull by the horns she appoints him as Chef and recruits another Sous Chef as Tony's number two. This leaves her more time to look at other aspects of the running of all her enterprises.

Daniel comes to the opening of The Pines, the first time that Ella has seen her son for several months. He is really impressed with the restaurant, saying "It is my turn to be proud of you for a change mum. Well done, it is just what this town needs".

"What are you doing now son, are you still investigating local news items".

Well I have been, but I got called into my boss's room the other day and he told me that Harry is intending to retire shortly and that he wants me to take over his job".

"I'm so pleased for you Daniel, you must be thrilled and delighted; at least I assume you are"? says Ella, detecting a hesitancy in both her sons voice and posture. But she is reassured when he replies "I most certainly am, because from my point of view it will give me more opportunities to investigate serious crime, which is something that I have always wanted to do".

Before Daniel returns to London, he visits his grandparents with Ella and is shocked to see how ill Alf is looking, as he struggles to breathe, his pallor grey, his face lined with pain. Elizabeth although cheerful is also looking strained, due no doubt to having to look after her husband.

They spend the afternoon reminiscing before Daniel takes Charlie for a walk across the fields where he grew up, the dog barking excitedly at anything that moves, even leaves that fall from the trees as the change in the season approaches, their colours of red and gold carpeting the floor beneath them.

It is obviously a rare treat for Charlie and Daniel suddenly realizes that Alf's condition has stopped him from doing even this simple chore. As he and Ella take their leave from his grandparents, he little realizes that it will be the last time that he sees his grandfather, this rather gruff old man with a heart of gold, who has meant so much to him growing up in this magical village.

Ella is also disturbed to see just how much her father has degenerated even since her last visit, just over two months previously. This length of time is unusual for her, but is due mainly to the fact that her every waking minute has been spent on the opening of The Pines. She berates herself for not finding the time to visit earlier, but determines that she will see them much more regularly in future, beginning by inviting them both to The Pines the next week, saying that she will both collect them and return them home afterwards.

On her return Ella contacts her sister Rachel and explains her concern about her parent's health, before asking "do you realize just how ill Dad is, because he looks terrible".

"Of course, Ella, but I didn't want to tell you just yet, not until at least you had got the Restaurant up and running. I should have told you I know, but every time I spoke to Dad, he insisted that you had enough on your plate without having to worry about the two of them".

Ella is shocked once more that she has been so absorbed with her own problems that she has completely overlooked her parent's welfare and resolves that she will never let it happen again.

She is as good as her thoughts from this point on, making sure that she spends at least one-half day a week with them, usually in Chadlington, because it is becoming ever more difficult for Alf to leave his cottage due to his poor health. Her time here is usually spent on washing clothes and cleaning the cottage, to relieve Elizabeth as much as possible so that she can attend to Alf.

As Christmas approaches, Ella is inundated with extra work. Her restaurant has been booked to capacity for the whole period, as indeed is her catering operation, so much so that she has to recruit several women from Chadlington to assist her.

There are a number of corporate bookings for both the Restaurant and Catering which is both very satisfying and stressful at the same time, but she will not let anything detract her from giving her parent's the attention they deserve.

The catering operation is also particularly busy at this time of year, which causes Ella the most work, because although it is lucrative, it is sporadic and by definition requires an immediate response. The bookings generally are for weddings, mostly in the summer and corporate bookings mostly in the run-up period to Christmas, although christenings and birthdays also occur. It is therefore difficult to forecast, which means that Ella cannot afford to appoint anyone to run it, because bookings only happen approximately forty times a year. One other major factor is that because it is Ella's personal baby, she is not prepared to hire someone to visit clients, preferring to sell the product herself, because she understands their needs and requirements far better than anybody else.

Having no other alternative, she soldiers on, responding to client's requests and hiring staff for waitress and other services on the day, relying heavily on Fiona to assist her preparing the food, which she delivers to site on the required day. The system works for now, but she also knows that if orders increase substantially, she will have to consider more permanent staff.

As Christmas draws ever nearer, Ella is determined that she will host a family get together and although that this is something that she does more often than not, her main consideration is to take pressure off of her mother, who is beginning to look as frail as Alf.

Rachel readily agrees to help, so Christmas day finds the whole family in Chadlington ready to celebrate the festive season: that is with the exception of Daniel who unexpectedly has to work, due to the fact that a huge robbery has taken place in a bank vault at a location near Hatton

Gardens during the night of Christmas Eve and in his new role of criminal reporting he needs to investigate and write a report for publication.

Ella is mortified but understands, telling him that she will visit him in London for New Year's Eve.

As they gather together on Christmas Day in Chadington, Alf is on top form, relishing seeing his children and grandchildren, as he relates stories of Christmas growing up.

"My father worked in the cowshed and he still had to milk over sixty cows by hand morning and night, even on Christmas Day, so we didn't see much of him but he always came into our bedroom at five o'clock before he had to go to the dairy and watch us open our stockings. These usually contained an apple, an orange and if we were lucky a banana. Sometimes there might be a wooden toy, a train, or a soldier or a doll for my sisters, but that was about it. Then in the afternoon, after he had a nap, we would listen to the Kings speech and then we would play charades or cards".

"The Lord of the Manor usually gave a bottle of whisky to all his workers and my dad would pour a small amount in our tea for breakfast. It tasted horrible, but we never said anything, because it made him happy. We never had television, or a radio either come to that, but we always seemed to have plenty to do. Dad kept chickens in a run in the garden and he used to kill one for Christmas dinner. He would kill several and either sell them to local villagers or give them to someone who had helped us during the year. It was very much an exchange or barter system in those days, people only used money when they had to buy something in the shop".

As she listens to her father, Ella is surprised; because it is the most animated that she has seen him for a long time. He still has a cough that seems to start somewhere from within his very soul at regular intervals, and when it happens, she can see the pain etched upon his careworn face, and she feels her love for her father threaten to overwhelm her. But she is happy for him at the same time, as he holds court over his family.

On the other hand, Elizabeth has taken the opportunity to sit back and relax as her daughters take control from her. In this way the afternoon and evening passes with them all talking and laughing enjoying each other's company. They sit in front of a roaring log fire and nobody turns the lights on, preferring to sit and watch its flickering flame which illuminates their faces as Alf continues to tell his stories, one of the others only interrupting him occasionally to query or expand on something that he has said.

But eventually Alf's exertions get the better of him and he falls silent, almost as if he has achieved something intangible to everyone except himself, but which Ella interprets as an urgent need for him to reveal parts of his life that they had never heard him talk about before.

It is with a sense of mounting loss that Ella suddenly realizes that Alf is saying goodbye to his family, even though he probably is completely unaware that he is doing so. Fortunately, other than Ella, nobody else has recognized this unconscious revelation, for which she is profoundly grateful, although it means that she has to bear the burden on her own.

As she silent meditates his unconscious admission, tears begin to run down her cheeks, which she hurriedly brushes away, but not before she looks across to Alf, only to see him smiling back at her, as if acknowledging his secret between them.

As they all prepare to leave at the end of the evening, saying their goodbyes, Alf suddenly says to Ella "I am so sorry that Daniel couldn't make it today. Tell him from me that he needs to come and walk Charlie more often, cos I can't do it anymore. One other thing Ella, I have never told you how proud I am of both you and Daniel. You have both achieved so much despite losing Richard, and things have not been easy for you, but ………".

Ella stops him at this point, putting her hand over his mouth before saying "That is because I have the best parents and sister in the world and without whom it would not have been possible. So, thank you Dad for everything".

As she leaves her parents Ella knows that she and Alf have both been saying goodbye to one another and cries inconsolably to herself all the way home.

* * *

Ella travels to London on New Year's Eve, to meet Daniel who has arranged to take her to see "The Mousetrap" an Agatha Christie mystery play, and then for a meal afterwards. Gathering up her courage she tells him about Christmas and Alf in particular, and of her conviction that he was saying his goodbyes to them.

"I have never been so certain of anything in my life before Daniel. It was if he knew and I felt so helpless".

She stops speaking with tears streaming down her face until Daniel holds her to him saying "I am so sorry mum, but I am sure that you are right. Alf has seen enough of life both with people and animals, to recognize the signs of his own mortality. Try to be positive and not be upset, because he wouldn't want that; anyway, you will need all your strength and energy to help grandma at the time when something happens"

"I know that you are right son, but it feels like someone is playing a sick joke on us, pulling us first one way and then the other" and then, pulling herself together "but I suppose that we must put a brave face on things for mum's sake.

They walk down to see the lights on the bridges and The Embankment which illuminate The Thames as it snakes through the Capital on its way to the sea. It is a strangely comforting moment as they join hundreds of others singing and partying as they wait for the New Year to come in. When Big Ben at Westminster strikes midnight, a great cheer goes up as people kiss, and wish each other A Happy New Year, which only makes Ella even sadder, because she has great reservations about the coming year. As she stands together with her son with the tumult of noise and merrymaking going on all around them, she is suddenly aware that Daniel has not said very much about his life and work at the paper. Summoning up her courage she inquires "so how are things with you Daniel, you haven't mentioned you work all evening; did you find out anything about the robbery in Hatton Gardens that made it not possible for you to come to us at Christmas".

Daniel looks pensive for a while before replying "well the robbers managed to break into the vault below the bank and get into the room where customers' personal safety boxes were kept; things like jewelry or valuable paintings. The problem is that the police don't know just how much has been stolen because the owners are loathe to tell them for one reason or another, probably in some cases because the goods concerned were already stolen, or in others that some clients were claiming for items that were not in their boxes anyway. The long and short of it is that I have managed to identify a number of likely suspects who carried out the raid, but proving it is a little more difficult".

"How did you manage to do that"?

"Well I quickly learned from Harry, that to find anything out about the criminal underworld you have to have someone on the inside that is prepared to inform on them for the cost of a few quid. The only problem is that the informer's identity must be protected at all times, because once it is revealed, they are as good as dead men. The master criminals who run these operations rule by fear and retribution. I know who some of them are, but without concrete proof I am unable to put their names in print. The major problem is that my informers are not prepared to go into the witness box and reveal what they know, because they know if they do that they will go missing, their bodies probably being put into the foundations of a new motorway. Anyway, if they did, their evidence would be ignored once the defendant's barrister revealed that they had received many convictions, because they are all members of the criminal underworld. The only thing that I can do is to allude to these master criminals without actually naming them, to ensure that readers can understand what is happening mostly in London, but also in other places as well. But at least I know now where to look and if I can get hold of more information legitimately, either by following them to see who they mix with and perhaps get more reliable witnesses, then I can make a more watertight case that I can give to the police once I have gone to print".

Ella is horrified at her son's revelations and retorts" Oh Daniel, what you have told me sounds dangerous; you will be careful won't you"?

As he looks at his mother Daniel is aware that he has frightened her and tries to lighten the mood saying "Oh don't worry mum, I will be very careful in my report so that even if they recognize themselves from it, their names will not appear".

He continues "it seems incredible in this age of The Beatles, Flower Power, Free Love and Carnaby Street, that such things can be going on under our noses, but they are" and then" come on let's get you back to your hotel; it's nearly morning already".

"Now that you mention it, I am really tired" replies Ella, shaking herself to try to stay awake "but I want to go to the sales in Oxford Street in the morning before I go home".

CHAPTER 22.

1967.
ELLA'S GRIEF.

Ella's worst fears are made fact within a few short days after the New Year when she gets a hysterical telephone call on the fourteenth of January from her mother telling her that her father's condition has suddenly deteriorated and that he has been taken in to The Radcliffe Infirmary in Oxford. Quickly dropping everything she makes her way to the Hospital to meet her mother who greets her, stricken by grief and tells her that her father was declared dead on arrival.

Within minutes Rachel joins them and the three of them spend several hours consoling each other, but also not knowing what to do next. It is as if their boat has suddenly become rudderless and they don't know how to find a new course, or a way to set sail, and even if they could, which way to proceed.

A doctor eventually sees them and after offering his condolences tells them that he thinks that Alf had developed lung cancer, probably brought on from smoking cigarettes, which caused emphysema originally but that there was only palliative measures that could have been taken by the hospital even if he had not died today.

The next few weeks pass in a blur for all of them, but Ella and Rachel try not to show their sense of desolation and loss, at least while they are with Elizabeth.

Daniel manages to get to the funeral which is in Chadlington Church on the thirtieth of January. The church is full to capacity as the villagers come to say goodbye to one of their own, and afterwards there is a reception at Elizabeth's cottage, which most people attend, some of them standing out in the garden because there is not enough room inside.

Eventually most of them leave but not before they relate stories of their own recollections and experiences of Alf.

Bert Sugden makes them all laugh when he tells them of the time that he and Alf, together with a couple of other lads of their age were crossing the fields to the Church for evening service to sing in the choir.

"It was mid-winter, so it was pitch black as we made our way across the fields, all dressed up in our choir boy cassocks. Well eventually we reached a field with a stream running through, and we were all mucking about as usual and Alf for no apparent reason suddenly fell into the stream in his full choir boy regalia. He was so embarrassed, because he couldn't possibly go to the church, with his clothes wet and muddy, so the rest of us went on without him, while he hung around the village trying not to be seen until he had dried out. Waiting until it was the normal time for the service to finish, he returned home as if nothing had happened.

Everything seemed to be all right and it looked as if he had got away with it until his mother met someone while shopping in the village the next day who inquired if Alf was O.K. When his mother assured her that he was, she then went on to ask the woman why she thought that he was ill, only to be told that she had noticed that he wasn't in Church. We all had a good laugh at Alf's expense about that, but Alf always insisted that one of us had pushed him into the stream" finishes Bert.

"That's true "came a voice from behind Bert, who swinging round says "How do you know Tom Grant, you weren't even there".

"That is also true" replies Tom "but I know because my brother Wills, who was with you all on that night confessed that he did it the next day, but it has taken all these years for me to tell you. It was funny though, although Alf never missed evening service again".

"You devils" laughs Elizabeth for the first time "Alf told me all about that many times and he never did find out who did it" and then as her face crumples once more "I wish he could have been here to hear it, he would have thought it so funny. Thank you, Bert and Tom".

Both Ella and Rachel stay the night with Elizabeth, but dread the coming days when they can't be with her all the time, so they discuss ways of sharing their time so that one of them is with her as much as possible. But Elizabeth's pain at her loss is deep, and even at times when they are with her, she still feels alone, and despite their efforts her health deteriorates as she mourns her partner of over fifty years.

Ella is seriously concerned for her mother, but her next source of loss comes from a quite different quarter when Mr Souch's wife Julia, telephones her in May with the devastating news that Mr. Souch has died.

Although he was not related and it doesn't feel quite the same as that of losing her father, Ella never the less experiences a sense of such sorrow that she is at first, unable to comprehend life without him. How will she manage without the good counsel, advice and encouragement of this man who has been her friend and guide for so many years. His wife assures Ella that it was his wish that things continue on in much the same way as they have always done and that he has left her a small bequest in his will with the notation "to my friend Ella Thornton who I have watched achieve great things that even she thought was not possible, with my hope that she continues to grow and do good things for the people of Chipping Norton".

The funeral is attended by all the good and the great of Chipping Norton, but the service is quickly over as Mr Souch had indicated was his wish to his wife some years previously.

"He was never one for pomp or false idols" his wife told those who attended the hotel afterwards. "He believed in individuals and what they could contribute. That's why he took such a shine to you Ella. Although you didn't have a really good education, you were prepared to take a risk, but he knew that your experience of life and of never having very much, had taught you to be careful. But much more than any of that he knew that you would work hard once you were given the chance; and you did. He was so proud of you Ella and I know that he would want you to know that".

* * *

Although Ella has experienced two terrible losses of both family and a friend within a few months, her business enterprises continue to build and flourish, despite the fact that she is spending more and more time looking after her mother, who is showing no signs of recovering in any way from the loss of her husband. Although concerned for her mother's health, she is happy to be able to do what little she can to help her. Both she and Rachel take turns to visit Elizabeth to wash clothes and clean the cottage, but no matter what they do, Elizabeth's health continues its slow deterioration. Both of her children are at their wits end with worry, not knowing what they can do to stop the decline.

Things continue this way until late October when Ella senses something more sinister in Elizabeth's condition. Both girls have always assumed that the cause of Elizabeth's decline has been caused by Alf's death, but suddenly Elizabeth begins to complain of pains in various parts of her body; so much so that Ella decides that her mother needs to see a doctor.

Dr Gavin takes his time and examines her thoroughly, after which he sits back in his chair and considers before saying "well Elizabeth I think that you need more investigation, so I am going to write to The Radcliffe Hospital for further tests, because your symptoms could have any number of causes, so we need to eliminate the obvious first. By doing this we will eventually be left with the real reason for the discomfort and pain that you are experiencing".

Ella starts to speak, but a warning look from Dr Gavin quietens her.

"Well Elizabeth" the doctor says, (handing her a small plastic bottle)"do you think that you could squeeze a water sample while you are here, which I can send off for test purposes".

When she has left the room, Dr Gavin turns his attention to Ella, and begins "I am so sorry Ella but your mother is seriously ill. I will wait until I get the results from her tests but things don't look good. The best thing that you can do is to keep her happy and as comfortable as you can. The other thing is that do you think that she will be able to hear the truth about whatever is causing her pain, or shall I not tell her. Modern medicine generally says that the medical profession should tell the patient the truth, even though it could make them more stressed and hasten the outcome, but insists that they have a right to know. Have a think about it and let me know; perhaps you could ring me before the day I get the results and we can talk more at that time".

Ella is absolutely devastated as she hears Dr Gavin's resume, before saying "Of course doctor, but I need to think about what you have told me before then, because it has come as a bit of a shock".

"Naturally "says the doctor who Ella has known and respected all her life, his first attendance to her being on the occasion of her birth. "I can only reiterate how sorry I am and hope in fact that I am wrong, but I don't think so and thought it only best that you should know so that you have time to think about it".

* * *

On the appointed day Ella telephones Dr Gavin who tells her that his suspicions about Elizabeth are unfortunately correct, and that all indications are that she has ovarian cancer." The problem with this type of cancer is that diagnosis is invariably too late, because by the time the symptoms start to appear it has spread to other organs of the body. It is known unofficially by some as The Silent Killer for this very reason. I am so sorry my dear, but there is nothing that we, the medical profession can do, apart from giving her some palliative care in the form of drugs to lessen the pain. Have you thought whether I or you should tell her; I must say that I think that we should, because she can then get her affairs in order"?

The prognosis when it is stated in such cold terms, hits Ella like an exploding bomb and she cannot catch her breath as the shock paralyses her respiratory system. Taking deep breaths and gasping for air she eventually manages to say "I am not surprised really doctor, but I just hoped that I was wrong. The most amazing thing is that I am sure that she knows, because she keeps telling me where things are, like her will and what little money she has as well as who should get what of her personal possessions when she's gone.

"Very well then my dear, we are agreed, so I will see you both tomorrow and explain things to her".

* * *

Much to Ella and Rachel's surprise, Elizabeth accepts Dr Gavin's diagnosis of her terminal condition, and looks almost as if what he has told her has come almost as a relief.

"I thought that it was something like that Doctor, thank you for being so honest with me. At least I know now so I can prepare things in advance".

"Well I will pop in to see you as much as I can and make sure that your pain level is controlled Elizabeth".

"One final thing Doctor; can you tell me how long I have got"?

"That is very difficult to determine my dear, but I would think in terms of weeks rather than months".

* * *

Both Ella and Rachel are determined that Elizabeth will not be left on her own, so they draw up a roster in which either one or both of them will be with their mother. To their great surprise and delight for the first few weeks, while the drugs keep her pain at bay enough for her to remain alert and conscious, Elizabeth is a joy to be with. It is as if knowing that she has very little time left to her, she wants to bond with both her daughters as much as possible.

She relives her youth, telling them stories of her growing up in Chadlington, making them laugh at things they never knew about her. How she and her school friends would knock on villagers doors and run away before those inside could see who did it: or of the games they played after school, hunt the treasure was one, in which one of them would write out clues which would lead the rest of them onto the next clue, and so on until the treasure could be found, which was usually a token apple or a sweet. This would often involve going over the surrounding fields, so the clue might be a specific tree or farm building. At other times Elizabeth would tell of leaving school at thirteen, to start work on the farm. At first helping the farmer's wife with the household chores, or helping to milk cows or at harvest time to gather the corn.

But although they are fascinated to listen to Elizabeth's stories of her life, by far the most astonishing thing that they find so endearing is the humour that she manages to invariably colour them with. Every day she has something new to tell them and keep them in raptures. How she met and married Alf, keeping him waiting by going out with other boys, although she knew that he wanted to be her beau.

"I just wanted to keep him on his toes" she told them "but I always knew that he was the one for me".

She seems to be telling her life in sequence, first schooldays and living with her parents, then her courting days, followed by her wedding and marriage, before finally she got to giving birth to her "beautiful" daughters. She repeats little stories of when they were children, most of which they have heard previously, but the way she tells them again, makes them laugh, even if to only see the love in her eyes and the pleasure in her voice.

Like the time that she walked with Rachel into Chipping Norton in her pram, a journey of several miles. Then leaving her baby daughter outside she went into Boots the chemist to shop. Coming out she caught the bus to Chadlington and was over half way home before she remembered that she had left her daughter outside the shop in her pram. But the story ended well as Rachel was still there even after Elizabeth had run all the way back, still playing happily with a punnet of strawberries that she had managed to open and smear all over her face.

Rachel and Ella treasure these last few weeks with their mother, both the happy times and the bad, but are just grateful that they have had this rare opportunity to share with her at the end of her life.

Elizabeth seems to be pacing the little that remains of her life to order, because as she reaches this point, her condition takes a turn for the worse and she begins to experience severe pain. When the Doctor calls again he increases her diamorphine with the result that she is induced into a coma, sleeping most of the time.

Ella and Rachel are devastated when this happens, but grateful that their mother is not in pain, as well as that they have had the opportunity to spend so much time finding out the things about her that they never knew. A week later, only six weeks after her cancer had been diagnosed, Elizabeth slips peacefully away to join her beloved Alf, leaving her daughters to grieve once more.

Daniel is distraught when he hears and returns immediately to be at his mother's side, to support her. The funeral and service are carried out at Chadlington Church and she is buried by the side of her beloved Alf, only a few short months after him.

Ella spends Christmas with Rachel and her family, which is a subdued affair, nobody feeling like celebrating, that is until after lunch when Ella starts to tell Daniel and Rachel's family some of the stories that Elizabeth had related as she lay dying. Suddenly they all feel better as Ella and Rachel have them in stitches retelling the things that Elizabeth had told them. As they progress Ella begins to appreciate just how much her mother had achieved by both describing her life and showing them that death was not something to be feared, but a natural part of life.

On her own later, Ella offers up a silent prayer to her mother, knowing that she will always be sad at her passing, but be forever grateful for the time that she has spent with her at her end.

Daniel and Ella spend New Year together, before he has to return to London. So ends Ella's Anus Horiblis Year, not one that she is likely to ever forget.

CHAPTER 23.

1967- 1973.
DANIEL THE CRIME REPORTER.

On his return from Chadlington, Daniel begins to follow up rumours and innuendos that are prevalent in the criminal underworld, of gangsters that are operating in The East End of London. Their operations are said to include armed robberies, drugs, assaults, prostitution and protection rackets.

But unlike other gangs that have pursued such activities previously, they are smarter, because they have people of The Establishment, public figures, and politicians on their payroll. They rule their empire ruthlessly, enforcing who they consider wrong doers i.e. people who would betray them, with broken bones, or even death.

Daniel spends many hours visiting pubs in The East End of London speaking to small time villains, trying to obtain information about the gangs who are operating with impunity in the area. His efforts are not completely without reward as he finds one or two of them who are prepared to tell him what they know for the cost of a few beers. His problem is that they are at the bottom of the food chain and anything they know is of very little significance. But nearly all of them know the identity of the people operating in The East End.

Their names, which are whispered in corridors of power and seedy pubs in The East End, are twins Ronnie and Reggie Kray and the gang they run is called The Firm.

As West End nightclub owners they mix with politicians and prominent entertainers such as Diana Dors, Frank Sinatra and Judy Garland.

The police have investigated the Krays on several occasions, but the brothers' reputations for violence have always made the witnesses afraid to testify.

Just only three years previously, in 1964 an expose' in The Sunday Mirror insinuated that Ronnie had conceived a sexual relationship with a Lord, a Conservative politician at a time when male homosexuality was still a criminal offence in the U.K. Although no names were printed in the piece, the twins threatened the journalists involved, and the politician threatened to sue the newspaper.

In the face of this, the newspaper backed down, sacking its editor, printing an apology and paying the politician£40,000 in an out-of-court settlement. Because of this, other newspapers were unwilling to expose the Krays connections and criminal activities.

In 1966, the year that Ella experienced the loss of her parents, Ronnie Kray shot and killed George Cornell, a member of the Richardson's (a rival gang which operated south of the river), at the Blind Beggar pub in Whitehall. The day before, there had been a shoot-out at *Mr Smiths,* a night club in Catford, involving the Richardson gang and Richard Hart, an associate of the Krays, was shot dead. Cornell's killing was in revenge for that of Hart.

Daniel is aware of all of this, as indeed he is of many others, but getting evidence to prove anything is nigh on impossible, so he has to write articles that give the facts of any incidences that occur and ignore references to those who actually give the orders and instigate theses atrocities. He realises that he needs to find a more senior insider of the Krays, who can keep him informed of their plans and how they operate, to enable him to obtain concrete evidence.

After some considerable time, he is directed to someone, via one of his existing contacts, who he is assured, is in close contact with the hierarchy of The Firm, who is in turn both disillusioned and frightened of them in equal measure.

In this manner, Daniel is able to establish a number of occasions when members of the gang are due to collect protection money from small shopkeepers in the East End. Not only that but he also discovers when the gang is due to take action against those who are in arrears and have been chosen to be made an example of to those other shopkeepers, who may be contemplating not paying for The Firms "protection".

By first informing the police at Scotland Yard, Daniel, accompanied by a photographer, is able to be close to where the incidents are due to occur and hopefully get a "scoop" for The Daily Compass.

Police are distributed in plain clothes in the area in the hope that one or more of the small shopkeepers will not pay the sums demanded. If this should happen, the police will step in to arrest gang members when they start to destroy premises and stock.

Neither the police nor Daniel has warned any of the shopkeepers of their presence, believing that by doing so the gang will not take any further retaliatory measures against them.

In this way Daniel manages to get front page headlines on a number of occasions which earns him some "street cred" but does not cause much collateral damage to The Firm, because neither he nor the police have any evidence to the people who cause the damage back to the Krays. The latter, are merely muscle men acting for the Krays, who know better than to divulge any information of their infamous employers to the police, any such information being rewarded by violence and death.

But a number of gang members are arrested and named and some even get short jail sentences. But Daniel realises that although some of the gang are being taken off the street, the damage to the many headed hydra that is The Firm is relatively non-existent. However, over a period it does have some small effects, because the gang's protection operations are gradually squeezed. After several months, Daniel's informer becomes very agitated, because the Krays are beginning to realise that they have a betrayer in their midst.

The informer fearing for his life, makes his arrangements for meeting Daniel become more and more convoluted, making changes to his appearance by using glasses or a false beard; or meeting in large crowds, in fact by doing or using anything that will give him anonymity. But eventually none of this is enough to make him feel safe and he tells Daniel that he can't help him anymore. Daniel, although disappointed, understands and accepts that his contacts life is in jeopardy, only to learn just a few days later that he has gone missing.

The Firm has dealt with its informer in their usual ruthless, efficient manner.

From Daniels standpoint the one positive thing that he has achieved is a close rapport with Scotland Yard, who recognise the information that he has given them is accurate, but also that he has always contacted them first and let them know when and where a crime is likely to happen. They in turn are prepared to drop him hints when they know other crimes are likely to happen, which gives Daniel time to be there with a photographer to get another "scoop".

The Firm continues on its course of murder and mayhem, but without sufficient evidence the police are helpless to act until 1967 when Inspector Leonard "Nipper Read is promoted to the murder squad and his first assignment is to bring down the Kray twins.

Eventually, after arresting the Krays and the 15 other members of the gang, Read then conducts secret individual interviews with the other members of the gang, offering each member one last chance to come onto the side of law and order. By so doing, and later by also finding a witness to the killing of George Cornell, (a barmaid who was working in the pub at the time and by giving her a secret identity), she testifies to seeing Ronnie Kray shoot and kill Cornell.

When the arrests are made, Scotland Yard informs Daniel unofficially, which enables him to be there for the last and final time to the biggest scoop of his career so far.

Later, he follows the trial avidly to listen to the stories of murder and corruption, before they agree finally convicted in March 1969, when they are both sentenced to life imprisonment.

By now Daniels reputation as a consummate reporter of crime has put him in the top echelons of his profession. So much so in fact, that he is invited onto television for his opinion on news items. Drugs are now a major source of news; their proliferation has grown more than anyone could have possibly thought possible and is beginning to ruin many lives of those people who are vulnerable to it.

The Daily Compass is leading the field in their revulsion and opposition to the people and gangs who are smuggling such evil contraband. Daniel runs a public campaign in The Daily Compass, against both the smuggling and use of these drugs and asks for information that anyone may have regarding the illegal import of them. He assures them that any such information will be treated in the strictest confidence.

The response he receives is enormous, much of it unreliable and unusable, but a small number are worth pursuing. These indicate some of the methods used to smuggle drugs through customs, but even more importantly they often reveal the names of operators who are carrying out this vile trade.

After researching some of the people named and the methods they employ, Daniel decides that he needs to build a team of informers who can tell him when and where certain consignments are to arrive. He has no problem finding people who are prepared to inform on suspects, which some do for small cash payments, while others are happy to do for no reward, other than that of reducing the flood of drugs into the country.

By using this method Daniel is soon being informed of where and when specific consignments are going to happen. It may be for instance that a lorry arriving at Dover Docks on a certain Ferry from Holland has a consignment hidden in a secret compartment in the petrol tank or in a tyre, or behind a false bulkhead. Or an alternative scenario might be that Daniel is made aware of someone arriving at Heathrow might be carrying drugs which they have concealed by swallowing them wrapped in cellophane or plastic bags, and are undetectable by sniffer dogs. The methods that are employed are limitless, making detection, recovery and convictions extremely difficult.

When Daniel manages to gather information relating to this type of subterfuge, he notifies H.M. Customs on the understanding that they will allow him to be available when they take action against the perpetrators, so that he can witness the arrest and get the scoop for The Daily Compass.

These are similar methods that Daniel has already used when notifying the police of criminal activities of burglary, protection or other nefarious crimes. Once H.M. Customs can see that Daniels information is accurate and that it leads to the apprehension and arrest of those responsible, they are only too happy for him to witness their arrests and get the scoop that his efforts and organisation so richly deserve.

Daniels profile is now so high that he is appearing regularly on television, not only on news items but is becoming involved in documentaries exploring drugs and crime. It seems almost inevitable that eventually one of the major television companies will offer him a place on their reporting news staff.

During all this time, Daniels work has precluded him from having any sort of a social life apart from having an occasional beer with colleagues at work. Women have been notably absent, as he spends sometimes eighteen hours a day totally absorbed in the job at hand. To his absolute shame when he does have time to consider the situation, he remembers that his mother is also a casualty. He has managed to visit her very infrequently and telephone her when the thought comes to him, which unfortunately for Ella means that she might hear from her son at any hour of the day or night.

She in turn is concerned for her son, but extremely proud when he appears on the television offering his opinions on anything from crime to drugs. But she also knows that he is doing that which he has always sought, so a small part of her is grateful for that at least.

Although he still sees his old flatmate Chas, Daniel has lived on his own, in a flat in Tudor Street, just north of The Victoria Embankment since 1967. This was not of his choosing, but rather because Chas had decided to ask his girlfriend Fay to marry him. The result of her emphatic yes meant that she moved in with Chas on a permanent basis and Daniel felt that it was only fair that he should find his own place.

The main advantage for Daniel living in this new location is that he is on the seventh floor in a large block of flats where his living room and two bedrooms both look out south across The River Thames. At night the view from here is mesmerising with lights strung across both side of the river and boats of all description making their way up and down this, the artery of London for over two thousand years. He just loves living here and takes great solace from the views and surrounding area with its hustle and bustle.

Both Chas and Fay had implored him to stay, but Daniel decided that their friendship was too precious to him, and that rather than risk damaging it, moving on would be a safer option. In retrospect, he felt that his decision was justified because the three of them remain good friends, seeing each other frequently, sometimes Daniel entertaining them at his, and sometimes the other way around. Strangely, although he is now very experienced and accomplished in what he does, Daniel still occasionally seeks his friend's advice. When he considers why he does this Daniel realises that Chas offers a completely fresh viewpoint from other colleagues who are nearly always on the same wavelength as him. Chas's advice and approach, although not very often taken by Daniel can sometimes see a way to release the log jam in his mind, giving him options that he had not considered. But more than any of this Daniel just enjoys Chas and Fay's company. They make him laugh and relax, something that he has very little time for when he is working.

Then in September 1973 Daniels world changes dramatically again when he is contacted by The B.B.C.'s World News Editor, Alistair Graham, who asks to see him at their Shepherds Bush studio.

Arriving at the appointed time, Daniel is ushered in to the great man's plush suite of offices. He begins by saying "Thanks for coming Daniel I expect you are wondering why I asked to see you. Well it's quite simple really, your powerful writing, combined with your uncanny ability to get stories before most of the other media, is becoming a byword in the industry. To be frank Daniel I can use your journalistic skills, although in a wider sphere than that in which you have been operating so far. Your appearances occasionally on our news programmes and other crime documentaries have proved that television is a natural medium for you. But the role I would like to offer you is that of foreign affairs correspondent. Basically, what this means is that you would be required to go to anywhere in the world at a moment's notice, where there is conflict or a story of a political nature occurring. If we take a look at the recent past for example it may have been to Israel to report on the seven-day war with Egypt, Syria, Lebanon and Jordan. Actually, it could be anything anywhere. You would be told by us when something of national or international interest is happening. When this happens, you will be expected to drop anything that you are doing and get yourself to wherever it may be P.D.Q.".

Daniel is surprised when he hears the offer, but as he begins to discuss it in more detail with Alistair, he finds himself becoming more and more excited at the prospect, because he realises that at this stage of his career he is definitely in the right place. Apart from his mother he has no other ties, wife or girlfriend to consider, while the other positives are that the money on offer is way beyond that which he earns currently, as well as the fact that his reputation in the industry can only be enhanced.

Eventually Alistair says "Well, have a think about my offer Daniel. I would like you very much on our team. But before you go why don't I get the people in who you will be working with. Terry James is the sub editor who you will be responsible to and his assistant who I won't name, because she says she knows you. Just wait there and I will go and get them".

Daniel is mystified at this announcement, but before he even has time to consider the situation Alistair is back, followed by a tall thin sandy haired man of about forty years of age, who has a ready smile and a firm handshake. Just for a moment Daniel is unable to see the women following who says that she knows him. But as Terry steps aside, she steps forward and is revealed to be Theresa.

"You no doubt remember Theresa Port" says Terry, as a way of introduction.

Daniel stands hypnotised by the vision of Theresa, who even after so many years still evokes such strong emotional feelings in him. She is even more beautiful than he remembers. No longer a girl, she is now a mature woman of poise and elegance, her hair now dark, long and lustrous, hanging to her shoulders. She looks at him with her dark brown, melting chocolate eyes, which he remembers so well. She is dressed in a dark blue navy suit comprising a jacket and pencil slim skirt which emphasises her slim figure (again which he remembers vividly) with a white silk scooped blouse under her jacket. Red high heel shoes complete her attire. A small smile plays on her lips as she says "It's lovely to see you again Dan", relapsing back into her abbreviated version of his name. "Just to reassure you, it wasn't me that recommended you for this position. That is down entirely to you and all your achievements".

CHAPTER 24.

1973 -1974.
ELLA AND GEOFFREY.

By late September 1973 Ella's life has been extremely busy since her parents died. Her business interests continue to take up most of her time. Additionally, she has joined the local Chamber of Commerce soon after she opened The Pines, which gives her an overview with what is happening locally as well as the opportunity to help others within the community. This is sometimes in the form of collections of donations from businesses, the money from which is distributed to the local needy. Another important area which interests her considerably is that of apprenticeships for young people. There are several businesses in the area, an engineering company that makes parts for the car industry and a furniture factory. There is also a small brewery that supplies pubs and hotels within a thirty-mile radius of Chipping Norton.

She is a voice of reasoned persistence in these matters and together with her colleagues they first concentrate their efforts on these and eventually are able to get them all to offer apprenticeships to young people. But she is not satisfied just with this and looks to extend training to other businesses, targeting retail shops, as well as for people in her own area of expertise of catering, cooking, waitressing and retailing.

For her part individually she has instigated training of her kitchen staff as she appoints them. Sous chefs now not only learn from Tony, Ella's chef, but also attend the local college, where they are taught other aspects of running a business.

Another initiative that Ella, with other colleagues at The Chamber of Trade and Commerce concert their efforts on is to attract businesses both large and small to the area. Agriculture has always been the major source of employment, but mechanisation has greatly reduced the need for manual labour and so other methods of employment need to be found.

She urges the Chamber to approach local government with a view to building a small trading estate, say a collection of small buildings that can accommodate activities, such as motor repairs, because more and more people have motor cars these days. There is also a need locally where individuals or businesses can go to get printing done, the only alternative currently being Oxford or somewhere even further afield. Another option is to build some units for warehousing purposes, where business can store wholesale stock which can be distributed to customers, individuals or retail, as and when demanded. Once she gets started Ella thinks of a host of other activities that could enhance the town and help people develop their lives at the same time. She is constantly thinking of ways to develop and enhance her community.

All these activities leave Ella with very little time for anything else, although she always makes time to see Rachel at least once a week when they go out to the cinema or for a meal. With Daniel away, Rachel is Ella's only family source left and they are both determined to stay close.

Apart from Rachel, Ella has no other social life. She still lives in the accommodation at the Café, so she sees Fiona on a daily basis, and although she gives her a free hand to run the business, she helps her out at busy times or is available if she needs help with any problems. However, she never offers an opinion unless asked, because she trusts Fiona and knows that she will only seek help when absolutely necessary. This only happens when Fiona has perhaps thought of a way to improve the business which may need a capital injection, or if she needs more staff.

She also spends two or three evenings a week at The Pines at the front of house welcoming customers and making them feel relaxed. In this manner she can see first-hand how clients respond to their surroundings, and the food on offer. This enables her to hopefully ensure that the restaurant not only produces good food, but also ensures that any problems that may arise can be resolved quickly and without fuss.

Her time spent at The Chamber of Commerce has introduced her to many other representatives of local business, some of whom appear to be there to represent their own interests, which is at odds with Ella's own more inclusive outlook of support for the less able. But most of the others she finds that she likes and can get on with to a greater or smaller extent. One of the former in this category is Geoffrey Thompson, who is in fact a distant relative of Mr Souch. Apart from liking him for his attitude and approach to developing local business, a view that she shares whole heartedly, she also feels desperately sorry for him, knowing that he is a widower, having lost his wife to cancer only three years previously; something that she can assimilate with from her own experience so many years ago, but which still remain vividly in her memory.

Geoffrey owns and runs a hardware shop further up the High Street from Ella's Café which is the only shop of its type in Chipping Norton. She has known of him for many years but their paths have never crossed until now.

Having similar interests in business they spend a lot of time together, which seems to inevitably draw them closer in more personal ways, which somehow triggers feelings in Ella that she thought that she would never feel again after the loss of Richard. But she thrusts all such thoughts to the back of her mind, particularly because, although Geoffrey shows her a side of himself that he does not show to anyone else in the Chamber, he nevertheless does not want or is unable to pursue the matter any further.

He is ten years older than Ella, who is now fifty-four, but her looks still defy nature, giving her the appearance of someone much younger. Her figure is still very much the same as it has always been, which she puts down to genetic genes passed down from her mother. The only visible sign of the ageing process is that her hair is now whiter, giving it a "salt and pepper" appearance, which gives her a statelier and more authoritative look. That's how she feels anyway,

Geoffrey by contrast is of medium height with a slightly portlier appearance, with hazel eyes and a long noble nose and a ready smile which is nearly always playing at his mouth. He has two sons who are now grown up and live in Oxford and he sees them often.

One of the features that Ella finds most endearing about him is that he is able to make her laugh almost at will; the most disappointing being that he smokes copious cigarettes and sometimes cigars. She knows from personal experience of both her parents that this is a bad habit which often causes health problems at some stage, but as they spend more and more time together, she is reminded just how much she has missed Richard's company. Although she has managed perfectly well making major decisions about Daniel growing up and running her businesses, she often regrets that Richard was not there to discuss the problems with her.

Geoffrey and Ella speak often together about Chamber of Commerce issues and inevitably talk sometimes turns to those of a personal nature. Ella tells him about Daniel and his progress in journalism, while Geoffrey tells her about his sons and their work. This in turn leads to both of them confessing their sense of loneliness without having partners to just listen to and offer advice if asked.

Matters continue in much this way through the year and although Ella finds some consolation from his company, their relationship doesn't develop any further until late in December when Geoffrey suddenly tells her "Oh Ella, I can't tell you how much I dread Christmas. Since I lost my wife it just reminds me of how wonderful it was when she was alive, when the family would all gather together and we would all have such happy times. Now there is only the boys, who always come, in fairness to them over Christmas Day, but once they are gone, my life returns to the same old, same old………..in fact if I didn't come here to meet people, in particular yourself, then my life would be completely empty".

Ella can see how difficult this confession has been for Geoffrey, because it has a resonance with her own situation. Before she even realises it, she blurts out "Oh Geoffrey, I know just how you feel because I have a similar situation, although it is fair to say that my sister Rachel (you remember Rachel) has always been there for me." And then as the idea strikes her, she continues "Look, I am going to Rachel's on Christmas day, but why don't you come to mine on Boxing Day; we can be company for one another. I will make dinner and we can put the world to rights. What do you say"?

Geoffrey looks pensive for a moment, before a huge smile envelope his face. "Are you sure Ella, I don't want to put you to any trouble, but I must admit it would be nice to have some company. Everybody else seems to have someone that they can go to, so the thought of seeing no one and being in the same four walls all day alone is frightening".

"It's no trouble Geoffrey and it will be good to have company for me too, so it's agreed. Come around on the morning and we will have a nice relaxing day".

It is in this way that Ella's life changes, imperceptibly at first, but with growing speed as their relationship gathers momentum.

Boxing Day is all that they both hope that it will be. Geoffrey arrives midmorning bearing gifts, a dozen red roses, chocolates, wine and a small personal wrapped gift for Ella, which is revealed as a gold cross and necklace as she opens it with trembling fingers.

"Thank you its lovely, but you really shouldn't have" Ella exclaims, and then "Oh just a minute, I forgot, I have something for you too". Going to the table she picks up a small present and hands it to Geoffrey, who holds it to his ear and shakes it saying "Well it's not ticking, so it is not a bomb, or a watch or even an alarm to help me get up in the morning. Whatever can it be".

"Well open it and you will find out you ninny" laughs Ella.

There is silence for a moment as Geoffrey struggles to get the wrapping paper off, until suddenly a pair of gold cuff links is revealed. "Thank you too Ella, you don't know how fortuitous these are, because I lost my one and only pair only the other day. You must be able to read my mind".

The day passes leisurely, both of them content in each other's company. Geoffrey helps her to prepare the vegetables for dinner, while Ella cooks a leg of lamb rather than have turkey for the second day running.

As they sit down for dinner Ella produces Christmas crackers saying" come on Geoffrey, you must wear a silly hat and read out the jokes".

They do this, Ella congratulating herself on this small rouse which helps to break down slightly, both of their inhibitions.

Once dinner has been eaten, they clear away the dishes before sitting down and chatting about just anything and everything, just because they can.

"It is so lovely to have someone to talk to" Geoffrey says after a long conversation together. "Perhaps I shouldn't say this, but I sometimes find that I am talking to myself when I am on my own at home".

Once again Ella is reminded just how lonely Geoffrey has become since the loss of his wife and her heart goes out to him.

"Never mind, you are here now and perhaps we can do this again sometime. I would certainly like that and I think that you would too".

"I most certainly would Ella, I just can't thank you enough for today" replies Geoffrey. "But the next time you must come to mine".

Later on, Ella prepares tea for them consisting of chunky bread smothered in butter with a selection of cold meats, sausage rolls and salad, topped off with pickles and mustard.

"What are you trying to do to me "chuckles Geoffrey. "I won't be able to get up for work in the morning at this rate".

"Get it down you, tomorrow you can go on a diet. Come on how do you fancy a game of cards, gin rummy perhaps, or whist.

In this manner the evening dwindles imperceptibly with neither of them wanting it to end, but eventually Geoffrey says "well I had better take my leave of you, we wouldn't want the neighbours to talk. Once again thank you so much for today. I have had the best time for ages". Pecking her on the cheek, he leaves and for some strange reason Ella feels distraught, as if she has been widowed all over again, which, when she thinks about it, is because today has been the first day since Richard died that she has spent in the company of a man just for social reasons, other than male relatives.

As she continues to dwell on the day and how happy she feels, she automatically wonders where this relationship is leading the two of them. For her part she knows that both of them are pleased to have found someone to fill the void over the loss of their partners, but for herself Ella realises that although she enjoys Geffrey's company, she is not looking for anyone to replace Richard in any other way. She worries that Geoffrey may want to extend their relationship to include sleeping together, before consoling herself with the thought that he is still grieving about the loss of his wife, so like Ella he is happy just for her friendship and company.

Anything more than that is a bridge too far thinks Ella as she settles down to sleep with the happenings of the day going around and round in her head.

Ella is confirmed correct in her assumptions as the months roll on. Geoffrey seems content just to be in her company as indeed is she in his. Her work commitments at The Pines means that they cannot see each other for three or four nights, although he does usually drop into the restaurant at least one night each week, which ensures that he can see her and saves him from having to cook for himself. But they go out regularly to the cinema in Oxford, or shopping, while they continue to visit each other, Ella teaching him the rudiments of cooking skills, something that he had never bothered to learn while his wife was alive.

Their presence as a couple is becoming recognised in Chipping Norton and despite their protests that they are just good friends who find solace in each other's company, tongues inevitably begin to wag.

Rachel is happy for her little sister and both she and Fred tease Ella unmercifully, despite her protests. Eventually, realising that Geoffrey's company means so much to Ella, Rachel invites them round for an evening and soon sees how relaxed and happy they both are in each other's company.

She takes an instant liking to Geoffrey and although she finds him a bit mundane on his outlook on life, she is happy that Ella has at last found someone that can at least fill a small part of the huge hole that Richard's death left in her life. He both makes her laugh a lot and is attentive to her every need. So much so Rachel reflects that although Ella assures her that their relationship is that one of good friends, she questions her objectivity in the matter but does nothing to persuade her sister otherwise.

Ella has not heard from Daniel for several months until suddenly in late March he telephones saying "Hi Mum, I thought that I would give you a ring to let you know that I have a few days free and so I thought that it would be nice if I came to see you next weekend".

"That would be lovely, it seems ages since you were here last"

"Well there's a good reason for that, but I will explain everything when we meet, so I look forward to seeing you on Friday night".

* * *

Daniel arrives in the evening on Friday as promised, by which time Ella is beside herself with excitement. She hears him coming up the road riding his father's motorbike, the sound of which brings back haunting memories of Richard's arrival all those years ago.

"Are you still riding your Dads old bike Daniel" she says greeting him with a hug of affection.

"Too right Mum, I couldn't do without it getting around London. But I must say that it's getting a bit long in the tooth now, so I may have to invest in a replacement soon".

"Well come inside, I have made a meal for us because I expect that you are quite hungry and anyway, I want to hear about everything that has happened to you since I saw you last".

Once they have sat down Daniel begins "well mum, quite a lot has happened since the last time we met. Last October the B.B.C. television contacted me and offered me a job as a Foreign Affairs Correspondent. I was absolutely stunned when it happened and quite frankly I didn't know what to say as first but after thinking about it I decided that it would be a good career move so I said yes, but not until after I had spoken to The Daily Compass, because they had always been good to me, giving me my first break in journalism and helping me in so many ways. But after I spoke to my boss Graham Morton, he understood completely and said that I would be daft if I turned such an offer down and wished me every success in my new venture. The only thing that he asked was if I would write an occasional weekly Saturday column for the paper, as and when events or changes in legislation occurred".

"I assured him that I would be more than happy to do that and after serving out my notice which took longer than I thought, mainly because the paper had to appoint someone else in my place, which took some time. The result is that I start on Monday at B.B.C. television centre. I will be in house for a while learning the ropes but eventually, I could be sent at a minute's notice to anywhere in the World. So, follow the news Mum and I might be waving to you from Moscow or Africa very soon".

Ella has listened as Daniel explains, thinking that she has always been so proud of his achievements. To see his name attributed to articles in the paper has made her sometimes pinch herself in disbelief, but his latest news gives her goose bumps as she thinks about it. "

"I can hardly believe it. You have surpassed everything that I could have possibly wished for you. Your father would have been so proud of you, as indeed so am I". This thought seems to trigger her next comment when she says "I think that your news deserves to be celebrated; wait a minute I have got a bottle of Champagne here somewhere".

After toasting his success in his new job, she goes on to question him in depth asking him if he has met any of the newsreaders that she has seen on T.V. Daniel replies readily as much as he can, but Ella knows her son very well and senses that there is something that he is withholding from her, which she ignores knowing that he will tell her eventually. Although she is pleased beyond measure for Daniel's achievements, she is concerned that he has no one else in his life, his work being his whole world. He is now thirty-two years of age and she wonders if it will ever happen for him, but she is loath to pursue the matter and cast a shadow over the proceedings.

"What about you Mum, how are things with you, Aunt Rachel writes to me occasionally and says that you are friendly with Geoffrey Thomson who runs the hardware store".

For the first time in years Ella is lost for words. She has obviously thought that this question might come up and has rehearsed her answer in her head for just such an eventuality, but now that she is confronted with it her mind goes blank. As she considers what this means the answer comes to her; she feels guilty!!

Why do I feel guilty she asks herself, because my relationship with Geoffrey is purely platonic and anyway even if it wasn't I am old enough and we have both been widowed for so many years that nobody has a right to question it? No, the real reason she feels guilty is because she is frightened that Daniel might think that she has deserted him and that their relationship, which has always been so close, will somehow be damaged because of it.

But she says none of this as she replies "Oh, so Rachel told you, well I was going to tell you anyway. The truth is that Geoffrey and I have been working a lot on projects for The Chamber of Commerce for some time and things just went on from there. He was widowed some three years ago and was very lonely. We both enjoy each other's company and go to the cinema or for a meal every so often, or he might come here and I will cook him a meal. It's all very innocent I can assure you Daniel; I am not looking for someone to replace your father in my life, just someone who can be a companion occasionally".

As she finishes speaking Daniel is suddenly aware of the huge effort that it has taken his mother to explain her relationship with Geoffrey, revealing just how guilty that she feels about it, and he feels humble and ashamed. Why shouldn't she find solace with someone, because although she has a busy work life, she has very little time for socialising and she must be extremely lonely during whatever time she has remaining.

From here it is just a small step for Daniel to recall the many sacrifices that she has made for him over the years and his sense of guilt threatens to overwhelm him.

"Look Mum I am only asking; it goes without saying that you have every right to see whoever you like" he begins, his voice breaking with emotion. "I am really pleased for you, and hope that it continues" and then more assuredly "I am a big boy now and if you decide to that you want to change your relationship from companions to something more intimate then I will have absolutely no problem with that either. I don't say it very often Mum but I love you very much and only want whatever you want for yourself. As for memories of my father, I will always love him too, but life moves on and so should we". He continues "I tell you what, why don't the three of us go out tomorrow for a meal or something so that I can get to know him better".

Ella has tears running down her face as she hugs him to her saying "If you are sure son, I would like that. Rachel has invited all of us to hers on Sunday as well, but I think it would still be a good idea for the three of us to go out tomorrow. Leave it to me, I will ring Geoffrey and arrange it".

The following evening finds the two of them at The Pines, and when Daniel takes issue with his mother saying "I thought that we might go somewhere different for a change" Ella cuts him short saying "why would we want to do that, The Pines is still the best restaurant around here by a country mile, now put on a smiley face, here comes Geoffrey. Please be gentle with him Daniel because I know that he is apprehensive about meeting you".

Daniel replies "As if I would say anything confrontational Mum", before being introduced to a nervous looking Geoffrey and saying "It's good to meet you Geoffrey, my mother has told me so much about you. I remember you from the time when I was very young and Mum would send me to your hardware shop for nuts and bolts and various other things".

Geoffrey is visibly relieved at Daniels tone and replies "Oh yes I remember those occasions as well, but apart from your red hair I doubt very much if I would remember you now. You have grown into a fine young man and are a credit to your mother, who I know is so proud of you. Every time you name is mentioned in the paper, she points it out to me. I have watched avidly some of the television documentary programmes that you have been involved with and now your mother tells me that you are going to work for the B.B.C. as a foreign correspondent".

The three of them are visibly more relaxed now that the introductions have taken place and as the evening proceeds Geoffrey asks Daniel to relate some of the stories that he has written about in The Daily Compass while Ella goes out to inspect the kitchen and make sure that their meals are as good as the Chef can make them.

Eventually they take their leave of the restaurant and while Ella and Geoffrey say goodnight to one another and make arrangements for the following day at Rachel's, Daniel walks slowly on until she catches him up.

"Well I thought that was a lovely evening, what about you Daniel. Geoffrey was amazed by your stories of criminals"

"Thank you, he seems like a very nice man. I am so pleased that he is in your life Mum. Just to change the subject I have to tell you that I am looking forward to seeing Rachel and Fred. By the way, will George and Harry and their wives be there, it has been years since we were all together".

Daniel has attended both George and Harry's weddings several years previously and has managed to keep in touch with both of them, albeit on a very infrequent basis, mostly birthdays and Christmas, but whenever they have all managed to get together in one place, they seem able to pick up just where they left off. So much so in fact that they have a little ritual when they meet again that one of them will finish off the last sentence spoken when they met the previous time, no matter how long ago that may have been. It is a source of great amusement when they meet on the Sunday after Daniel, Geoffrey and Ella have got together the previous day.

As soon as the three of them see each other Harry pronounces with a great air of authority "five gold rings" to which George replies immediately "Six Geese a laying" with Daniel completing the ritual "Seven Swans a swimming" at which point they all hug each other and fall about laughing, pleased that they have all remembered their own part from the last time that they met. Each off them subconsciously aware that the ritual, silly as it is, somehow bonds them together. Just the fact that they all remember their own small part indicates the respect that they all have for each other.

"Dan, you know my wife Maria" says George, introducing his family." However, you haven't met my son William yet".

After first hugging Maria, Daniel looks down to see a small boy of about six years of age who is instantly recognisable as George's son. There can be no other explanation, he has the same blond hair as his father, although much more of it, which hangs down in locks to his shoulders. Pale blue eyes and a ready smile, also similar features that his father has bequeathed him complete his countenance.

"Well hello William, it is lovely to meet you at last. I have brought you a present" says Daniel, passing him a book shaped package.

William excitedly opens the present which is revealed to be a Beano Annual.

"Thank you so much Uncle Daniel. I love the Beano I get the comic every week".

"As did I when I was your age"

Before any more can be said Harry steps forward, saying "You remember my wife Briony, Daniel, but you haven't met my daughter Gwen".

"Of course, I remember Briony, we were at school together in Chadlington. I seem to recall that I had a boyhood crush on you" says

Daniel embracing his unrequited love of many years ago. "Now let me have a look at this pretty little girl. How old are you Gwen"?

Gwen replies "I am nearly five years old Uncle Daniel"

"Well I have brought you a present too Gwen" says Daniel producing a wrapped box shaped parcel. "I hope that you like it".

Ripping off the wrapping paper Gwen reveals her present to be a Cindy doll.

"Oh, it's just what I wanted, thank you".

"Well I seem to have got that right" replies Daniel, not revealing that he had asked Ella previously what their interests were and what they might like.

Gwen also has blond hair, her eyes again pale blue, but her complexion is the colour and texture of fine porcelain. She is petite and reminds Daniel of her mother who he can still remember so vividly from their time at school.

George and Harry are curious to hear some the more intimate details of Daniels more infamous stories, but after a while he asks them about their own lives, from which he learns that George is still working with his father decorating and doing small building work, while Harry is a self-employed qualified electrician. All of them work at some of the many houses that are being built on estates locally.

After spending the afternoon and evening renewing and reinvigorating their relationships and with all of their good wishes for his future ringing in his ears Daniel, together with Ella and Geoffrey, make their way back to Chipping Norton in time for him to return to London.

As he sets off Daniel is very aware that he has not made any mention to his mother of his encounter with Theresa and that he will be working with her, while Ella for her part is conscious that there is something that her son is withholding from her and she wonders what it can be.

CHAPTER 25.

1973.
DANIEL AT THE BBC.

Daniel is strangely excited and apprehensive as he makes his way to The B.B.C. studios at Shepherds Bush the next Monday morning.

As he travels, he tries to analyse just what these feelings mean. He knows that he is exhilarated to be starting a new career and looking forward to its challenges, but is apprehensive about his reunion working with Theresa. Thinking about this last aspect he suddenly realises that although they talked about his appointment and the scope that his new job entails neither of them had made any reference to each other about their personal circumstances.

Daniel was so blown away by seeing her again that he didn't even look to see if she was wearing an engagement or wedding ring. If he had, and if she was wearing either he would know that she was lost to him for ever. Following these thoughts to the next stage he realises that his feelings for her remain unchanged. Just seeing her, has stirred up wonderful memories of the good times that they had experienced on Dartmoor, before she had been effectively abducted against her will, which in turn had led him to believe the worst of her and spurn her entreaties of innocence.

He is still pondering the unanswerable as he reaches the studios and makes his way to reception where to his amazement, he sees his name on the welcome board. Just as he reaches the reception desk Theresa comes hurrying out to meet him saying "There you are Dan; I was hoping to be here when you arrived but I got held up at the last moment. Follow me and I will show you to your desk. Space is tight but after you have been here a short while I think that you will be travelling quite a lot, so that the times that you are here will only be spasmodic".

"Terry has asked me to show you around and get you acclimatised, so once I have shown you where your desk is, I will do that". Then lowering her voice "I can't tell you how glad I am that we are going to be working together Dan. I have followed your career closely over the years. In fact, it took me awhile to realise that it was you". And then "come on, once I have showed you the various departments, we can look at the most important place in the building".

"What's that then" Daniel replies, intrigued.

"Why the canteen of course, dummy. It's where I do my best work".

Daniel laughs, mostly with relief at Theresa's laid-back approach, some of his fears abated. It means that even if she is married or has a boyfriend, her attitude suggests two things, the first being that she has at least forgiven him for not supporting her when she needed him most and the second that she finds no difficulty about working with him for the same reason. He, on the other hand, finds her closeness to him slightly disturbing, being aware of just how beautiful she looks.

The morning continues with the tour of the studios which are the latest state of the art and contain the latest that technology can provide. There are several studios, a couple in which two drama programmes are being made. The news department takes Daniels breath away. It is huge with a couple of rooms with banks of monitors and state of the art equipment, where newsreaders can present their latest offerings to an insatiable public.

Apart from the rooms for the newsreaders there remains a huge area which teems with untold numbers of people, the majority of which are on the telephone garnering news from reporters and agencies from around the world, while other rush hither and thither holding pieces of paper. Everything is done at pace and to an outsider like Daniel is bewildering. Among all this debris, cables are running everywhere like snakes waiting for passing victims.

As she has promised once the tour is completed Theresa takes him to the promised land of the canteen where they consume coffees and cakes.

"I will show you in more detail where we decide which items of news to develop for showing. While on the subject Dan, I can tell you that we took up many of the items that you sourced from local papers; for example, we followed up on the story of the little boy who fell into a frozen pond. It was exactly the sort of thing that we were looking for. By the way I found out during the course of talking to the man who saved the boy, that you had gone out of your way to find him employment. That was very kind and way above anything that was necessary; I must say that I looked at you in a new light from that day on".

This then has been Theresa's only reference to what had occurred between them all those years ago and Daniel feeling guilty again replies "I guess that you had no reason to think of me in a good light, because of the way that I treated you on Dartmoor. I will be forever haunted for that experience and the way that I reacted and I hope that someday you can forgive me". Then continuing, "Do you have any problems with us working together Theresa, because if you do, I will move on"?

To his surprise she relies immediately "Of course I don't Dan, it was such a long time ago and in fairness to you who didn't know the truth it must have looked as if I had deliberately gone of my own free will to the other tent. But don't let's talk about it anymore, we are older now and I hope that experience has taught us how to forgive each other".

So, they talk of other things, mostly about Daniels job, while he is hardly able to keep his eyes of this beautiful woman who he once won and then lost. She laughs often, her eyes sparkling as she does so, while occasionally shaking her head to keep her long lustrous hair in shape. Her laugh is genuine, her mouth reacting to her eyes, producing the irrepressible smile that Daniel remembers so vividly.

Unable to supress his curiosity any longer, Daniel asks the one big question that he has wanted to ask, but for which he has been dreading the answer. But he needs to now for better or worse, because it will determine how their working relationship will develop.

"Tell me then, did you marry Peter" he asks hesitantly.

"Peter" she replies questioningly, and then as if remembering who he means "Oh I would rather not talk about him if you don't mind. I will tell you some day, but not just yet. Anyway, whatever happened to you and April".

Daniel is wrong footed for a moment until he resolves in his mind to tell Theresa the truth. "Our relationship didn't last the course; I think for two reasons. The first was that she was happy working in Bristol while I too was happy working in London for The Daily Compass. Travelling back and forward took its toll eventually and so we decided to split".

"What was the second reason Dan"?

Daniel is silent for a moment as he gathers himself for his confession.

Speaking in a voice full of emotion he replies "well, if you must know I couldn't forget the woman that I spent a few days with on Dartmoor". Then before Theresa can respond he continues hurriedly "April and I did keep in touch for a while on a friend only basis and the last I heard was that she met and married a Don from Bristol University and has two young children.

I have to tell you that since April, I have lived like a monk: not necessarily from choice but just because my work became all-consuming; my mistress even. I have never had any regrets on that score before, until this very moment. But that's enough about me, what has been happening with you. The last time that we talked you had plans to follow a career in the Police, so how come you are here".

He has not dared to look directly at Theresa as he has been speaking, but now as he raises his head for the first time, he can see her eyes glistening, with tears threatening to flow down her face. She hurriedly applies a tissue in an attempt to stem the flow.

"It seems that we have both been burying ourselves in our careers Dan, perhaps trying to avoid the truth about each other. The reason that I decided that I wanted to be involved in television and specifically the news department was because immediately after I graduated, I took what I thought would be an interim position with B.B.C. Bristol News. How wrong can you be, because it turned out to be the most wonderful opportunity, which I grabbed with both hands? I progressed rapidly, eventually running the newsroom, which was at the point when someone put my name forward for this position. I have been here now for five years and I have loved every minute of it".

As she finishes speaking Daniel asks her tentatively "I don't know what happened to Peter because you won't tell me, but there must have been other men in your life; are you married or is there anyone at the moment "?

Theresa looks pensive before she replies "there have been several, well three men to be exact over the years, the last of which I have known for about six months and am still seeing periodically, although our relationship doesn't seem to be going anywhere. If I am honest neither of the two other relationships meant very much to me although I did live with the second one for eighteen months or so before I began asking myself why I stayed because there was nothing there for me. Does that answer your question Dan"?

Daniel is devastated by her reply; his hopes dashed on the rocks of despair as he hears that Theresa is in a relationship, and he doesn't know how to reply, until eventually saying lamely "Yes, thank you for being so honest with me. I guess that it was too much for me to hope that you would be foot loose and fancy free. But now I know I will keep our relationship on a strictly work basis. It's probably better that way particularly at the moment when I am learning the ropes on my new job. I think that it would be best if you showed me how I need to get televised items to the studio from wherever I am while I am on location".

To his surprise Theresa smiles gently and laying her hand on his replies "Don't be sad and unhappy Dan, you know how I feel about you; nothing has changed in that regard, but I just need to get my own act together. My only tiny reservation about getting together with you is that although we were both smitten with each other all those years ago, it was only for a few days and who is to know if it would have lasted. Just give me time to get used to the idea. Although your feelings for me are still as strong, as indeed mine are for you, I didn't know that you still felt that way until a few moments ago. Let us just take our time and see what happens. If we are to be together at some stage in the future, we need to be sure, I wouldn't want either of us to regret it later, so it's got to be right".

Daniel's mood is lifted slightly at her words, although he knows that she has not offered him a definite future with her. He replies "I understand, but I have no doubts or reservations about the way I feel about you. It feels that I have been marking time since the day that we separated on Dartmoor for this moment. But I will respect the way you are feeling and wait for the time, however long it may be, for you to let me know that you feel the same way too".

So that is how it is left, with Daniel feeling that Theresa has chosen her words carefully, as if to let him down gently about their future together.

They return to the newsroom with people greeting Theresa warmly as she passes them by, introducing Daniel as they go. Once they are ensconced in the newsroom Theresa introduces Daniel to specific people who he will need to work in concert with on location. The first of these is Mark Jerome who is a camera man; the next is Johnny Broad who is responsible for the sound by means of a boom microphone which is usually held above the presenter's head, out of camera shot when the presenter is reading from the autocue.

The latter is a screen with a rolling word presentation that the presenter reads from when reporting from outside locations and is held just below the camera. It is an unwieldy contraption which is operated by hand by the camera man who has to wind it at just the correct speed for the presenter to read. If he winds it too fast, the reader has trouble keeping up with it; conversely exactly the opposite occurs and the reader is left speaking so slowly as to make him look ridiculous, so it is important that the cameraman and presenter are in tune with each other. During the next few days Daniel and Mark rehearse this part of the presentation again and again.

The presenter prepares his speech that is then typed up onto the autocue ready to be read. When done professionally the presenter appears to be reciting his piece from memory and avoids the necessity for, he, or she to be referring to written notes.

This then completes the team that are needed to produce televised reports from abroad. They will develop and grow together over the next few years, sometimes in places of luxury and opulence, but more often in dangerous places where war is being waged and where their complete trust and understanding of each other is paramount. To get to this stage will take some time, but it helps enormously that they all like each other immediately.

Daniel spends several days "learning the ropes" until after nearly two weeks Terry calls him in to his office where Theresa is already present and says "I have a project for you Daniel which means that you will have to leave to get there by plane tomorrow latest"

"Where is it that I have to go Terry".

"Well as you know General Idi Amin led a military coup d'e'tat in Uganda in January of nineteen seventy-one against the incumbent President Milton Obote, and rumours of atrocities have been rife there ever since, so we need to get you over there to find out just what is going on. Your job will be to go and get an interview if possible, with Amin, but also to visit as many places as you can to assess what the regime is doing. There have been reports of many people being killed and many thousands being displaced. I suggest that you get in touch with our Embassy first and see if they can arrange a meeting with General Amin. It may be that you have to speak to someone in the Ugandan Junta which has set up its own Government. I can't tell you anymore because the situation is so fluid out there at the moment, but I am sure that you will be able to achieve something. As for how long that you will be there is a matter of pure conjecture".

"Only you can decide when you have exhausted as much as you can, because at the moment it is a moving feast out there and changes appear to be being made on a continuing basis. Theresa here will go through things and tell you what paperwork you need as well as giving you a list of contacts and anything else that is relevant. I will expect a daily report of say five hundred words, which can be transmitted by radio for our news bulletins, and at least three or four video tapes which can be flown back to us for inclusion in the television news. It just remains for me to wish you good luck in your first assignment, so break a leg as they say".

As Terry finishes speaking, Theresa motions for Daniel to follow her to her office where Mark Jerome and Johnny Broad are already gathered.

"Here are your air flight tickets for tomorrow. Your flight leaves at midday from Heathrow she begins".

Theresa spends the rest of the day explaining in more detail the scant information that is known about the new regime in Uganda until she eventually says "Well that's about all I can tell you boys, but you know that we are always here to help you if possible, but don't forget to keep in touch with The British Embassy as well, although I think that is more likely that if you do somehow offend the Amin administration, that you will be deported. So, for now, Goodbye and Good Luck".

Time between Daniel and Theresa has been minimal since they spoke of their feelings for one another and the subject has not been raised again, leaving Daniel to assume that he is correct in his assumption that she has given the matter more thought and has decided against pursuing their relationship any further.

Returning to his flat Daniel packs in readiness for the next day and is just thinking whether he can be bothered to make a meal for himself or to go out to eat when there is a ring on his doorbell. Wondering who it can be, on the basis he rarely receives house calls he is stunned when he opens the door to see Theresa looking ravishing in a pale blue short sleeved summer dress, which follows the contours of her figure. It is cut low at the front, with a blue and pink silk scarf. She wears high navy-blue heeled shoes which accentuate her long slim legs and she carries a matching blue summer jacket slung carelessly over one shoulder.

Before she can even speak Daniel lets out a small groan of approval, at which she smiles, saying "Hi Dan I hope you don't mind me coming round like this but I would like to explain the reason why I have not spoken to you about the two of us anymore since your first day at work. Can I come in"?

Daniel, still dumbstruck at seeing her replies "Of course, come in, you are the very last person that I expected when the bell rang. But before you do, let me take a look at you". Standing back he takes hold of her hands in his, before standing back and staring directly into her warm chocolate eyes, saying "I am finding it difficult to find the words to explain how beautiful you are and just how overwhelmed I am to see you here, but it's important that I get it right. I have dreamed of this moment, or something like it for so long. I honestly thought that I would never see you again. Then more recently, seeing you every day and not knowing if you wanted us to get together again has been sheer torture".

"Dan stop wittering on and let me in" Theresa says with a laugh as she brushes passed him into the small hall, after which he ushers her into the large living room.

"Wow, what a fabulous view of the river and The South Bank that you have from here". Moving over to the large panoramic windows she stands entranced looking out, before turning to Daniel.

"It is so amazingly beautiful Dan; if I lived here, I don't think that I would be able to drag myself away from this stunning view". Then as Daniel closes the gap between them she moves forward to meet him and for the next few minutes they are totally absorbed with each other as he bends to gently kiss her, first her eye lids and then her neck, inhaling in the smell of her musky perfume and the feel of her hair, before tasting her soft tender lips that seem to melt as they meet his.

After what seems only a brief moment to Daniel but is in fact much longer, Theresa pulls almost apologetically away, before smiling and saying "before this goes any further, let me tell you why I came. So why don't we sit together on the sofa and I will explain".

They sit together, Daniel with his arm around her, not wanting their closeness to end.

"Remember Dan that I told you that I was already seeing someone when we spoke last but that it was very infrequent. Well he rang me last night and invited me out. After you and I spoke I knew that I only wanted to be with you, but I went to see him, only because I thought it was the right thing to do, to tell him face to face".

"Did you"? Daniel is impatient now thinking that Theresa had changed her mind when she got there.

"Of course, I did you ninny, why do you think I am here"?

Daniel cup of joy runs over as he grabs her and hugs her in a bear grip, lifting her off her feet and swinging her round, while simultaneously smothering her with kisses. Much more time elapses on this occasion, until they eventually come up for air.

They spend the rest of the evening talking about each other, filling in the gaps from their days at University until Daniel suddenly asks "Hey, have you eaten yet because I have just remembered that when you came, I was just on my way out to the restaurant. Would you like to do that"?

Theresa ponders for a moment before she says "No, I went straight home to change and then came here; but why don't we order a take-away and stay in here. I would rather that it was just the two of us".

"I hadn't thought of that, there's a Chinese restaurant just up the road and they deliver meals, is that o.k."?

"Great, we can sit by the window and watch the river and then afterwards you can show me the rest of your flat".

Once the meal arrives, Dan pulls the dining table up to the window so that they can watch the world go by.

"I think that this special occasion deserves Champagne; just give me a minute, I think I have one in the fridge"

Disappearing into the kitchen, he returns triumphantly carrying a bottle from which he pours into two large glass flutes and raising one of them aloft says "Here's to us, but more importantly, here is to you, the woman I have waited for, without always realising it for so long".

Theresa acknowledges Daniels homage to her and replies "Never mind Dan, there is nothing that we can do about it now, but if it's any consolation just think how great it is going to be catching up".

They sit to eat but both soon become aware that they are not hungry, the sense of occasion becoming too much for them, until Theresa says "come on Dan you haven't shown me the rest of the flat yet".

"Well there's not much to see really, but sure, if that is what you want" he says leading the way into the kitchen which is well appointed with cream cabinets and cupboards. The ceiling has two rows of spotlights which floods the room with artificial light, while there is a large window at one end just above the sink. All the tops appear to be of marble and there is an island extending out into the room, which has a number of high stools around it.

"I don't spend much time in here although I am getting better at cooking. I do a mean chicken curry, if I say so myself, which will knock your socks off. Why you would want that to happen I don't know, but that is what I have been told" Then leading her back into the hall he shows her the bathroom which has a bath with a shower facility. There is a separate toilet next door. Finally, he says" all that remains is the bedrooms of which there are two, the first of which is quite small and which is used if I have someone to stay. That just leaves my bedroom which is larger, behind this door" he finishes, standing back to allow Theresa to go first.

"Oh yes I can see that it's a man's room "she exclaims, noting the minimalistic appearance. There are no pictures on the walls and the only furniture consists of a double wardrobe a bedside table and a three-foot single bed.

"Well I have never felt the need to do anything with it because of the hours that I worked. Invariably I would get home late and crash out for a few hours before it was time to go out again".

He turns to lead her out again, but before he can do so she takes him by the hand and whispers "Well, we will have to change all that, won't we", before leading him across to the bed.

Their lovemaking is feverish and all-consuming as they offer themselves to each other. Daniel remembering vividly where and how to please Theresa, places that she taught him so many years ago.

As the night continues so does their need for each other, until finally Theresa, who is sitting astride Daniel climaxes for the final time, moaning and shuddering in ecstasy, before collapsing beside him. They both fall asleep in each other's arms, totally exhausted.

Waking suddenly Theresa shakes Daniel saying in a voice filled with panic "wake up Dan, its three o'clock and I have to get home".

"Don't worry my love, why don't you stay the rest of the night and I will run you back in the morning in plenty of time for you to change and get to work. That way we can first have breakfast together. I don't need to be at the airport until midday which will give us plenty of time".

"Are you sure Dan, I can get a taxi if it is easier for you".

"Yes, I would like it very much if you stayed; anyway, if I get another couple of hours sleep, I should be able to continue our physical conversation, if you know what I mean". Laughing, Theresa replies "Oh, I know just what you mean Dan. Why didn't I think of that"?

Daniel encompassing her replies in soft earnest tones "we must make the most of the opportunity because I don't know how long it will be before I am back from Uganda" to which Theresa nods her head in acknowledgment.

"I know, it is so ironic that we finally get back together and you have to go away almost straight away".

The rest of the night passes until Daniel's alarm clock wakes them. The thought that they won't see each other again, possibly for several weeks adds impetus to their lovemaking. Their emotions are an intoxicating mixture of elation on their reconciliation and a sense of loss that they will soon have to part.

Eventually and reluctantly they dress and have breakfast, but Theresa cannot resist spending time just looking out of the living room window. She stands transfixed watching commuters of all nationalities and genders making their way along The Victoria Embankment, to their jobs in the Financial Centre in the city. As she raises her eyes, she can see right across the river to The London Television Centre and The National Theatre just beyond it. Small river craft scurry up and down like water beetles on a pond. Scanning right to left she notes the myriad amount of people crossing Blackfriars Bridge, like locusts searching for their next meal.

"Oh Dan, this is such a lovely spot to live; you must spend all your time just looking out watching the world go by".

"Not as much as I would like, but I hope that you will have lots of time to see it again in the future. By the way where is it that you live, I have forgotten to ask in all the excitement"?

"At Chiswick in Asbourne Grove; my place is not as swish as this, but it's handy for the B.B.C Television Centre at Shepherds Bush: speaking of which we had better go, because I have to be at work by nine. Look I have written my home telephone number so that you can ring me whenever you have the chance from Uganda. I am sure that we will speak while I am at work, but it will all be about work; there will be no opportunity to speak personally".

Daniel takes her home to Chiswick on his motor bike, where they sit outside for a while saying their goodbyes. "Well good luck in Uganda Dan, don't forget to ring; I will miss you".

"Me too" he replies as he leaves to return and get ready to go to Heathrow.

CHAPTER 26.

1973.
UGANDA.

Daniel and his crew arrive at Entebbe airport at three in the afternoon of the second of November 1973. As they step from the plane, they are hit by a blast of humid heat that has them perspiring immediately. Eventually negotiating their way out of the airport, they hail a taxi of dubious vintage to take them to their hotel in Kampala.

Once here Daniel consults the notes that he has made in England about Idi Amin's regime change although he is aware of most of it. He knows that Amin led a successful coup de 'tat against the incumbent President Milton Obote in January nineteen seventy-one while the later was out of the country attending the Commonwealth Heads of Government Meeting in Singapore.

Obote's regime had terrorised harassed and tortured its own people. Frequent food shortages had blasted food prices through the roof. Obote's persecution of Indian traders had contributed to this. During Obote's regime flagrant and widespread corruption had emerged. The regime was disliked, but Amin's regime change was to prove even more feared and hated. Neither was Amin's action taken to improve life and repeal Obote's corruption, but rather one of self-preservation on Amin's part, when he found out that Obote had left instructions while he was out of the country, for him to be arrested by loyal officers in the Army.

Once in Amin's control, Uganda then effectively became a military dictatorship. He had no other experience than the military, which determined the character of his rule. Uganda was in effect governed from a collection of military barracks scattered across the country. The Ugandan State Research Bureau (SRB) which had its headquarters at Nakasero, became the scene of torture and executions over the next couple of years. The army itself was an area of lethal competition, in which losers were usually eliminated.

In 1971 and 1972 the Lugbara and Kakwa (Amin's ethnic group) from the West Nile were slaughtering northern Acholi and Langi, who were identified with Obote.

Only the most trusted military units were allowed ammunition, although this prohibition did not prevent a series of mutinies and murders.

Daniel is also aware that the in the previous year (1972) an attempt by an American journalist, Nicholas Stroh, and his colleague, Robert Siedle, to investigate one of these barrack outbreaks at the Simba battalion in Mbarara, led to their disappearance and later, deaths.

Amin made the usual statements about his government's intent to play a mere "caretaker role" until the country could recover sufficiently for civilian rule. He repudiated Obote's non-aligned foreign policy, and his government was quickly recognised by Israel, Britain and The United States.

In the two years since Amin had seized power the economy had been devastated by his policies, including the expulsion of Asians, the nationalisation of businesses and industry, and the expansion of the public sector.

In August 1972, Amin gave most of Uganda's Asians 90 days to leave the country, and then seizes their property homes and businesses. The expulsion took place against a backdrop of India phobia in Uganda, with Amin accusing the minority of the Asian population of disloyalty, non-integration and commercial malpractice, claims Indian leaders disputed. In response Amin argued that he was giving Uganda back to the ethnic Ugandans.

Sixty thousand Asian's were deported, about half of which, being citizens of The United Kingdom, emigrated there.

This then is the situation as Daniel arrives against the further background of reports of disappearance of anyone who opposes Amin. Troops loyal to Obote are tortured after which they disappear off the radar.

Amin switches allegiance as and when it suits his mood, first rejecting Israel's help, which had been considerable, only to secure financial and military aid from Libya.

Daniel decides that his first objective is to visit as many places as possible to get the feelings of its inhabitants, and draws up an itinerary with each place having its own separate time scale. Once he has done this, he decides that he will also try to get an interview with Idi Amin, but knowing that it will be very difficult to achieve.

It is in this background of terror and corruption, that Daniel begins his journey to investigate truth from rumour. Hiring an old four-wheel drive Toyota and driver called Thomas who has been recommended, they set off first for Masaka, a chief town about one day's drive south of Kampala. The reason for this is because it is on what is classed as a main road, but what appears to be in Daniel's eyes, a track of flattened earth, making him to idly wonder what secondary roads are like.

Although he knows the background to these events, Daniel is appalled at the scenes of horror and devastation that they meet as they make their way, passing villages which have been first pillaged and plundered, and subsequently torched. It is obvious that some, if not all of the inhabitants have been slaughtered, by the mounds of hastily dug graves that are everywhere. In one or two villages there are a few villagers who have escaped the conflagration, only to return after the attackers have left.

Daniel tries to talk to some of them, but if they do not flee from him, they are too afraid to tell him who has caused such devastation, only muttering that "soldiers came when we were asleep, before most of us could escape", but other than that they will not reveal their names or anything else for fear of reprisals. Some of them have horrific injuries caused by machetes, some with lost limbs and some with burns which have become open sores, while escaping from the fires.

While Daniel, together with Johnny Broad on sound is interviewing as many of the villagers that are left, Mark is filming the evidence of the violence. After a while Daniel does get snippets of information which reveal who the attackers were, but invariably they are from one faction or another from the military.

This scene is repeated at regular intervals as they make their way to Masaka, each one a repetition of the last.

As they get to Masaka the picture is even more graphic. Here there were once many Asian shopkeepers and businesses who have now been expelled from Uganda. The people who emerged as the beneficiaries of their expulsion, were not, as Amin claimed at the time "the common man", but rather the Ugandan army. Shops, ranches, farms and agricultural estates were confiscated, along with cars, home and other household goods. This expropriation has proved disastrous for the already declining economy. Daniel's guide has told him in addition that the new owners, many of whom have no experience in how to run a business, soon ran them into the ground, from mismanagement and abuse of power.

In addition, cement factories at Tororo and Fort Portal has collapsed from lack of maintenance and neglect, and sugar production has ground to a halt as unmaintained machinery jammed permanently.

Finding a room at a dilapidated and run-down hotel, Daniel prepares his piece of five hundred words which he then telephones to the B.B.C. in readiness to be broadcast over the radio within the next couple of days, signing off as "your foreign correspondent in Uganda".

Finally, before retiring to bed, the three of them go out and about in the town, filming and recording Daniel's commentary of the scenes of devastation and neglect that Amin's new regime has caused. Once this is completed, they return to the hotel to eat before making their way to bed.

Their meal is basic, the only form of food available seeming to some form of maize, which is one of the staple foods, not only in Uganda, but throughout most of Africa. Daniel resolves to try and find some fresh food and fruit, which they can take with them, if at all possible.

They are all utterly exhausted, not only from their travel, but mostly from the oppressive heat and extreme humidity; but sleep doesn't come easily as the temperature in the bedrooms is even higher than outside. They all have taken the precaution to bring mosquito nets which they lay under, the threat from malaria being very real.

This then is the pattern for the next two weeks as they travel around the country. Their days are met invariably with scenes of horror and devastation, which are usually even worse in isolated places. Their guide Thomas tries to keep them away from places where the military are, because he is unable to know which factions are more hostile than others, but that neither is sympathetic to their objectives. There are countless incidents in the coming days when Thomas takes avoiding action when he spots columns of either military units or renegade bandits, knowing that either will attack them to loot and possibly kill them in the process. On several occasions they are chased by unidentified gangs who, travelling in old military vehicles, open fire as Thomas accelerates to keep ahead of them. The sound of bullets whistling past their vehicle, some even striking it, is a chilling experience, reminding them that they are effectively in a war zone and as much at risk as the villagers, many of whom have already died or been maimed.

But despite this Daniel manages to file a daily report for radio as they progress, although he is not able to telephone it through in those places where telephones do not exist. Eventually, after eleven days they return to Kampala where Daniel tries to contact someone in authority who can arrange him an interview with President Idi Amin.

Eventually after three days he is put through to an unnamed senior officer in "The Command Post" which is Amin's new name for Government House.

"My name is Daniel Thornton and I am the foreign correspondent for the B.B.C., and my job is to report on the new Ugandan Government. Would it be possible to get an interview with President Amin, so that he can explain the progress that the country has made since his rise to power"?

"Well Mr. Thornton, I have to tell you unequivocally that the answer to your request is no. You may not realise it, but your actions in my country have not gone unnoticed by those of us in authority. I have to also inform you that you are no longer welcome here". Then more chillingly "Therefore if you have not left Uganda by tomorrow, I cannot guarantee your safety; do I make myself clear"?

Daniel understanding the threat replies "perfectly sir, we will be on the evening flight tomorrow, but if President Amin ever wants to give the B.B.C. an interview I would be honoured to fly out and meet with him".

For the very first time Daniel is brought face to face with the perils of his new job and feels fear not only for himself, but for his team as well.

Deciding that discretion is the better part of valour, Daniel does not pursue this objective and makes immediate arrangements to fly home. He has only managed to speak to Theresa a couple of times since he first got to Uganda, the time difference making it difficult, but when they speak after his conversation with the representative in Government, Theresa can hear the fear in his voice as he repeats it.

"Oh God Dan, that sounds horrendous, have you arranged your flight. If it's any consolation, Terry is delighted with your verbal reports, some of which have already been broadcast. Have you managed to get any films that we can show on television because they will be even more effective than radio"? Then "I have missed you so much Dan and I look forward to seeing you in a couple of days".

"I love you Theresa "says Daniel simply; something that he has always known but has been reticent to declare before. He has not meant to say it now, but hearing her welcoming voice after the unmistakable threat that he had received earlier, triggers his response.

Their last day before returning to Kampala is spent at Jinja, which is the place where Lake Victoria drains into The Victoria Nile, the river which flows north through Uganda is effectively the point of the source of the Nile itself. It is a mesmerising place, a humbling experience as they watch the sheer volume and power of the mighty river at the beginning of its long journey to Egypt and the Nile Delta.

As they lift off from Entebbe, Daniel is surprised to realise that although his journey has shown him the corrupt and devastating effects of Amin's regime, he is also leaving with unforgettable memories of the sheer beauty of this land, and reflects on how different things might be under a more benign, democratic autonomy.

Places like Nakasongola, which although devastated by regime change, sits on the edge of Lake Kyoga. The views across the lake he finds almost indescribable, which he thinks is surely a testament to its beauty, if he, a man who spends his life describing things, finds it so difficult.

He has been amazed at how vivid and varied the shades of green are in the lush vegetation, so colourful that at times it hurts the eyes. Finally, he reflects what a wonderful, beautiful country Uganda could be if it was run by the right people who cared for its citizens and its future, rather than those corrupt few who just want to take what they can at everyone else's expense.

CHAPTER 27.

1973.
DANIEL AND THERESA.

Arriving at Heathrow, the three of them make their way to the B.B.C. at Shepherds Bush studios. They are by now totally exhausted after their long overnight flight, but Daniel wants to finish some of the videos which he needs to put on some audio introductory voice overs as well as checking everything for content.

Terry and Theresa welcome them back, she noticeably with a hug for Daniel, before saying "You have done fantastically well with your reports for radio which have already been broadcast; how many videos did you manage to film"?

"Well I don't know how many hours you want to put out on television, but we have got something like nine or ten hours' worth, although I am sure that it will be a lot less once it has been edited. Do you want me to do it now"? Oh by the way I have couple of reports which I got Johnny Broad to put on tape for the radio, the last one of which finishes with a recording of my conversation with the official who threatened us that if we did not leave Uganda he could not guarantee our safety".

"Wow that is a scoop of gigantic proportions Dan and it will demonstrate to the British public what sort of man and regime that Amin is operating, if your reports haven't done so already. Don't worry about editing the videos today, there is no immediate hurry. Perhaps we could look at them together in a day or so, just to make sure that there is nothing politically sensitive that will offend people who we don't want to offend. Meanwhile thanks to all three of you for your great work".

As Daniel starts to make his way out if the building, Theresa catches up with him. "You must be exhausted Dan; just get yourself home and get some sleep and I will see you in a couple of days".

"You are right about that, I think that I could sleep for a week, but I was hoping that you could come to mine tomorrow night. It seems so long since we were together on our own".

"Oh good, I was hoping that you would ask. I would offer for you to come to me but I have one of the newswomen staying temporarily with me which could cramp our style.

* * *

Theresa arrives as promised the next evening and is met at the door by a refreshed Daniel. As soon as she is inside, they are kissing hungrily while trying to undress each other at the same time. As they break for air Theresa smiles at him wickedly before saying breathlessly" We are not having any preliminaries tonight then Dan. Nothing to eat first, no celebratory drinks, just bed, is that it"?

Daniel looks nonplussed for a moment before saying "Oh I am sorry my love, I just thought that…….before he can say anymore Theresa laughs "I was only joking Dan, of course that is what I want too".

"Are you sure, because I have bought a new bed for the occasion, but the way I am feeling about you now, I don't think we are going to get there in time".

"Wow a new bed, I have got to see this" Theresa exclaims excitedly, pulling him forcefully behind her. Throwing open the bedroom door, she stands transfixed, taking in the view before her, then immediately collapsing with uncontrollable laughter into Daniel' arms as she sees the small two berth tent that he has erected where his bed used to be.

"I just love it Dan, what a great idea, we can relive our time on Dartmoor" Theresa says huskily, her mood changing from one of laughter to need.

"I am so relieved that you like it, I only did it for a joke, but we can use the bed in the other room if you would rather".

"No chance Dan" says Theresa crawling into the tent. "I wouldn't miss this for the entire world; now come on and get yourself in here" and then "Oh you have got all the kit as well, inflatable mattresses, sleeping bags, even a ground sheet; you seem to have got everything".

"More importantly" says Daniel as he enters the tent "I've got you" as he reaches for her.

Their lovemaking is as intense as always, that is, until after some time just as they are reaching a crescendo, the guide ropes of the tent, which Daniel has only secured by putting books on them, gives way and they are left floundering, enveloped in canvass and helpless with laughter. But once they have recovered nothing can daunt their amore.

This then is the turning point for their relationship, a reaffirmation of their feelings for one another. As he reflects on it, which he often does, Daniel realises that this is the happiest that he has ever felt.

Within only a few weeks Daniel suggests that they both move in together, either him moving to Theresa or vice-versa. Hesitatingly he puts it to her, and is overjoyed when she replies "Oh I would love to Dan, but the only stipulation I would make is that I move into yours. Although it is further from where I am in Chiswick to work, I really love your flat and where it is. The views from your window and the locality it is in are stunning" and then, although she has called him her love, for the first time she says "You must know that I love you Dan, I don't know why I haven't told you earlier, because I have always loved you from the first time we met on Dartmoor".

Moving in together gives them both a sense of security, taking away any uncertainties that they may have had at the beginning, so much so in fact that on one day in June she suddenly says "How would you feel if I asked you to come with me and see my parents. I speak to them regularly and I have told them about you and I know that they would love to meet you".

"Of course, my love, I would like that, but on one condition, that we also go to meet my mother. I know that she will love you as much as I do".

"I would like to meet her too Dan. From what you have told me about her, she is obviously a woman of substance; she has to be, to have achieved all that she has on her own. Let's go to my parents this weekend and to yours on another weekend in a few weeks' time".

* * *

They travel by train from Paddington straight through Bristol Temple Meads, continuing on to West End in Nailsea, where they hail a taxi which takes them to Theresa's parents address in Eastway Square. As they draw up outside the house, Theresa's parents come running out to greet them, her mother first, a beam of pure delight on her face as she embraces her daughter, saying "Oh it's so good to see you my love" before standing back and adding " and you are Dan of course, I recognise you from your reports on television. Welcome, I am Val and this is my husband Daryl".

Daniel is stunned to see an older version of Theresa as he stands back; the same mischievous smile, intense brown/ black eyes and brunette hair, albeit with streaks of white. Tall and still slim for her age, she exudes both confidence and warmth.

"Hi Dan" says Daryl" I have heard so much about you from Theresa; how strange that you two met again so many years after leaving University".

Dan is met by a giant of a man, standing something like six feet four inches tall, with a build to match. He has a bush of black unruly hair which has flecks of grey at the temple and sides giving him an air of authority. He has blue piercing eyes that at this moment are examining the man who is of such interest to his daughter. He is dressed casually in a short sleeved shirt and jeans .He smiles readily as he continues "come on, let's go inside and we can catch up with what the two of you have been doing" adding as an afterthought to Theresa "you will be pleased to know that your brother and his family have just arrived".

"Oh great" she replies before turning to Daniel and saying mysteriously" I think that you will like him Dan; anyway, he remembers you".

As they enter the house, they are met by a man who can only be Daryl's son. He is tall with broad shoulders and has long jet-black hair. Thinking about it, Daniel decides that he is as much a young clone of Daryl as Theresa is to her mother Val. But even more than that he is vaguely familiar

But as Theresa introduces Dan to her brother, everything clicks into place as she says "Dan I would like you to meet my brother Peter, his wife Christine and their son Liam who is ten, going on fifty".

She says nothing more, waiting for Daniel to react, which he does immediately when he says "Hi Peter, you're her brother now are you; I think that you were her boyfriend the last time that we met".

"Yes, I'm sorry about that, but it wasn't my idea Dan; Theresa didn't want to be on her own at her graduation, although our parents were there. I think that she wanted to prove a point to you, but whatever it was I think that you will both have to work it out together".

"Oh, I think that he has worked it out already Peter" interrupts Theresa, laughing "o.k. I was just trying to make you jealous, but it didn't work, did it"?

Daniel's face is serious as he replies" You couldn't be more wrong my love, I was absolutely devastated at the time" then brightening, "still, all's well that ends well. No wonder you didn't want to tell me anymore about Peter you little minx".

Val has made lunch which they consume while the family catch up with each other's news. Some of this now includes Daniel of course as he and Theresa tell the others of their work and lives in London.

"Where is it that you work Daryl? I think that Theresa informed me many years ago that you worked for a Shipping Agent".

"Yes, and I am still there. I work in Queens Square in Bristol most of the time but we have an office in Avonmouth as well which I have to sometimes go to. Val works a few hours a week at the supermarket in Nailsea, but we both hope to take early retirement in five years' time".

"What about you Peter"? Daniel enquires.

"Well, I am Manager of a building Society in the centre of Bristol" is the reply. "I have been there since leaving school. It is where I met Christine who worked there as well. We live in Clevedon now which is just a few miles away".

"I am sorry but our other daughter cannot be here to meet you today Dan" continues Val "because she is married and lives in Gloucester. Not that it is a problem; it's just that she has had a baby girl a few weeks ago and is not yet ready or able to make the journey at the moment".

"That is understandable" says Daniel "but perhaps Theresa and I can go and see her sometime when we visit my mother, who lives not a million miles away in Chipping Norton."

Changing the subject, Daryl enquires "So what do you want to do with the rest of your day"?

"Well dad I would like to show Dan around the village this afternoon and then I thought it would be nice if we all went up to the Queens Head this evening and played skittles. They still do that don't they"?

"You bet, but why don't Peter and Christine join you while we look after Liam and spoil him rotten" retorts Daryl, before adding" I tell you what, why don't we all go early and grab a pub meal. It will save your mum cooking".

Once agreed, the four of them leave Eastway Square and wander slowly around the village, both Peter and Theresa pointing out place of interest. Daniel can see that the village was very old village originally, from the parts that he can still observe which must have been enchanting. But much of it is still is being extended massively by new estate houses.

"What happened" he asks Theresa.

"It's now a dormitory town for people who work in Bristol. There is just not sufficient land available for everyone who wants to live and work there, hence this unsightly compromise, new brick housing surrounding the village of local stone, destroying its quaintness and a way of life that has remained untouched for hundreds of years. I do understand the reasons, but I just think that it could have been done more sympathetically".

* * *

The Queens Head is still as Theresa remembers it from her youth, although there are only one or two locals who she can recall. The evening passes in a flash as they first eat, most of them choosing pasty and chips (a Queens Head speciality) before playing the local Queens Head team at skittles, the latter who seem to practice every night according to Daryl, being prepared to take on all comers as and when necessary.

As expected they are thrashed but unbowed and not a little the worse for wear after heavy consumption of the many choices of beers and wine available as they wind their way back to Val and Daryl's, while Peter and

Christine say their farewells before driving home to Clevedon, but promising to visit Theresa and Daniel in London soon.

Daniel and Theresa are slightly concerned about their sleeping arrangements which they have discussed prior to arrival, but their doubts are soon dispelled as Val tells them "I have put you both in your old bedroom Theresa. Then smiling "it's a little late to try and make you have separate rooms".

Sunday is spent lazing after a late start due to hang overs of varying intensity, but once they have all consumed English breakfasts washed down with mugs of steaming tea the ice is broken and Daniel becomes the main source of interest as they quiz him about his work in journalism.

He makes them both laugh and cry as he describes some of his more adventurous experiences. They listen enthralled as he tells them some of the unknown and salacious details about the Kray and Richardson gangs until it is nearly time for both Theresa and him to leave in time to catch the train back to London.

"Why don't you both come up to see us Mum? You could stay for a couple of days and we could all go out to a show or shopping in Oxford Street"

"Yes, I think that we would like that, wouldn't we Daryl; we could see the sights as well".

* * *

"I think that went very well, don't you"? Theresa remarks, as they find their seats on the train. "Thank you for coming Dan, I think that they liked you a lot".

"You don't have to thank me my love; I really enjoyed it and their company immensely. You have parents who care for you very much, which is pretty much how I feel about you as well".

"Your mother is next Dan. I feel very guilty because you haven't told her about us yet, have you"?

"No, I wanted to surprise her. Obviously, I will have to tell her that I am bringing a female friend with me but I don't want to tell her that it's you, because I have a strong feeling that she will be over the moon when she does find out. I remember seeing the disappointment on her face at our graduation when you and I obviously had meant something to one another at some time, but for reasons that I could not explain to her, we were unable to take any further".

The next few weeks are hectic for both of them as Daniel makes a number of trips to Europe visiting either the heads of state or their finance ministers in various countries. The U.K. had joined the EEC on the first of January and the B.B.C wanted to gauge Europe's response to it so far, because there was a feeling generally of resentment that the British public had been dragged into the union without first being consulted in a referendum.

Daniel's visits are done on an ad hoc basis, rather than all at once. He visits France and Germany first, before returning, after which he visits Holland and Belgium. These visits are of only two-or three days duration which is ideal for he and Theresa's burgeoning relationship.

Their spare time is of paramount importance to both of them, which they grab avidly, after long periods of intense pressure at work. Free weekends are spent exploring London, going to the theatre or out for meals. Despite both of them having lived in London for several years they never tire of exploring its many facets; museums and art galleries is a never-ending source of interest, as is The British Library which holds periodic special exhibitions. But even more than any off these they love the sights and sounds and the history of this magnificent city that has been England's Capital for hundreds of tears.

Occasionally Theresa plays host at their flat to a number of their circle of growing friends. She loves cooking and entertaining and Daniel is happy to help her, knowing the pleasure she gets from it.

On one such occasion Daniel's new colleagues, Mark Jerome and Johnny Broad, together with their wives, as well as Chas, his old roommate and Fay, his wife are all invited as well as some of Theresa's work mates. The flat soon resounds with the sound of their laughter as they get to know one another, intermingled with their appreciation and delight of Theresa's cooking extravaganza.

When they finally leave, chattering and jostling out onto the street below Daniel takes Theresa in his arms saying "Thank you my love, you did a great job. They all seemed to get on famously with each other" then he looks at her in a way that she recognises instantly. "Come on let's go to bed, we can sort the dishes out in the morning". But before he has time to say more, she replies "I know what you are thinking, but you have no chance tonight, I am shattered".

But she surprises herself as she responds to his lovemaking once they get into bed.

* * *

After telephoning Ella and arranging to visit her in Chipping Norton, Daniel adds briefly and mysteriously "Oh by the way, I will be bringing my girlfriend with me Mum, she is just dying to meet you".

"Girlfriend, what girlfriend; you never told me that you have a girlfriend"? Says Ella in a voice filled with excitement and pleasure that her son has at last found someone significant in his life. "How long have you known her, who is she, what does she do, how old is she......"?

"Whoa, hold your horses a minute Mum, all will be revealed when we get there on Friday evening after work in my new car. I figured that it was about time that I got one because the two of us travelling on the motorbike in all weathers is just not viable. I am keeping the bike though, because it is still handy for me getting around London when I need to in a hurry"

"I will see you on Friday evening then son; I can't wait, you have got me intrigued about your lady".

"O.K. mum; don't bother to cook for us when we arrive. I thought that we could go to The Pines, I have told my friend all about it and she is dying to see it, but most of all she is looking forward to meeting you".

* * *

It is now late August as Daniel pulls up outside Ella's Café on the designated Friday evening. She has been eagerly awaiting their arrival and comes hurrying out to greet them as he and Theresa clamber from the car.

As Theresa stands upright Ella looks at her and her face is transformed by a look of wonder, unbelief almost, before she says in a voice filled with emotion, her eyes verging on tears "Oh, its Theresa isn't it" before continuing "I hoped so very, very much that it would be you".

Theresa mystified responds "Thank you, but what do you mean, I don't think that we have ever met".

"No, we have never been formally introduced and in fact the only and last time I saw you was on your and Daniel's graduation day. But it was enough to tell me of the strength of feeling that he held for you and the despair that he felt that you could not be with each other. That is why I am so pleased and happy to see you together at last. Please come here and give me a hug my dear".

Daniel has stood transfixed while all this had been going on, until he can contain himself no longer "I never realised that you had witnessed my downfall all those years ago mum. You never gave indication at the time".

"Well I didn't want to make matters worse because I could see how upset you were, but that's all behind the two of you now, so let's go inside and celebrate. I have a bottle of bubbly in a bucket of ice waiting for this occasion, after which we can go to The Pines to eat".

As they go inside Theresa whispers to Daniel "Your mother is amazing. Fancy remembering about the last time we met at graduation. By the way when are you going to tell her about us".

"I think that now is as good a time as any" comes Daniel's reply.

As Ella returns with champagne and fills their glasses, Daniel raises his, saying "I have a toast to make, please raise your glasses to my mother, for everything that she is and means to me." Then he quickly follows this saying "My next toast is to Theresa who has agreed to be my wife".

Ella is stunned and amazed with delight at this unexpected news and it takes her several seconds before she responds enthusiastically "Congratulations to both of you. What a lovely surprise" and then "I think that this calls for another bottle of champagne; you have made me so happy. Have you given any thought about when you will get married"?

"Well we don't have a date yet" replies Theresa "but soon, within the next three months. We both feel that we have wasted too much time already".

"Wow" says Ella as she rushes to embrace them both, completely unable to conceal the joy that she is feeling.

"Well I think that's a yes" says Daniel, smiling at Theresa.

They are slightly "squiffy" after consuming a bottle of champagne as they leave to walk the short distance to The Pines where Theresa can see just how venerated Ella is to both staff and clients alike.

"This place is beautiful Ella" Theresa says "Although Daniel told me about it, I never expected something quite as exquisite as this. You must be very proud".

"Thank you my dear, now what would you like to order" says Ella, blushing slightly and not knowing quite how to respond. "Now tell me how you met and got together again" and then "I am sorry if I am going on too much my dear but I can still hardly believe that it's you sitting here".

Once they are all seated Theresa relates the story of how she and Daniel found each other again. Ella notes with joy, in every word and syllable that she speaks, the depth of feelings that she and Daniel have for each other.

Daniel then tells his mother about his work, much of which she has either heard on the radio or seen on television, but he explains in more detail the operational side of it, but at the same time omitting to mention any of the dangers that his work sometimes entails.

As they leave the restaurant to return home Ella tells them that she has arranged all of them to visit Rachel and her family the next day, adding that Geoffrey will be coming as well, then on the following day, the

Sunday, she is returning the invitation and will be cooking lunch for all of them, which they can eat in the Café because it will be closed.

"We are going to have a party to celebrate your engagement. I am so excited; I just can't wait"

Ella has tormented herself since Daniel has said that he was coming with Theresa about the sleeping arrangements. It is only when they reach the Café that Daniel tells her that they are living together and have been for some months. She heaves a sigh of relief, because she has only two bedrooms and has dreaded the moment when she has to ask where they want to sleep. But Daniel's confession obviates the need for such drastic measures.

Ella has invested a considerable amount on the interior of the rooms at the café; redecorating and replacing new furniture everywhere. Daniel is stunned at the transformation when he and Theresa go to bed in his old room. Gone is the old single bed, to be replaced by a queen size double. Fitted wardrobes with matching drawers and bedside cabinets in white are shown to their best advantage by pale warm dusky pink walls, with a matching coloured carpet. Additionally, there is a new small en-suite shower and toilet. But Ella has retained some of Daniels posters from his school days which she has put on the walls in the places where they were originally.

The next day is a blur as Daniel shows Theresa the beautiful area of The Cotswolds where he was born and brought up. Setting off in his new Vauxhall car they head first for Chadlington the village where he was born and grew up. He shows her the cottages where his parents and grandparents had lived, before walking with her around the village.

It is a beautiful warm summer day, which showcases the local honey coloured stone buildings, giving them a warm glow. The walls which surround both the cottages and fields are also of the same material and are constructed only by placing the stones in layers without the use of cement or mortar. Flowers of many descriptions grow between the rock layers, making the walls appear to be living entities in their own right.

Returning to the car they move on travelling south to the picturesque town of Burford with its ancient buildings and history. Its wide streets denote that they were used in previous centuries to drive sheep through to market. But now its quaint shops offer local people and visitors a varied selection to satisfy almost anybody's taste. Entering the town from the south, the road in slopes down, passing clusters of centuries old houses, built high above, giving the impression from the car that the road is in a valley.

Here they stop for a repast of coffee and cakes, after which they browse the shops, each with its own niche offering. Theresa is in her element, so much so that Daniel has to remind her that they have to be back in time to go to Rachel and her family.

"O. k. but we must come here again soon "she complains.

With time running out they make their way to Stow on the Wold which again is an old market town higher up in this beautiful area. Like Burford and many other Cotswold towns, Stow owes its prosperity to sheep and the wool industry which was at its height several hundred years ago.

Its centre has a large space, again originally devoted as an area where sheep where driven to market many years ago, but which now serves as a trade market twice a week and as a car park in the intervening periods. Because it has a similar appeal as Burford, Theresa is soon exploring its many shops, scurrying round its alleyways and hidden passages.

"This area is so beautiful; I can see why you love it" Theresa remarks, as they make their way back to the car.

With their time nearly up they make their way back to Ella's at Chipping Norton, in time to all leave together with Geoffrey to go to Rachel's at Charlbury. Here they are all welcomed enthusiastically.

"Come in all of you and make yourselves at home" says Rachel before introducing Theresa to all her family. "Well Daniel, you are a dark horse, fancy not telling us about Theresa; come on spill the beans, how long have you known each other. No wait, don't tell us yet because as it's a lovely day, we are having a Bar-B-Que in the garden, so let's all go out there first".

Once they are all settled outside Daniel relates how and when he met Theresa first on Dartmoor and then more recently when he joined the B.B.C.

"You mean that you lost touch for all those years, why was that".

Daniel skates over the question, evading the need for a reply, until Rachel asks next "when are you thinking of getting married then".

"As soon as possible within the next three months, we both think that we have wasted enough time already. We hope to marry in Nailsea, which is in Somerset and is where Theresa lived with her parents before moving to London".

Theresa then outlines the few details that they have decided on for the wedding. "There is still a lot to do but I am sure that it will happen within the time scale we have set ourselves, although Daniel has to go to Bangladesh soon which will slow things down a bit".

Rachel is pensive for a few moments before saying "Look if it will help, I can make your wedding dress for you; it's what I do. But it really doesn't matter if you have already decided where you are going to get it from".

Theresa smiles broadly before saying "I would like that very much Rachel, both Ella and Dan have sung your artistic praises so much that it would be churlish to refuse".

"In that case I will measure you before you go. I have lots of this current year's design upstairs, but if you don't like any of them, we can design one together. You will need a couple of fittings, but that isn't a problem, because you can either come back or I can come up to you. I would like that, because it would give me a good opportunity to go to London; I don't go there often enough".

The afternoon continues with Fred dressed in a casual top and shorts, a beer close at hand, in control of the bar-b-que, while the rest of them sit on lounge chairs drinking their respective poisons. While this is happening Daniel can't help noticing just how much Geoffrey is fitting into the picture, being accepted completely by everybody, which makes Ella's son happy. Over the years Daniel has been concerned for his mother' future, but he can see that now that Geoffrey is in her life, she is more relaxed and happier than she has been for some time.

While Harry and Georges children are playing happily in the garden, Daniel takes the opportunity to get up to date with their parents. However infrequent his visits Daniel still has strong emotional attachments to this area, so the talk is of the people they all know.

"Did you know that Ken Braithwaite immigrated to Australia last year? He got a job teaching in a school in Brisbane. He was teaching in Charlbury so I guess that helped him; but he invited all of us to go and visit him whenever we wanted too". And then "you remember old Mrs Johnson who lived in Chadlington, well she died last week, but she had a good innings; she was ninety-five".

As the afternoon progresses, Rachel and Theresa disappear to look at wedding dress designs and for the latter to get measured. Eventually Theresa finds a design that she likes, to which Rachel responds "good choice, it's lovely, but if we change a couple of things, I think that it will look even more stunning". She goes on to explain and Theresa's eyes light up at her suggestions.

Eventually it is time for Daniel and Theresa to leave, Ella and Geoffrey deciding to stay on at Rachel and Fred's.

Now that the subject has been broached Theresa and Daniel are full of ideas and things that they need to do to start their wedding arrangements. "I think that it was all a bit unreal until today, when Rachel offered to make the wedding dress. Now I can't stop thinking about it; how about you Dan"

"I feel exactly the same my love. I think that we need to see your parents and book the church and somewhere for the reception, what do you think"?

The conversation continues as they drive back to London, both of them excited at the thought and prospect of the wedding and marriage, but even more than that, the thought of always being together.

CHAPTER 28.

1973.
A SOMERSET WEDDING.

On the twenty-eight of September 1973, Nailsea's small Church is packed to the rafters as Theresa and Daniel make their vows on this late warm autumn day. They have both been true to their word that their marriage should be as soon as possible. All the hard work and heartaches are forgotten however as they stand vowing to love each other "until death do us part".

Theresa's parents sit at the front on one side and Ella and Geoffrey on the other; they look on proudly, smiling, both women also stemming the flow of tears of happiness and nostalgia at the same time.

The reception is held at a country club just a few miles away. Daniel has arranged for a horse and trap to get them there, while the rest of the guests make their own way in cars, but his plan goes massively awry as a sudden hailstorm threatens to engulf their open carriage. The driver in charge of the horse manages to pull up the cover, to stop their clothes becoming sodden and their journey continues. However, the horse is to put it mildly, not in the first flush of youth and the further that the journey goes the slower it gets. What was originally intended to be completed in about forty minutes has now already taken over an hour and they still have a couple of miles to go.

Daniel, quickly summing up the situation, realises that their guests will have been at the venue for some considerable time already. The second factor which forces him to make the decision to abandon ship is that the horse is by now virtually at a standstill, so jumping from the carriage Daniel tells the driver that they cannot wait any longer, and after helping Theresa down, proceeds to flag down the first available vehicle. Fortunately, within a short space of time he manages to stop a small Citroen car which is carrying two young men.

Daniel apologises profusely, and after explaining the situation, the two men are only too happy to take the newly wedded couple the rest of the way to their reception, but not without making a number of jokes at the couple's expense.

But all is well as they reach their destination to be met by their guests, who in turn make a number of similar jokes. Daniel realises that his wedding will be the source of much ribaldry and fun over the years to come, and thinking about it in the cold light of day, he too can now see the funny side of the situation.

Fred who is the best man makes a speech full of jokes at Daniels expense which is to be expected and finishes on a more sombre note, with a resume of Daniels life both growing up and to date, which has the guests both laughing and crying alternately.

Theresa's father Daryl eulogises his daughter, unable to hide the pride and passion that she has engendered in her parents. He makes reference to the day of their graduation and how Theresa had inveigled her brother Peter to act as her boyfriend to make Daniel jealous, which caused no end of laughter and no little comment to his face as the day wore on.

Many of the guests are staying here overnight, as is Daniel and Theresa's parents, but the happy couple leave to catch their plane from Lulsgate airport for their honeymoon to Venice.

As they say their farewells Ella whispers to her son" now just you look after her Daniel, she is all that I could have wished for you. Don't leave it too long before you come and see me".

"I will mum; I know just how lucky I was to find her again".

* * *

Their honeymoon is all that they hoped it would be. Unfortunately, they can only be here for a few days because the demands of their work. This determines them to see as much of the sights as possible. They love waking up each morning to look out over the Grand Canal with Gondolas and waterbuses (Vaporetti) carrying sight seekers to other parts of the city. It takes a little while for them to adjust to the fact that people move from place to place by boat rather than car, bus or train. But once they slow down to the appropriate pace, they begin to enjoy the experience more and more.

They discover to their surprise that Venice is made up of over one hundred small islands which are separated by canals. These islands are linked by over four hundred bridges.

Their Hotel is close to The Rialto Bridge and from here they can walk along the Grand Canal to St. Mark's Square and look round the magnificent Basilica with its thousand years of history. Another day they catch a boat to the island of Burano where beautiful fabrics and lace can be bought. Theresa finds several items of lace exclaiming "Oh I would love these Dan they will look fantastic in the flat".

"Then you shall have them" says Daniel, not wanting or being unable to deny his beautiful wife anything.

The island of Murano is the place of their next excursion, where exquisite glass has been made for hundreds of years. They cannot resist the lure of some of the beautiful items, some of which they buy to take back as presents for family.

They visit The Doges Palace and marvel at the Bridge of Sighs, so named because of the prisoners who once walked over it under sentence of death, the sighs they make because of their inevitable fate being heard from below as they crossed it.

Their days are spent exploring the many small streets and canals which are so numerous that they frequently lose their way. But it does not matter as there is always something new and interesting to discover. They are entranced at the many shops in St. Mark's Square, Daniel buying a full-length leather coat for Theresa to keep her warm for the coming English winter. But more than all of this, they love the Italian people and the food which they stop to eat at regular intervals.

They make love often and passionately, now that they have more time to enjoy the experience, while recognising that this is a special time and that normal life will inevitably follow.

All too soon it is time for them to return home because Daniel has instructions that he has to go to Bangladesh the next week, but they vow that they will return again at some future period and relive the experience.

* * *

Daniel presents himself at the B.B.C. on his return, together with Mark and Johnny. Terry James fills in the background to the events which have happened in Bangladesh since its war of liberation from West Pakistan in March 1971, some of which they already know. He begins;

"Formerly East Pakistan, the rise of the Bengali nationalist and self-determination movement sparked a revolution and armed conflict during the 1971 Bangladesh genocide. The war began after the Pakistani military junta based in West Pakistan launched Operation Searchlight against the peoples of East Pakistan on the night of 25th March this year. It pursued the systematic elimination of nationalist Bengali citizens, students, intelligentsia, religious minorities and armed personnel. After a bitter war of attrition, West Pakistan surrendered.

The Provisional Government of Bangladesh was formed on 17th April 1971.

India joined the war on 3rd December 1971, after Pakistan launched pre-emptive air strikes on North India. The subsequent Indo-Pakistan war witnessed engagements on two war fronts. With the rapid advance of the

Allied Forces of Bangladesh and India's air supremacy established, Pakistan surrendered on 16th December 1971.

Sheikh Mujibur Rahman later took the office of Prime Minister and helped Bangladesh enter into the United Nations. He travelled to The United States, the United Kingdom and other European Nations to obtain humanitarian and development assistance for the nation. He signed a treaty of friendship with India, which pledged extensive economic and humanitarian assistance and began training Bangladesh's security forces. Major efforts were launched to rehabilitate an estimated 10 million refugees who had been displaced by the war.

A constitution had been proclaimed and elections held earlier in 1973, which had resulted in Sheikh Rahman and his party gaining power with an absolute majority. He had further outlined state programmes to expand primary education, sanitation, food, healthcare and water and electric supply across the country".

As Terry finishes his resume, it is at this stage that Daniel is asked to visit and report on the progress of this huge initiative. Because of the intensive background of war being waged by so many factions it had not been possible for journalists from any nations to gain entry into this new young state. But the B.B.C had judged that now that there was a recognised Government in place, it was the appropriate time to let the world see the progress that had been made and to show the sacrifices that it had cost.

"When do we leave Terry" asks Daniel.

"Tomorrow at midday" comes the reply. "I have produced some notes of who to see and where to go if it is possible. Good Luck; I know that you will do a great job".

Daniel's last night before he has to leave for Bangladesh is fraught for both he and Theresa. "I know that you have to go Dan, but so soon? We have only just got back from our honeymoon for God's sake".

"I know love, but it's my job. I don't want to be away from you either, but you know deep down that I have to do this. Now let's go to bed and I will comfort you".

"Oh, that's what it's called is it, comfort" says Theresa, laughing, but she doesn't care what it's called as they get into bed and Daniel' arms are around her.

* * *

Arriving after a long tiring flight at Dacca, Daniel and his companions are hit immediately by the tropical monsoon climate that is both hot and very humid. They find their hotel which they have booked into for two days to give them time to assess their next step.

The intensity of the sun, combined with heavy seasonal rain ensures that the terrain is both green and excellent for growing food stuffs, of which rice is the main crop. Unlike Uganda the people are welcoming and subdued in equal measure. The last few years have taken its toll of its inhabitants who are among the poorest of any in the world.

Once they have organised their transport, in this case an old four wheeled land rover, Daniel and his party set off to explore the countryside and how its people are coping after so much bloodshed and upheaval.

They know that Bangladesh is densely populated, low-lying, mainly river country on the Bay of Bengal. The delta plain on which Bengal stands is fed by the Ganges, Brahmaputra and Meghna rivers and their tributaries occupy 79 per cent of the country, which is where most of the population live because of its fertile ground for growing crops. Unfortunately, it is this area that is flooded regularly when the monsoon rains feed into the rivers which burst and flood the delta plain. The inhabitants are regularly subjected to floods caused by natural disasters such as cyclones, accompanied by storm surges. Most of the terrain in the south within the Bengal plain is generally at sea level.

When the floods occur, they bring mud and silt which washes through towns and villages, destroying everything in its path. There is higher ground to the north of the country which is crossed by swiftly flowing rivers.

Daniel, Mark and Johnny spend the next two weeks travelling through the country. The most striking thing that they witness everywhere they go is the sheer poverty of the inhabitants who live mostly in huts made from reeds and rushes. Their garments are worn and threadbare and there is hardly work for anyone that Daniel can see.

Most villagers have a small patch of land on which they grow rice or vegetables, some of which they take to the local market to trade for cooking pots and utensils. It is life at its most basic and Daniel and his team are often at the point of tears as they witness poverty at its most degrading and humiliating.

They travel to most of the major cities and conurbations, first south to Chittagong then North West to Khulna, Jessore, Barisal and Narayangan, before travelling further north to Rangpur. The population is now some 69 million souls who live in an area less than half the size of England.

They can see that huge efforts and commitments are being carried out by the Government, but despite all of this, their efforts are akin to a drop in the Ocean. The only evidence of manufacturing of any description is that of making garments and fabrics for export.

The difference between Daniels visit to Uganda compared to here in Bangladesh is stark; where they experienced threats of violence and a fear of the authorities, here they travel at will and experience only their own concern for the inhabitants of this beautiful impoverished nation. They record as much as they can, which is considerable as they are not inhibited in any way. Daniels objective is to show this beautiful country and its people in the most tragic perspective, hoping that by so doing that it will stir the emotions of the world to react and support them. They meet numerous people, both at local and central government level who are only too happy to tell them or indeed show them whatever they want.

At the end of two weeks Daniel, Mark and Johnny return home. They are reluctant to leave Bangladesh, but hope desperately that their work will help it, even if only in some small way.

Theresa meets him at the airport excitedly throwing her arms around him as her swings her round and off the floor. "It's so good to see you home again Dan, I thought that you were never coming. How was Bangladesh, did you manage to get some good material"?

"It was a very moving and humbling experience my love. I will show you some of the material when we get home, so you can see what I mean".

Saying his farewells to his colleagues Daniel and Theresa make their way home to begin living a normal existence once more.

As they sit and watch some of the videos that Daniel and his team have made, Theresa is both astounded and strangely ashamed at the poverty of the people of Bangladesh.

She watches in silence, with tears running down her face until it is finished. "Wow Dan this is potent stuff and If it doesn't make Governments all over the world get up off their butts and do something, then I don't know what will".

The B.B.C shows Daniels reports, which are taken up and shown by television companies in the major developed Countries, for which he achieves international acclaim. When he is asked how proud he feels, he always replies "I didn't do it for acclaim, but rather to highlight the plight of the impoverished nation of Bangladesh"

As December 1973 approaches, Daniel telephones his mother and when she replies he asks her" hi mum, how are things? I just wanted to invite you and Geoffrey to ours for Christmas. It is our first Christmas together and we would like you both to share it". They talk for several minutes; Ella being delighted at the thought of spending time with her son. Just as they are about to say good bye, Daniels says "Oh, by the way, Theresa is pregnant". He doesn't have time to elaborate any further, because Ella is shrieking with delight. "Put her on Daniel, I must congratulate your clever girl"

Daniel hands over the telephone to Theresa, who has to withstand Ella at her most voluble. After what seems an eternity to Daniel, Theresa passes the phone back to him saying "Your Mum wants a word with you".

"Yes mum, what is it"

"Well Daniel, I too have some news, which I hope that you will approve of. The thing is that Geoffrey has asked me to marry him and I have said yes, providing that you have no objection".

It is Daniel's turn to be gobsmacked and he spends the next half hour both congratulating and assuring his mother that he thinks that her decision is the best thing that could happen to her. He finishes by asking her "when are you thinking of doing the deed then mum" only to hear her reply "well if we are coming to you at Christmas, we had best be married before then. I can't come to your flat with Geoffrey and sleep with him without being married. What would my son think"?

Daniel laughs uproariously, but deep down he knows that his mother is serious; it is ingrained in her very character that she must not be seen to be going to bed with anyone other than the one that she is betrothed to. She continues "anyway, neither of us wants a grand wedding and we have decided that we will get married in The Registry Office, so I had better get my skates on, because it's only a few weeks to Christmas. We will only have close family, Rachel and hers and you and Theresa (and the baby to be, of course). There are only Geoffrey's two sons, Rex and Ben and their families on his side, so there shouldn't be too many".

"O.K. mum, just let us know the date and we will be there. I am so pleased for you mum; you deserve someone in your life again"

As he puts the telephone down for what he hopes is the final time this evening he remarks to a smiling Theresa "well, what are your thoughts about that my love. What a year 1973 has been".

CHAPTER 29.

1941-1943.
NORTH AFRICA AND EL ALAMEIN.

At the end of April, Richard, along with most of his unit are given seventy-two-hour passes. The significance doesn't escape them and leaves them wondering when and where their next actions will be.

The quickest way to get home from Aldershot, Richard has found from experience is to thumb a lift, knowing that members of the public with cars understand and are sympathetic to servicemen who need to get home to see their loved ones, or return back to their units. He is lucky today as an older man, who is a representative for men's clothing stops. "I am going to Oxford, is that any good" he enquires, much to Richard's delight.

Ella is standing at the sink at the back of the cottage as Richard let's himself in at the front door, hoping to surprise her. Tip toeing up behind her he grabs her around the waist and lifting her off her feet, spins her round and round until she is dizzy. Once he stops her delight is overwhelming "Oh you silly idiot, you frightened the life out of me" she manages to say, and then "What's this then, how long have you got".

"Seventy-two hours my love, so let's make the most of it, because I think that there is something big in the wind, which makes me wonder how long it will be before I get another posting. Now where's that boy of mine".

"Don't wake him, he is having a little nap; he still needs a couple of hours every afternoon".

"Well then, why don't we do the same Princess" retorts Richard, "Then I can see him when he wakes up" as he leads her upstairs.

The intensity of their passion for each other never dims, reflects Ella, thinking that the reason must be that they have to grab each fleeting moment when they can, because they don't know when, or indeed if, they will see each other again.

The next two days disappear in a blur as Richard bonds with his son, the three of them taking him for walks together with Bonny, Alf's black Labrador who Daniel will come to rely on so much in the coming years.

All too soon it is time for Richard to return to his unit and he leaves his little cottage at Chadlington, this time to the sound of Vera Lynn's latest haunting ballad on the radio "I'll be seeing you". Once again Ella stands watching him go with tears cascading down her face, wondering if in fact she will be seeing him again.

*　*　*

In early May and upon his return to barracks Richard's Royal Army Service Corp (RASC) is transported to Dover, where they stay for three weeks under canvas, awaiting further instructions.

Rumours and counter rumours are rife, some saying that they are going to invade Norway, or possibly a surprise incursion into France, Holland or even Denmark; anywhere to draw Nazi Germany's attention and make it react to the situation. Nobody thinks that such action can be anything more than a diversionary tactic, but that if such action can make the enemy wonder where and when such attacks might come from in the future, its purpose will have been served.

It is with considerable surprise to most of them, when all army personnel are embarked onto several converted cruise liners which act as troop carriers, while equipment, tanks, artillery, armaments and other supplies are loaded onto several merchant ships. The convoy sets off at the beginning of April accompanied by four Royal Navy Destroyers and head south west into The Bay of Biscay, all the time keeping over a hundred miles from the coasts of Portugal and Spain.

This is a new experience for Richard, as it is indeed for many of them, who all suffer sea sickness for several days. The whole operation is carried out in strict secrecy, the planners not wanting to draw attention to the convoy or its destination, fearing attacks from German bombers from the air or U-Boats from the sea.

The convoy successfully docks at Alexandria in Egypt after several days at sea, ready to join the Allied forces in its battle for the control of North Africa. After disembarking all personnel are put once again under canvass until all the merchant ships are unloaded of their invaluable cargo of weapons and machinery.

While the men are still in situ in Alexandria, they are addressed over a period of days by a senior officer, who explains in detail what has happened so far in the North Africa Campaign. He begins his address; -

"The battle for North Africa has been raging since June 1940, starting with the Italian declaration of war. This is a struggle for control of the Suez Canal and access to oil from the Middle East and raw materials from Asia. Oil in particular has become a critical strategic commodity due to the increased mechanization of modern armies".

"Since the Italian declaration of war against the Allied forces, battles have swung back and forth right across the region, from the Libyan and Egyptian deserts, as well as in Morocco, Algeria and Tunisia.

There have been several battles since June 1940, commencing on 14th June when the Britiish Army's Hussars and 1st Royal Tank Regiment crossed the border from Egypt into Libya and captured the Italian Fort Capuzzo. This was followed by an Italian counter offensive into Egypt and the capture of Sidi Barrani in September 1940 and again in December 1940 following a British Commonwealth Offensive, "Operation Compass". During this last operation the Italian 10th Army was destroyed.

The German Afrika Korps are commanded by Erwin Rommel, who has become known as "The Desert Fox". He was dispatched to North Africa in February of this year to reinforce Italian forces in order to prevent a complete Axis defeat. Although Rommel had been ordered to hold the line, an armoured reconnaissance soon became a full- fledged offensive from El Agheila in March. The Allied forces were pushed back and leading general officers captured. The Australian 9th Infantry Division fell back to the fortress of Tobruk, and the remaining British and Commonwealth forces withdrew a further one hundred miles east to the Libyan-Egyptian border. With Tobruk under siege from the main Italian-German force, a small battlegroup continued to press eastwards, Capturing Fort Capuzzo and Bardia in passing. It then advanced into Egypt, and by the end of this April had taken Sollum and the tactically important Halfaya Pass. Rommel has garrisoned these positions, reinforcing the battle-group and ordering it onto the defensive.

Rommel's successes are even more remarkable when it is considered that he only has about one hundred and fifty German Panzer's and a couple of hundred largely obsolete and poorly armed Italian tanks. This is because Hitler has committed most of his tank units to" Operation Barbarossa" in his attempt to invade Russia and is thus unable supply further men or supplies to The North Afrika Campaign.

Although isolated by land, Tobruk's Australian garrison continues to receive supplies and replacements, delivered by the Royal Navy at night. It is quite apparent that Rommel's forces do not have the strength or training to take the fortress. This has created a supply problem for his forward units. His front-line positions at Sollum are at the end of an extended supply chain that stretches back to Tripoli and has to by-pass the coast road at Tobruk. Further, he is constantly threatened by a breakout of British Forces at Tobruk. Without Tobruk in Axis hands, further advances into Egypt ere impractical.

To summarise Gentlemen, it is now up to us to take the offensive and defeat the Axis Powers once and for all".

* * *

They do not have to wait very long before they are moved forward to join a small –scale attack called "Operation Brevity", which is an attempt to push the Axis forces off the key passes at the border. This gains some initial success, but the advanced position cannot be held. Brevity is then followed up by a much larger-scale offensive, "Operation Battleaxe" on 15th June, which is intended to relieve the siege of Tobruk., but this again fails.

These are Richard's first -hand experiences of desert warfare, and they are a salutary reminder of the cost of war. The RASC responsibilities are to ensure that supplies of armaments are available, behind the lines within a reasonable distance from the place where action is being taken. So, shells for tanks and artillery fire are transported behind Allied Forces lines and left in boxes waiting to be collected as and when necessary.

If supplies are left too far in the rear of the offensive, momentum is lost, but if they are too close and the Allied forces are overrun then apart from the fact that retreat is necessary, there is a very good chance that supplies can become spoils of war to the other side, so tactics and logistics are a key consideration. If retreat is inevitable, it is the R A S C responsibility to attempt to recover supplies before they are overrun.

But the most single important factor is that this war is being waged in extreme heat of over forty degrees centigrade, making every movement a challenge. With no water locally, the RASC has to build pipelines several miles long to within distance logistically of troops and tank crew, because dehydration is very real. This is exhausting, reserve sapping work, but Richard counts himself lucky when he thinks of the poor bastards who are waging war, while being sat in enclosed steel Tanks. The temperature inside these doesn't bear contemplation, because there is no form of air conditioning and whatever little air is inside them is shared by the four or five crew members. This small amount depletes rapidly once the crew go into action. Advances also cause logistical problems of supplies which have to be moved up accordingly. Usually when not on operation most personnel sleep under small tents, but some do not bother and make the stars their canopies.

But there is no hiding from the heat of day as the sun pours down in its evil malevolence. The men wear hats with shades to protect their necks and take whatever protection that they can, but the sheer heat sometimes causes some of them to collapse, due to hydration and there is nothing that can be done other than transport them back to base when this happens.

The other major factor that confronts combatants of both sides is sandstorms which occur when winds, travelling at high speeds sweep across the desert picking up sand in its path. This phenomenon can often be several thousand feet high. The sand hits anyone or anything in its path with extreme force, working its way into every corner and crevice. It is almost impossible to stop exposed faces or hands from being attacked, causing lacerations to skin which if not treated can become infected. Nobody is immune to this, tank crew, infantry, motorised crew, or support staff.

When retreat occurs, it is a demoralising moral sapping experience, after days, weeks or months of moving forward, with all the effort it takes, then only to have to reverse everything that has been gained.

Back in Cairo Richard finds life unreal after his time at the front. It is as if war doesn't exist. He spends time writing letters to Ella or sometimes going into Cairo with friends who he has come to trust, something that is absolutely essential in the heat of battle. They all train regularly trying to improve logistically the means and methods of distributing supplies which can mean success or failure.

After the failure of "Operation Battleaxe" there is a period of consolidation. Then it is announced that Archibald Wavell has been relieved of command of The Western Desert Force and has been replaced by Claude Auchinleck.

For Richard and his colleagues all they hear is rumour and innuendo; small pieces of information that may or may not be true. Then they hear that The Western Desert Force is to be reinforced with a second corps, 58th corps, with the two corps forming the Eighth Army. Eighth Army will be made up of army forces from the Commonwealth nations, including the British, the Australian, and the British Indian, the New Zealand, the South African armies and the Sudan Defence Force.

After a lengthy period of inactivity, during which time Richard and his colleagues become more and more bored apart from training, but not wanting to see action either. Eventually they come around to the view that if action is the only way to defeat the Axis powers and return home, then the latter is slightly more preferable.

Then on 18th November 1941 the new formation launches a new offensive, "Operation Crusader". After a see-saw battle, the 71th Division garrisoning Tobruk are relieved and the Axis forces are forced to fall back. By January 1942, the front line is again at El Agheila.

1941 ends with skirmishes continuing on an almost daily basis. Richard has been in North Africa now for over seven months and is totally exhausted from his contribution to "Operation Crusader". He has experienced both death and maiming in all its brutal forms so much that he has difficulty sleeping. The memory of tank crews being blown to pieces are vivid, when an artillery shell hits their tank, penetrating the interior and then spinning around inside it, either slicing through flesh or detonating the ammunition, causing injuries and death by the former and certain death by the latter.

Another scenario that haunts Richard is the sight of Allied infantry being mown down by the machine guns of Axis tanks; completely at their mercy as they try to cross vast open expansive areas of desert, leaving them defenceless with its lack of cover. Wherever possible the infantry walks behind or to the side of their own tanks as they advance using them as cover, but once the tanks go into attack or retreat mode, the infantry are at their most vulnerable because they cannot keep pace with the tanks, which results in them being isolated.

In January, Rommel launches an Axis offensive, capturing Agedabia and Benghazi, but as the fighting continues through 1942 the Eighth Army reverse some of their losses and manage to capture positions throughout May.

But after receiving supplies and reinforcements from Tripoli, the Axis attack again, defeating the Allies at Gazala in June 1942 and capturing Tobruk. The Axis forces drive the Eighth Army back over the Egyptian border but their advance is stopped in July only 90 miles from Alexandria in the First Battle of El Alamein.

At the end of June 1942, the Axis Forces make a second attempt to break through the Allied defences at El Alamein, but are unsuccessful. On 13th August 1942 General Auckinleck, although he has checked Rommel's advance at the First Battle of El Alamein, is replaced by General Harold Alexander, while Lieutenant-General Bernard Montgomery takes command of the entire Eighth Army.

On 23rd October, Montgomery launches a major offensive, decisively defeating the Italian-German army during the Second battle of El Alamein, eventually leading to the Axis lines at El Alamein being broken and the capture of Sidi Barani, Tobruk and Benghazi.

These are major gains by the Eighth Army causing severe logistical problems for the RASC who are stretched almost to breaking point, but to their credit do a magnificent job ensuring that armour, ammunition, water and food keep up with the advances.

Leading up to the Second Battle of El Alamein, the allied forces practises a major deception, code named "Operation Bertram". This is devised to deceive Rommel about the timing and location of the Allied attack. The operation consists of physical deceptions and camouflage, designed and made by the British Middle East Command Camouflage Directorate. These are accompanied by electromagnetic deceptions codenamed "Operation Canwell" using false radio traffic. All of these are planned to make the enemy believe that the attack will take place to the south, far from the coast road and railway, and take place about two days later than the real attack.

"Bertram" consists both in creating the appearance of army units where none exist, and in concealing armour, artillery and material. Dummy tanks and guns are made mainly of local materials including calico and palm-frond hurdles. Real tanks are disguised as trucks, using light Sunshield canopies. Field guns and their limbers are also disguised as trucks, their rear wheels visible, under a simple box-shaped Cannibal canopy to give the shape of a truck. Petrol cans are stacked along the sides of existing trenches, enabling them to be hidden in the shadows. Food is stacked in piles of boxes, and draped with camouflage nets, to resemble trucks.

In September they dump waste material (discarded packing cases etc.) under camouflage nets in the northern sector, making them appear to be ammunition or ration dumps. The Axis naturally notice these but, as no offensive action immediately follows and the "dumps" do not change in appearance, they are subsequently ignored. This allows Eighth Army to build up supplies in the forward area, unnoticed by the Axis, by replacing the rubbish with ammunition, petrol or rations at night. The RASC are instrumental in this aspect of the operation, making Richard feel very proud when he and they all see how effective it is to prove.

To achieve the deception, trucks are parked openly in the tank assembly area for some weeks. Real tanks are similarly parked openly, far behind the front. Two nights before the attack, the tanks replace the trucks, being covered with Sunshields before dawn. The tanks are replaced that same night with dummies in their original positions, so the armour remains seemingly two or more days' journey behind the front line. To reinforce the impression that the attack is not ready, a dummy water pipeline is constructed, at a rate of 5 miles per day. Dummy tanks, guns and supplies are built to the south. "Bertram" has thus succeeded in all its objectives. The Eighth Army continues to advance and on Christmas Day 1942 captures Sirte in Libya and Tripoli on 21st January 1943.

Richard is by now and for several months in fact, has been working by automation. Every day appears to be the same, rising early to resupply existing armoury dumps or move supplies forward to new positions. It is a backbreaking mind depleting job, every sinew aching after just a few minutes work, irrespective of how much rest beforehand. He has now been here for over eighteen months but he doesn't have the will or the inclination to think about home or Ella anymore, because the war is all consuming.

The advance continues more or less unabated through February and in late March Operation Supercharge is launched, which outflanks and makes the Axis position at Mareth untenable. Then on 6th April the Eighth army links up with the First Army, led by the American General Eisenhower. On 22 April Allied forces launch "Operation Vulcan", followed by "Operation Strike" on 5 May.

On the following day, 6 May the British enter Tunis and the Americans enter Bizerte, leading to the Axis Power surrender in Tunisia on 13th May.

The North African Campaign is over, but the there is a need to recover supplies and equipment from both the Allies and also the Axis power, including German and Italian tanks, trucks and ammunition rifles and any other equipment that can be reused, before the theatre of war can move on. When all of this is finished towards the end of June, no one, least of all Richard, or any of his colleagues, have any idea what this might mean, or where this may be, although all of them are desperately hoping that they will get a few days back in Blighty before starting on a new campaign.

At home the defeat of the Axis powers in North Africa is received with euphoria and the country goes wild with celebration, but for Ella the longer that Richard does not return home, the more her sense of happiness turns to one of concern.

CHAPTER 30.

DECEMBER 1973.
ELLA AND GEOFFREY'S WEDDING.

On a warm wintry Saturday in the second week in December 1973, at three o'clock in the afternoon, Ella Thornton is married to Geoffrey Thomson at Chipping Norton Registry Office. If she is completely honest with herself Ella knows that she has strong feelings of affection for Geoffrey and is grateful and happy that he is in her life. She hopes this is enough to ensure their marriage will be one of contentment, and hopes that her feelings will grow with the passing of time. He makes her laugh and is considerate and kind in all manner of things, but she has never experienced the same thrill as those of the years when she was married to Richard.

"O.K she thinks to herself, you are being unreasonable, you can't expect to experience those feelings again at your age", but she can't help comparing the times when Richard and she were courting and when she was married to him; remembering the longing and the need just to see and be with him. Quite often there was no conversation between them, but the silence spoke volumes to both of them, just to be in each other's company; it was enough.

"Just pull yourself together my girl" she chides herself as she makes her final compromise before saying "I do".

In the few years to come that they have together she never regrets her decision to marry Geoffrey, but she knows that it isn't love in the same way that it was the first time. Neither does she let Geoffrey suspect anything to the contrary, making him happy beyond measure.

But today after the wedding they all return to The Pines which is closed to the public for the day, for their wedding breakfast.

Ella has decided on the menu and her staff, from the chef and his helpers in the kitchen, to the waitresses who serve them, have produced and delivered a magnificent meal in honour of Ella. Everyone is welcomed with a choice of a champagne or a soft drink before sitting down to the meal.

The starters include a selection of Tomato soup with croutons: or Duck comfit with orange marmalade: or Prawn tempura with sweet chilli sauce. Next comes the Main Course with a choice of Pan-fried plaice, cauliflower roast and royals, fondant potato in red wine sauce: or Pressed shoulder of lamb, black olive jus, mash potato: or Pot-roast corn-fed chicken, mushroom and leek pie, seasonal vegetables.

The meal is followed, by a selection of mouth-watering Desserts, from; Raspberry cheesecake with lemon sorbet and seasonal berries: or flaming coffee brulee with caramel ice cream: or flaming baked Alaska, vanilla chocolate ice cream. Each course has its own choice of wine.

Afterwards, there is a choice of tea or coffees.

* * *

Rex, acting as the best man makes a speech both honouring and debunking his father in turns, but it is plain to see the respect and love with which he holds him.

Next it is Daniels turn, acting as the father of the bride to illustrate to those present just how much his mother means to him. His words flow effortlessly from the heart as he tells them of the courage, fortitude and love that she has shown him time and time again. He continues on relating the various periods and events of their life together when he was growing up. "She has been my rock and my shield" he finishes, before glancing at Geoffrey "So look after her please". He finishes by saying "Would you now please all raise your glasses to my mother Ella and her husband Geoffrey".

There is an audible clearing of throats and paper tissues being applied to tears that are welling, as they all reply "To Ella and Geoffrey".

The rest of the day passes in a blur as everyone get to know one another. Ella has tried to avoid having photographs taken, thinking that she and Geoffrey are too old for such things, but Rachel has arranged for a local photographer to take some. What nobody realises is that the local newspaper, The Chipping Norton Chronicle has got news of their wedding via The Chamber of Commerce where both Ella and Geoffrey are members, ensuring that their wedding will reach the front page on the following edition.

The invitations have made it plain that the reception finishes at five o'clock, Geoffrey and Ella having arranged to leave for a short honeymoon immediately afterwards, although Geoffrey has not told her where it will be. There are emotional scenes as people say their farewells and good wishes for the happy couple, until all that are left with them are Daniel and Theresa and Rachel and her family. They stay for a while, their closeness not wanting them to leave. Theresa comes under considerable pressure to tell them when the baby is due and what sex it is. She is more than happy to tell them that it is due in late July and that she is expecting a boy.

This news sends Ella and Rachel into raptures, much to Daniels amusement.

Eventually it is time for them to leave, but not before promises are made and dates set to see each other again.

Daniel and Theresa leave to return to London with the other's congratulations ringing in their ears, while Rachel kisses her younger sister goodbye saying "Well Ella thank you for a lovely day. I am sure that Geoffrey will make you very happy. I am so glad that you have found each other" and then conspiratorially "You must try you know. I realise that nobody can replace Richard, but you wouldn't want them to would you. You can't hide these things from me, because I always know your innermost thoughts. I always have, I don't know how or why".

Once again at this moment, Ella is confronted with Rachel's wonderfully kind and considerate knowledge. She understands how Ella is feeling and has always been there for her in her moments of need; for her sister to know how she is feeling today is a source of comfort and reassurance.

They all part, promising to meet as usual the next week as Geoffrey says "come on Mrs Thomson we had best get a move on if we are going to get to the place that we are going".

"Well, I think that you had better tell me where it is, don't you, if you want me to hurry up" says his new wife, laughing.

"Very well" replies Geoffrey with a sigh, before continuing" I suppose I had better tell you now that we are on our own. Because it was only for a short period, I thought it would be best if we didn't go abroad, but stayed in Britain, so I have booked The Dorchester Hotel in Mayfair for three nights and the theatre for tonight, so get your clogs on. We can do all the sights on the other days, what do you think"?

To Ella, the sound of such a prestigious hotel in London is something that she can never have envisaged and she gives out an involuntary gasp, before saying "Really, the Dorchester, are you sure that we can afford it".

"Of course, my love, for you, the top brick of the chimney" and he hugs her saying in a conciliatory tone "You know you don't have to worry about us going to bed together. Take as long as you like; I would prefer that you did, rather than you have to force yourself. I couldn't bear it if you had to do that".

"Oh Geoffrey, it's not that, it's just that it has been so long since, you know, and I am not a young woman any more".

"Of course, you are bound to feel that way, so let's take things slowly and not try to rush things".

In this way the subject is left unresolved, as they get a taxi to Oxford where they catch their train to London.

To Ella's complete surprise their time in London is a magical experience as they first go to the theatre to see Agatha Christies production of her play "The Mousetrap" before checking in to The Dorchester where Geoffrey orders a bottle of Champagne to be sent up to their room. The sheer opulence and elegance of her surroundings just stuns Ella, who wanders around exclaiming "Oh look at these drapes Geoffrey, they are just to die for" and "have you seen the en-suite bathroom and toilet, I am sure that the taps are covered in gold". The litany goes on with Geoffrey secretly delighted that his bride is obviously enjoying the experience and that she is pleased with his choice for their honeymoon. But it gets even better for him as Ella is now more relaxed and once they are in bed together, she makes the first move to their lovemaking.

"Are you sure" Geoffrey asks anxiously.

"Absolutely Mr Thomson" replies Ella, thinking to herself "it's just like riding a bike or swimming; once you have done it, you never forget", but there is still some small part of her that makes the inevitable comparison with Richard.

Waking the next morning Geoffrey orders breakfast in bed, which throws Ella's thoughts back to the days when she cooked for Lord Stevens at The Manor House in Chadlington so many years ago. "What goes around comes around" she reflects wryly to herself, as she devours her devilled kidneys, washed down with strong hot coffee, finishing with toast and marmalade.

Out in the cold of this winter's day, they hurry from place to place, first from The British Museum, after which they move on to shops in Oxford street which they browse before getting another taxi and going into Harrods in Kensington where they go to the café and consume coffee and cakes. The day is a complete intoxicating whirl for them both, neither having experienced anything remotely like it before.

But the day continues to get even better as they find an Italian restaurant in Kensington and have pasta dinners, where Geoffrey springs yet another of his surprises.

"Once that we have finished here, I have booked us tickets to see Swan Lake, performed by the Kirov Russian Ballet company at The Royal Albert Hall; do you like ballet Ella"?

"Well that sounds wonderful Mr Thomson and no I have never seen ballet of any sort, but I have always wanted to; and I have always wanted to visit The Royal Albert Hall, so it's all good".

"When you are ready then we will make our way there, it's only a short walk from here and we can have a look at The Albert Memorial opposite".

There follows a magical evening which is all that either of them could hope that it will be. They are both stunned at the Albert Hall and its welcoming grandeur. Ella would have preferred to have had a seat in one of the many tiers that rise up around the building, but Geoffrey assures her that the view and the spectacle of the performance can best be experienced from the floor. "At least that is what I was told when I telephoned to book the tickets" he finishes.

He is proved right as the ballet begins and the haunting refrain of Tchaikovsky's music floods through the hall, while the performers begin their compelling dance.

Ella loves everything about it, the music and dance lifting her up to a place that she has never been before and she is suddenly aware how much she has missed because of her limited education and background growing up. But on reflection she does not feel upset or angry in any way, knowing that her parents did everything that they possibly could do for her and she is grateful for it, however limited it might have been. Her thoughts are finally reconciled as she realises that she has at least managed to have the experience, something that Alf and Liz never did.

They wander out at the end of the show with hundreds of others bustling and jostling as they all make their way back to their homes. Ella finds it strangely reassuring to be in a crowd of this size who are all chattering and smiling as they tell each other of the parts that they have liked the most.

It is cold but invigorating as they hail a taxi and return to The Dorchester where they have a night cap before retiring to their rooms.

The next two days are spent in much the same fashion, sightseeing and shopping. On the final day, just before they check out of The Dorchester, Ella makes a sudden request. "Geoffrey, would you mind if we visit Daniel and Theresa before we go home. It may not be possible because they may be working, but I know that Daniel in particular doesn't always have to go to the television studios, because some of his work can be done at home. What do you think; shall I give them a call"?

"Of course, anything for you" declares Geoffrey, still in a honeymoon haze.

Daniel answers the phone to his mother's call and is delighted when she asks if she and Geoffrey can call and see him before they return home to Chadlington.

"Of course, mum, we would love it if you can make it. Theresa will be home very soon; she had to go in early today because of a crisis, but I heard from her just now and she thinks that it's all been resolved".

Upon reaching the flat Ella and Geoffrey are welcomed by her son and his wife who are excited to see them." Come on in, out of the cold, I have put the kettle on and there is a Victoria Sponge Cake in the cupboard waiting to be eaten".

As they sit and talk Theresa asks them where they have been during their stay in London and she can see and hear the excitement in Ella's voice as she tells them about their stay at The Dorchester Hotel and of the various places that they have visited. "I loved the theatre, but the Ballet just blew me away; the colour and dance, in fact the sheer spectacle of it was just amazing. We have had such a wonderful time, haven't we Geoffrey".

She then goes on to say "well are you going to show Mr and Mrs Thomson around your flat, I for one haven't seen it for a long time and I am sure that Theresa will have updated it from your bachelor days Daniel".

"You are right there" agrees Daniel with a smile "Luckily Theresa has an eye for interior design and has transformed the place. I was never here long enough to notice and even if I had been, I doubt if I would have changed anything. Come and see".

As they enter the living room Ella can see how Theresa's input has added light and space to it. Gone are the darker shades of reds and greens, only to be replaced by warm creams, with pale shades of blue picked out on cushion covers and curtains. There is a large tan leather brown three-piece suite which envelopes them as they sit. Cream curtains run the length of the wall, behind which is the panoramic window which has such beautiful views across the river and beyond. They stand for several minutes absorbing the sight of people scurrying along the Embankment, leaning forward to fight their way into the south easterly wind which started its journey from Siberia and is by now at the height of its power as it barrels its way across southern England and London in particular.

There are people of all types and denominations battling their way into the wind, their features bleak and pinched, while others moving in the opposite direction are swept helplessly along, holding on to hats that the wind is threatening to blow into the river, where river craft of every description bustle their way hither and thither in what appears to be an aimless purpose.

"I could stand here forever watching the great tide of humanity as it goes about its business and see the river in all its moods. I find the whole scene captivating, exciting even" declares Ella, before adding" come on show me the rest of the flat".

As Daniel shows them round, Ella can see the amount of influence that Theresa has had. For the better too, she thinks to herself as she notices the new subdued lighting, original pictures by up and coming artists and fresh flowers carefully placed for maximum effect. There is a new large double bed in the main bedroom and new fitted wardrobes have replaced the old double wardrobe which has been consigned to the smaller bedroom.

"We have not done anything to the small bedroom yet because we are going to turn it into a nursery for the baby eventually" says Theresa before continuing "we have left the kitchen for now because it is in good order, but we have replaced the bathroom and toilet suites because they were looking a bit dated. So, Ladies and Gentlemen that concludes the tour of the flat. We hope that you like it as much as we have enjoyed doing it".

"It's fabulous declares Ella, I think that you have done really well, haven't they Geoffrey".

"They certainly have" replies her husband, anxious to support his new wife.

The afternoon disappears rapidly as they all sit and discuss the arrival of the baby and how much life will change for its parents, until Ella eventually says "Well husband, I think that we had better move if we are going to catch the train that will get us home by early evening. We don't want to leave it until it's too late because we have to get back to work tomorrow".

Suddenly a thought occurs to Daniel and he says "By the way where are you both going to live now, at your accommodation at the café, or at Geoffrey's house".

"Well we have given it a lot of thought and decided that we will both live at Geoffrey's house; it will be a bit cramped at the café, so I have told Fiona that she and her husband can move in. She was delighted when I told her and anyway, she deserves it because the café wouldn't have been half as successful if she had not been there all this time. Eventually we may look to move somewhere local so that we are not living with memories of our previous partners, but we will just have to see on that one".

"I think that is a great idea mum, I just hadn't thought of where you were going to live until this very moment. Anyway, it has been lovely to see you and we will see you again at Christmas which is only a couple of weeks away".

As Ella and Geoffrey leave to catch their train, both of them in isolation reflect on the last few days and the experiences of their honey moon.

* * *

Christmas 1973 is a huge success; arriving at Daniel's flat on 24th December they are both immediately taken on a shopping expedition to Oxford Street because neither Daniel or Theresa have had time to buy presents for each other.

The street is alive with crowds who throng their way excitedly to the stores, filled with anticipation for the events of the next day. As they reach Selfridges a Salvation Army band is playing Christmas carols outside, which people continue to hum along to, even after they have moved away from it. Street sellers are busy heating chestnuts over a charcoal fire, while acrobats dressed as clowns entertain the crowds with their athletic routines. Two of them walk on stilts which makes them stand over ten feet high, while amazingly other acrobats perform feats of athletic prowess by forming a pyramid four people tall by standing on each other's shoulders. Before the audience can catch its breath the acrobat on top projects himself downwards and at the last second forms himself into a ball just before he reaches the floor and rolls forward, the majority of his impact being dissipated by his adopted pose.

Entering Selfridges Daniel eventually buys a gold Swiss made watch that Theresa chooses, before she in turn buys him a leather wallet and a pair of black brogue shoes.

As they finish Ella declares "come on, I think that we deserve coffee and cakes", to which they all agree.

Once this has been consumed, they all go their separate ways to buy little gifts for each other. Ella buys a mobile and a cuddly teddy bear ready for the baby's nursery, before purchasing two books for Geoffrey. She has already bought other presents with her, so is finished quite quickly, before the others. She spends the rest of her time in the maternity and children's departments looking at things that she will buy once the baby is born, being loathe to getting any now in case she tempts fate.

Meeting up they spend several hours shopping, Ella buying luxuries to augment those which Theresa has purchased for Christmas Day; chocolates, dates, nuts and fruit as well as a bottle of champagne.

Feeling exhausted they return happily to the flat where they collapse until late evening when they go to attend midnight service at the local church.

Waking late Ella and Theresa begin to get the turkey ready, while Geoffrey and Daniel prepare vegetables.

Because of their late night, which results in everyone sleeping until mid-morning, they first sit down to watch the Queens speech before having Christmas Dinner which Ella and Theresa have prepared, after which Daniel suggests a walk along The Embankment to blow the cobwebs away.

Ella finds that walking it is almost as good as watching events from the flat as people they meet all greet them with a smile and a "Happy Christmas", leaving her to contemplate why this should be on this one day a year, while on any other they would just look straight ahead and ignore eye contact.

They return refreshed and play cards and charades until they have had enough and just sit and talk, content in each other's company. During this conversation Ella takes the opportunity to ask Theresa how long she intends taking maternity leave.

"Well I am not sure yet, but I don't think that I will be able to stay away too long because if I do The Corporation will appoint someone else and I will either lose my job or alternatively be downgraded, which I don't want to happen. It's not about the money because we can manage on Dan's earnings, but rather that I enjoy my job and I am very good at it and that it has taken me a long time to get where I am. I will need to look for someone to look after the baby so that I can return to work ASAP".

Ella can see the stress in Theresa's eyes and feels the pain that she is going through, before an idea comes to her which she will need to discuss with Geoffrey before anything more is said.

After dinner on Boxing Day Ella and Geoffrey leave to catch the train home relaxed and happy in the knowledge that her son and his wife have enjoyed their company as much as they have theirs.

CHAPTER 31.

1974-1976
ELLA'S FIRST GRANDCHILD.

For all of them nineteen seventy-four is a year of great changes, the most significant of which is in late July as Theresa gives birth to a boy which they name Richard in memory of Daniels late father.

When she hears this Ella is in floods of tears in gratitude to her son and his wife's thoughtfulness and her own memories. She and Geoffrey delay their visit to her grandson for a few weeks, anxious to give Daniel and Theresa at least a little time to adjust to their new life.

* * *

As she opens the door Theresa gives them both a hug before saying "you are just in time, I have just fed the baby and Dan is changing him, which is not to be missed".

"You are right, I wouldn't want to miss that" replies Ella with a smile as they all go into the kitchen where Daniel has the baby stretched out on his back on the table, preparatory to changing his nappy. To her surprise the baby is relaxed and happy, letting his father do whatever is necessary. His eyes are pale blue and what little hair he has bears a tinge of red, which to Ella is so distinctive of both Daniel and his father. The connection is so strong that Ella gives an involuntary shudder as she sees her grandson for the first time, the hairs on the nape of her neck seeming to stand up. She is unable to speak for several seconds, eventually managing to murmur "well now aren't you the spitting image of your father when he was your age". She omits to mention any reference of Daniels father, not wanting to upset Theresa. Instead she says to her daughter in law "can you see any likeness to your family" and she is glad when Theresa replies "well my mother says that she can see me in him when I was young".

They spend the day fawning over the baby, at least during the times when he is still awake. Eventually Ella asks Theresa "when are you planning to return to work"?

A cloud passes across Theresa's face for a second before she replies in a worried voice "well they want me back when the baby is three months old but quite honestly I don't know if I will be able to, because I have tried advertising for someone to look after him, but the only replies that I have had are from young girls of sixteen or seventeen who have had no experience. Although they are all very nice, I don't think that I am prepared to take anyone of them on who are so young and inexperienced".

Then as she pauses, she adds "there was one young woman of about twenty-seven who had experience and would have been ideal, but she could only do three days a week so I had to discount her".

As she hears this Ella looks across to Geoffrey who nods imperceptibly. Upon seeing this Ella says "well both Geoffrey and me have given some thought to your predicament because you mentioned it some time ago. Now stop me if you think that this is a silly idea, but what if I came up here two or three days a week and looked after Richard. I would have to stop over, but I could sleep on the settee. That way you could take on the young woman who you thought was ideal for the three days that she could manage".

Theresa is stunned momentarily, until looking across to Daniel she says" what do you think Dan, it could solve the problem for now, until such time that we could find a more permanent solution".

Daniel replies unhesitatingly "well if mum is prepared to do it, I think that it would give us more time to resolve the matter in the longer term, so thank you mum".

After further discussion, it is agreed, and Ella can see the sparkle returning to Theresa's eyes as she realises that what to her has been an intractable problem has, for now anyway, been resolved.

* * *

For Ella and Geoffrey, the year has been one of adjustment and learning as their relationship develops. After much thought and consideration, they both decide that they can both live in Geoffrey's house, neither of them feeling the presence of his previous partner, all pictures and items that might do so having been taken down. However, Ella is concerned that Geoffrey's sons, Rex and Ben may consider her as a "gold digger", someone who will now become between them and their inheritance if their father dies before her.

Although neither son has ever given any indication that they feel this way, Ella feels the need to quell any fears that they may have on this score, so she discusses the matter with Geoffrey. After explaining how she feels, she goes on to offer her solution. "What I think that you should do Geoffrey is to draw up a new will, leaving the house and everything to them in the event of you dying before me. Once you have done that, I think that we both need to tell them, so that they know, because I don't want them to think that I have any wish to take their inheritance"

Geoffrey is pensive for a while before saying" are you sure Ella, because I couldn't bear the thought of dying and leaving you with nothing, so I think that we will have to arrange that they get perhaps half of my estate when the time comes".

He is surprised when he hears Ella laugh at his reply and when he asks why she replies "Don't be silly Geoffrey; I certainly don't need anything, because I have three very viable businesses which are growing daily. If and when anything happens to you, I can move into The Pines accommodation, but who knows it could be me who goes first. The only thing that I will say is that in the event of me dying first I would like to leave my assets to Daniel, so perhaps we can draw up new wills together to reflect this".

"If that is what you want my dear, then that is what we will do, and we will tell the boys when it has been done, but I intend putting a clause in my will which states that in the event of my death before you, that you be allowed to live in this house rent free until such time that you are ready to arrange accommodation at The Pines".

"Deal" says Ella "I am glad that we have got that out of the way; now let us speak no more about it".

Life for Ella and Geoffrey becomes much less stressful as time goes by. He has found someone reliable who he employs full time who can take over the running of the hardware shop if he is not there. This means that for the very first time both he and Ella have time to do things without having to worry about not being missed. For the first time travel has become a very real option for working class people, with cheap inclusive holidays to Spain, Italy and France well within most people's reach. Their first venture is to Benidorm in June and Ella is amazed to experience the hot summer sun and the beaches, with their long stretches of golden sand, where they can both lie under huge parasols all day, while sipping sangria or wine.

She loves walking around the town after dinner at the hotel and experiencing the shops which are heaving with people from all over Europe and which remain open until late. Neither can she resist buying things to take back to Theresa, Daniel and young Richard; a leather purse, a psychedelic shirt and a soft toy.

She and Geoffrey both love the whole package, which for both of them is completely outside of anything that they have experienced before, and vow to repeat it as soon as possible.

However, Ella's grandson slows down their travel itinerary somewhat, because as Theresa begins working again in the middle of

October, Ella in turn has to begin spending two days a week in London looking after Richard. But she doesn't consider it a hardship in any way because she has time to get to know him as he grows up. By spending two days here, she only has to stop over one night on the settee which isn't long enough to cause a problem. Occasionally Daniel will be at home preparing for a trip, in which case he looks after his son, thus sparing his mother the journey, but this is often effectively cancelled out when Theresa sometimes has to work weekends, meaning that Ella has to make the journey again, but she doesn't mind, because the train journey fascinates her and she can see her grandson once more.

Julie Sandom who Theresa has employed for three days per week proves to be a godsend and is wonderful with Richard, but she can't work weekends having a child of her own which her mother looks after during the time that she cares for Richard, thus enabling her to work.

* * *

Sometimes Geoffrey accompanies Ella to London and returns home at the end of the day, while Ella sleeps over. He doesn't seem to mind, in fact he is very supportive, for which Ella is grateful.

The following year, 1975, Daniel and Theresa take Richard for a holiday in France which gives Geoffrey and Ella time to take another holiday in Italy.

This time the experience is slightly different as they book a coach tour and fly out to Florence where they spend two days visiting places that they have only heard of from the radio or the newspapers. They wander through its streets that are so narrow that even the hot Mediterranean sun cannot penetrate. They visit the wonderful Uffizi portrait gallery where there are paintings by a number of Italian masters before moving on to the Galleria del Academia where they stand transfixed at Michael Angelo's immense statue of the David.

But Ella is totally staggered when she sees a number of unfinished statues by the same artist, in which partially carved figures appear to be trying for to extricate themselves from blocks of marbles. It impresses her so much that she is sure that it is something that she will never forget. As they make their way back, they come to the medieval Florence Cathedral of Santa Maria (Duomo) which can be seen from miles away with its huge dome covered by terracotta tiles, which was added to the church in the 14th century. They take a conducted tour of this magnificent building and marvel at its grandeur. From here they meander slowly on until they reach a cobblestone square which is surrounded by shops, restaurants and cafes where they stop and order coffees while sitting outside under huge umbrellas to protect them from the sun.

As they finish, Ella, who has been looking at a local guide book, says "look why don't we go down to the river (Arno) and cross the Ponto Veccio Bridge. It has shops on both sides on the bridge. It says here that it is constructed of medieval stone. I think that I would like to see that, how about you"?

"That sounds great my love" replies Geoffrey rising and taking his wife by the hand to assist her over the cobblestones. They are fascinated as they cross the bridge and investigate the shops which to Ella's delight mostly sell jewellery. Here she buys silver earrings for Theresa and a pair of cufflinks for Daniel before finally buying a gold tie pin for Geoffrey which he has been showing an interest in. Descending the other side of the bridge they make their way to the Palazzo Pitti where they enter to visit the Boboli Gardens which are to be found at the rear of the building. The gardens are renowned throughout the World for their fauna and flora. They wander languidly, entranced by the sheer variety of plants, stopping periodically to sit on a bench because they are by now tired, not being used to so much exercise or the intense Italian heat.

At the end of the two days they board a coach which will take them to their next destination, Naples. After checking in to the hotel they wander down to the sea where they book tickets to visit The Isle of Capri and Sorrento the following day, before returning to the town to look for somewhere to eat. They are amazed at the choice of restaurants and the volume and variety of the meals that they offer, Ella showing great interest in some that she thinks she would like to introduce into The Pines restaurant.

As they stand undecided outside one particular place a man appears from the inside and says "Do you want to eat" in very broken English and seeing their indecision says" come in then" and grabbing them both by the arm he almost drags them inside where he leads them to a table. Although slightly alarmed Ella and Geoffrey can see the funny side and looking at each other, burst out laughing. The menu is in Italian and after perusing it unsuccessfully for several minutes Geoffrey attracts the same man's attention, who appears to be not only the owner of the restaurant but also the waiter.

"What is this, and this" asks Geoffrey, pointing to several items on the menu and after the contents have been explained to him and Ella, they both decide to order the one which has been described as a beef dish of some description.

Wanting to know how it is to be cooked, Geoffrey tentatively enquires" and how is this cooked please" meaning well done, medium or rare.

The waiter looks puzzled for a few moments, obviously unsure how to answer, before he finally takes the plunge and says "It is cooked with electricity".

Ella and Geoffrey can contain their laughter no longer, much to the waiter's alarm, but order the beef anyway.

The next day they catch the boat to The Isle of Capri and Sorrento, riding the cable car which, they find exhilarating and from which they can see so much of the Island.

Rising early the following day the coach takes them to the ruined city of Pompeii which lays at the foot of Mount Vesuvius the volcano whose eruption nearly two thousand years ago engulfed and subsequently entombed the city in six metres of ash and pumice-stone. It has been undergoing excavations on and off since the eighteenth century and because it has lain unseen for so long. it is the finest example anywhere of a Roman town which still shows so many facets of how its people lived two thousand years ago. Meeting up with their guide he explains to Ella and Geoffrey that there were twenty thousand people living in the city, but most moved out at the first sign of the eruption, so when the final flow descended like a tidal wave, only about two thousand people remained trapped. As a result, those left were entombed in a poignant time stopping moment. Plaster casts were made from almost perfect moulds left in the solidified ash by the bodies of those caught in the sudden destruction. As these spaces were found by excavators, they were carefully filled with plaster forming images of the victims as they tried to escape. It is these together with the implements of everyday life that bring those final moments into grisly reality.

Their guide shows them the major features, the roman baths, then the Anfiteatro, the oldest known Roman Amphitheatre in existence which originally held up to twenty thousand spectators. Then he shows them the bakeries, small family restaurants and even a brothel, where frescos appear in abundance in nearly every building.

Ella finds that it is a strangely moving experience and she is moved to tears at the plight of those who chose to stay and died in such tragic circumstances. But the sight is so vast that they can only manage to see a fraction of it before they have to call it a day, leaving her to vow that she will return whenever she gets another chance.

They spend another two days in Naples, the first visiting Hurculaneum, a town quite near to Pompeii, which had suffered a similar fate from the same volcanic eruption. There second day was spent relaxing by their hotel pool in readiness for their visit to Rome the following day.

Their final two days are spent in Rome which they both agree is a totally inadequate length of time to see enough of this ancient and absorbing city.

A number of excursions have been arranged by the coach organisers in which guides are provided, the first of which is to the Colosseum, built in 70-80 AD, the largest Amphitheatre built in the Roman Empire. Originally capable of seating 60000 spectators it was used for gladiatorial contests. But words cannot fully describe this incredible building which in its day saw Emperors being asked by the crowd to decide life or death for vanquished gladiators by means of his hand being raised with his thumb up or down.

They continue to the ruins of the Roman forum which is a rectangular plaza surrounded by several important government buildings at the centre of the city. Their guide tells them that The Forum was the centre of the day to day life in Rome, the place of triumphal processions and elections, also the venue for public speeches, criminal trials and gladiatorial matches, as well as the nucleus of commercial affairs.

The second day they are transported to The Vatican, where they queue for a tour of St. Peter's Basilica and The Sistine Chapel, something that Ella has wanted to do since visiting Florence and seeing Michelangelo's sculptures, knowing that he left the city to travel to Rome after being offered a commission by Pope Julius 11 to paint the ceiling of the Sistine Chapel, a project that was to take him from 1508 to 1512 and was eventually to become a source of wonder and beauty throughout the Christian world. On the sanctuary wall there is a large fresco The Last Judgement by Michelangelo, while the main ceiling decorations are nine scenes from the Book of Genesis.

Ella is blown away by the sheer beauty and scale of Michelangelo's work and wonders how this genius found the inner strength to lie on his back, while being suspended nearly a hundred feet above the floor for several years and still manage to produce art of such mesmerising quality.

Their next visit is to the Pantheon, which their guide tells them was built two thousand years ago as a Roman Temple and is now a church. It is a circular building with a portico of large granite columns. Inside is the rotunda which is under a concrete dome with a central opening to the sky. The Pantheon is still the world's largest unreinforced concrete dome, a testimony to its builders.

As they come outside again, they find themselves in the square called Piazza delia Rotonda which has restaurants all along its three sides where meals are served outside under awnings to protect customers from the heat of the sun.

They are only too happy to take advantage of its facilities and sit contentedly eating pasta and drinking Chianti before reluctantly deciding to move on.

By now they are both culturally sated and decide to spend the rest of the day getting some retail therapy as they leisurely visit shopping areas before returning to their hotel.

For both of them this has been a voyage of discovery and Ella realises that her limited education has resulted in an almost unquenchable thirst for more knowledge and experiences that her visit to Italy has given her, and resolves silently to do more, hoping that it will set the pattern of their future holidays.

* * *

Returning home Ella and Geoffrey's life returns their normal pattern. She continues to look after her grandson Richard who is beginning to walk and demand more of her, but she is only too pleased to be able to spend time with him watching him grow and learn. She takes him for walks in his pushchair, all the while pointing out things and places of interest, or takes him along The Embankment, stopping to buy him an ice cream, or sometimes wandering to find a park where she can put him on a swing and hear him shout excitedly as she pushes him very gently.

She looks forward to the time when he is a little older so that she can take him to the Zoo or a museum or to any of the host of places in London which are on his doorstep.

For his part Daniel has been busy preparing documentaries for the B.B.C. on the developments in Uganda and on an in-depth analysis of General Idi Amin, the head of its Military Junta.

As 1975 progresses the world is becoming ever more aware of an even bigger and potentially much more destructive conflict, again in Africa; specifically, in Angola. Daniel has followed its development for eighteen months and realises that is inevitable that he will need to go there to let the world see just what atrocities are being committed in the name of freedom.

In November 1975 Angola becomes independent from Portugal, the last African state to do so from colonialism. There are three Angolan rebel movements which had their roots in the anti-colonial movements of the 1950.'s, the MPLA, FNLA and UNITA.

As the three combatants, who generally represent their own tribal interests take up their positions to seek power for their own movements, other interested parties begin to become embroiled for their own particular ends.

The MPLA, the largest of the parties is supported by several African countries, as well as by The Soviet Union and Cuba, the latter becoming its strongest ally, sending significant contingents of combat and support personnel.

By contrast the FNLA has very little support although the U.S. does supply aid.

UNITA is supported by the United States with the onset of the civil war which is the stage currently that Daniel has instructions to go and report on.

* * *

Leaving with his usual team of camera man Mark and sound recordist Johnny in early January 1976, Daniel flies out to Luanda in Angola, the place where the MPLA have set up their seat of government.

He can see immediately the effect that the civil war is having on its people, which is not so obvious in Luanda, but it is unavoidable once he ventures any distance inti the countryside. Here the devastation and desolation are only too apparent with villages destroyed and bodies still littering the ground in a state of putrefaction.

This is the picture that is repeated everywhere they venture, the result of the countries people tearing themselves apart. It is a depressing and frightening scene as on several occasions Daniel and his team have to take avoiding action to being attacked, but as they camp one particular night they find themselves suddenly woken up by a group of militia bursting into their tents carrying automatic rifles and gesturing for them to go outside where they have to form a line.

Daniel doesn't know which faction the militia represent and from the attitude they have adopted he fears not only for their safety but also their lives.

Speaking to who can only be the leader of the armed group, he shows him their journalist authentication and equipment, although most of his conversation is in the form of a charade, because none of the group appears to speak English.

After what seems to Daniel and his team to be a lifetime, the leader orders them to be tied up and put into the troop carrier that they have arrived in. They are bound and blindfold while they travel with the militia and only released after long intervals to be given small drinks of water and maize, which appears to be the staple food.

After two days they meet up with a larger group of militias and after some discussion between them the three of them are untied and brought before the leader of the larger group who speaks fluent English. After questioning them at length and examining their paperwork he says "you are very lucky; my men were not sure of your credibility and were considering liquidating you, but decided to hold you until they met up with us. Now that I have seen your papers, I am satisfied that you are who you say you are. We are on our way back to Luanda and once we get there you will be free to go".

Daniel realises that the troops must be members of the MPLA, and for the first time since their capture he is able to contemplate his survival and the thought that he will see Theresa and his son again.

From what he has seen Daniel can also see that Angola's civil war will take years to resolve and cost many lives in the process.

On his return to Luanda, Daniel contacts Theresa who has been distraught with worry at not hearing from him, which is heightened even more when she hears his story. To her relief, he assures her that everything is now under control and that they will all be leaving Luanda in a couple of days to return home.

As they board the flight Daniel experiences a small shudder as he realises that his visit has been the most terrifying of his career so far.

Theresa is at the airport to welcome him home, her tears evidence of her concern and relief.

Daniel's report is shown the following night's news, which shows the world for the first time the extent of viciousness and depravity that the civil war in Angola is enduring.

Theresa's fear is such that she tries to talk Daniel into changing his job, but he takes her gently in his arms and says "but this is what I do my love. I admit that it was worrying for a while, but never the less I still love doing it with a passion"

After several hours' discussion, some of it quite heated, Theresa can see that she is not able to change his mind, so compromises saying "look Dan if it is still what you want to do, fine, but I just want you to realise the agonies that you put me through when you are on assignment, so do please, please, make sure that you contact me as much as you can, because I am in torment when I don't hear from you. I just cannot think of something dreadful happening to you which might mean that I have to bring Richard up on my own".

For the first time Daniel can understand Theresa's fears and determines to do as much as he can to allay them in the future.

CHAPTER 32.

1977-1989.
MOLLY.

When a larger, four bedrooms flat, one floor above them becomes available early in nineteen seventy-seven, Daniel and Theresa decide to seize the opportunity with both hands and to their delight their bid gets accepted.

"Now we can have my, or your parents, or friends even to stay Dan, something that we haven't been able to do before".

"Not only that, but my mum can have a bed when she has to stay over when she is looking after Richard, rather than having to sleep on the settee".

As she snuggles up to her husband, Theresa murmurs in a seductive voice "we also have another bedroom which means that we can have another baby, what do you think Dan"?

"Well it would be nice for Richard to have a brother or sister my love, let's see how things go for now".

* * *

Ella loves Daniel and Theresa's new flat which has even wider and better panoramic views than their previous flat, as well as a separate bedroom that she can use when staying over.

Life for her has got better and better as she and Geoffrey take more holidays exploring Europe. They look for more cultural breaks now, after their experience in Italy, rather than spending time burning themselves on a beach. On one occasion they visit Austria and go to a Mozart music concert in Saltsburg, on another they visit Prague in Czechoslovakia and wander its medieval streets that remain virtually unchanged. Ella soaks up the experiences like a sponge, just grateful that she has had the opportunities to see places and things that were only words in her schoolbooks.

Her world is pretty much complete as between times she continues to look after Richard, who now has a vocabulary which is growing daily. She loves watching him as he tries to grasp new words and their meanings and spends endless hours encouraging him.

Arriving at Daniel's flat one day in late October she is met by a deliriously happy Theresa who is jumping up and down in excitement. After she manages to calm her down, Ella asks "whatever is it Theresa, I have never seen you like this before".

"Oh mum" Theresa cries "I have just had my results back and they confirm that I am pregnant".

There is a stunned silence before Ella too is jumping up and down in excitement with her daughter in law, the two of them unashamedly crying with tears of joy.

* * *

On the ninth of June in nineteen seventy-eight, Theresa gives birth to her and Daniel's second child, a girl, who they name Molly, for no other reason than that they both like the name.

When Ella sees her new granddaughter for the first time, she has no hesitation in saying to Theresa "well my dear, there can be no doubt whose daughter this beautiful child belongs to; she has the same colouring and features as you".

"Daniel says something similar and I agree, but she still has things that remind me of her father; the way she looks sometimes, or the way she holds herself and her smile which is his, the thing that made me fall for him all those years ago".

"How much maternity leave are you taking this time" Ella asks "I know that you didn't want to be away from your job last time, in case you either lost your job or got demoted. I only ask because I don't want you to go through that trauma again and to tell you that I am quite happy to continue to look after both Richard and Molly when you have to return to work"

Theresa literally heaves a sigh of relief before replying "Are you sure, I have been so worried and didn't know how to mention it, but if you could, if only for a year or so, it will give us breathing space until we can arrange something more permanent. We have been so grateful to you for all that you have done and I don't want you to think that we are taking you or Geoffrey for granted".

"Nonsense, I have loved having the opportunity and wouldn't want it any other way my dear, so let's not mention it any more. Just let me know when you want me to start again and I will be here. Anyway, now that you are home again for a while it will give Geoffrey and me time to arrange a visit to Egypt to see the pyramids, something that we have wanted to do for a while".

* * *

Not wanting to visit Egypt in the height of its summer, Ella and Geoffrey book a ten-day tour commencing in October. They are both extremely excited as they take off from Heathrow on their journey to Cairo where they are met by their tour guide who takes them to their overnight hotel.

The next day they journey to Giza and visit the Pyramids and the Sphinx which they have seen on various documentaries on television and which Ella has learned about in school all those years ago. Here are the huge monoliths which were built thousands of years ago for the Kings and Queens of Egypt by its people using only primitive tools. They both stand in awe, completely unable to comprehend the scale of the achievement. The next day they catch a plane to Aswan and start their tour to visit Philae temple by motor boat on the Nile.

They spend several days cruising on the Nile visiting Abu Simbel, the temple of Komombo and the Edfu temple, before moving on to Luxor and the valley of the Kings and the Colossi of Memnon.

Even though it is late in the season, it is still hot and they are glad to be able to return to the boat after a day spent in the relentless heat of the sun, to where it is cool and they can relax with a cold gin and tonic or a beer.

They return to Cairo and spend a day exploring some of the myriad markets which seem to sell anything from goat's meat to fine silk cotton material.

As they leave, they reflect on the amazing sights that they have seen and the places they have visited and agree that it has been a magical experience for both of them.

* * *

Life returns to normal as Ella begins to look after both of her grandchildren in early December as Theresa's maternity leave expires. To her surprise Ella finds that looking after two children is much more exhausting than she expected. Although Richard is undemanding, Molly like most second born children fights her corner when she wants something.

But Ella loves watching each child learn and grow, just grateful for the opportunity to observe this miracle of nature evolve. Richard now calls her Nan which she loves. She makes jig saws with him and teaches him the alphabet rote fashion and takes them both to the park most days that she is there and looks forward to the time when she can explore the exciting local places of London.

Sometimes Geoffrey travels to meet her on her second day and they go out for a meal or to a show before returning home to Chipping Norton.

Life is very busy for both of them, Ella because she still wants to keep her finger on the pulse of her enterprises as does Geoffrey on his.

Ella sees Rachel and her family as often as time will allow as well as both Geoffrey's sons and their families.

In September 1979, Richard begins at primary school already having spent three mornings a week at playschool. Theresa is nervous for the first two weeks but she has no reason to worry as he settles in from the very first day, some of his friends from playschool also in the same class. On the days that Ella is involved, her first job is to do the school run holding Richards hand while she pushes Molly in her buggy.

When she thinks about it, Ella considers her life almost perfect, until that is, the day in November 1980 when Geoffrey suffers his first stroke, which changes everything.

* * *

Soon after their marriage Geoffrey and Ella had decided to allocate Friday evenings as the one in which they can indulge themselves, be it going out for a meal, or to the cinema or possibly to the theatre in Oxford. It isn't always possible, but whenever it is, it becomes their objective. This particular Friday evening is no different from any other as they visit The Pines to eat.

They are welcomed by the staff as usual, although Ella has already been in earlier checking the menus which she and the chef have changed that day, as well as acting as the Maitre De, welcoming and showing the clientele to their tables as they arrive.

After a sumptuous steak meal for Geoffrey and sea bass for Ella, washed down with a Malbec red wine, followed by apple and plum crumble, they finish the evening drinking coffee, before returning home. Arriving they slump down, each separately into one of the two settees which have soft down filled cushions that envelope them as they relax. They discuss the events of the day while half watching television.

Suddenly Ella becomes aware that Geoffrey's replies are becoming a series of incoherent mutterings and looking across to him she sees to her distress that he is lying back against the cushion with his head to one side. On closer inspection she can see that his face is drawn and sagging all down his left-hand side. By this time although still awake and conscious, he is unable to answer her or to hold a conversation.

Damping down her feelings of fear and dread she telephones immediately for an ambulance, reasoning that it might be several hours for her to get a doctor to come out, if at all at this time of night. The ambulance arrives after a couple of hours and after examining Geoffrey the driver and nurse decide to transfer him to the John Radcliffe Hospital in Oxford.

Ella prepares to go with Geoffrey in the ambulance but manages to telephone both of his sons and explain the situation before she leaves.

What follows in the next few days is for Ella a roller coaster ride of highs and lows as the doctors first try to determine a diagnosis, after which they can begin the best treatment available to give him the chance of a recovery, however good or bad that may be.

A consultant, Mister Jardine comes to see Ella after several hours, but what seems to her a lifetime, to explain what has happened to Geoffrey and to let her know the procedures that he will be taking and what his prognosis will be once it has been done.

"Well Mrs Thomson I have now had time to examine and establish that your husband has suffered a stroke, the type of which is called an Intracerebral haemorrhage, which occurs when brain tissue becomes flooded with blood after an artery in the brain bursts.

To correct this, your husband is being given a course of drugs which will reduce the pressure in the brain, control his overall blood pressure and prevent seizures and sudden constrictions of blood vessels. Having said all that, I cannot predict with any degree of certainty the extent that he may recover. Unfortunately, by the time he reached us several hours had elapsed and we know from experience that the sooner the patient reaches us and is diagnosed, the better are their chances of a full recovery".

Noticing that Ella has become more and more distressed the longer he continues, the consultant softens his tone and says "I don't want to upset you any more than I have to my dear, but I have a duty to tell you how things are as I see them. Your husband may make a full recovery but in my experience that is unlikely and he will possibly be left with some element of paralysis, perhaps only minor, but whatever it is you will need to start getting your head around it, and decide how to deal with it".

"Now we can help you and advise you, so you will not be on your own. For example, we can arrange for speech therapy and physical therapy should they be required. We can also advise on occupational therapy which can be used to help him improve his ability to carry out daily activities, such as bathing, cooking, dressing, eating, reading and writing.".

As he finishes speaking Ella asks timidly "Can you tell me how long that he is likely to be in hospital".

"Well it depends how he responds to treatment, but the best scenario is at least two weeks so that we can monitor his progress. There are facilities that you can use here; there is a bed in an adjacent room where you can sleep for a few days so that you can be with him. It is here as a form of support which is a vitally important part of his rehabilitation and ongoing treatment".

They talk at length for another half an hour or so until the consultant can see that Ella has calmed down, before he takes her to Geoffrey's bedside where he is sleeping peacefully.

Later Geoffrey's sons arrive and Ella updates them on all that has happened. They are naturally concerned but defer to Ella as she explains that she will be staying at the hospital for several days until Geoffrey has stabilised. Both the boys offer to take it in turns with her to be at his bedside once this period is over, to ensure that there is someone with their father at all times, at least until he is fit enough to leave hospital.

Over the next few days Geoffrey's condition improves to the point where he can speak, but only in a slurred manner. More importantly he has been left virtually paralysed down his left-hand side. The consultant tells them that he has probably recovered as much as he is likely to, but that he will stay in the hospital for a few more days because there is a risk that Geoffrey may suffer another stroke.

Ella is distraught when she hears this, fearing that the worst might happen, but as the days go by Geoffrey continues to improve, albeit only slightly, until after three weeks the hospital tells her that he is being discharged. She is over the moon when she hears this but when they arrive home in the ambulance, she is made aware of the sheer scale of the problems that she and Geoffrey have to face.

The first problem is that Geoffrey is immobile, although the hospital has given her a wheelchair to push him around the house, but she has difficulty getting through some of the door openings because they are not wide enough.

Rex and Ben, Geoffrey's sons have already brought a single bed down from one of the upstairs bedrooms and put it in the living room as a temporary measure, until the time that a stair lift can be installed. Luckily there are two bathrooms, one on the ground floor, the other on the first floor, so that Ella can bath Geoffrey. The only problem is that she is not strong enough to get him in and out of the bath, so she has arranged for a carer to come in and help her each morning.

The doctors have already stressed the importance of a nutritious diet as well as warning that not smoking tobacco and drinking moderately or not at all, are essential to maintaining good health.

As the weeks, months and years roll by, Ella's life is transformed from one of sheer joy at seeing her grandchildren growing up on the one hand, to one of monotonous drudgery on the other.

Geoffrey's condition means that she has to be on hand at any time night or day looking to his every need, not that he is very demanding. But even more importantly Ella is determined not to ever complain at her lot, in fact quite the contrary as she realises that if she does it might make Geoffrey's health much worse.

Sometimes they still manage to enjoy each other's company, despite all their problems, but often Ella is herself at breaking point, feeling like a prisoner almost, in her own home; not being able to see her grandchildren, although Theresa and Daniel visit when they can with them. Neither is she able to keep up to date with her cafe and restaurant business, although Rex or Ben both arranges to take a day off very occasionally from their work, so that they can look after Geoffrey. When this happens, Ella takes the opportunity to catch up with what is happening with her businesses.

Because Geoffrey is immobile his weight balloons up, which in turn puts more strain on Ella as she tries to move him either from the settee to his wheelchair to the toilet or to his bed. It takes all of her strength and fortitude when this happens and as time goes by adds to her feelings of inadequacy and frustration.

* * *

But things become much worse in the summer of 1986 when Geoffrey suffers another stroke. This time he is left virtually paralysed, completely unable to do anything for himself. He spends much of his time sleeping and shows no sign of recognising anyone even when his eyes are open.

He returns to hospital for further checks and to give Ella some respite, but they can do nothing more for him, so have no alternative than to discharge him to return home, leaving him to be left to Ella's ministry.

It is now that she is at her lowest ebb, but still manages to cope as best she can to look after her husband. The ambulance men manage to get Geoffrey upstairs to his bedroom which he hasn't used since his first stroke.

Because he is unaware of what is happening around him Ella doesn't spend as much time at his bedside, only checking on him periodically, which in turn gives her some relief, although she feels even more trapped in the house than before, because there is no discourse between her and Geoffrey at all now.

Things continue in much the same fashion until suddenly in February 1987 Geoffrey's condition deteriorates dramatically and before she can even contact the doctor, he takes his last breath.

Ella is inconsolable, questioning herself that she could have done more, as well as feeling her sense of loss once again. But both of her and Geoffrey's families assure her that she has no need to chastise herself.

When she tries to analyse her feelings, she realises that some small part of her feels guilty because although she has loved Geoffrey, her feelings for him have never been as strong as those she had for Richard, her benchmark by which she compares it, rightly or wrongly. But in some strange way she has cared for Geoffrey even more because of it, as if somehow compensating to make up for how she feels.

Daniel, together with Rex and Ben arrange the funeral which takes place in the local church in Chipping Norton which is packed with family, some of whom Ella has never met, as well as friends and business colleagues from the chamber of commerce. Rex gives the eulogy of his father bringing tears and smiles in equal measure as memories are rekindled.

Ella has arranged for the funeral breakfast to be at The Pines which is closed for the day for this purpose. By this time Ella is physically and mentally drained and seeing this Daniel makes his apologies for her and takes her back to her home where Theresa and the children are waiting.

Ella's spirits lift as she spends the next few days with them, reacquainting herself with her grandchildren who have now grown up so much that she can hardly recognise them. But she has no reason to fear that they won't recognise or remember her as they begin talking to her saying things like "do you remember when you took us to the zoo Nan" and "when you met me from school and bought us ice-creams" and "when you took us to the park and we went on the swings".

She has to swallow deeply when she sees Richard, to avoid saying involuntarily out loud how much he looks like his grandfather. He is now nearly twelve years old and tall for his age, with a characteristic flaming head of hair, piercing blue eyes and freckles on his face.

Conversely Molly, who is nine, is the spitting image of her mother, both in looks and mannerisms. Not only that but she has a mischievous smile and wicked sense of humour, continually hiding her brother's toys or clothes, driving him to distraction in the process, which only makes her laugh more.

At the end of four days Daniel has to leave, but promises to return as soon as possible, and as she closes the door on their departing backs, Ella is suddenly aware that she is on her own again and collapses slowly into the nearest chair, weeping.

* * *

The next few months for Ella are spent acclimatising and adjusting to her new single life. She begins by spending more time at the café and The Pines, slowly getting to grips with them again. As much as anything she does this to block out the feeling of loss by working to the point of excess.

Eventually her thoughts turn to moving; Geoffrey's house now only holds bad memories for her, and although neither Rex nor Ben have ever questioned her right to be there, she knows that the house is their inheritance eventually. She has had time to look at what space is available above The Pines restaurant; a space that was originally designed to be used as a flat with living accommodation.

At present some of the space is used to store some stock for the restaurant, as well as old fixtures fittings and furniture, but if it were all put somewhere else the space could be returned to its original use as a flat, with two bedrooms, a living room, a small kitchen and a bathroom: more than enough in fact for her requirements.

She throws all her energy into converting the flat back to its original use, her creative skills coming to the fore once again to create a comfortable living space big enough for her new requirements.

In January 1988, Ella moves in to her new flat after explaining to Geoffrey's sons that they can now claim their inheritance.

Living at The Pines has a number of advantages that she hasn't even considered up until now, but by being above the restaurant Ella can keep an eye on it and retain an element of control of her business, something that she has not been able to do for a very long time. She also enjoys the interaction with shopkeepers and shoppers in the town, meeting people that she knows and hasn't seen for a long time. She welcomes these opportunities and takes the time to speak and ask how they are, sometimes meeting for coffee and a chat.

She is now nearly seventy, an age when most people are winding down, but Ella doesn't feel the need at all, being totally absorbed in her work and family, whenever she can get to see them. Looking after Geoffrey for the last few years has kept her body slim and mobile, but the stress and worry have taken its toll in other ways; her hair is now pure white, while her face carries the cost of sleep and energy loss, with lines across her forehead. She bears other lines on her face, but these have a very different cause, because there are crinkles around her eyes and mouth that disappear every time that she laughs, which she hasn't done for years, but is beginning to once again.

Other than Daniel and his family, she has always remained in touch with Rachel, the latter's encouragement and sheer persistence offering help and support whenever Ella needs or asks for it, which has been considerable recently.

She also visits friends regularly in Chadlington that she has known all her life and it is while she is here at her old school friend's, Jane Harris cottage, on a lovely spring day in April 1989 that she learns that the Manor House Hotel has changed ownership.

"I had heard that the hotel wasn't doing very well, several years ago, but I didn't realise that things had got that bad" Ella says, before continuing "Do you know who has brought it"?

"Oh yes, but it is only a rumour at the moment" replies Jane.

"Well who is it then, don't lead me on and then leave me suspended" says Ella, laughing.

"Don't blame me if it turns out to be wrong then, but if it's true, it's that famous artist and oil painter Martin Fleet"

"What, the one that was so badly injured and burned during the war" says Ella who remembers seeing several television documentaries about the person in question and how he overcame his severe disabilities and learned how to paint as a form of recuperation when he recovered.

"His injuries were terrible and if I remember correctly it was a miracle that he survived. The explosion, or fire that caused it even almost destroyed his larynx and voice box, because I can remember from the documentary that he could only speak in a sibilant whisper; it was quite eerie to hear him, the poor man.

What I do know is that his paintings are beautiful, so I suppose that it is a form of compensation, a way of him learning to come to terms with his dreadful disabilities. The last time that I saw him on television was when he exhibited at The National Gallery. I would have loved to have gone and seen it but it was when Geoffrey was so ill and it wasn't possible for me to get away".

"That's him, but as I say I am not one hundred percent sure, because although it is supposed to have happened a little while ago, nobody has seen him around the village. The only thing that I will say is that if it is him, he must be totally transforming the Manor House, because there have been builders and landscape gardeners going there daily for months".

"How intriguing" replies Ella, before changing the subject and enquiring after other friends that she knows who still live in the village?

CHAPTER 33.

THE INVASION OF ITALY 1943.

Richard and his colleague's hopes of a few days leave home after El Alamein are dashed as they find themselves wading ashore at the south eastern region of Sicily near Syracuse on 10th July 1943, after a short journey by sea from Tunis. He is part of The British Eighth Army under General Bernard Montgomery, who together with the U.S Seventh Army under General George S. Patton forms the landing forces.

The American forces meanwhile are launching their invasion simultaneously on the Gulf of Gela on the south coast, the objective being that the British forces will head north to capture Messina and cut off the Axis forces of Germany and Italy, thus stopping them from evacuating to the Italian mainland. While all this is taking place, airborne landings are being carried out simultaneously by parachute brigades.

Sicily has been chosen as a prelude before the invasion of mainland Italy although nobody has told Richard or any of the allies' combatants, the knowledge being held by only the top echelons in the military.

Like many of his colleagues in the R A S C, he has been temporarily drafted into the infantry until a foothold can be gained on Sicily, but this is of little interest to him as he steps from the amphibious Duckw transporting him from the ship to the beach.

The landing forces are met by a withering hail of machine gun fire and shells as they get closer to the beach and Richard thinks for the very first time in this war that he might very well not survive this morning. Everywhere around him men, some of whom he has known for many months are being slaughtered by the relentless onslaught, but slowly, as shelling from the destroyers offshore return fire at the German and Italian positions, the battle begins to turn and the Allies forces begin to build a foothold.

Miraculously Richard remains unscathed, the only evidence that he was ever involved in such carnage being a small flesh wound to his ear, caused by a machine gun bullet which would have ended his life were it a fraction nearer his head. He has experienced emotions from sheer exhilaration to that of fear, cowardice or possible death on his short one-hundred-yard journey up the beach. Even as he runs, he had flash backs, visions of his life with Ella and Daniel his young son, which acts as a spur to achieve his objective, although when he reflects later, he realises he never had time to fire a single round in anger at his enemies.

Ella is never far from his thoughts during the many months they have been apart; she writes regularly to him and he replies as often as possible, but their correspondence often takes one or two weeks to reach each other. He keeps a photograph of her and Daniel is his wallet and takes it out whenever time allows, so that he can see her sweet face and recall their moments together.

Once the beaches have been secured the next two days are spent consolidating their positions, bringing in tanks, artillery and other heavy paraphernalia of military destruction, before moving north along the east coast towards Messina, with the Americans in a supporting role along their left flank.

The British forces are met with relatively little resistance after their initial landing and they manage to clear the south eastern region in the first three days. This is due in no small measure because where they encounter Italian troops who are not supported by German forces, the Italians, who are very often Sicilians, surrender, rather than see their beautiful island destroyed.

The Eighth Army takes the town of Vizzini on the third day and Richard experiences for the first time how the Italians live. Most of them are poor agricultural workers who come out into the streets to welcome them, glad to be rid of their German oppressors, despite their government having declared war on the Allies in the first place. It is quite apparent that the majority of Italian citizens do not wish for this conflict, but fear the fascist regimes under both Mussolini and Hitler.

Their welcome even extends to invitations for some of the troops into their homes; Richard and two of his close friends being among them.

The village is several hundred years old and is built on a hill, as indeed are many others in the surrounding area. With space being at a premium it is inevitable that the village is made up of a maze of narrow streets that either climb upwards to the summit or plunge downwards towards the valley floor, depending on which way people are travelling.

Their particular villager's house is a revelation to Richard. Looking unkempt and run down. It is in the middle of a terrace which has another terrace only a few feet opposite, the two together forming a narrow passageway which the searing heat from the sun cannot penetrate, while the small narrow road is made up of cobbled stones, not the easiest material to walk on.

As they climb the path that reaches the house where they have been invited, Richard notices that it has wooden green shutters covering the windows at both ground and first floor level. The front door also is made of solid wood with no aperture for a window of any description. The outside walls are of brick which is plastered over in stucco and painted a light brown colour, which has become dirty and worn with the passage of time.

Every house has a balcony at the first and second floor level, over which washing is invariably hung to dry. But to Richard and his companion's utter amazement when they enter into the house, they find that all the floor areas are either covered in tiles or marble. This, together with the shutters has the effect of keeping the house cool, stopping the overpowering heat outside from entering the interior.

They are made very welcome by the older male of the house who introduces himself by pointing at his chest and saying "Vito" before using the same method to introduce the rest of his family, as firstly Angela, a more elderly lady who is about the same age as Vito and who Richard assumes to be his wife is indicated. The next person is Pia, who is a young woman of about twenty and is dressed in little more than rags, but even these cannot disguise her sheer beauty, her dark brown eyes, olive skin and slender shape forming an intoxicating mix. Finally, the third person is pointed at and named as Nicola, a boy of about ten years or so who is nervously hiding behind his mother's skirts.

The conversation is limited, but they get by with a mixture of pigeon English from the family and the few Italian words that Richard and his friends have learned in the last few days, sign language filling the gaps in between. Angela has made them a meal of pasta and bread which they wash down with a bottle of Chianti that Richard has managed to buy before arriving.

Amazingly, despite the conditions they all find themselves in, they manage to all laugh together, mostly at each other's contortions as they try to hold a conversation in a manner not unlike playing charades. Eventually as they take their leave, Richard notices that one of his colleagues, Bernard, a young single lad from Burnley has becomes smitten by the beautiful Pia who responds in a similar fashion.

They are in the village for several days, during which time Bernard and Pia's relationship develops rapidly before the invasion moves on. Richard is surprised when Bernard tells him that he has told Pia that he will return to see her once the war is over, and wonders idly how he managed to convey his feelings to her, before reflecting on his early relationship with Ella and realising that love will always find a way, however difficult.

By now Richard has reverted to his role in the R A S C, getting supplies of shells and ammunition for tanks and artillery to forward positions. It is back breaking work carried out in the extreme heat of an

Italian summer, in precarious and dangerous conditions. Good progress is made initially, but the campaign takes an unexpected turn as they began to encounter German forces in the hills leading to the Plain of Catania.

It is here that the German Luftwaffe has airfields and they are able to launch attacks, bombing and strafing the British forces whose offensive becomes bogged down in protracted and bloody battles on the Plain of Catania and in the mountain's northwest of Mount Etna and they experience heavy losses. The main thing that sustains Richard through this testing time, when he thinks that all is lost, is the support and positivity of his pier group. Individually they are all feeling the same, but as a group they are as one, implacable, immovable and undefeated.

Their faith in each other is justified as on the 23rd of July the British Eighth Army nears Catania, but they still have to break through the German Etna Line, an area north of Catania which encircles the volcano, before extending northward across the Nebrodi Mountains to the sea. Here they experience their heaviest fighting of the invasion, the Germans illustrating once again their resilience and superb fighting qualities.

The Eighth Army progresses north, first capturing Catania before moving on onto the mountain slopes. It is here in the almost impenetrable dust and heat of battle that Richard has a near death experience. With the rest of his group he is unloading supplies of artillery shells and petrol behind the British lines, when from over the brow of a hill several hundred yards away appear two German Panther tanks which are advancing rapidly towards the R A S C and its supplies. This is the one single thing that they all fear, a counterattack which breaks through the British lines leaving the rear positions exposed. Richard knows that the two essential things that are necessary in this situation are (a) not to leave the supplies so that they can be used by the Germans and (b) to get the hell out. The Panthers are now using machine gun fire against the British infantry who are retreating and are exposed with no tanks to cover their retreat and are being mown down like coconuts at a fair.

By this time Richard and most of the team have fallen back on foot trying to avoid the hail of German machine gun, fire but not before receiving a number of causalities, including their senior commander. Seeing the German tanks and infantry approaching the British supplies Richard, who seems to be the one person capable of making a decision, orders the survivors to open fire on the Lorries loaded with shells and ammunition and by doing so hoping that it will cause them to explode.

Nothing happens for several minutes, during which time the German tanks keep on advancing towards both the ammunition and the British.

Just when they think that they have failed in their objective, the supplies of munitions and petrol explode with a roar that is deafening. A huge ball of fire erupts almost simultaneously as they throw themselves onto the ground to avoid being caught up in it.

Both German infantry and tanks that are moving toward them are caught up in the maelstrom of fire and death and are decimated as artillery shells and ammunition explode all around them.

This brings the German offensive to a halt for long enough to enable British tanks and infantry to organise their own counterattack and to quell the German advance. The following day Richard is called to his commanding officer's, Major Wilson's tent, where he is thanked for his quick actions when he tried successfully to explode the fuel dump. He goes on to say "Your response saved untold British lives and I am pleased to tell you that I am mentioning your actions in despatches. I am also pleased to inform you that you are promoted to Corporal with immediate effect. Well done".

Although he is pleased that his action has been recognised, Richard is not so thrilled to hear that he has been promoted, knowing that it might distance him from the men that he has come to know and trust, but when they hear, it is obvious that they are pleased for him and congratulate him warmly.

The German with overall responsibility for Sicily, General Hube, by utilising his army's dogged resistance, is able to delay both British and American advances long enough to begin evacuating Sicily on 17th August across the Straits of Messina. This is the one thing that the Allies have tried desperately to avoid, wanting to destroy or capture the Axis forces and take them out of the next phase, the invasion of mainland Italy.

The Americans arrive in Messina just hours after the German evacuation, with the British arriving days later.

As for Richard, he has no knowledge of the tactics or objectives of those in command, just being grateful that he is still alive and in one piece as he arrives in Messina.

* * *

The Allied forces gather together in Messina awaiting their next move in the game of chess being played out in this part of Europe. They don't have to wait very long as on 8th September 1943 the surrender of Italy is announced by General Eisenhower, which is then confirmed by the Bagdoglio Proclamation by the Italian Government. By now Italian popular support for the war is declining, particularly after the overthrow of Benito Mussolini and his fascists in July.

Then on the third of September, part of the Eighth Army, the British 5th infantry division, which includes Richard and the R A S C, find themselves boarding landing crafts that take them across the Straits of Messina to land near the tip of Calabria on the north side. At the same time the 1st Canadian Infantry Division, are landing at Cape Spartivento on the south tip of the toe. The short distance from Messina means that landing craft can be launched from there directly, rather than be carried by ship, which is a good thing as far as Richard is concerned, due to the fact that he suffers from sea sickness.

There is a feeling of excitement and success among the troops, that stems from knowing that the Italy has surrendered and to some extent this is borne out as they land and meet very little resistance, the Italian forces surrendering almost immediately. The Germans have decided not to defend southern Italy because now that their Italian allies have surrendered, they can no longer trust them not to reverse their roles and attack them. To avoid this happening the Germans, have to spend much time and effort disarming the Italian Army and to occupy important defensive positions.

But there can be no let-up in the pace of the invasion and the next day finds them some twenty-five miles north at Bagnara Calabra where they link up with the 1st Special Reconnaissance Squadron which has arrived by sea. Here they encounter a battalion of Panzergrenadier Regiment and drive it from its position.

Progress north is slow as demolished bridges, roadblocks and mines delay the Eighth Army. The nature of the countryside in the toe of Italy makes it impossible to by-pass obstacles and so the Allies speed of advance is entirely dependent on the rate at which their engineers can clear obstructions.

Most of the demolition has been caused by the German Army, which no longer has the support of the Italian Army and who have chosen not to defend the "boot of Italy" but rather withdraw to a line several hundred miles north to a position opposite the Gulf of Salerno.

By the 11th September the ports of Bari and Brindisi still under Italian control, are occupied by the British.

Richard has seen very little action so far, but this is about to change very soon as the Eighth Army receives instructions "to maintain pressure upon the Germans so that they cannot remove forces from your front and concentrate them against Avalanche" (the landing at Salerno by the American Fifth Army and the British X Corps on 9th September which had received considerable German resistance).

Life for Richard has become one long monotonous ritual of rising early from his sleeping bag, then grabbing breakfast from the meagre choice available, before joining his unit to move forward north. Supplying arms and fuel in this terrain and heat to forward troops and tanks is gut wrenching, back breaking work. The mood between his team fluctuates wildly between ecstasy and demoralisation, depending upon the success or failure of the advance. Once they are in countryside that is hilly or mountainous there is an increasing chance that either side can overlap the other, the result being that they can find themselves cut off and surrounded without even realising it until it's too late. Once the day is done and evening arrives, they slump exhausted to the ground and talk of the things they miss back home.

"I can't wait to get home to my Misses and kids" exclaims one.

"Nor I" say's a second. "I'm going to take them all to Brighton and to the pier where we will get fish and chips. Then we will play cricket on the beach and then go swimming and get candyfloss, the kids love that".

"You will have to wait until the tide goes out then mate" replies a third, because the beach is all shingle and stones".

"I expect the beaches are all mined anyway" says another.

"Just let me get to my local pub, I can't wait to get a decent pint".

"I just want to see my girlfriend and take her to the flics; that is if she hasn't gone off with someone else" replies yet another, to which there is a murmur of agreement, many of those who were courting at the time that they left obviously worrying about just the same thing; and one or two married men also with the same concerns.

Richard listens half-heartedly to the comments, but his thoughts are of Ella and Daniel, wondering how they are managing and wishing he could be there with them.

It is like this most of the time when they stop , everyone disclosing their most intimate longings and desires for the time when they return home, but all too often some of them are missing in the ranks when they stop for the next time, because they have been either killed or wounded.

By the 27th September they capture a large airfield at Foggia, after first linking up the British 1st Airborne Division at Tarranto, before pushing north along the Adriatic coast through Bari. They then advance to a line from Compobasso to Larino and Termoli on the Biferno River.

If the men thought that they had experienced a hard war of attrition up until this point, they are soon to find out that it has been as nothing to that which they now face.

By early October 1943, the whole of southern Italy is in Allied hands, and the Allied armies stand facing the Volturno Line, the first of a series of prepared defensive lines running across Italy from which the Germans have chosen to fight delaying actions, giving ground slowly and buying time to complete their preparation of the Winter Line, their strongest defensive line south of Rome.

It is here that Richard discovers for the first-time details, from other British troops of "Operation Avalanche" the second invasion of Italy, which had taken place beginning on the 9th September at Salerno. It was carried out by the U.S. Fifth Army and the British X Corps, with the 82nd Airborne Division in reserve.

Its primary objectives were to seize the port of Naples to ensure resupply, and to cut across to the east coast, trapping Axis troops further south. In addition, there was a naval task force of warships, merchant ships and landing craft of some 627 vessels. The assault was carried out without preliminary naval or aerial bombardment, in order to secure surprise, but tactical surprise was not achieved.

"Salerno was a victory that was borne out of an almost certain defeat" says a sergeant from the British X Corps as they gather with men of the British Eighth Army as both groups gather in the evening to compare notes on their experiences. "Both the Yanks and ourselves lost thousands of lives getting ashore and establishing a bridgehead. I guess that the Germans had anticipated that we would try to land at Salerno because they were certainly waiting for us with tanks and artillery, which they followed up by bombing by the Luftwaffe. Luckily for us The Navy came to our rescue and bombarded them. German resistance was fierce from the 16th Panzer Divisions battle groups and the Luftwaffe, whose planes began strafing and bombing the invasion beaches, until X Corps seized the Montecorvino airfield, destroying three dozen aircraft German Planes in the process. Unfortunately, we couldn't use the airfield because it was within the range of the German artillery".

One of Richards pals then remarks "so consequently they (The Germans) left virtually all of southern Italy below this line undefended, except for two Panzer Corps and a parachute division, knowing that the main attack would come at Salerno".

The discussion goes on well into the night, which eventually gives Richard a much clearer view of the whole picture of the Allied invasion, rather than the severely restricted version that he knows from his own limited experience.

From this point on, the next stage of the campaign becomes for the Allied Armies a grinding, slog of attrition against skilful, determined and well-prepared defences in terrain and weather conditions that favour defence and hampers the Allied advantages in mechanised equipment and air superiority. It takes until mid-January 1944 for them to fight through several defence lines to reach the Gustav line, the backbone of the Winter Defences.

However, Richards war in Italy comes to an abrupt halt in the most innocuous and painful way, just before this has been achieved.

On the 6th January he is descending a hilly slope together with the British 5th Infantry Division when he stumbles into an entrance to a rabbit warren and loses his foothold. Trying to stop himself from tumbling down the rest of the steep incline he falls, hearing a loud snap from his left leg which remains stationary, even though the rest of him continues its momentum forward, or more correctly, downward. From the instant sensation of searing pain, he knows immediately that his leg is broken, if not worse.

He is carried back to camp by his colleagues and once the medics have set and plastered his broken leg, arrangement is made to return him to England by troop ship.

But before he leaves, he has the sad and onerous task of writing to Pia, the young woman on Sicily who his young friend Bernard has become so endeared, to inform her that he was killed in action just the previous day.

Using an Italian translator, Richard tells Pia that Bernard has been killed and to tell her how much he loved her, taking every opportunity that Richard, or anyone else for that matter would listen to him to declare his feelings for her.

"I know that you will understand when I tell you that Bernard died bravely, going to the assistance of some of his colleagues who were trapped and under fire from all sides. I reached him as he lay dying and his last words that he said, were to tell you that he loved you very much and hoped that you would find happiness once this terrible war is over".

Sitting back Richard reflects on his message to Pia, knowing perfectly well that Bernard had died almost immediately from his wounds, without ever having the time to speak. Although the circumstances of his death were perfectly true, Richard wanted to assure Pia of Bernard's love for her, which he declared to him constantly, so he has no qualms in using this minor indiscretion.

The journey home on the troop ship from Naples is free from attacks of any kind, the Battle of The Atlantic having been almost won, the threat from U-Boats being virtually negligible.

It has been two years since Richard was last in England and his mood is a mixture of happiness and tears, although why he weeps quietly to himself is a mystery until the straights of Dover appear with their iconic white cliffs welcoming him home and the reason becomes all too apparent, as love of country and family consume his every thought.

He has a fourteen-day pass, with orders to return to Aldershot at the end of this period, so he makes no delay in catching the next train to Reading, before changing to Oxford and finally catching a bus to Chadlington, where Ella and Daniel are waiting for him at the bus stop.

Daniel is now five years old and a junior version of his father, their flaming red hair and steely blue eyes proof of their genetic traits.

January 1944 is cold, and within a few days of Richard being home there is a heavy fall of snow that makes going out anywhere almost impossible, but this suits the Thornton family as they get to know each other all over again.

Daniel has started school in Chadlington in September of 1943 so Ella takes him there each day, fighting her way through several inches of snow, before she returns home to Richard and inevitably to bed, where they make love, sleep and then talk, usually in that order. Making love is not only therapeutic and deeply satisfying for them both, but is also a source of laughter and hilarity as Richards leg which is still in plaster causes all sorts of problems as they try to find positions that can accommodate it. On several occasions one or the other of them are dumped unceremoniously onto the floor as their feelings of excitement get the better of them, leaving the other one of them sprawled solitarily above on the bed helpless with laughter.

They live every day as if it is their last, not knowing how long Richard will be away the next time that he is sent, because he knows from several years' bitter experience just how much of a lottery living or dying can be, having lost so many comrades to the vagaries of combat.

Once the snow has melted, they go for walks, although these are limited to how far Richard can go using his crutches, or they take Daniel shopping to Oxford at week-ends. In between Richard spends time servicing and maintaining his motor bike so that when the plaster comes off his leg, they can go out for rides to surrounding villages. Daniel is always at hand to pass a spanner, a can of oil or whatever may be required as he maintains the vehicle, always insisting that he has to wear a set of blue overalls just like his dad.

Ella is dreading the day that Richard will have to return to barracks at Aldershot, fearing that when he is fully fit that he will be returned to Italy.

But there are other, much more important things on the horizon that neither of them can foresee, so Richards future in Italy is put on hold, awaiting the largest invasion fleet ever assembled to release Europe from the Nazi yoke.

During the time that this is all taking place Richard is allowed several forty-eight hour passes right up until the end of April when all leave is cancelled.

He waits, unknowing, a sense of something life changing invading his soul, while gradually building his strength, exercising his leg which he is now able to use, while troops of British, American, Canadian, Australian and a host of other commonwealth countries can be found all over the South of England awaiting for the order to go.

CHAPTER 34.

THE MANOR HOUSE, CHADLINGTON 1991.

Life for Ella continues to be busy; she sees Rachel more regularly, because although she hasn't quite retired completely, her sister has taken a step back from full time working and appointed a manager in both of her shops. She and Ella visit Oxford regularly together, to go to the Theatre or to the Cinema or just for some retail therapy. They still find as much joy in each other's company as they have always done since they were children, something that they both are grateful for.

Rachel often raises the question of going on holiday together. "Why don't we all go to France or Austria next summer Ella; just you, me and Fred. We could get a cheap flight and then hire a car when we get there, so that we can get around and see the sights. You haven't been anywhere since Geoffrey died; it would do you good".

Although they talk about it on numerous occasions it never seems to happen, but just the thought that it might be a possibility at some time in the future is enough for Ella; a temporary escape route, if or when her life becomes less demanding.

She still finds time to go to London to see Daniel, Theresa and her grandchildren, although she has to be more selective when this happens, because Daniel is sometimes away reporting, even though a date has been agreed. But as he tells her when an earthquake occurs in Turkey or an uprising happens in some far-flung corner of the world "these things that happen, or the people that take these actions never consult me to see if it is convenient for me beforehand".

Never the less, Ella goes anyway, her main reason being that she wants to keep in touch with her grandchildren as much as she can before they grow up and leave home. Richard is now seventeen and has taken his G.CS.E's and is continuing to study to take his A levels the next year, while Molly, who is now thirteen has completely different interests that include playing pop music and going to gigs to see her favourite bands, or to go out with friends from school.

 She has not yet begun to be interested in boys, but has developed a keen sense of clothes, or rather clothing design. This sometimes shows when she buys items, only to take them apart and change them to a design of her liking. When she first did this, her mother was horrified until she saw the end result and recognised the latent talent that her daughter possessed, before making the connection between Molly and her Great Aunt Rachel.

For all these reasons, Ella delights in seeing them and taking them out to places of interest, to The Natural History Museum, or to The Science Museum, even to Kew Gardens. Wishing to broaden their horizons she takes them to the theatre to see the musical, Phantom of the Opera and even Covent Garden to the ballet.

But Ella gets the most pleasure when she is with one or the other of them when she is alone with them. It is at these times that they pour out their hearts and concerns to her, finding that they can tell her both their hopes and problems, in some cases rather than their parents, knowing that she will always have a ready word of advice, or even more importantly that she will never divulge their conversations with anyone else.

"Why can't I wear a bra; all of the girls in my class wear them, but mum says I must wait until I am ready. Some of my friends don't have boobs but still wear bras. It's not fair" complains Molly on one occasion when the two of them are alone.

"Oh my love, your mum is right" replies Ella, not wanting to challenge or undermine Theresa's decision in any way, but then goes on to add " Look, it's your birthday in six months, so why don't I buy you some then, by which time you well probably need them anyway. That way your mum can blame me and I will say that I didn't know that it was a problem".

Molly's face lights up at Ella's suggestion, who knows that if her mother had made the same offer, she would still not have accepted it.

On another occasion when Ella is out shopping with Richard, she asks him if he has any thoughts on what he wants to do when he finishes his A levels.

"Well I hope to go to University and study law" Richard replies.

"With a view to do what"

"I would like to either to become a solicitor or a barrister eventually. I could take a qualifying law degree at University, after which I would need to decide which one to pursue, because their pathways diverge"

"You have obviously given it serious thought Richard, but what do your parents think".

"Well I have discussed it with them and mum is fine with it, but I think that dad wants me to do something similar to him, but to be honest it just doesn't grab me. I know that he has been hugely successful and I am proud of him, but I want to do something different"

"Then you should stick to your guns. I am sure that when he sees how determined you are, he will understand"

In this way Ella watches her grandchildren grow and develop on their way to adulthood.

* * *

Life in Chipping Norton follows its familiar pattern that is until one Wednesday in late June she receives a call from a Penelope Charteris who introduces herself before going on to say "I am speaking on behalf of Mr Martin Fleet who lives at The Manor House in Chadlington. He has asked me to call because he has heard from a number of local people, who speak very highly of you, that your company arranges catering for functions in situ.

Now that he has lived here for a while, together with the fact that all the necessary alterations have been carried out on The Manor House, Mr Fleet feels that it would be a good time to have a summer party for the villagers so that he can get to know everyone. To that end I would like to arrange an appointment with you here, to give us some ideas of what you might be able to do. How does next Friday at ten a.m. sound"?

Ella sits transfixed as she listens, so much so that it is several seconds before she is able to reply "Why that sounds like a lovely idea Penelope, may I call you that, I am Ella by the way. I have a number of options at various price ranges, depending on what is required. I will bring copies with me on Friday so we can discuss them then. Who shall I ask to speak to"?

"Just ask for me and we can take it from there. I look forward to seeing you on Friday then".

* * *

At the duly appointed time on the Friday concerned, it is with a mounting air of excitement that Ella drives up the long avenue which has a row of maple trees either side. This is the first time that she has visited The Manor House since she left in 1956 and she can't wait to see how it has fared since then.

As she turns the final bend in the drive the house stands in front of her, but the drive continues on in a circular fashion immediately in front of the porticoes which lead to the front door. The circular area within the drive is mostly a lawn, within which at the centre is a large rose garden in full bloom.

Wanting to experience the Manor from a suitable distance she stops the van just after the final bend and tears fill her eyes as she looks at the beautiful eighteenth century house, built of distinctive honey coloured

Cotswold stone. She knows that the original house was quite small and narrow at the front, but extra wings were added each side of the front during the nineteenth century. Its windows are leaded and wisteria covers the whole of the façade.

Ella sits lost in thought as she recalls the many happy years that she spent here as maid and then cook, before restarting the van and drawing up outside the large wooden door which lies behind the two large porticoes and up three stone steps. She can smell the roses as she steps out of the van even though she is several yards away, and breathes in deeply to get the maximum effect from their glorious aroma.

She hesitates perceptively before ringing the large buzzer, feeling strange to be gaining entry by the front door, when all her previous experiences were from the back at the servant's entrance.

She hears the sound of hurrying feet and then the door is opened by a young woman who Ella recognises immediately as the daughter of one of her close friends in the village. "Hello Dawn" she exclaims "are you working here then".

"Oh yes Mrs Thornton" Dawn replies, acknowledging Ella's first marriage but not her second," I have been here for a year now, along with a couple of the young men from the village who do part time gardening for Mr Fleet. I love it; he is so kind. But you have come to see Penelope Charteris, Mr Fleet's P.A. haven't you. She told me to expect you and to show you in when you arrived, so please follow me".

Ella dutifully follows Dawn as they pass through the small vestibule which leads into the magnificent hall, the area which Ella remembers with such clarity. It is huge, its floor covered with Italian marble tiles, while its walls are panelled in light oak. At the far end there is a wide balustrade staircase leading up to a landing at first floor level, which proceeds to go around the four corners of the hall. As she looks up Ella hopes to see the glass covered dome which is on the third floor at the top of the house and covers the central part of the hall. She has always loved this feature with its glass painted panels, through which the light pours, throwing its reflection on everything it touches.

There is a large Persian mat which covers a major part of the central area of the hall. On the wall where the staircase leads up to the first floor there are two huge oil paintings which Ella recognises as those painted by Martin Fleet; the first a portrait of a beautiful young woman with dark hair which tumbles down to her shoulders, and green eyes which seem to follow Ella as she walks around the room. There is a smile playing at her lips, as if she knows something that nobody else does, or maybe that the artist has just said something to make her laugh.

The second picture is a landscape and is at least six feet long and three feet high. It is on the landing and to Ella's amazement is of The Manor House. It is beautiful and is just how she remembers it when she last worked here.

There are several high-backed armchairs with lamps next to them scattered around the hall and a large antique sideboard which Ella thinks is probably French eighteenth century in the area under the staircase. Finally, there is a large glass chandelier which hangs suspended from the dome on the third floor until it reaches the first-floor landing level, where it cascades down directly over the hall, its hundreds of pieces of glass glittering as it hangs above them.

The whole effect is stunning and Ella realises that although it is not much different in appearance than when she worked here a considerable amount of money has been invested to reach this point.

Her reveries are interrupted as a woman of about thirty years of age enters the Hall saying "Dawn told me you were here, come on through, we can talk at our leisure in my study".

Ella has no difficulty recognising Penelope Charteris from her portrait on the stairs and follows her to her study wondering about her relationship with the artist.

As they sit down Penelope begins "I will just explain again what Martin wants to do. He fell in love with the village as soon as he saw it and when he heard that The Manor House was on the market, he just had to have it. To show just how much he likes the village and the people in it, he would like to start a tradition in which he can throw a summer party for them all and perhaps even a second party at Christmas time. The summer one will be held outside on the lawn at the back, but if it is successful the Christmas event will be here in the house.

As Penelope finishes speaking Ella can't stop herself from saying "It all sounds like old times. Lord Stevens used to do something similar back in the late twenties and early thirties before inheritance tax took its toll. I was only young then but everyone looked forward to it".

"Does that mean that you are from the village originally" replies Penelope, before Ella nods her head. "I'm sorry I didn't know, but if you can remember them your knowledge will be useful for what we want to achieve".

Well it's a bit more than that Penelope, because you see I worked here for Lord Stevens as cook up until he had to sell The Manor House in 1956".

"Did you really, well that's quite an amazing coincidence. Please let me show you round before you leave. You can tell us how much things have changed, and even those things which haven't changed".

"I would like that very much, but first tell me in more detail what sort of thing that you want".

They discuss the catering options and it is soon apparent that what Martin wants is a buffet style meal selection. Ella shows her a number of options and they agree on a salad and rice-based meal, with chicken, curried lamb and various kebabs as well as a selection of ham and cheese. New potatoes for those who don't like rice are another choice. Puddings are easier to select; these are raspberry roulade, fresh strawberries and cream and lemon cheese cake.

"Before we go any further "remarks Ella "I shall need to know how many to cater for. The other thing that you may need to consider is whether you may need to hire a marquee. It doesn't have to be a huge one, but just big enough to put the food in if it rains that day. People are usually adaptable if things like that happen, but wet and soggy food is another matter. The other thing to consider is seating; if you like I can arrange to hire collapsible canvas chairs, but again I will need to know numbers. I can also arrange to hire a marque it you like".

They discuss numbers, logistics, costs and the date for this to happen for a while until Penelope suddenly pushes back her chair saying "come on, I think that we have done all that we can for now; I will establish numbers and the date and I well get back to you A.S.A.P., but I am happy for you to do the catering as we have discussed. Before you go let me show you round, I will be interested in your comments".

Ella can't wait for her tour to begin but as they both move toward the door it is suddenly opened and a man, who she recognises from documentaries on television and photographs in the paper as Martin Fleet enters.

"There you are Penny, I wondered where you were" come the words in the sibilant whisper that Ella also recognises. As he stands before her, she observes his mutilated face and head that has suffered so much. Skin-grafts cover most of his face and neck, but amazingly his blue eyes return her gaze unblinkingly. It is difficult to see how tall he once was thinks Ella, but a combination of old age, together with the result of his terrible injuries have left him stooped so that he stands just a little taller than she does.

His nose has no recognisable form, but instead there is rather a small mound of scarred flesh covering the small portion of bone that is left, where it once was; his hands too are scarred almost out of recognition, one of his fingers missing their end joint on his right hand. He is totally bald and his ears have obviously burnt, leaving them scarred and deformed, all due no doubt from the same source of the rest of his catastrophic injuries. He wears full-length sleeved shirt and trousers, to cover what Ella realises are his other injuries, and she wonders how he manages to paint such glorious, fantastic pictures and what courage he must have to overcome such adversity.

Strangely she is both neither shocked, repulsed nor offended in any way by his appearance, and as he suddenly looks at her for the first time and gives her a lop-sided smile she is moved almost to tears emotionally. She experiences feelings that she has not experienced since she was a young girl. Her heart begins to race and she experiences palpitations that almost stop her from speaking.

"And you must be the lady who is going to do the catering for us" he whispers, to which Penelope retorts "Yes, this is Ella and we have just agreed most of the details. But you will never guess the most amazing coincidence" she pauses to give her story maximum effect......" Ella used to work here as cook until Lord Stevens sold it in 1956. How amazing is that"?

"You mean that you lived here in the village" was the hissing question.

"Well yes I was born just down the road in Bull Hill, but I often lived in here at The Manor House as well, when Lord Stevens threw dinner parties".

"Martin stands stock still for a moment, a puzzled frown on his face, before continuing "Ella......that's a lovely name. I used to know an Ella, but for the life of me I can't remember where or when".

"Perhaps she was a nurse when you were in hospital convalescing all those years ago" offers Penelope.

"Yes, maybe that was it".

"I was just going to show Ella round the house so that she can see her old stomping ground; would you like to join us Martin" questions Penelope?

"I would love to, if Ella doesn't have any objections. I would be interested to see what she thinks of the house now. Just give me a moment so that I can get my wig, I'm sorry my dear, I didn't mean to frighten you, but I don't wear it when I am in the house and not expecting visitors".

Ella is at a loss for a moment, because contrary to what she thought that she might feel when she did eventually meet Martin, she doesn't feel horrified or shocked in any way; rather she feels a comforting warm glow in his company that she cannot explain.

When he returns, the three of them set off around the house and Ella is agreeably surprised to find that a lot of the original features have been preserved, but Martin explains that this is because The Manor House is a listed building and as such most of the features have to be retained. The only major alterations are those where bathrooms and toilets have been installed as en-suite facilities in the bedrooms. This has had the effect of reducing the size of some of the bedroom space in some rooms but some of the others have taken adjoining cupboard space to achieve the same thing.

"The Hotel Group had to make those changes to bring it up to people's expectations after the war. But the Manor as it was then didn't have enough rooms, so the Group applied for as extension to be added to the Manor which was granted, making the place a whole lot larger "whispers Martin. "I didn't need all these extra rooms, so once I owned it, I applied to turn the extension into a number of flats which I sold off once it had been converted. This worked out well because the sale of the flats helped to offset the cost of buying The Manor House. So now I have the house back to its original size. A new access road was made for the tenants of the flats so that they don't have to use the original drive to the house; the one that you came in on this morning. Once that had been done, The Manor House reverted back pretty much to its original format".

Ella is thrilled as Martin and Penelope begin showing her round the Manor, starting on the second floor. All the bedrooms are immaculately furnished and decorated.

"I can't believe how much this has been transformed" she exclaims.

"Why is that" queries Martin in a whisper.

"Well when I was employed here this top floor was effectively the attic and as such was only occupied by servants and staff. Most rooms had two single beds and a marble washstand in which we washed. There was one single wardrobe for both of us to put our clothes in and there was one toilet outside at the end of the corridor".

"Crikey" says Penelope, unable to stop herself "I thought those days went out with the ark".

"No, they were very much alive and kicking up until the late 1930's; still are in fact in some rich houses" confirms Ella.

The first-floor rooms are even more exquisite than the second and although they conform to how Ella remembers them, she cannot associate the level and quality décor that they now possess.

"This is my room" says Martin, opening the door into a huge room which has a beautiful corniced ceiling, with two large leaded windows at the opposite side from the door. Noticing her gazing at the windows Martin ushers Ella in saying "go and take a look. I think that you will like the view".

Walking across to the window Ella knows very well what she will see, because she remembers that this room was Lord Stevens and it was at the front of the house. The view is, as it always was, breath-taking. Directly in front is the drive with its circular approach, below which is her van and the rose garden; but to her extreme left she can see the beginning of the walled vegetable garden, and she wonders idly if it is still maintained. Beyond the drive on both sides are fields which disappear into the distance, which Ella remembers with clarity from her youth. She had always enjoyed the views from this window, sometimes making excuses to visit the room to do so.

She turns eventually saying "Thank you for that. I always loved the view from here. It brings back so many lovely memories".

"I have commandeered the room next door as well to use as my studio. The light is always so good in there" says Martin in the same sibilant whisper. But Ella is getting used to it by now and is able to recognise more easily what he is saying.

The tour continues with Ella pointing out differences to places in her day, while recognising the immense amount of work and money that Martin has invested.

They return to the ground floor via the staircase which brings them down into the Hall again.

"When the hotel owned it, the hall acted as the reception area, but we just want it to be a space where people, friends and visitors can gather. In fact, thinking about it, I reckon that it will be an ideal space to throw a party for villagers at Christmas, but let's just see how the summer party goes first" says Martin, his whisper at an even higher pitch as his excitement grows.

Passing out of the hall they enter a passage from which there is a doorway on the right which leads into a massive room which is obviously used as a lounge. Ella can see that serious money has been spent here; there are three large pale blue settees which look as if when they are sat in, that they will envelope the occupant with their beautiful feather filled cushions. In addition, a number of high-backed chairs in the same pale blue furnishings are placed strategically around a beautiful eighteenth century fire place. On the wall farthest from the door are two large leaded windows through which the rays from the sun floods.

Table lamps stand on occasional tables placed beside each chairs seating position as well as each end of the settees, their light giving a warm glow to this exquisite room. The carpet is cream and there are cream curtains running from ceiling to floor. Ella notices a number of what she thinks are large Chinese Ming vases, before she sees another of Martin's large paintings of Oxford on another wall. She recognises Magdalen College and its grounds that are so real that it makes her feel that she is standing in the garden.

"This was the lounge for guests to use when The Manor House was a Hotel" says Penelope. But Martin liked it so much that we decided to keep it as a lounge just the same"

"Yes, it was used as a lounge during the time that I worked here. It was always a lovely area, but you have made into a stunning room".

"Thank you" says Penelope "Some of the furniture and other items as well as some fixtures and fittings we purchased from the hotel group when Martin bought the house. Others were purchased from auctions or house sales".

The next room is on the opposite side of the passage and is of a similar size to the lounge, but it is obviously used as a dining room. A mahogany table, probably of eighteenth-century date runs about twenty feet down the centre of the room, above which is a chandelier at each end. The walls are covered with what looks like to Ella, a green damask material, with matching ceiling to floor curtains covering the windows. The floor is covered with rich mahogany tiles, the whole giving an overall effect to the room of rich opulence

"This room was used by the hotel for dining purposes, but it had a number of smaller tables distributed throughout the room, to seat two, four or more people. But we always wanted it to look this way" says Martin giving Ella another lopsided smile, which she suddenly realises, is his only smile, his mouth also having been another area of damage. He continues "we bought the table at auction; it is in fact much larger than we have here, because we have taken out a couple of leaves. My objective is to get enough people to dinner to justify putting the other leaves back. Other than that, it is plenty big enough for our needs. "But I am digressing, come on and I will show you the kitchen, your area of expertise".

"I would like that very much" says Ella. "It has got to be a million times better than when I worked here. There was no money for improvements of any kind back in those days, and even if there had been there were no dishwashers, fridges, freezers or any of the other multitude electrical appliances that there are now".

They descend the steps that take them to the Kitchen which is on the ground floor at the back of the house. Ella knows that the house is built on a slope, making the ground floor in the rest of the building, different from that where the kitchen is positioned.

As they enter the kitchen Martin ushers Ella forward saying "I would be interested to know what you think; Penny and me designed it but neither of us have very much experience in cooking or the logistics of where equipment needs to be".

The first impression that Ella gets as she enters the room is that it is flooded with light. At first, she is at a loss to see the source because the two leaded windows are the same as they were in her day. Then as she looks closer, she can see that the original cupboard at the end of the room which was always used as a pantry has been taken out. This also had a window which has been retained and the light from this is now an addition to that which she had experienced all those years ago.

A continuous mirror has been mounted on the wall directly opposite the existing two windows on the top of the floor cupboards reaching up to the bottom of the top cupboards. The result of doing this means that light coming through the windows, where it strikes the mirror, is reflected back into the room. The door through which they have all entered is of glass, which is surrounded by a wooden frame. Finally LED lights run all round beneath the top cupboards, while lights hang suspended at strategic positions; one above the sink, another above the islands, of which there are two as well as others which highlight areas where they are needed.

Now that the pantry has been taken out the whole room is much larger than Ella's time and it has been put to good use, with cupboards running around three of the walls, as well as under the islands. These are all covered by what Ella can only assume is marble or quartz. There are two double ovens as well as a dishwasher and an American style fridge freezer.

The sink is on one of the islands, the top of which again is either quartz or marble.

She is blown away at the sheer opulence that the room exhibits and emits a low wow!

Martin hearing her voice of approval is pleased and turns to Ella" you approve then. We didn't want to keep the kitchen that the hotel had because it was used for commercial purposes and we just wanted it for a normal family home; admittedly a large family home, but one none the less. Is there anything that you don't like"?

"Well you have certainly created a beautiful kitchen. I notice that you have a coffee machine that makes cappuccinos over there which gets my vote already".

"You like coffee then Penny replies. But is there anything that you don't like. We may as well pick your brains while you are here".

"Well there are just one or two things that spring to mind. The first is just a personal thing, which is that I think that the best place for the sink is directly under the window from where the best natural light can be got. Another is that as many facilities as possible should be close together to cut down on unnecessary footfall. Too much time can be lost walking, when what is needed is as much equipment and facilities to be within reach to save time and energy".

"I think that the sink where you prep the food needs to be close to the fridge and as close as possible to the ovens, although it is not critical. But do you see what I am saying; your sink is built into the island, which doesn't have the best natural light, while the two ovens are on the wall opposite to the windows, which means that there is a lot of walking between the sink and the oven. Similarly, the fridge freezer is at the far end of the room, which again increases the amount of walking and even more importantly, it wastes time, particularly if some ingredients have been forgotten, making another journey necessary. The dishwasher also needs to be near to the sink so that dishes can be rinsed before being placed in it. Having said all that your kitchen is lovely; it's just that my working life and experience has taught me the best ways of managing a kitchen. I hope that I haven't offended you, because that is not what I intended, but have just tried to be constructive".

"Blimey" retorts Penny "well I suppose we asked for that. But what you say makes eminent sense so I think that we need to go back to the drawing board, don't you Martin"?

Before he can reply, Ella says "Please don't go changing things because of what I have said. I am sure that whoever uses it thinks it is perfectly OK".

This time it is Martin who interjects "I am most impressed with your analysis Ella, for which I thank you. It makes me realise how arrogant I was to think that I knew the best way, when in fact I should have consulted someone like you, or preferably you, before I went ahead. I will make changes as you have suggested, but I would like to sit down with you first to ensure that there is nothing else that we have missed, will you do that for me"? I will of course pay you for your time on a consultancy basis. Perhaps we can do that once the village party has taken place".

Ella agrees reluctantly, realising that if she has not said anything that the kitchen would not have to be changed.

The kitchen completes the tour, much to Ella's dismay, because she has enjoyed visiting the place from which she gained so much experience to enable her to begin her own business.

Martin and Penelope (please call me Penny, everyone else does) return with her to the hall where they say their farewells.

"I will let you know the date of the village party once we have discussed it later on today" says Penny, while Martin finishes by saying "it has been lovely to meet you Ella. I hope that this can be the start of a beautiful friendship between us".

CHAPTER 35.

JULY1991.
CHADLINGTON VILLAGE PARTY.

Penny is as good as her word when she rings Ella the next day saying "Martin and I have talked things over and we think that the best date to have the party will be the last Saturday in July. That will give me time get invitations printed and to send them out to everyone in the village as well as giving those who want to come, time to reply.

We also talked over the options that you put forward and have one or two things that we would like to change Don't worry they are additions and we realise that they will affect the cost. If you have the time perhaps you could pop up and see us again; perhaps Monday, if that would be convenient".

On arrival on the Monday Penny meets her saying "Martin will be down later. He is working on a painting for his Gallery in London, but we can go through things which will save time".

After Penny has explained the nature of the additions that they wish to include, Ella says "well I can include these which will not affect the price because they are only marginal costs, but do you want me to source a marquee and canvas chairs for people to sit on"

"Oh yes please, I had forgotten about them".

"What else do you intend doing at the party; I am sure that the villagers will love a nice meal, but I think there needs to be other things going on or else they will just fade away once they have eaten".

"What sort of thing were you thinking of".

"Well you could have games for the children for example. Sack, and egg and spoon races are always good to get people's attention; some of the parents quite enjoy getting involved with those, and if you can spare the expense a local brass or silver band is nice to listen to. Better still, if you can get some of the local farmers to bring some farm animals the children would love it. Perhaps a few sheep or goats, which farmers could put in mobile pens so the kids can pet them. Obviously, all of these need to take place before food is served or else there is a good chance that some of them will be throwing up".

"Blimey" exclaims Penny, which seems to be her stock phrase when she is impressed. "neither Martin or I had thought passed giving everyone a meal, but you are right, the event needs to be more encompassing, if not it will be all over in no time. Thank you for pointing out the obvious".

They discuss the options for a while longer until Martin pops his head round the door saying "How are you two getting on".

Penny then explains about Ella's suggestions, at which point he holds his head in his hands. "How did we miss that? Thank you so much Ella, you have probably saved our village party from almost certain disaster, extinction even".

"Well I have been doing this sort of thing for a long time, so to some extent it's fundamental".

Ella returns home after Penny requests her to let her know if she thinks of anything else that might enhance the party.

In the coming days Ella sources both a marquee and enough canvas chairs for one hundred and fifty people to sit on, the number Penny has confirmed as necessary.

* * *

The day of the village party arrives and to everyone's relief is warm and sunny, although there is a small breeze which Ella, Penny and Martin are all grateful for. People are due to start arriving at three o'clock, but Ella has been in action since six am, preparing food with two youngsters from The Pines. It has been a flat-out operation, but it can be done no other way.

The previous day she was at The Manor House when first the marquee arrived and then the chairs which she supervised to where they should be put on the huge expanse of the lawn. The spot that she has chosen is only a short distance from the rear of the house, only some thirty yards or so from the kitchen. She has agreed this with Penny and Martin who think that it is a good idea, because she can fill the fridge with food and then bring it out as and when required. Last but not least she has supplied several trestle tables on which the food can be put.

It is now mid-day and she has just three hours to get the food to The Manor House in readiness for the start of the party. It takes her two trips and she is only just ready when the villagers begin to arrive.

At Ella's suggestion Penny has booked a children's entertainer who gathers them round him as they excitedly arrive. She has also got her gardeners to lay out white lines for the children's races later on.

The marquee is surrounded by several large oak trees, under which the chairs are spread in a random manner, because Martin wants to achieve a feeling of relaxation for his guests.

Shortly after three the villagers begin to arrive in a straggling procession, all of them on foot, because none of them have had to travel more than half a mile to get here. As they reach the front of the house before making their way around to the back Ella who is standing with Martin and Penny witnesses a most extraordinary act of courage from the artist as he steps forward to greet each and every one of them. He wears gloves so that none of them can see his disfigured hands although he cannot hide his face, but he wears a straw panama hat which covers the top of his head.

"Welcome to The Manor House Mr and Mrs Edwards and this must be Jimmy and Karen". (When she sent out invitations Penny had enclosed a sticker with each person's name on it for them to wear on the day, which makes it easy for Martin to identify them) "Don't you live next door to the butcher's shop? I think that I saw you the last time that I went there. Or to Mrs Edwards" I noticed you talking Karen to school the other morning, does Jimmy go to a different school now?

For every person Martin has a remark or a question to ask and although some of them are obviously disturbed by his appearance, nearly all of them feel more relaxed once they talk to him. Ella watches him, in awe of the courage that it must have taken for him to be able to do it.

As for herself Ella has the best time that she has had for a long time as she greets friends and villagers that she has known all her life. True there are one or two newcomers that she doesn't recognise, but by and large she knows most of them, so much so in fact that she is able to introduce some of them to Martin and Penny.

When they get to the back of the house, drinks are available in the marquee, with a choice of wine, beer and soft drinks; the food is also ready, which Ella has also lain out on trestle tables. The time scale for how long this should be is open ended, meaning that the villagers can leave food until later, or go up again for second helpings if they want to. Ella has ensured that there is sufficient for all eventualities. She has also arranged for the two young ladies who helped her prepare the food to attend, their function being to circulate with trays of drinks and also to keep the food topped up as and when necessary.

Another of Ella's suggestions arrives as they all sit around under the trees, with the dappled sunlight filtering through the canopy of leaves. As they all sit round eating and drinking suddenly a well-dressed man of about forty years of age appears who Penny introduces as a magician.

This is someone who Ella has seen when she has done other catering functions, whose act has entertained and baffled people, leaving them shaking their heads and asking each other "how did he do that", so she had no hesitation in recommending him.

He moves around the crowd, concentrating on six or seven people at a time, doing sleight of hand card tricks or making things disappear, a watch or wallet from an unsuspecting victim, which then mysteriously reappears form someone else's pocket. Next is the three cups trick, which he places upside down on to the top of the table. Under one of them he places a pea and then proceeds to shuffle them around on the table. Once this has been done, he asks one of his audiences to tell him under which cup the pea can be found. Inevitably they guess wrong the first and even second times as there is nothing at all under either. The magician finally lifts the third cup to reveal not a pea but an egg.

No matter how hard or how closely they watch him they fail to see how he manages to deceive them. He spends about twenty minutes with each group before moving on to the next, leaving the first group discussing how it has been done.

Both Martin and Penny are delighted to see the amount of interest that he has created and determine to thank Ella for her suggestion.

For those who are looking for other things Penny has arranged for several local farmers to bring a few animals, sheep or goats, even a few chickens which they place in separate pens further down the lawn. These are a huge hit particularly with the younger children who can stroke them or even hold the chickens.

The afternoon passes in a mixture of quiet tranquillity and excitement, as once people have eaten and rested, they make their way to the area where the races are to take place. Egg and spoon and sack races are contested, first by the children and then by the parents, who all too often can do nothing but laugh uproariously as they fall over into each other in the sack race, or keep dropping the egg from the spoon in the other.

As the afternoon fades into evening, people begin to drift away, parents with young children first, then the more elderly and finally those in between, but without fail they approach Martin before leaving and thank him for inviting them, or invite him in turn to the local pub one evening, The Malt and Shovel just up the road.

Watching all this Ella is in awe of the public relations exercise that Martin has pulled off; not cynically, but as a gesture of goodwill to get to know these people who he has come to live amongst.

Finally, once everyone has left, Ella too says goodnight, while promising to return the next day to clear up.

"We cannot thank you enough" says Martin who is clearly very tired. "In fact, we couldn't have done it without you, could we Penny".

* * *

Having slept better than she has for ages Ella returns the following morning before anyone else in the Manor is awake. Her two waitresses of the previous day accompany her and they get stuck in clearing away the leftover food, paper plates and all the other detritus that occurs in these situations, putting it in large black sacks before placing them in her van.

Just as they are putting the last of them into the van Penny comes hurrying out to greet them. She has obviously just got up, her long dark hair wet from showering, her green eyes looking tired from lack of sleep.

"I'm so sorry that I wasn't here when you arrived, but I was dog tired after yesterday and just couldn't wake up".

"Please don't give it another thought, we have just finished anyway" replies Ella. "The men will come and dismantle the marquee tomorrow, and others will collect the chairs".

"Martin is still sleeping as far as I know, but he and I talked for a while after everybody had gone. Now that the party is finished, I am going to return to my house in Oxford, my husband, bless his heart keeps asking when I am coming home. I only stayed this long to make sure that everything went smoothly, although I need not have worried, because you did such an excellent job".

This news is a complete revelation to Ella, who replies before her head can control her mouth, and says "Oh I assumed that you lived here all the time as Martin's P.A., how do you manage if you are needed urgently"?

"Well there are very few things in the art world that are that urgent. I may have to talk to Gallery owners if something is going wrong, like Martin's health for example, which happens fairly often as you can imagine. One of the major problems is that the smoke inhalation that damaged his vocal cords also caused considerable havoc to his lungs. He carries a nebulizer with him constantly and if that doesn't give him enough relief, he has a bottle of oxygen by his bedside. There are not many days when he doesn't have to use one or the other. Anyway, I am here most days, so I know pretty well what's going on from day to day. It's just that my husband is an airline pilot, which means that we don't see each other as often as we would like anyway, so I really need to get back".

As they continue speaking, the figure of Martin appears from the back of the house. Contrary to what Penny has said it is obvious that he has been up for some time, because he is fully dressed in shirt and trousers, over which he wears his artist's smock which shows marks of recent activity.

"There you are Ella; Penny and I were hoping to see you before you left, weren't we Penny". Then before Penny can reply he continues "Have you told her what we discussed". Hearing this Penny shakes her head. "No, I haven't got around to it yet".

"Well Ella, we both wanted to thank you for your efforts of yesterday, and to show our appreciation we would like to take you and your husband out for a meal. We asked around and from what we were told, there is a really good restaurant in Chipping Norton called The Pines that most people recommend. Have you heard of it"?

Ella is silent for a few seconds, not knowing how to reply; eventually she begins "Well Martin you don't have to do that because I was only doing what you have paid me for. It's true that I enjoyed doing it because it was here in the village that I was born and The Manor House was where I worked for so many years, so I have been rewarded".

"I have been a widow now for four years, my second husband dying in 1987". She finishes by saying. "Anyway, I was delighted to hear that so many people were recommending The Pines restaurant, because I own it, and after what you have just told me I insist that you come one evening as my guests; your husband too Penny. Can you make it one day this week"?

After they get over their astonishment, Martin and Penny agree after much persuasion to visit The Pines on the next Wednesday, but not before Martin has insisted that Ella accompanies him to London when he next visits his gallery, which is the following week.

Ella is only too delighted to agree, getting to like and respect Martin more and more. She cannot put into words, or reconcile why she feels this way, but she suspects that a small part of her selfishly wants to continue the connection with The Manor House. Another reason might be that she also knows that by far the most important reason is that she would like to continue to see the artist, who moves her in an inexplicable way that she cannot explain. Although Martin is seriously disfigured, she has no feelings of repugnance or disgust, but rather in fact an overwhelming sense of respect and warmth and a need to continue seeing him.

It can't be love as her age, can it, she thinks? No, no, she is way past the days of yearning, perhaps it is just the thought of male company again after such a long time. But she eventually ceases to try and analyse her feelings, finding them confusing and unanswerable.

* * *

Wednesday evening arrives after what seems to Ella a lifetime, but at the appointed hour Penny, her husband Phillip and Martin are at the entrance to The Pines, where she meets to greet them. After Penny has introduced her husband, she shows them to their table which she has carefully selected as being both fairly isolated and not too far from the kitchen. All of her staff has been made aware that the evening is important to her and that she wants it to be a success, for her own and the restaurants sakes.

But she has no need to worry, because as the evening progresses, they all relax as they begin to discover things about each other. "You said when we last spoke Ella that your second husband died in 1987, so what happened to the first" questions Penny, before adding "Oh don't answer that, I have no right to ask".

"That's perfectly O.K. Penny it was all so long ago. My first husband, Richard was killed in France, during the Second World War. We had been married six years and our son was only five, so life was quite traumatic; but that's enough about me, tell me about you, how did you come to meet Martin and work for him".

Penny thinks carefully before she says "well it was through my father really; you see he owns a gallery in London and is always looking for new talented artists, so when Martin approached him many years ago he could see that here was one to watch for the future, and had no problem in offering to hang a number of his pictures in his gallery.

Martin's pictures took off straight away and Dad couldn't get enough to satisfy demand. Not only that, but Martin was also getting commissions for portraits and landscapes from individuals and corporate bodies and the whole thing was getting too much for him. This went on for several years until one day my dad had a brainwave and asked me if I would act as Martin's P.A.

I had been to University in Manchester and got a Masters in media and consultancy, after which I had a job in advertising in the city, where I was perfectly happy, so I needed some persuading, but I eventually agreed and I must say that I have never regretted it or looked back ever since".

Ella turns to Phillip "What about you, how did you meet Penny"?

"We met at University in Manchester didn't we Pen. While studying, we both joined the theatre productions that were being run and knew immediately that we were meant to be together. After I got my degree, I left to get my pilots licence, after which I joined British Airways to train as a commercial pilot. Penny stayed on to get her masters which meant that we had long periods when we weren't able to see one another, which was dire, but everything worked out O.K. as you can see. We lived in London until two years ago, but moved to Oxford when Martin bought The Manor House, because Penny needed to be near him. It wasn't a problem for me because I work shifts and can be away from home for several days at a time, so I only need to go to Heathrow when I begin my shift and when I return home. In between I have a lot of days off so it doesn't matter too much where I am based".

Finally, it is Martins turn, although Ella knows some of his background from watching documentaries of his life and work.

She asks "I know a little of you from television programmes that you have been made about your work Martin, but there is also a lot that I don't know. For example, I know that you were badly hurt in the war, but I don't know anything about your life before you enlisted. Where do you come from, where is it that you call home and how did you learn to paint? Did you go to an art college or were you good at painting before the war"?

Martin looks pensive for a moment, before saying "Well just to change the subject for a moment I would like to thank you for inviting us tonight. I must say that the glowing recommendations that I heard about this place don't even begin to do it justice. My beef wellington was just to die for".

"However, to return to your questions, the first thing that I would say is that I don't know the answers to most of them. As you so rightly say I was wounded in the war. I don't remember any of it I am afraid, because when I was injured, I lost my memory completely and I never regained it even to this day".

"What I was informed had happened afterwards, is that I was travelling with a convoy of petrol tankers and other lorries carrying supplies of weapons for troops, as well as shells and ammunition for tanks. It was a pretty potent cargo. There were a number of troop carriers travelling with us in case we encountered the enemy, but this was thought unlikely because the Germans were in retreat at this point".

"We were travelling towards Falaise where the British, Canadian and Polish forces were trying to encircle the Germans, in an exercise called the Falaise Gap, a few weeks after D Day, in an effort to cut them off and to stop them retreating and reforming later".

"The assumption was that we had been travelling for several hours when our commanding officer decided to stop for a comfort and food break. We had pulled off from the road into a wooded clearing and formed a circle, much like they do in the western movies".

"The cooks had broken out rations inside the circle and had begun to make a meal. Meantime I must have been told to take up a position some hundred yards away to guard the camp. From what others discovered later there were only a couple of us and we were back under a tree off from the road that we had just left. There were other guards who were spaced out round the main camp, but because the trees were denser where the camp was, they were nearer to it."

"I must reiterate that I am only telling you this as it was explained to me afterwards. Nobody knew for sure what caused it, but evidently a bomb from a German plane, (although it is unlikely because the allies ruled the skies by then), or maybe a lucky shell from a gun had a direct hit on the camp. The other possibility was that we had camped on a minefield and one of us set it off. Whatever caused it with the amount of weaponry and petrol that we were carrying nobody stood a chance. Everyone was killed that terrible day, except me".

At this point Martin stops and takes a swig of water from a carafe. His squeaky high-pitched voice is becoming less discernible the longer that he speaks and it is several minutes before he can continue.

"Anyway, the first thing that I knew was several days later when I woke up in a hospital in Surrey that specialised in burns and trauma. I had been flown home as soon as they found me, which wasn't very long after it happened, because the conflagration could be seen from miles away; the hospital had sedated me to give me chance to adjust to the shock and had already carried out several skin grafts which were necessary if I were to live. This was to be the pattern of my life for the next two years. But the most devastating thing for me, was, and still is, that I not only had no recollection of this terrible event, but that I have no memory of anything since".

"The authorities only knew who I was because I was still clutching my dog-tag in my hand, although how it came to be there I cannot explain, because it was always round my neck until then, according to army rules; I must have snatched it off when the explosion happened".

"When I was found, according to the people who saved me, I was completely naked partially behind the tree that I had been stationed at. They told me afterwards that they thought that it was the reason that I survived".

Ella sits transfixed in her seat as she listens to the suffering that Martin had endured, both then and now, before saying "So you were told who you were from your dog-tag and presumably once your army records were examined you could find out where you lived and to try to contact family and friends who would at least be able to fill in some of the blanks for you".

"Yes, you would think so wouldn't you; the records showed that I was born and lived in Nottingham before I signed up in 1939 and that I was living in an orphanage.

In 1947, some three years after I had finished rehabilitation, I caught a train to Nottingham and made my way to the orphanage only to find that it had been totally destroyed in a bombing raid in 1943. I visited the council offices to see if I could look at any records that might have been saved from the bombing but I was told that they had all been burnt in the fire following the direct hit by the bomb".

"My army records showed that I was born in May 1922, so I was just seventeen when I signed up. Whether I was working somewhere before that I have no way of knowing and wouldn't know where to start anyway, so after making as many enquiries as I could think of, I had no option than to return to Surrey. Since then I have tried to come to terms with it but there are times when I get very depressed. But on the positive side I might never have become an artist if I had returned to my roots, because it was the wonderful Hospital staff that got me interested. Once that I had recovered to the point that life was boring, the staff tried, as part of my therapy, a number of different hobbies that might grab my imagination. After trying to make pottery, which I was hopeless with, I then attempted to write but the words just wouldn't come. Then someone came up with oil painting and I was hooked. It became my entry into a new world, one that I had not seen before. "When the therapists saw the results of my labours they were amazed and encouraged me even more. There was talk of sending me to Art College, but it just wasn't possible at that time, so I taught myself" he finishes proudly.

"I continued for a couple of years, by which time I had a large portfolio of work which I didn't know what to do with. Eventually I took some of them up to London with the idea of touting them round some of the art galleries. My luck was in for a change that day, because the very first gallery that I approached belonged to Penny's father and the rest as they say, is history".

Ella has been totally absorbed while Martin has told his story but as he finishes she enquires "but what made you buy The Manor House and how did you come to find it, because if you didn't know the area then you could have no reason to visit Chadlington".

"Well I have Penny to thank for that" continues Martin, "because you see that before she moved to Oxford, her father purchased another gallery there, and asked me for a selection of paintings to go in it. I spent several days in Oxford, a place that I have grown to love. During that time Penny and I would explore the area, for no other reason than that we wanted to. Our pilgrimage brought us eventually to Chadlington and while we were here, we stopped off at The Malt and Shovel for refreshments, where the landlord happened to mention in passing that The Manor House Hotel was up for sale. I had only been here for a few minutes, but I already felt a strong connection with this lovely unique little village which, …. oh, I don't know, this may sound a little dramatic, but it seemed to be pulling me here. I can't explain it in any other way, but the feeling was strong and strangely comforting. So much so in fact that I took the plunge and have never regretted it since".

Penny interrupts at this point saying "yes it was really strange because as we progressed towards the village Martin would issue instructions; turn left here, go straight across the roundabout or go right at the big house on the right. It was really quite eerie because although there were signposts most of the way when there weren't, Martin seemed to know exactly which way to go".

Ella has listened attentively as Martin describes his affection for the village where she was born and suddenly feels overwhelmed by her feelings of affection that are growing for this physically damaged but warm hospitable man. They have all talked so much that she suddenly realises that their meal has nearly finished and that the only thing that remains is the coffee course.

Not wanting the evening to be over just yet she says "If you like we can go up to my flat upstairs for a night cap before you have to go. What do you think"?

Penny and Phillip look tentatively at each other, but Martin has no such qualms and says "I think that we would like that very much my dear. We don't have to worry about driving because Phillip and Penny drove to my place, after which we got a taxi here. They are staying over with me tonight, so we will get a taxi back to The Manor House"

The decision having been made, Ella leads them upstairs to her flat saying "it's not very big, but it suits me fine. Not much washing and cleaning you see".

Entering the living room Martin immediately notices Richard's watercolour paintings that Ella has hung at strategic points in the room, and remarks in a voice full of admiration" who painted the pictures Ella, because they are very good. In fact, they are good enough to be in a gallery". Then looking closely at the signature "I would like to meet Richard Thornton, whoever he is, so where can I find him".

There is a pause before Ella replies in a voice filled with emotion "Richard was my first husband who was killed in the Second World War, the one that I told you about earlier. Richard enjoyed painting watercolours and we would travel out to places locally whenever we could, and I would read a book, or knit while he painted".

As she finishes, she is unable to stop the tears from slowly wandering down her face, and in a bid to avoid her embarrassment she continues "just stay there for a moment and I will get you all drinks so that we can celebrate a lovely evening".

When she returns Martin apologises profusely, saying "I am so sorry my dear, but I just didn't make the connection. You must have loved him very much; and he you in fact, because the portrait of you is both very good and expresses the love that he so obviously felt".

"How do you know that the portrait is of me, because it was done nearly fifty years ago and I look nothing like that now"?

"My dear, beauty can be defined in many ways, but by far the two most important are 1, bone structure and 2, the ability to enjoy life and overcome adversities no matter what it throws at you. These two things you have in abundance and are also what I see reflected in Richard's painting".

Ella is silent in the face of Martin's perception which she finds uncanny to say the least. Discussions continue for a while until Penny says "look at the time, it's nearly midnight. We had best leave so that Ella can get to bed. Can I use your phone to ring for a taxi please"?

In this manner the evening ends, but as Martin says goodnight he says "Now don't forget that I am taking you to London next Tuesday to the gallery. I will pick you up in the morning just after nine, will that be O.K."?

Ella replies, meaning every word "I am looking forward to it very much, and before she can understand why, she moves forward and kisses him gently on his ravaged cheek.

CHAPTER 36.

1991.
ELLA AND MARTIN.

Martin is true to his word as he picks Ella up on the following Tuesday in a chauffeur driven car. "Well this is very nice" she remarks as they sit together in the back, the luxury leather seats enveloping her.

"To be honest I never learned to drive and after I was wounded it just wasn't possible" was the whispered reply. "I have been thinking, once we have visited the gallery, which shouldn't take too long, perhaps we could have lunch somewhere; what do you think"?

"That sounds perfect" says Ella, who is enjoying every minute of her day out, without having to think of train times, or the weather, or anything else for that matter.

Dressed in a blazer and wearing a pink shirt with a navy-blue tie, Martin is the picture of sartorial elegance. Pale grey trousers and crocodile shoes complete the image, while as usual a wig covers his skull, hiding some of the damage; a wide brimmed straw boater hat conceals the top half of his face, leaving only his jaw and throat exposed. He is obviously used taking as many precautions as he can to avoid shocking people thinks Ella, who has no such qualms regarding his appearance.

They reach the gallery which is in Kings Road, Chelsea, where the driver drops them outside before arranging to pick them up when Martin calls him on his mobile phone.

Upon reaching the front door they are met by a man who appears to be in his late fifties and greets Martin, saying "well how are you keeping old man. It's good to see you. I presume that this is Ella who I have heard so much about. Welcome my dear, both Martin and my daughter Penny have sung your praises, so if you can do that you must be very special, because they are both hard taskmasters. I am William Charteris by the way".

"Thank you, I am very happy to be here; I can't wait to see Martin's paintings".

"Come on in then, but first let me get you some tea or coffee".

Penny's father is dressed flamboyantly in a pale, sand-coloured linen suit with a light blue shirt which is open at the neck, where he wears a navy cravat. A handkerchief, matching the colour of the cravat is in the top pocket of his suit, which tumbles out, as if it were alive. As he reaches out to shake her hand Ella notices his gold cuff links and makes a bet with herself that they are nothing less than that of twenty-four carat gold. Light brown moccasin shoes complete the picture, which Ella thinks is probably par for the course in gallery owner's parlance.

As they walk around the large airy gallery Ella is in awe of Martin's paintings and even more of the money that they command. A number are of London scenes which show the majesty and variety of this wonderful city. Scenes of the Thames flowing past Westminster as it makes its way to the sea, with watercraft of every description scurrying every which way, while the reflection from the sun ripples its way the length of the river; or of Oxford street with its mixture of traffic and iconic double decker buses, with people of every nation weaving their way between it and the shops; a moment in time captured and suspended to perfection.

But as Ella reaches the end of the last row she is utterly stunned to see a large canvas, some six feet long by four feet high; but it is the subject matter that is the cause of her surprise, because it is of The Manor House at Chadlington taken from the drive in such a position that the extension, which is now comprised of flat's is not included. It is a beautiful picture, painted in an almost impressionistic style, which is the cause of Ella's amazement, because she too has a painting, although only in watercolour, at home on her lounge wall of exactly the same subject.

She takes a large intake of breath, which draws Martin's attention. When he sees the cause of her surprise he remarks "Oh you noticed that too did you. I wondered if you would when I saw your picture on your wall. It looks as if both Richard and I stood at the same place when we painted the house which is quite surprising because there are any number of places that we could have stood, but we both chose this one. I did mine in the summer last year and it looks as if Richard's was done about the same time of year, only fifty years earlier".

"I agree, but not only that, although Richard's is much smaller and painted in watercolours, they both manage to have the same feel about them. What a coincidence".

Their tour now completed they say their farewells to William, Penny's father, after Martin has confirmed that there are several paintings in progress which he will send to the gallery in a few days' time.

"The sooner the better" replies William "demand for your work is heavy Martin and I can sell them almost as soon as I get them".

As they leave the gallery Martin says, "What would you like to do now my dear".

"Well your earlier suggestion of lunch sounds good to me".

"Good, well there are several lovely little restaurants down here, one of which does Italian cuisine that I particularly like. How does that sound"?

Once agreed they spend the next three hours enjoying a leisurely lunch; Ella has linguini with clam sauce followed by a Panna Cotta with raspberry coulis, while Martin decides on a Mushroom Risotto followed by Tiramisu, all accompanied by a bottle of Chianti.

As they sit drinking coffee Ella's mind is racing with the thought of introducing a few Italian dishes on to The Pines menu. This is followed by the thought that dishes from other countries ought to be considered as well. French cuisine is highly regarded as indeed is Asian food. She makes a mental note to follow up her thought processes when she gets back. Meanwhile they sit and talk as if they have known each other forever in a relaxed stress free-way. Eventually Martin asks her "You told me that you had a son the other evening but you didn't say anything else about him. Where does he live now and what is he doing? Please tell me to mind my own business if you don't want to answer".

"No, I am happy to tell you all about him because I am very proud of him. Daniel has for years now worked for the B.B.C reporting from trouble spots all over the world. He also produces documentaries, so you can see that he is very successful".

Martin stares open mouthed for a moment before clapping his burnt and ravaged hands together and saying "You mean THAT Daniel Thornton; well I must say that you are full of surprises my dear. No wonder that you are proud of him, I would be too. I have watched a good deal of his investigative journalism over the years and would love to meet him sometime".

Ella is overcome with emotion to hear Martin speak in such glowing terms of Daniel and replies "well I will arrange that if you like the next time that he visits me, but I think that you will find that he will want meet you just as much as you want to meet him. I have heard him speak admiringly of your work many times". Then looking at her watch she is surprised to note that the time is now just after four o'clock and says with a start "How on earth did it get that late. If you don't mind Martin, I think that we ought to be going back soon; but I have enjoyed today very much, so thank you for asking me".

"It has been my privilege my dear. Although I have been on my own since the war, to some extent I have got used to it, but there have been times when I crave someone else's company other than my own; when that happens, I become very depressed. Penny has been marvellous at such times, so I am lucky in that respect. However, I have to tell you that

I enjoy your company so much, because I feel that although our lives are completely different, the ways that we think and feel are similar".

"Oh, I am so glad that you think that, because I agree" replies Ella "I don't know how or why that is, but it is true. Perhaps it is because we grew up in the same era and it is our shared experiences of that time which set the way that we think about things". Then, once again as if she can't help herself, she says "Why don't you come over to me perhaps one evening a week, and maybe we could reverse the process on another night when I could come to you. We could start this coming Friday if you wish".

A wide lop-sided smile envelopes Martin's face, totally changing his scarred features, making them almost invisible as he replies "That sounds wonderful Ella; it is more than I could possibly have hoped for".

Ella is perfectly happy to agree, but she questions why she has spoken in such a manner. "Brazen", her mother would have called it, but she knows that it is so much more than that. She asks herself "is it because I feel sorry for him and I just want to ease his pain and the fact that he is lonely", but she rejects the thought, because she can't stop the butterflies in her stomach or the intense feeling of contentment whenever he is near.

Now that they have reached this position in their relationship, the die is cast, from which there is no turning back.

* * *

Within a very short space of time their relationship grows and they are seeing each other regularly several times each week. Ella no longer questions why, but is content to just go with the flow. The suggested arrangement of a couple of days each week is soon consigned to the dustbin of history as they both seem to feel the need to be with each other most of the time.

When she thinks about it, Ella can't quite believe it, because she is very often the one who is making the first moves, but she doesn't feel embarrassed or encumbered in any way.

As if to convince herself, it is she who one evening first makes the suggestion that Martin should stay" It will save you having to turn out late at night and go back to an empty house. You can stay here overnight, have breakfast in the morning and then I can run you back in the van".

Martin looks stunned at first before offering" Thank you Ella, you are quite right, but have you got another bed that I can use, and what will people say. I don't want to compromise you in any way, and by so doing jeopardize our relationship".

Ella smiles before saying "Quite honestly Martin, I don't care what people say. I am much too long in the tooth to worry about things like that, and as for a spare bed, yes I do have one that you can use but I was thinking that we could sleep together in my king size bed; but if you would rather have your own then that will be O.K. too"

"Of course, I want to sleep with you. It's just that I haven't slept with a woman ever, to my knowledge, I just can't remember. My main concern is that I am terrified that when you see me naked you will find me repulsive and I will lose you, in which case I would rather that it didn't happen".

Ella can see the stark terror in his eyes, and hear it in his voice and determines to allay his fears. "Oh Martin, neither of us are in the first flush of youth. My body has gone south and I get aches and pains in places that I didn't know I had; who doesn't at our age? It is just that I think that if we could hold and comfort each other that would be enough. I'm not expecting passion, just someone to hold me. On the other hand, if you want any more, then that would be O.K. too".

As she speaks, she can see him wavering, not completely persuaded by her argument, and realises that if she has to do something positive. She quickly closes the gap between them and says "come on Martin, let's go and lay on my bed. We can keep our clothes on and just hold each other and I am certain that you will find it comforting. There is no need or rush to do anything more".

Martin is persuaded and follows her into her bedroom where they lay down together on the bed fully clothed. Ella reaches across and lays her arm on his chest before snuggling her head onto his neck and shoulder. "There now that's not so bad is it" she enquires after about twenty minutes, only to hear a soft snore.

"Well, I'll take that as a yes shall I" she mutters to herself, before sniggering helplessly, which wakes Martin.

To her surprise he puts his arm around her shoulder and hugs her to him. "This is lovely he whispers; thank you".

"You don't have to thank me Martin, because the feeling is mutual. As I explained we can comfort each other".

Now that this particular barrier has been overcome it seems to open a door to other areas of their lives that they have not yet already spoken about. Ella tells him about Geoffrey, her second husband, explaining that he was always kind, loving and generous. "I did love him, but never in the same way that I had Richard. You probably think that is a cruel thing to say, but although I felt like that, I never ever let it show to Geoffrey because I respected him too much, because he introduced me to things that I had never thought possible before; foreign holidays, the ballet and the theatre for example".

In turn Martin gives her glimpses into his life, explaining that he still has to go to have plastic surgery from time to time. "It's on ongoing exercise, as bits of me start to split, so the surgeons take skin from areas that weren't damaged in the first place. Unfortunately, there are not too many of them left now. On the positive side, the last time I went they said that technology has improved so much recently that I could have a replacement nose if I wanted it".

"You are going to get it done aren't you" says Ella. "Apart from anything else it will improve your breathing and give you more confidence. Make the appointment and I will come with you".

"I think that I will, but are you sure that you want to come".

"Of course, I do".

He then goes on to tell her how he made his reputation as an artist, the long hours developing his skills and the highs and lows he experienced along the way. Ella can tell by the way that he is speaking that it wasn't an easy path that he had to tread and her heart goes out to him once more.

Their conversation eventually exhausted, they lie contentedly together until sleep drifts in like an old friend and overwhelms them until the next morning, when they wake only to discover that they are still fully dressed. But, thinks Ella gratefully, our relationship has moved on.

Martin too is different; more relaxed and dare she think it, more tactile with her, laying his hand on her arm when they pass, or smiling abstractly at her when he remembers being with her on the bed. They are just little things, but things that Martin has not done before last night.

As agreed, after a full English breakfast, Ella runs Martin back to The Manor House, where he immediately goes into his studio to work on several canvases that he had already started.

* * *

Penny telephones Ella two days later to let her know that she has arranged for Martin to have the operation on his nose the following week, adding "I don't know how you managed to persuade him, because I have been trying to make him get it done for ages. I have managed to get him into a private London specialist burns unit".

"Oh you know what it's like, he needed more than just one person to tell him" replies Ella, knowing that it was a lot more than that, but not wanting to reveal the real reason; "I am seeing him later today, but tell him that I said that I will be there for him".

* * *

She is true to her word as she accompanies Martin to the burns clinic the following week, encouraging him when he meets the surgeon, and is with him two weeks later as he is wheeled down to the operating theatre, assuring him of her love, because she recognises by now that this is what she really feels. When he returns after the lengthy procedure, she is waiting for him in his private room as he recovers from the general anaesthetic. The clinic has arranged for her to have a small bed next to him, so that she can be with him.

The surgeon has told them that the procedure will be to take off the original skin graft that had been put on Marin's nose all those years ago, and then to build a new nose from bone fragments which they will take from his thigh, covering it with another skin graft. Once they can see that the bone graft is growing and that the skin graft has taken, he will be able to leave, but he will have to return regularly for check-ups. He finishes by saying that the rate of recovery varies from one person to another, but that it will probably be between seven and fourteen days.

Ella stays with Martin for the whole time, talking to him of their future together, reading to him, because he is unable to do so, the operation leaving him with two bruised eyes. But much more than all of this, her presence by just being there helps to keep his spirits up.

At the end of the second week, Martin's bandages are taken off and the surgeon declares that he can go home to The Manor House, but with a list of things that he can and can't do, as well as enough medications to sink a battleship.

Gradually, Martin recovers, his new nose giving him a boost, because not only has it improved his appearance markedly, it has also made his breathing much easier.

In October Ella is given a glimpse of the other side of Martin's life when he contracts a serious chest infection and she realises for the very first time just how precarious his hold on life is when Penny explains to her just how often Martin is subject to things like chest infections, bronchitis and pneumonia. Finally she says to Ella's utter dismay "He is only too aware that one day he will succumb to one of them; with the amount of damage that was caused to his lungs, it's a miracle that he has survived until now", and then seeing the look of horror and distress on Ella's face she continues "Oh I am so sorry my dear, I thought that you knew".

"Well I suppose that I did, when I think about it, but that's just the point, I chose not to think about it. But now that I know, it makes me more determined than ever that the two of us make the most of our time together".

* * *

November arrives, by which time Ella and Martin are virtually living continuously together, although it is not always in the same house. The majority of the time they spend in Chadlington at The Manor House because Martin needs to use his studio regularly. Ella sleeps there most nights but invariably returns to Chipping Norton during the day to keep up with the café and The Pines restaurant.

However, the beginning of the month seems to trigger memories of her friends and family that she has neglected since the summer, when she and Martin got together. But now that she has time to think about it, a sense of shame envelopes her and she takes immediate steps to rectify her mistake. She has of course told Daniel and Theresa as well as Rachel and Fred about Martin, but only on the telephone, so after discussing it with Martin they both agree that the best thing would be to invite them all either to The Manor House or to The Pines.

For his part Martin wants to invite them all to The Manor House, while Ella thinks that it will be easier if they meet at The Pines, because food can be more available. But as she gives the matter her full attention she understands Martin's reluctance, realising that he will be able to cope better with so many new people if he is in his own environment. Eventually she says "why don't we have it at The Manor House and I well get one of the chefs from The Pines to come and prepare food".

Martin is delighted at this suggestion, so Ella contacts Daniel and Theresa realising that he might have work commitments for the proposed date, but she is over the moon when he confirms that he can make it and finishes, saying "I can't wait to meet Martin since you first told me about him; I have looked up a number of documentaries that have been made which tell all about his amazing life and work. In fact, last year before you got to know him, there was an exhibition of his work at The Royal Academy at Burlington House in Piccadilly which Theresa and I went to see. I have to tell you that I loved his work, so to get to see Martin and speak to the man would be fantastic".

"Well, it's even much better than that Daniel, because when I told him about you, he said much the same thing about your work, so the two of you have already got a mutual admiration society going. We would like it if you stayed overnight and made a weekend of it. Bedrooms are not a problem and it will give you a chance to see The Manor House again after all these years".

Daniel laughs and replies" That sounds just great, I can't wait mum".

In her turn Rachel says "about time too. I thought that we were never going to meet him, you have kept him so long to yourself".

CHAPTER 37.

NOVEMBER 1991.
ELLA AND MARTIN'S SURPRISE.

The eighteenth of November is the epitome of a mid- autumn English day. Trees are already losing their leaves of red, gold, green and brown, but there are still enough to stir emotions with their beautiful tapestry. Early morning shrouds the countryside in a mist as Daniel, Theresa and the children travel up the drive to The Manor House. As they reach it, the mist clears leaving the house visible for the first time, its golden façade welcoming them.

Ella rushes out to greet them, Martin following along as fast as his legs will let him. After hugging them all in turn Ella introduces them to Martin who smiles warmly saying "You are most welcome, Ella has told me so much about you all". Then turning to Daniel "I have followed you career with interest Daniel and admire what you do so much. I can't wait to talk to you about it later".

"It's funny that you should say that Martin" Ella's son replies "because the feeling is mutual, I can assure you. I love your paintings and saw your exhibition last year at The Royal Academy, which was brilliant".

Ella stops any further discussion saying "come on you two, there are other guests that you should meet before you get engrossed talking about your lives".

As they return to the house Penny and Phillip are waiting in the hall and are introduced, before they all move top the large living room where Ella has put several flower arrangements, their bouquets intoxicating, their colours eye catching and vivid. A log fire burns merrily in the fireplace, its flickering warmth a reminder of the time of year.

It is only a matter of minutes before Rachel and Fred arrive, their two boys and their families following close behind.

"Ah, so this is where you worked all those years ago, has it changed very much; doesn't it feel strange" says Teresa to Ella.

"Well it did at first, but no, it hasn't changed all that much because Martin has restored it beautifully and kept all the best bits. The furnishings are all new of course, some of them bought at auction".

Daniel greets his cousins as usual with Harry exclaiming "eight maids a milking" which George follows with "nine ladies dancing" leaving

Daniel to complete with "ten lords a leaping" at which point they all high five each other.

Tradition having been maintained they all catch up with each other before Ella announces that dinner is ready.

They all move into the dining room which has been laid out in all its finery. The chandeliers shimmer above the mahogany table, each crystal reflecting its own faceted lights down onto the rich red-brown surface. Ella has arranged the table settings; the cutlery of silver and all of the plates of Worcester porcelain are hand painted. A large flower arrangement in the centre of the table completes the picture, which raises several "Wows" a couple of "Fantastic" and an almost inaudible "Fuck me", the last from cousin George.

Ella has arranged the seating plan and has mixed up both the sexes and family members, which she hopes will break down barriers, which seems to work as people start to talk to one another. She has also arranged for Tony, her head chef from The Pines to cook for them which he is delighted to do after seeing the facilities at The Manor House. He has brought a waitress with him and has been hard at work since mid-morning. The food is soon being served, warming home-made vegetable soup or crab pate to start, followed by either beef wellington or saddle of lamb, all washed down with a Malbec red or Chardonnay white wine. A selection of puddings or cheese and biscuits complete the feast, after which they move back into the lounge.

Penny and Phillip have proved to be both proficient and able, explaining all about Martin and how he came to live here to any of those that ask.

Picking up on conversations that she has overheard, Penny offers to show people around the house if they are interested. This is something that she and Martin have agreed in advance, knowing that most of the guests will remember The Manor House from their youth.

Ella is only too happy to accompany them, which leaves Martin and Daniel alone after the rest have all gone. Daniel has in fact deliberately chosen not to go, although he very much wants to, but prefers to stay behind so that he can talk with Martin.

He begins by saying "my mother tells me that your wounds were incurred during the war. That must have been a terrible experience. Do you think that you could tell me how it happened? The reason I am asking is because I have been asked to do a documentary on the D-Day landings and the invasion of France. Please say no, if you don't want to talk about it, but your experience is just one of the sorts of things that I am looking to include. I am sure that you understand, looking at the operation from the ordinary soldiers' perspective rather than of the planners and those in command".

For a moment Martin says nothing and Daniel thinks that he has overstepped the mark, but eventually raising his head the other replies "No, of course I don't mind telling you Daniel, after all it is common knowledge, but if I do, will you tell me about your journey from a child to your now prestigious position in journalism".

"I don't know about prestigious, but it's a deal".

Making themselves comfortable in the voluminous high-backed chairs either side of the fireplace, Martin repeats the story of his life in a similar fashion to the one that he told Ella all those months ago. Daniel listens mostly in silence, making notes in the book small book that he always carries with him; occasionally interrupting for a point of clarification. As Martin finishes, Daniel says "when exactly did this happen"?

"Well I was subsequently told that it was on the 10th of August Daniel".

"That's good, because it gives me a starting point to look up the records. From what you have told me I would very much like to give it a mention in my documentary; would that be O.K.".

"Sure, if you think it will contribute something relevant to your piece, now let's talk about you".

They have been talking for several minutes when Ella and the others return from their exploration of the house. As she walks in, she is struck forcibly by the two men facing each other across the fireplace, both waving their hands distractedly to emphasize points that they are making. What is even more pronounced is the way that they hold their heads; upright and "in your face" when making a definite statement, but on one side, their voices questioning rather than dictatorial when seeking answers or clarification. She wants to laugh at the sheer absurdness of it; that is before she notices the way that Daniel holds his right hand to his jaw, with two fingers splayed on his cheek, while listening to Martin. This is something that she has not noticed before in Daniel but has seen countless times when Martin is contemplating a problem. She wonders idly if these are things that a lot of people do, but that she has never noticed before.

She has no further opportunity to think any more about it as Rachel grabs her by the arm saying "right, I've got you at last, now let's find somewhere, so that you can spill the beans about you and Martin. I'm beginning to think that you don't want to tell me anything."

"That's not true Rach," says Ella using the diminutive form of her sister's name, the way that she has always used as an indication of the feeling of closeness for her sister. "Let's go into the dining room; we won't be disturbed there".

As they enter the dining room Rachel is already interrogating her sister." Now, come on Ella, tell me, how are things progressing with Martin. He seems a lovely man, but aren't you even slightly put off by his appearance? Is your relationship one of just friends or is it something more"?

"Hold on, one question at a time please" says Ella, laughing at her sisters' normal direct approach. "The first thing that you need to know is that I don't even see his terrible injuries as a problem or disadvantage in any way, because my feelings for him outweigh all other considerations. To be quite honest I feel as if I have known him for years. Secondly, our relationship is much more than that of just friends. In fact, I think of us as soulmates who have been searching for each other all our lives. As for the "S" word, yes it happens occasionally, but it's not high on our agenda, but I guess it doesn't need to be at our age"

Ella finishes by saying "look Rach, I have not felt anything like this since Richard, so try to be happy for me, please".

Seeing the mixture of concern and elation on Ella's face, Rachel immediately adopts an attitude of happiness. "Oh Ella, of course I am pleased and delighted for you, because your happiness is all I ever want for you, so if Martin makes you feel that, then it is good enough for me".

"Thank you, sister of mine, how could I have managed without your love and care all these years". Then "let's get back to the rest of them. I don't see them often enough these days".

When they return champagne is being served with the instruction "it's for a toast, so don't drink it yet".

Ella makes her way to Martin's side where he is stood at the fireplace. Clapping his hands to get everyone's attention he begins "I have an announcement to make which I perhaps should have made when we were all at dinner, but Ella and I discussed it and decided that now would be the best time".

Seeing them all looking confused, even concerned he hurries on "I hope that we have your blessing, because the reason for the toast is to tell you that Ella and I were married at Chipping Norton Registry Office last Saturday. We apologise for not letting you know but we decided that we didn't want any fuss at our age, so without further ado I give you a toast to Ella my lovely bride. My only fear is that you will not approve of out union, and that is the last thing in the world that I would want to happen".

As Martin finishes speaking, mouths around the room hang open at his announcement until Rachel stands, saying" well you two, you certainly know how to shock an audience, but for me personally I can only say that I wish the very best for both of you. As for you Martin you must be very special if my sister has given you her seal of approval".

But before she can propose the toast Daniel moves forward towards his mother, giving her a kiss on both cheeks and whispering in her ear "congratulations mum, I think that he is a great guy and feel as if I have known him forever".

Turning to his new stepfather he shakes him by the hand saying "You old fox, you certainly kept that a secret. Now I have even more reasons to include you in the documentary".

Finally, he turns to face the assembled crowd and addresses them saying "dear friends and family, please join me in a toast to the happy couple; to Ella and Martin, my Mum and Dad".

Glasses are raised and the anthem is repeated, "To Ella and Martin".

Once the formality of the wedding announcement is over, the lull in the conversation becomes filled: everyone needing to catch up with each other before the time comes for them to depart. Dates for future times when they can all get together are exchanged, everyone wanting to ensure that they see each other more regularly and that it is not left so long again.

Ella and Martin make sure that they speak to everyone individually, the latter showing a great interest in them all because "I want to get to know you because you are such an important part of Ella's life.

To Fred he inquires if he can give him a quote for some decorating that he and Ella want doing and to Rachel he inquires if she can talk to Ella about curtains for several of the rooms. As he reaches Daniel, Theresa, Richard and Molly: Ella joins him saying "You haven't had chance to speak to Theresa and my grandchildren yet, let me introduce you".

After the introductions have been made, Martin speaks to Richard, asking how he is getting on at school and if he does any sports. As Richard raises his face to answer him Martin is struck by how much he looks like his father and says "well there can be no doubt who your father is" as he looks at the flaming red hair and steely blue eyes and freckles which confirm his paternal genes.

The two of them talk of Richard's ambitions to which Martin says he will follow with interest, before he turns to Molly and asks her how she is doing and what her hopes are for the future, only to hear her reply "well I would like to get into music or design clothes".

Before he can address Theresa, she takes the initiative saying, much to her husband's surprise "we have met once before Martin, although it was several years ago. I interviewed you when you had one of your first exhibitions at The Tate Gallery. I was very new at presenting and you were very kind and understanding, which made my job so much easier. I have often thought of it and vowed that I would thank you if I ever got the chance, but I never for one moment thought that it would be today and, in these circumstances, so thank you".

She hugs him as Daniel says "well I'll go to the foot of our stairs; the day just gets more and more unbelievable. You never told me that my love" he says to Theresa;" but to change the subject Martin you did offer to show me your studio earlier, so would now be a good time"?

"Certainly, my boy, why don't we do that now? You are also welcome" he addresses Theresa, Richard and Molly, giving them one of his lopsided smiles.

Climbing the stairs from the hall, they all go up to the second floor and along the corridor to Martin's studio. As they enter Daniel can see a large landscape painting, some seven or eight feet long by four feet deep, which he recognises as that of the indoor market in Oxford. It has all the movement of the market, with customers selecting vegetables and fruit from one stall, while others queue at bread and cake stalls from another. Others are entering a tea shop, while yet more stand outside a jewellery shop, looking avidly at things that none of them can afford. Martin has captured the exuberance and essence of the market, his colours vivid and his customers and stall holders a living testament to the market.

Moving along to the next picture Daniel is even more surprised to see another landscape, smaller this time, of Stow on the Wold a village not too far away, the next a painting of Bourton on the Water.

"These are lovely Martin Daniel exclaims, before adding "you may not believe it but my father did watercolours of each of these, from very much the same positions as yours, is that a coincidence, or what"?

"It certainly is Daniel. I have seen your fathers work which your mother has on the walls of her flat at The Pines, which I may add are very good. I did in fact paint the last two recently after I had seen them, but the one in the market I did two or three years ago. It is really strange that both your father and I not only painted, although in different mediums, but also from similar viewpoints".

Eventually Martin says "well if you have seen enough, I think we should return downstairs, because there is a wedding cake which we had made specially for today".

Martin is as good as his word when they return to the living room, the wedding cake is there waiting to be cut. Photographs of the happy couple are taken performing the obligatory cake cutting ceremony. The waitress hands out a portion to each and every one of them on plates, some of which are eaten straight away. Others however ask if portions can be wrapped for them to take home because the time is now getting late. As the party starts to break up and people start to say their farewells, Martin promises each of them that he and Ella will ask them all again in the near future.

Daniel, Theresa and their children, being the only ones left, make their way to their bedrooms totally exhausted by the day's events.

As they prepare to leave the following morning, they invite Martin and Ella to stay with them on Christmas Day. "No, thinking about it why don't you come up on Christmas Eve, that way you don't have to worry about travelling on Christmas Day says Theresa".

"We would love to, wouldn't we Martin".

"Oh yes, I can't think of anything that I would like more. Thank you".

* * *

"I think that went well" declares Martin as Daniels car disappears up the drive, its rear lights winking in the dark November morning, until it turns the last corner, leaving the avenue of trees empty once more.

"Oh, it was much better than that" replies Ella;" and you were brilliant by the way".

CHAPTER 38.

CHRISTMAS 1991.

The next few weeks are hectic for Ella because the Christmas period is always the pinnacle of her culinary year, with office parties and groups of friends and families filling The Pines during the whole of December. Christmas Eve steals up on her almost as a surprise, virtually unannounced, before she is even ready.

What am I going to do" she complains plaintively to Martin "I haven't even bought presents for any of them yet"?

"Don't worry my love. We can leave early and stop off at Oxford Street or Kensington and do the shopping before we go to Daniel's. I will arrange for the driver to pick us up in an hour or so".

Ella is only too happy for Martin to take the strain of the arrangements from off her shoulders, leaving her to just fill a suitcase for them both, making sure that she includes Martin's nebulizer which she has noticed him using frequently lately.

Within an hour or so they are being dropped off in Kensington, Martin telling the driver that he will call him when they are ready.

Harrods is their first place of choice, where they look for suitable gifts for Daniel's family, a bottle of exclusive perfume for Theresa which Ella knows is her favourite, a biography of H.G Wells for Daniel, leather driving gloves for Richard who is taking driving lessons and a selection of materials for Molly so that she can make some clothes to her own design.

Feeling pleased with their efforts they decide to have lunch in the restaurant while they are there, after which Ella leaves Martin to settle the bill while she goes to the jewellery department where she buys a gold watch for Martin.

Their last act before they leave, is to go to the food hall where they purchase champagne and wine as their contribution towards the Christmas dinner.

"There we are my dear, job done; I told you that you had nothing to worry about. Now I think that I had best call the driver so that he can take us to Daniel's place".

Molly meets them at the door, unable to contain her excitement "Hi Nanna and Grandad, come in, we've got my favourites for tea, salmon and cucumber sandwiches, and chocolate cake and ice cream".

"Wow, if we eat all that how are we going to have room for Christmas dinner" exclaims her Nanna.

"We will worry about that tomorrow" says Molly pragmatically.

Tea is served, after which Ella helps prepare some of the vegetables for the next day, while Martin, Daniel, Richard and Molly play cards

"Are you at home after Christmas Day" Ella enquires of her daughter in law.

"No, we are going to my parents in Nailsea for three days. It's been several years since we were all together as a family, so I am looking forward to it".

"Good for you, give them my love and tell them it's about time that they came to see me; I would love it if they could".

"I certainly will; now I think that we have done enough, so let's go and join the others".

When they enter the living room, they find that Richard and Molly are watching a Christmas film while Martin and Daniel are engaged in a serious conversation.

"Now, none of that" exclaims Ella, "we are here to enjoy ourselves".

"Martin asked me what I have been doing and I was telling him that this has probably been my busiest year" says Daniel. Well to be correct it started last December with the fall of the Berlin Wall, which was followed this year by a number of The Soviet Union's former satellites voting to restore their independence from what is now Russia. This meant that I needed to report on all these events as they happened. Then, during June, July and August I was in Estonia, Latvia, Ukraine, Moldova, Belarus, Kyrgyzstan, Uzbekistan, Tajkistan and Armenia.

Prior to that, in January and February I was in Kuwait when Iraq invaded, after which I reported on The Gulf War from Saudi Arabia where coalition forces were gathered for Operation Storm (the invasion of Iraq) and I followed them as the Iraq army retreated and finally sued for peace.

In May, Croatia held a referendum to vote to secede from Ugoslavia. This was followed by the collapse of Ugoslavia in June when Croatia and Slovenia declared their independence.

At the same time in June, Boris Yeltsin was elected President of Russia and began to dismantle the trappings of communism.

The Croation War of Independence began on 1st October as forces of the Ugoslavia People's Army invaded the towns of Bulrovaic and Vukovar. The war is still being fought and has no end yet in sight". Daniel leans back in his chair before saying "So you can see Martin that it has been a very demanding time and I haven't even told you all of them".

"I don't know how you can stand the pressure that your job demands" declares Martin.

"Oh, I feel it at times but most of the time I love it and wouldn't have it any other way. But as mum says let's talk about something else".

The evening continues until it is time for bed. "We had better not be late because Molly will be in to get her presents at some ridiculous hour in the morning" says Theresa. That hasn't changed even though she hasn't believed in Father Christmas for years", and then longingly "in fact sometimes I wish she still did".

* * *

But Christmas Day is magical as first Molly wakes her grandparents with a cup of tea and a mince pie at eight o' clock.

"Why thank you Molly, that's very thoughtful and kind. When are you going in to your parents to get your presents"?

"Mum says that we can't have them until after breakfast when we are all together"

"When did she tell you that" asks Ella"?

"When I went into see her at five o'clock" is the instant reply, which has Ella and Martin in fits of laughter.

After breakfast Theresa distributes their presents from under the huge Christmas tree that reaches from floor to ceiling at the end of the living room. Excitedly Richard and Molly open theirs, a computer for Richard, jewellery and clothes for Molly from their parents. They are just as delighted when they open the presents from their grandparents. "Gosh, thank you so much" declares Molly "now I can design my own clothes". Richard too is pleased with his driving gloves and the two of them cross the room to hug Ella and Martin.

Eventually all the gifts lay open, together with wrapping paper and cards that cover the floor and every other available surface. That is with one exception as Martin brings in his gift to Ella which is in the shape of a large cardboard box.

"How did you manage to keep that hidden" enquires Ella. "It wasn't in the car yesterday".

"Ah, well I had the driver deliver it last week, after first checking it out with Theresa".

"Well what is it" cries Ella.

"If you open it, you will find out. Come on, the suspense is killing me" says Theresa. "I don't know how I managed to not open it when it arrived".

Ella opens the package with trembling hands until at last the cardboard falls away revealing a portrait of herself, which Martin has painted in oils. Apart from it being an unmistakable likeness, showing her white hair which is now short and cut in an elfin style, tapering at the back which reveals her long swan like neck, then her dark brown eyes like pools of chocolate, while her mouth smiles back at the viewer mischievously, emphasising the laughter lines around her mouth and eyes. But much more than that, Martin seems to have captured the very essence of her being, the very core of her soul, the one indefinable thing that he recognises that no one else can.

"He knows me so well" thinks Ella as she kisses Martin while tears roll gently down her face. "Thank you, Martin, it's gorgeous".

"It certainly is" chips in Daniel, while Theresa murmurs "you have caught her in one of her pensive moods, you know, the ones where she is in a world of her own, lost in thought. It's magnificent".

* * *

The day passes in a welter of activity, with walks along The Embankment in the still frosty morning, (although Martin declines because he doesn't want to get another chest infection) followed by a late dinner, after which Martin and Daniel clear away the dishes. Party games follow, with a break to listen to The Queens speech. Theresa has prepared a game of pass the parcel with forfeits for whoever is holding it when the music stops. The forfeits can be anything from singing a Christmas carol to finding where a particular person is sitting, after being blindfolded and spun around several times. Charades follows after which a break is taken.

Once everyone's glasses are filled, Daniel lifts his and proposes a toast "to Mum and Martin who is most welcome into our family".

"To Ella and Martin, may they both have a long and happy marriage".

Martin has arranged for his driver to pick the two of them up at eight o'clock and he arrives strictly on time. After much hugging and farewells, Ella and Martin leave after arranging to invite her offspring to The Manor House at the end of February, although Ella knows that she will probably see them all again before that, because she and Martin have several visits to make to London for various purposes in the near future.

CHAPTER 39.

1992.
NEW YORK AND TORONTO.

Ella and Martin spend New Year's Eve with Rachel and Fred at Charlbury; just the four of them, their children attending celebrations and parties with friends and relatives from places as far apart as from Gloucester to London.

The three of them regale Martin with their stories of growing up in Chadlington until he suddenly says to Ella "which cottage was it that you lived in; do you think that you could show me sometime".

"Of course, I can, in fact I'm sure that the owner would love to show you around. It is now owned by Eric and Angela Croft who are teachers at the school. They are lovely people and they come to The Pines regularly, so we all get on like a house on fire. I will ask them when they next come in".

Ella is surprised how well Fred and Martin get on. Although their lives are diverse, they seem to have common interests that are not apparent at first glance, the main thread running through their conversation as Ella hears Fred begin to tell Martin stories about his grandchildren.

"I can remember a particular evening many years ago when we were asked to baby sit for George's son Charlie who was only three at the time. He's a lovely lad, but this evening he was just full of mischief. He had already taken all the cushions off the furniture and spread them all over the floor so that he could dive on them from one to the other, which he followed by writing all over the coffee table with coloured pens. But after he had turned the dog out of her basket and decided that he would lie in it, I only just managed to stop him from eating the food from the dog's bowl. This was the final straw as far as I was concerned, so pointing my finger at him I told him to behave".

"A look of utter confusion crossed his face as he said in a trembling voice "but I can't behave grandad". The look of frustration together with the complete lack of understanding had Rachel and me in fits of laughter.

On another occasion when we were again looking after him for the day, we took him to a café for a bite to eat. Everything was going well until a waitress dropped some cutlery just as she was passing our table. Thinking that this was a new game to play, as quick as a flash Charlie picked up his knife and fork and threw them on the floor. We had a hell of a job explaining why it wasn't a game, but we did have a laugh".

They count down the last few seconds of the old year and raise their glasses as the clock strikes twelve, welcoming in 1992. Hugging, they wish each other a Happy New Year, which whenever Ella looks back on it, causes her untold grief and pain.

* * *

A few days later Ella shows Martin around the cottage in Bull Hill that she had lived with Richard when they were married, after first getting permission from the owners.

A strange thing happens that gives Ella goose bumps as they enter the living room when Martin suddenly says, looking at the modern fire and its surround "whatever happened to the old black leaded grate and oven where all the cooking used to be done. That's progress for you I suppose, as is the clothes tumble drier in the kitchen which has replaced the old wooden airer in front of the fire".

Before Ella can reply or question him about this amazing statement, Martin shakes his head as if in pain and complains of being dizzy. As she looks at him Ella can see the perplexed look that has come over his face and the beads of perspiration that are beginning to stand out on his face. As she makes him sit in one of the armchairs she asks "whatever made you say that my love", but even though she asks him several times his only reply is that he has no recollection of saying it.

It is a while before Martin feels well enough to proceed further and when he does both Ella's amazement and the suspicion which has been niggling at the back of her mind are aroused even further, as he points out places where he thinks that he would have hung Richard's pictures if it were him. In every instance his choices are in the same places as they were originally, which Ella puts down to a large degree to the fact that both Richard and he were artists so it follows logically that they would have similar thoughts on where the pictures ought to be hung to achieve the most impact, but she still has that niggling feeling that will not go away that leaves her both euphoric and stressed at the same time.

* * *

In the middle of January Martin experiences another chest infection, much to Ella's distress. Once again, the doctor prescribes antibiotics which work their magic, but leave Martin exhausted and spent.

But as Martin convalesces, Ella spends more and more time getting to know this man who has had such a dramatic effect on her life. Gradually as she questions and probes, she begins to unravel the story of his life since the time he was so traumatically and devastatingly injured in 1944. It happens as they sit each day, usually in the afternoons which has become the time for her to discover more about him.

He begins "after about three years I was allowed to leave the hospital completely, apart from periodic visits for check-ups. By this time, I had already established myself, albeit in a minor capacity in the Art World".

"The first thing that I did after leaving the hospital was to try and find somewhere close to the centre of London, because I realised quite quickly that this was where things happened in the art world. After several months I found premises in Holgarth Road, West London, where there was a row of terraced houses, in each of which there what was termed as artists' studios in the top of the buildings. This proved to be true and proved brilliant for my purpose. The light flooded in through windows that stood from floor to ceiling on the fourth floor. This was in the late nineteen forties and the area was still suffering from war damage, so as you can imagine it was pretty run down. However, I couldn't afford to rent one complete building, but I managed to do a deal with one of the owners to rent just the studio area, where I began my painting career in earnest. Luckily, the entry to the studio was by means of a separate stairway, so I could come and go as I pleased. Because I couldn't afford anywhere else to live, I decided to both paint and live in the studio, although I was careful not to let the owners know".

"I already had a portfolio of my paintings which I had completed while I was at the hospital, so I tried to find a gallery which would be prepared to exhibit them to give me something to live off while I was getting established which is how I met Penny's father, William".

"He had only been in business for two or three years by then, but being the gambler, which is so often the case with entrepreneurs, he took a chance with me, something for which I will be forever in his debt".

"My life at this time was work, work, and more work, but I didn't mind because I was doing the thing that I loved. I had no time for a social life and even if I had, there was no way that I would venture out anywhere in public unless I absolutely had to, in case I frightened the natives with my scars. But this was also a plus because it meant that I had more time to paint".

As he pauses lost in thought at this point, Ella interrupts "You mean that you never saw anyone from one week to the next; that must have been very hard".

"It was for years and things didn't change until I began to accept how I looked, because you see although some people looked at me in horror, while others showed pity and sympathy at my predicament, the real problem was me, because I also felt horror, pity and sympathy for myself. Once that I recognised my problem I began slowly to return to the world, although not by much even then".

"After several years William offered to do an exhibition of my paintings in his gallery, which was when my work took off, so much so that it became recognised by other galleries who also did exhibitions of my work, some of which were lent to galleries for that purpose. But it took until the late seventies before major galleries in placed like Amsterdam, Berlin and Tel Aviv and finally The Tate exhibited my work".

"When all this happened, my world was turned upside down as I travelled in Europe attending galleries and meeting people of influence in the art world. But It wasn't until nineteen eighty-three that the Metropolitan Museum of Art in New York came calling, offering to exhibit my paintings, that my name began to be mentioned in international circles. Once they had made the commitment, other galleries from every continent followed their lead, so you can see that I have been very lucky".

"Nonsense" exclaims Ella "in this life you make your own luck, and anyway if you did experience a good roll of the dice with your work, you most certainly didn't earlier on during the war".

* * *

As the year progresses Martins health improves markedly, much to Ella's delight and amazement. Then at the end of May, to her complete surprise he tells her that he has been invited back to The Metropolitan Museum of Art in New York in June, who wants to do another exhibition of his work and would like him to attend.

"I thought that it would be a good opportunity for us both to go. We could extend our stay and take a look around the city; that is if you would like to".

"Like to? Like to? I should say so; it is right at the top of my "to do list", somewhere that I have always wanted to visit. How fantastic my love".

"Good, because I have also been invited to a gallery in Toronto's West End where they want to show my work later on in the year. I thought that we could kill two birds with one stone and travel there after we have finished in New York; we could call it our honeymoon, if you like".

By this time Ella is jumping up and down with excitement "I think that I must have just died and gone to heaven" she exclaims "are you sure my love".

"Never more so" declares Martin "I am sorry that we weren't able to go away before, but hopefully this will make up for it".

* * *

Ella contacts Daniel who is happy for them both, saying that if he and Theresa can get some time off that they will join them with the grandchildren for a few days. The next few weeks are a hectic merry-go-round as Ella and Martin draw up their itinerary which will mean that they will be away from the end of June returning in the middle of August.

Leaving Heathrow, they arrive late afternoon on 22^{tnd} June to Kennedy Airport and are whisked to their hotel, the Hotel Fifth Avenue, by a complimentary taxi, care of The Gallery. The first thing that strikes them is the heat which is over thirty degrees centigrade, and this coupled with the high level of humidity makes it uncomfortable for both of them, but even more so for Martin with his medical history. Ella quickly realises that she will have to control when and where they visit to counter its effects as much as possible while ensuring that his nebuliser is available at all times.

The next two weeks are the most exciting that Ella has ever experienced. They have carefully chosen their hotel because it has both an excellent reputation and is also central to the heart of the city, making it relatively easy to catch taxis to go to wherever they want to.

The first few days are spent visiting The Metropolitan Museum of Art, which is within walking distance of their hotel. Here Martin is feted and acclaimed as he meets and greets the luminaries who are involved with running the exhibition of his work as well as a number of wealthy people whose donations make the existence of the Museum possible. Ella accompanies Martin every day and watches him with pride as he manages situations as they arise.

The Museum's curator, Quentin Whitely makes a speech thanking Martin for loaning some of his paintings for the exhibition. He then goes on to thank him in advance for both attending and giving his time to answer questions thrown at him from the floor.

Martin is an old hand at this and is able to field questions, most of which he has answered many times and at many places before. He summarises his talk by telling his audience of his journey from novice to artist and of his experiences in between. He finishes to a round of applause as he says "I will be available to take any further questions you may have because I will be here for the rest of the day".

His spell of duty is completed at the end of the first week and Ella and he then have what he describes as "our time", when they can begin to explore this magical city.

They visit Central Park and take the mandatory horse and coach ride, which is followed by tea and scones in the restaurant by the lake. As they make their way back, they stop and sit on the edge of the fountain and watch New Yorkers scurrying on their way back to work after hastily taken lunches.

When she thinks about how far she has come since growing up in her little village of Chadlington so many years previously, compared to where she is at this moment, sitting with the man that she loves so ardently, Ella finds the situation almost surreal and she realises that the here and now is comparable with only a handful other periods in her life in which she has been so happy. It is up there with Richard and her marriage and Daniels birth and she can give it no higher compliment than that.

To ensure that they have a lasting record of all their experiences, they both take inordinate amounts of photographs, both having their own camera each, but also stop others to ask if they will take photographs of the two of them whenever they feel the need.

Other days are spent on mandatory visits to places like Radio City, or The Empire State Building (where Ella becomes giddy at the top and refuses to look out at the scenery, staying back to avoid seeing just how high they are). The Statue of Liberty is an absolute must so they catch the ferry which takes them to Liberty Island in New York harbour where they climb up inside the statue; Ella is again queasy but overcomes her feelings this time.

After her experiences of tall buildings they decide not to visit The Twin Trade Towers which are in fact higher than The Empire State Building, so find their way to Times Square where they stand transfixed as a tide of humanity swirls around them, jostling and bustling as they make their way on their journey through life, some to the subway, others hailing the distinctive yellow cabs of this city. The noise from vehicles passing over steel grids on the streets which cover miles of underground cables that generate steam for the city is deafening at times and steam rising from covers gives the impression of a landscape from another planet. There are people here of almost every nation on earth, making it one of the most cosmopolitan cities anywhere. Ella finds the whole effect of all these factors both exciting and strangely comforting at the same time, wondering how the city continues to operate at all under such extreme circumstances.

They return each evening to their hotel completely exhausted by their explorations, stopping only to dine before retiring to their room for the night, so that they can continue afresh for the next day, when retail therapy is next on their itinerary.

Ever since she first found out that New York was on their agenda, Macey's has been at the top of Ella's shopping list, having heard from a number of people that it is a "must", so they spend the next day shopping here, stopping regularly for coffee and cakes, or something more substantial.

Surreptitiously Martin buys her perfume and a gold bracelet as a memento of their visit which she has indicated that she likes, and presents them to her when they return to their hotel. As she throws her arms around him, he says" no thanks are necessary my love, the fact that you are here with me is all that I could ever wish for. Now get changed, because I have booked us seats for a musical on Broadway".

The next day, to their delight they are joined by Daniel, Theresa, Richard and Molly who have managed to grab a few days from their heavy schedules to be with them and are staying at the same hotel.

Daniel has visited New York before in the pursuit of his work, but for the others it is their first time, so they all revisit the places that Ella and Martin have seen before looking for new experiences which are to be found in abundance.

They take a tour guide of Chinatown with its blend of restaurants, cafes, sidewalk food stalls, street vendors, and traditional herbal medicine shops. Museums and temples contrast with bargains for perfumes and handbags. After, they visit the adjacent neighbourhoods of Soho and Little Italy.

As they sit in Starbucks drinking their mandatory coffee, taking a break from their tourist duties, Ella see Theresa trying to suppress a smile. When she asks her, what is amusing her Theresa replies "I was just thinking of something a friend of mine told me about the time she visited New York with her autistic son who was about twelve years of age at the time. They had been here for several days when she asked him what was the one thing that they had seen that he had liked most: He replied that it was The Grand Central Station and when she asked him why he said "because its Grand" and when she asked him if there was any other reason, he added in a tone which meant that he was stating the obvious "and because its Central". I laughed when she told me and being here brought the memory flooding back".

On another day they go up the Rockefeller Centre and, in the evening take a sunset harbour boat cruise and see the city from the waterfront.

All too soon their time is ended and after saying their farewells, Daniel and his family leave to return home, Theresa and the children still full of the sights that they have seen, while Ella and Martin prepare to get ready for the next part of their journey to Toronto.

As they arrive at Lester Pearson Airport, they can see the CN (Canadian National) Tower in the distance, standing majestically on edge of Lake Toronto. Built in 1976, it was at that time the tallest freestanding structure at eighteen hundred and fifteen feet.

They make their way to their hotel, The Sheraton Centre Toronto on Queens St. West. Although it has only been a two-hour flight, they are both tired and decide just to take a short walk to find their bearings before starting sight-seeing in earnest the following day.

"Shall we go up the CN Tower tomorrow" asks Martin as they sit in bed talking of the places they would like to see. "But I need to go to the art gallery the day after to arrange for the exhibition and see the facilities".

"Oh yes, but I will need to stand at the back of that glass fronted lift that goes up the outside of the building, and probably with my eyes closed too" responds Ella who both wants to go, but is frightened at the same time, and then as an afterthought "I am so glad to be with you here Martin, its lovely, but it doesn't really matter where I am as long as we are together. You know that, don't you?"

"I feel the same way my love" replies her husband, only to hear her soft breathing which tells him that she is asleep.

The next morning, they make their way to The CN Tower where Ella is as good as her word as she shrinks to the back of the glass fronted lift with eyes closed, not daring to look down and see the earth disappearing rapidly from her view.

At the top, the tower revolves, and they sit and watch the city from their three hundred-and-sixty degrees vantage point while consuming coffee and croissants in the restaurant. Eventually they make their way back to the lift, carefully circumnavigating the reinforced glass ceiling through which the view can be observed right to the bottom, where miniscule people are wandering around like a colony of ants queuing to buy tickets.

Ella once more takes up her position at the back of the lift with eyes closed and a prayer on her lips while Martin looks on, concerned for his wife. Within seconds they are deposited at the bottom and Ella's fears subside immediately, so much so that she begs Martin that can go up again before they leave Toronto, at which point he bursts out laughing, the reason for which she just cannot understand.

They move down to the waterfront which is only a few minutes away. They have already researched the area and know that ferries run regularly from the Queens Quay Terminal to the islands which are about a kilometre off shore. Their choice is either a cruise around the islands, of which there are several, or to disembark at one of them and explore, catching a return ferry later in the day.

Choosing the latter, they duly get off the Ferry at Centre Island and decide to hire bicycles so that they can see as much as possible. Apart from a few municipal vehicles there are no cars allowed on the islands so they follow the wide tarmac paths stopping regularly to enjoy the beautiful scenery. There are a number of parklands where people are sitting with children eating picnics. Eventually they ride right across the island which is only a few kilometres long, where they reach a restaurant and stop for salads, which they wash down with Canadian wine which has been produced from vineyards in the area around Niagara, an hour or so away. Like most people here they eat outside in the warm Toronto sun and take in the majestic view of the city shoreline just across the bay, with its towering skyscrapers and C N Tower.

Disposing of their bicycles they catch the ferry back and decide to return to their hotel and rest before changing and going out for an evening meal. As they lie resting, the events of the day making them totally relaxed, they both simultaneously seem to find the need to express their feelings for each other and without a word being uttered, make love slowly and luxuriously. As they lie spent, Ella thinks to herself that Martin must feel really relaxed, because it is only in these sorts of situations that sex occurs, so she determines that they will do more explorations, to see if they can recreate the same conditions again.

They spend the evening in The Distillery District, a Designated Historic Sight set in 19th century buildings that once housed a large whisky distillery. They wander around its cobbled streets that are lined with restaurants, bars and boutiques, as well as art galleries and outdoor sculptures. There are also outdoor stage performances and dance music at the areas several theatres

They are completely undecided to which restaurant to go to, the choice being vast and the quality even more so, but they finally plump for The Cluniy Bistro with its classic French Menu and wine selection, with its captivating marble bar and tiled floor.

They sit and eat and discuss the things that they would like to do in the next few days. "Well I would like to come back here to see more of the Distillery District, I think that we should come back in December as well, because our waitress just told me that there is an annual Toronto Christmas Market that takes over the streets, which she assures me is a wonderful experience. Oh, and The St. Lawrence market is close to where we are now, which sells fresh meat, fish and fruit, as well as cheeses of every description; that sounds lovely too. Oh, and the Eaton Shopping Mall. Oh, and I would like to catch the Go Train and go somewhere else. Oh, and there's still Niagara Falls, we haven't even mentioned them yet. Oh and.....

"Stop", cries Martin, laughing at this juncture, holding up his hand in a gesture similar to a policeman on traffic duty "I promise that we will do all of those things, but just let's take one at a time please".

They return to their hotel Martin with his arm around Ella for a number of reasons, mostly because he wants to, but also to stop her from stumbling on the cobbled streets, and finally because of the effect of the French wine that has taken its toll on her constitution.

Martin spends time the next day at The Screen Print Room, an art gallery built from a repurposed ammunition factory in Toronto's West End. His discussions are constructive as he and the curator and his colleagues of the gallery, who have asked to be able to exhibit Martin's work, agree on a date in May of the next year, and the material that they would like to show.

The purpose of his visit completed Martin returns to Ella at the hotel, after which they go to The Eaton centre for a shopping extravagance of unrivalled proportions.

Their next few days are spent doing the things from their itinerary. They first hire a car which Ella drives, going first to Niagara Falls which is only two hours distant from downtown Toronto. Here they stand in amazement above the falls which are in the shape of a horseshoe and are immediately opposite to the U.S.A border.

Here Lake Eerie empties into a channel which eventually finds its way into Lake Ontario. Water spray from the falls rises up from the bottom forming a perpetual mist in which rainbows form.

Making their way they move further down the channel to the place where they can get a small cruise boat that takes people back right under the falls where its thunderous effect can be felt at full force. The boat, "The Maid of the Mist" is tossed around like a rag doll in the surging water and although they are issued with protective water gear, they are all drenched by the sheer force of the spray and mist, which is both frightening and invigorating at the same time.

They have been recommended to visit another town called Niagara-on-the-Lake, which is only a few miles away. Built in the colonial period, its major features and buildings have been retained. Making their way they find it and fall in love with its quaint buildings, many of which are made of clapperboard timber, painted delicate colours of every hue, its shops offering a range of arts and crafts for tourists.

They fall in love with this little gem of a town, with its wide roads built to accommodate herds of cattle being driven through it to market many years ago. To their surprise there is a George Bernard Shaw society and theatre here in honour of the great man, where his stage plays are regularly re-enacted.

They like this place so much that they find hotel accommodation for the night, before returning to Toronto the next day in time to continue their pilgrimage of this fascinating city that they are beginning to know and love.

After a few more days, time as ever wins the day, and they leave reluctantly for the airport, promising each other that they will return again soon.

"We didn't even see a baseball match and The Toronto's Blue Jays Stadium is right there" complains Martin bitterly.

"Or go to the theatre" responds Ella. Then mischievously "perhaps we will go at Christmas; not this year but perhaps next".

"Deal" responds Martin, much to her delight.

They arrive back at The Manor House Chadlington on 10th August and as she sinks into their bed she remarks "I have loved our journey so much Martin, but I must admit that it is lovely to finally get back to our own home".

* * *

Daniel, together with his family, visit the next weekend and catch up with them to discover how much they enjoyed Toronto, at which point photographs are produced and their experiences are explained.

"You must come with us to Toronto next time" Ella says. "We loved it, and there are so many things to do. It is a lovely country and the people are so friendly and open. We thought that we would like to go just before Christmas next year, because they have a Toronto Christmas Market in The Distillery District, Not only that but there is an open ice skating rink down near the harbour, Oh and we could do and see an ice hockey match, I've always wanted to do that, and" …at this point Martin stops her in mid flow, knowing that she will go on forever. Daniel too recognises this trait in his mother and laughs, saying "You have worked that one out then Martin" to which the latter gives him one of his lopsided smiles.

"That sounds fantastic; I think that we would like that" replies Daniel, looking at Theresa for her assent.

"Definitely" is her strong response, with Richard and Molly nodding their heads in unequivocal agreement.

In the afternoon at Ella's suggestion they all agree to take a walk around the village and the surrounding fields which have meant so much to her and Daniel over the years. It is a warm summer's day, the sun's rays illuminating the honey colour stone of the cottages and field boundaries, making them glow, a testament to this geological area.

As they stroll through the long winding narrow village, they encounter people they have known forever and take the time to stop and chat, catching up with events as they go.

Reaching the bottom of Bull Hill, they climb the style which takes them out into the fields which Daniel knows so well from his youth and considers almost as his own domain. He shows them all features and places which he discovered in his childhood growing up. "Over there in that derelict farm out building, barn owls nested regularly every year and I used to go and check that they were O.K. whenever I could. In the bottom of that dell underneath the hill, there used to be a badger's sett and sometimes, if I was lucky and very quiet, when it was growing dark, they would all come out with their young and romp around. It was a magical scene which I saw a number of times and which I treasure and have never forgotten".

Daniel continues with his stories, holding them all enthralled as they meander through the fields until they reach another style which they all cross, until Martin, who is bringing up the rear, catches his hand on a bramble as he dismounts. Although it only a superficial wound it bleeds quite profusely until Theresa digs into her bag from which she produces a box of tissues. Thanking her, Martin manages to stop the flow after several minutes before looking around to see if there is somewhere that he can put the bloody evidence.

Seeing him struggling, Theresa says "I have a small plastic bag here somewhere Martin, so give it to me and I will put it in the bin when we get back".

They continue following Daniel as he describes some of his adventures when he used to walk the dog, most of them funny; like the time when Bonny chased a fox and got stuck in a hedge trying to follow it. "The thing was that she looked so surprised when I managed to extricate her, she, not for one-minute recognising that she was three times the size of Brer Fox".

Returning home to The Manor feeling tired but relaxed they spend the rest of the day on the patio talking and reminiscing of their travel plans and experiences until late evening.

As they leave after lunch the next day, Daniel and Theresa invite Ella and Martin to stay at the end of September, Daniel having to go to Serbia and Croatia in the between time.

"That will be lovely, thank you" says Ella" we want to come up anyway, so we can do what we have to before we come to you", knowing that Martin wants to take her to the Ballet at Covent Garden and to Claridge's for lunch.

* * *

To Ella's absolute astonishment the first place that Martin takes her, when they visit Daniel is to the building in Holgarth Road, where he had rented the studio on the top floor when he was beginning his career as an artist.

As they stand outside, she wonders why he has brought her here until he suddenly produces a key saying "come on, let's go up and I will show you where it all began for me".

"But how do you still have the key" exclaims Ella.

"Because I have owned it for years" is the reply. "After I became relatively successful the first thing that I did was to offer the owner a very good price so that I could continue to use the studio and make the rest of the building my home, a place, a sanctuary where I could live".

Ella is silent as she considers first the pain and isolation that Martin has had to endure over the years, then the joy of his journey to make his way after leaving hospital, and she marvels at the resilience and will power he needed to get there.

Together they visit the studio which looks remarkably as if Martin has used it the day before as indeed does the rest of the house from which Ella recognises his style of furnishing.

"Why does it look so clean and tidy".

"Well, that's because I have a cleaner that comes in regularly. After I moved to Chadlington I just couldn't bear to give this place up completely. I hope that you can understand; I have no wish to live here anymore because I love Chadlington, but for so many years it was a large part of me.

"How could you not think that I would I understand; you should have said" and then "I know, perhaps we could stay here overnight when we have to come up to London to a show or to go shopping. It will be easier than having to journey back at the end of a long day".

"Are you sure my love, because if so, I would like that very much".

Making their way to Theresa and Daniel's they are made welcome over coffee and cakes.

As they sit laughing and relaxed Daniel addresses Martin. "By the way, I forgot to mention that I went to The National Archives at Kew and looked up your war record as we discussed. You were quite correct when you said that it happened on 10th August 1944 in a wooded area just north of Falaise and that everyone, apart from yourself was killed pretty much instantly. There was some speculation that it may possibly have been caused by friendly fire, because there had already been several incidents, but nothing was ever proved in the heat of the battle.

So now that I have the confirmation, there is a starting point for your story. I will need more details about your life since then but I will need to bring my camera and sound man down to see you at The Manor House at some stage to record your story, but there's no hurry just yet. I have already interviewed a number of soldiers who landed on D Day and went on to gain a foothold, some who eventually reached Paris and some who reached Berlin. I have others still to see but I also have most of the archival material that I need to complete the project. So, between the people who have given their stories of events and the material that I have, there should be a good balance".

As he finishes Martin says "I am glad that you found confirmation of my story, because I only learned of it from word of mouth from those who picked me up after the incident. It's not appropriate now and we haven't time anyway, but I would be interested to see what you found when we speak again".

"I will bring it with me without fail when we come next. I will arrange a date when I am ready; will that be O.K".

No more is mentioned on the subject until Ella and Daniel are alone in the kitchen washing up the dishes. Suddenly Daniel says "look mum I hope that you won't be upset, but when we were last with you, if you remember, Martin cut his hand on a bramble when he was clambering over a stile. Well the thing is Mum that I have been thinking for some time that Martin isn't who he thinks he is; not that he has been trying to deceive anyone, but just because of the terrible injuries and loss of memory that he received in the war. My feelings had become so strong in fact that I saw an opportunity to try and discover who he really was when Theresa found his bloodstained tissue, still wrapped up in a plastic bag when we returned home from seeing you the last time. Anyway, to cut a long story short, I sent it off for a D.N.A. analysis".

Before he can continue Ella looks at him in astonishment, her face a picture of bewilderment. "Why would you do that Daniel; I'm sure that you must have had a very good reason, so tell me".

There is silence for several seconds, neither of them prepared to admit what they really think until Ella whispers in a small faltering voice filled with emotion, tears streaming down her cheeks "you think it too then, don't you, so it's not just me".

Daniel closes the gap between them and takes his mother in his arms. "I am so sorry mum; I am making a right mess of this. Yes, I did think that Martin was my dad; that was until I received the result back from the laboratory which showed quite clearly that there was no match between his D.N.A taken from the tissue and mine which I sent for comparison.

Everything seemed to point that way, the paintings and his mannerisms, which I recognise in both of us, as well as how he came to live in Chadlington; him seeming to know the way although he had never been there before. But I was wrong mum and I suspected that you also had similar thoughts, so I had to find out for sure one way or another. However, I have to tell you that I was so disappointed when I got the results, but thinking about it since I find that my feelings for him haven't changed. I still like him as much as ever and respect him for the way in which he has conducted his life after his dreadful injuries".

As he finishes speaking Ella says "are you absolutely sure son, because all my instincts have been telling me that he is your father" and then "I must admit that although I, like you, am absolutely distraught that he isn't Richard, I still find that I love him just as much, so don't be sad for what might have been and let's be happy for what we have. At least I don't have to look for things that aren't there anymore".

As she finishes speaking, she knows in her heart of hearts that she will not be able to stop looking for connections that don't exist, but wishes to allay Daniel's concern for her.

Leaving Daniel and his family, Ella and Martin make their way to Covent Garden Opera, to see a performance of Bizet's Carmen, where to her delight the sheer spectacle of music, colour and drama overwhelms her senses, leaving her no time to contemplate Daniels earlier revelation, although she knows that it will come back to haunt her in moments of uncertainty in the future.

* * *

After their long sabbatical from work, Ella spends time catching up with her business interests which takes her up until Christmas, while Martin is similarly engaged producing more paintings for his exhibition in Toronto the following year. As December approaches Ella suddenly remembers Martin's wish to invite the villagers to a party. When she mentions it to him, he agrees instantly saying "Thank you, I should have thought of it myself before now; let's get Penny involved, its right up her street".

Penny is only too pleased to offer her services, getting Ella involved in a similar manner to that of the garden party the year before. "Only this time it will need to be held in the house" she declares.

This time they have the earlier experience to call upon and once they have decided on Saturday 11th December, Penny sends out invitations. After much discussion they decide on hot food of a Christmas flavour, things like turkey with all the trimmings, followed by Christmas pudding, mince pies and custard. Ella decides that she will get the chef from The Pines to cook at The Manor House rather than preparing everything at the restaurant and having to then subsequently transfer it all to The Manor House.

A Christmas tree some twelve feet high is ordered and installed in the hall and Penny and Ella then do the decorations, installing fairy lights, balloons and other paraphernalia. When it is done, they stand back and admire their efforts and are astounded at what they have achieved. The green from the tree that is covered by lights compliment the wooden wall panelling, while streamers and balloons hang from the chandeliers. The lights reflect onto the wall panelling, highlighting the beautiful oak wood grain, while throwing shadows onto the Italian marble tiles.

"It looks beautiful "Penny whispers, standing back in amazement at their efforts.

"It certainly does" replies Ella "aren't we clever".

Deciding to have a break and to celebrate their efforts, Ella opens a bottle of her favourite Malbec red wine and they sit side by side on one of the settees chatting about the Christmas party arrangements. Eventually Ella falls silent and ever-astute Penny, sensing that her friend is troubled about something asks gently "what is the problem Ella, you look sad when you should be delighted that all our hard work has paid off"

Ella remains silent for a while and Penny can see that this woman who she has come to love and respect is having her own internal battle to decide if she should speak or not. But her thoughts are so overwhelming that she eventually has no option than to reveal them. She begins "I am telling you this in total confidence Penny, so I hope that you will not repeat any of it to anyone. You see I had thought for some time that I could see connections between Martin and my first husband Richard". She then proceeds to illustrate the occasions and similarities that had made her come to this conclusion.

"But it was not only me that experienced these same thoughts, because unknown to me Daniel had also been harbouring similar doubts of his own. So much so, that he decided to take matters into his own hands and sent samples of his own and Martin's blood for D.N.A. analysis". She finishes by telling an astonished Penny of the negative result from the tests and of her and Daniels's bitter disappointment.

Penny is pensive for several seconds before saying "My poor love, what a terrible thing to have to go through" before questioning her in depth about Ella's reasons for coming to the conclusion that she had.

They talk for hours while Penny absorbs just how much disappointment Ella and Daniel have experienced from the test result. As she sits contemplating the situation, suddenly Penny becomes alert and says in a questioning voice filled with promise "you say that Daniel sent his and Martin's bloods off for analysis" and when Ella replies with a quiet wavering yes, Penny smiles for the first time since they sat down.

"Well there is something I think that you ought to know Ella, which may or may not put a different light on things. You see nearly twenty years ago Martin was diagnosed with Leukaemia on top of all his other problems. Luckily, he was in a position to get treatment privately and after seeing one of the top consultants in his field it was decided to give him a bone marrow transplant. The main problem was that the best and quickest way to get it was from a close relative, but as far as he knew there weren't any".

"Eventually however, they managed to get a match from the database, which was being compiled for just this sort of purpose and after lengthy treatment involving staying in hospital Martin was declared cured. Now you must be wondering why I am telling you this, but the answer is very simple really, because when bone marrow is replaced from another donor the blood D.N.A of the donor replaces that of the host. This always occurs in this way, sometimes for only a while, other times for longer, but in a lot of cases forever. For you the implications might mean that Martin's blood D.N.A changed when he had the bone marrow treatment. Now I am not saying that Martin is Richard, but merely that Martin's D.N.A. might not now be the same as that of which he was born. I hesitate to tell you this but I feel it only right to tell you. Obviously, the changes, if that is what has occurred, will apply to saliva and hair samples as well, so your D.N.A. route will be closed as a means of identification. I think that you need to discuss the situation with Daniel before you take any further action, but I wish you good luck with that, with all my heart".

Ella's eyes fill with tears as she listens to Penny, unable to stop them from streaming down her face. Upon which the latter takes her in her arms and comforts her, the elder being comforted by the younger woman. Once she has recovered sufficiently to talk again Ella says "I will think about it but my immediate reaction is not to tell Daniel, because I don't think that either of us could face being disappointed again".

* * *

The day of the Christmas party arrives and is an even bigger success than the summer garden party. As well as the villagers, Ella and Martin have invited Daniel and his family and Rachel, Fred and their families.

As he did before in the summer, Martin welcomes his visitors together with Penny and Ella. Most of the villagers have never been inside The Manor and their curiosity is at fever pitch, but they are all allowed to wander around the ground floor while Ella explains to them what it was like when she worked here.

Suddenly there is a knock at the door and upon opening it Martin welcomes in the local Chadlington church choir: something that he has arranged but kept as a surprise. They are all suitably dressed in their cassocks and ruffs while carrying lit candles. As they file into the hall, they begin singing Christmas carols to the readymade audience of village guests. Gathering round the Christmas tree they continue, their voices echoing the story of the nativity. It is a magical candle lit scene, to which is added the voices of the guests as they join the choir.

Once they have finished, everyone is ushered into the dining room where the buffet that Ella and Penny have organised has been laid out.

Once all feelings of hunger have been sated, Ella has arranged for a small disco to be installed in the living room, after first moving out some of the furniture to make room for couples to dance. In this way the evening continues, with both Ella and Martin delighted to see how close the evening has brought the villagers together.

Eventually at midnight the villagers say their farewells and thanks, at which point the hosts collapse exhausted after what they all consider has been a great success.

Daniel, Theresa, Richard and Molly stay over for the night and as they leave the next morning, Daniel pulls Martin to one side saying "I have now got everything that I need on my project, except for your story, so I would like to come and record yours Martin. How does the 11th January sound"?

That's fine by me Daniel, but don't forget to bring the info that you found at The National Archives; I would quite like to see them to see if they stir old memories".

"We are going to Theresa's parents for Christmas, so January will be the first chance that I get to come again"

"That's O.K son "replies his step father who views Daniel as his son anyway even after such a short time." Rachel has invited us to hers for Christmas".

* * *

Christmas at Rachel's gives Ella time to slow down from her manic yuletide period. Rachel and Fred are without their children, who are spending time with their various parents-in-law, but it suits the four of them who can please themselves to do things at the pace they choose. Their day involves drinking coffee and talking to a large extent. Martin explains what Daniel is doing on his project, which leads to further discussions about his part on that fateful day. Ella then tells Rachel and Fred about how Martin overcame his disabilities and how he began painting to earn a living.

At this point Rachel says "what a coincidence though Ella, bearing in mind that Richard liked to paint, you must attract them like moths to a flame".

"Hardly, because Richard only used watercolours and it was a hobby" to which Martin replies "but he was very talented, so although it was only a hobby, he had an extraordinary ability my dear".

* * *

New Year's Eve brings 1992 to its conclusion, with both Ella and Martin looking to fulfil many more of their dreams in 1993.

Canada and Martins Art Exhibition beckons in May, as well another visit in December with Daniel and his family. But it is at just such times as this that life can deal its cruellest blows.

CHAPTER 40.

1993.
SUSPICION.

Daniel arrives with Mark Jerome and Johnny Broad on the eleventh of January and after they are all acquainted Daniel talks Martin through the questions that he will be asking him. "Don't worry about a thing Martin; just tell me your story in exactly the same way that you told me the first time. We can stop anytime you like, and we can do another take if you feel that you would like to expand on something that you have already said. What I would like to do, if you agree is to go through your war experience first, here in your study, after which I would like to question you about your working life in your studio. How does that sound"?

"That's fine by me Daniel, just tell me what you want me to do and I will try to oblige".

Martins contribution to Daniels documentary is recorded and completed, after stops for a number of retakes and lunch. Eventually Daniel is satisfied with the result, explaining that he will voice over it at various points to both emphasise and make it more inclusive to the rest of the programme that he is trying to create.

Thanking Martin, they leave, Daniel assuring him that his story will bring home the suffering and courage to viewers of those who had to face the invasion of Normandy and the subsequent fight across France, whose objective was to first overthrow its usurpers, before finally defeating Germany in 1945. "I think that I have all that I need to complete the documentary now, so it should be ready in a few months" Daniel finishes.

* * *

Towards the end of January, Britain experiences heavy snowfalls, the like of which it hasn't seen for many years, covering The Cotswolds in a mantle of white, making travelling impossible and leaving farmers whose lambs are giving birth, some of them out in the fields, serious problems.

It is at this vulnerable time that Martin contracts yet another chest infection, which only antibiotics can cure. Ella is beside herself with worry because although she can telephone the Doctors surgery, neither he nor anyone else can get to The Manor House, so it is several days before Martin can be reached, by which time his condition is serious, neither his oxygen or nebuliser having the slightest effect on his condition.

When eventually the doctor is able to reach them, he takes one look at Martin and arranges for an ambulance to take him immediately to The John Radcliffe Hospital in Oxford. Ella is by this time out of her mind with worry but tries not to show it to her husband.

Constant rest and antibiotics eventually work their magic on Martin, but it is nearly three weeks before he is allowed to return home. Ella has managed to stay at the hospital with him in a private room, but the worry combined with insufficient rest has taken its toll of even her strong constitution, leaving her empty and exhausted.

Not only that, but her suffering is compounded every time she sees things in Martin that remind her of Richard; the way he holds his head slightly to one side when listening to her, or his smile which is more a lop sided grin but which she recognises in both of them, or sometimes the way he stands with his hands held behind him when contemplating. The list is endless until she recalls with a jolt that these things are illusory and not possible, because of the result of the D.N.A. test.

When she is on her own, after she has once again experienced something that reminds her of both of her men, she cries inconsolably, unable to realise why, only knowing that she has experienced true love twice in her life, each time from men who are so similar in so many ways that she cannot differentiate between them. Thus, she cries for both of them.

* * *

Daniel, Theresa, Richard and Molly make the pilgrimage to the hospital several times, something that has lifted Martins spirits significantly, although Daniel is always subdued after they have left, saying to Theresa "I can't bear to see him looking so weak and vulnerable, because I have come to know and like him so much".

As Ella and Martin leave, the Consultant pulls her to one side "I don't know if you are aware just how ill your husband is Mrs Fleet, but I feel I must warn you that his lungs cannot take too much more of these incidents. It is almost a miracle that he pulled through this time, as you can tell from the fact that he has been here for so long. Other people recover in far less time".

"But what can I do that will help to reduce the chances of him having another attack" asks Ella tearfully. "It seems like we have only just found each other and the thought of losing him now is unbearable".

"I am sorry my dear but apart from the obvious, keeping him comfortable and not doing too much, there is nothing anyone can do. My advice is to make the most of what time you have left together. Your love will help too".

* * *

At the beginning of March, Daniel, Theresa and the children arrive unannounced, which is significant in its way because previously he has always telephoned to make sure that it is convenient.

They stay for the day, Daniel talking to Martin while Ella, Theresa, Richard and Molly go to Rachel's to catch up and discuss Molly's future in dress design.

Meanwhile Daniel is telling Martin that his documentary is going to be on air the sixth of June on B.B.C., to coincide with the anniversary of the D. Day landings. They then continue to talk animatedly for hours discussing each other's lives, as if wanting to empty themselves to each other.

Just before Ella returns with Theresa and her grandchildren Martin says "Well Daniel although we only met a relatively short time ago, I can tell you in all honesty that if I had ever had a son, I would have wanted him to be just like you. I am so proud of you".

"Daniel brushes away a tear before replying avidly "The feeling is mutual I can assure you Martin. I know unequivocally and for certain that you would have been as good a father as my own".

As Ella returns Daniel whispers to her so that no one else can hear "I need to have a word with you mum, can we go somewhere private"

"Of course, but whatever is the matter son. Let's go to the study".

Once ensconced in the study Daniel begins his carefully constructed speech. "Well mum I came here today specifically to tell you that I had occasion to go to The National Archives to follow up on a war record for the documentary and while I was there I suddenly thought that neither of us knew where or how dad died in the war, so I looked up his record".

He stops talking momentarily before continuing "I think that you had better prepare yourself Mum because what I have to tell you is mind blowing, well it was to me anyway. The truth is that my father died on the very same day and in the very same place where Martin was wounded. He was in fact one of the remaining men who died that day. Now you may think that is a huge coincidence, but to me, when other factors are taken into consideration, I feel that it's even more significant. So significant in fact that it made me doubt the result of the D.N.A. test that I told you about".

Before Daniel can add anything further, Ella stops him by saying "before you say anymore just give me a minute to collect my thoughts" and then she sits silent and still, fighting her inner demons, her hands covering her face.

Daniel waits patiently, giving his mother time to absorb what he has just told her. After what seems to him an age, Ella looks up.

"What you discovered is yet another piece in Martin's jig-saw life. I hope that you will understand and not be angry with me but I am now going to tell you something that I found out from Penny several months ago which I had decided not to repeat to you because of the bitter disappointment we both felt when we got the results of the D.N.A. blood test. But what you have told me I think changes things considerably".

Ella then goes on to relate her conversation with Penny, Daniels eyes lighting up at the sound of her every word. By the time she finishes his excitement is overwhelming and to her delight he says "I don't blame you for not telling me mum, in fact I understand completely. But as you say, now that we know where Martin and Dad were on the day that one of them was killed, everything changes. I think that we should send samples of hair and saliva from both of Martin and me for another D.N.A. analysis, don't you"?

Ella looks apprehensively at her son, this man that has been her rock for so long, not wanting to cause him pain. "No Daniel, don't you see that if Martins blood now has a different D.N.A. from that which he was born with, saliva and hair samples will all have changed as well. That being the case, unfortunately that particular D.N.A. route is closed to us".

While she has been talking, Daniel's body language changes, from that of being upright and confident to gradually that of slumping in defeat, while his face conveys his shock at her news. Seeing the haunted look on his face Ella takes him in her arms, the mother comforting her son after so many years. "Try not to be sad Daniel, if it's any consolation to you I still think that Martin is your real father, I just can't prove it, that's all".

It is several minutes before he can compose himself before asking "tell me again mum the reasons that you believe that to be so".

He watches her closely waiting for her reply, afraid of her reaction, but to his amazement she remains perfectly calm and composed. This isn't the way he has expected her to be.

She is quiet for a heartbeat before she replies, saying" Oh Daniel, I think that I have always known; there were too many things for it to be anyone else; the similarities between Martin and you for a start, the paintings for another, the wound on his leg that I have not told you about which is in the very same spot where your father broke his in Italy".

"I must admit that when you told me that the D.N.A. result was negative the first time, I was totally distraught and every time that I thought of it after that I would brace myself and try to ignore my feelings, but however hard I tried, I kept coming back to what my heart and intuition was telling me".

She then goes on to tell him about the strange things that Martin had said when they viewed the cottage in Bull Hill. "He seemed to know everything about the cottage Daniel. I can tell you it was eerie to say the least".

"But ignoring all of that, the one singular indisputable reason is the fact that I feel exactly the same way about him as I did when he left for the last time during the war. I felt it as soon as I met him that summer after all those years. Although his injuries scarred him so dreadfully, they couldn't hide the man that he always was"

Daniel interrupts Ella abruptly. "But what are we going to do Mum: do we let him know even though we can't prove it"?

"Why nothing of course, because I think the shock would be too much for him after all this time. I think it is best left to let sleeping dogs lie. He has gone through enough already. I am happy Daniel, even though I have thought for a long time that Martin was in fact Richard, but what I can't understand is why he was not recognised by the authorities all those years ago. He said that he had his identification tag in his hand when he was found, so what happened"?

"Well I have given that a lot of thought mum, and I know from talking to him that when they found him after the explosion, he was completely naked. This is something that I have had experience of seeing when I have reported from various war zones; the blast simply rips the clothes from the person if they are standing too close. Now, Martin also told me that he was on guard with another soldier and that they were together, near the road under trees".

"Putting two and two together, what I think happened was that as the blast hit them, Martin, or Dad as we now know him to be, perhaps instinctively threw his arm out to pull the other soldier out of the line of fire and grabbed his I.D. tag from around the other persons neck where they were normally kept. Dad must have been partially behind a tree, but Martin Kemp, who I can only think was the second guard, took the brunt of the blast. Dad's own tag must have been blown off with his clothes. As you can see if this is the way that it happened the authorities would have naturally thought that the survivor was Martin Fleet".

"Whatever we do Daniel, I have no intention of telling him. Does anyone else know about any of this? Does Theresa or the children know"?

"No, I haven't said anything to them because I wanted to talk to you first".

"You know Daniel, sometimes I think that Martin knows. Not all of it, just bits that he seems to recognise, things that trigger his memory, like those at the cottage, or the paintings, but even more than that is the fact that he returned here to this village. Something must have caused him to recognise this place, even though it lay deep in his subconscious. I don't believe that it was a coincidence Daniel. Penny has told me that when she and Martin first came to Chadlington when they were sight-seeing around the area, Martin had on several occasions corrected her when she took the wrong road, so although I am sure that he wasn't fully aware, his subconscious memory must have been telling him the way. Although he has no recognisable memory from before the explosion, some things seem to lie dormant and get triggered occasionally by certain events. It may be something quite innocuous, like his watercolour paintings, or knowing the way here from Oxford or even seeing the cottage for the first time after so many years. Whatever the cause, it is there struggling to manifest itself to him".

"As far as anyone else is concerned I think that it would be best to say nothing to them until we know more. With the best will in the world it is easy to say the wrong thing, quite accidentally, at the wrong time and to the wrong person. I will speak to you soon Daniel, once I have decided what is the best thing to do".

Daniel is silent for a while before saying mysteriously "O.K. mum, that's fair enough; I won't say anything, but I have just had an idea that I need to follow up on, so I need to telephone Penny before we go".

CHAPTER 41.

REVELATIONS.

Whatever decision Ella might have made, the choices are taken from her in the most tragic of circumstances in early May, when Martin suffers another attack of acute bronchitis. It comes, as it always does, completely out of the blue when he wakes one morning having difficulty breathing. The doctor attends and issues another prescription of antibiotics, with the warning that there is little else that he can do, other than to give him pain relief in the form of diamorphine, if the antibiotics fail to clear up the infection. Ella knows that if that happens, Martin's chances of recovery are miniscule.

During the first few days Martin seems to be making a good recovery, but as time goes on it becomes apparent that the antibiotics are losing the battle, giving Ella a sense of helplessness and despair. She calls the doctor again who takes one look at his patient, before telling her that there is nothing else that he can do other than to relieve Martin's suffering and asks for her permission to do so. By this time Martin is in a semi-coma, drifting in and out of consciousness. Ella wants desperately to say no, but seeing her husband fighting for every breath, a dry rattling sound coming from his throat, his pallor a mixture of grey and slate white, she relents, not wanting to extend his pain any further.

"Yes" she whispers to the doctor who is looking sympathetically at her, aware of the terrible torment that she is experiencing.

"Very well my dear" and then as if to comfort her "you are doing the right thing you know. I will give him an injection now and send round a nurse to administer another tomorrow morning, then again in the evening. If you think that he might want to see any friends or relatives I would suggest that you arrange it as soon as possible".

Hearing Martin's future told to her so bluntly, Ella is faced with the inevitable and sinks to her knees sobbing uncontrollably.

The doctor bends down and helps her up, placing her in an armchair, before saying "I'm so sorry my dear, but I think that it's best that you know. It will give you and others a small window to say your farewells.

Once the doctor has left, Ella picks up the telephone to speak to Daniel.

* * *

Theresa, Daniel and their children arrive in the late afternoon on the same day. Ella meets them at the door hugging them all, the last of whom is Daniel who is already in tears. Taking Ella to one side Daniel says "can you spare a minute Mum" to which she replies, aware of the intensity of his mood "of course, let's go into the study.

Once inside Daniel cannot contain himself for another nano second and blurts out "You remember the last time we spoke about the negative result between Martin and my blood test; well if you remember I said that at the time that I needed to speak to Penny, the reason being that I had a sudden inspiration that she might know where one of his original paintings was, that he had definitely painted before he contracted leukaemia and if she did, there was a reasonable chance that his original D.N.A. would be on it.

He pauses a moment for dramatic effect, the reason for which is all too apparent to Ella. "Well we got lucky mum" he says, his voice rising with every word. "After we had finished our conversation Penny sat down and tried to think of where just such a painting might be, before eventually having a Eureka moment".

"Ella is beside herself by now. "But what and where did she come up with" she says, her voice trembling, her body shaking visibly.

"It was so simple really" says Daniel, "she asked her father, who, as luck would have it had one of Martin's first pieces that he ever did, which her Dad had bought as an investment and was still hanging on his wall at his home. There was no trace of any D.N.A. on the frame but we managed to get some off of the painting, and guess what? I got the results back from the laboratory this morning which confirm that Martin is Richard, my dad and your husband. I am beyond being happy mum and I am sure you are too. It's such a damn shame that we have only found out now when it is too late".

Seeing her son in such pain Ella move swiftly to assuage his suffering.

"Try not to worry Daniel; your father wouldn't want you to see you like this. Remember he respects the man you have become and even though he doesn't know the real relationship between the two of you, he already loves you as if you are his son".

As mother and son stand and hug each other, Daniel, who is now more at ease with himself asks "can I go up and see him mum. Is he awake"?

"Well he comes in and out of consciousness son. If you are lucky you might catch him at the right moment".

Daniel leaves engulfed in tears again, to go to see his father. Once he has left Theresa says to Ella "I have never seen him like this. He has been distraught ever since this morning after the post arrived. He must have got so close to Martin when he was doing the documentary"

Ella realises with a jolt that Daniel has still not revealed Martin's true identity to his family and what is even worse that it is her fault for not letting him tell his family.

"Theresa my dear I have something to tell you that will make you see why Daniel is so upset. The reason that you don't know is my fault entirely, because I forbade him to tell anyone. The truth is you see my dear that we recently discovered that Martin is in reality my first husband Richard Thornton, Daniel's father".

Before she can continue Theresa, who is standing dumb struck, suddenly finds her voice and chimes in "That is incredible, but how is that possible".

Tenderly Ella relates the circumstances, including all of her and Daniel's suspicions until finally revealing the irrefutable proof of the D.N.A. results.

"I just wish that he had told me" cries Theresa breaking down in tears.

"Please don't blame him my dear. When we first suspected it, I didn't want to tell anyone in case that it got back to Martin. I didn't know how he would react if he discovered the truth. The shock might have been too much and I couldn't have coped with that".

At that moment Daniel returns saying that Martin is in a deep sleep. Looking at Theresa's tear stained face he realises that Ella has told her about his father, but before he can say anything she is in his arms, sobbing and crying "I am so sorry Daniel, but now that I know I understand everything; your intensity about getting the documentary finished as quickly as you did, the way you spoke about Martin and the awe in which you held him".

They sit together on the sofa while Daniel relates all the little niggling reasons that had first drawn him and his mother to question Martin's origins.

***

In the evening Rachel and Fred arrive after being summoned by Ella, who first tells them about Martin's prognosis. They are shocked, even though they know how fragile his health is. But this news is as of nothing, once Ella reveals Martin's true identity and how they discovered it".

"Oh My God, that is unbelievable and to think that he has been here all this time and we never knew" cries Rachel hugging her sister." Although now I know, there were little things, his manner of speaking and the way he held himself. He even told me once that he would like a motorcycle; that should have rung bells, but it didn't. I wish that we had known earlier, we could have done so much more".

"That's just the point Rach, I only knew for sure recently and I was frightened that if he found out that the shock might be too much for him".

They all sit talking, reliving both Richard's life when they knew him and his subsequent life since, while Ella explains about the various signs that made her realise who Martin really was.

"But really before any one thing gave me reason to question him, the way I felt when I met him and when we were together, was enough for me to know".

* * *

Rachel and Fred go upstairs to say their farewells to their brother-in-law, who is still either asleep or in a coma. They leave after first getting Ella to promise to send for them if anything happens.

Daniel and his family are staying for however long it takes, wanting to pay their last respects to Martin, but also to support Ella through her inevitable trauma.

Wanting to say goodnight to Martin, Daniel and Theresa, together with Richard junior and Molly go upstairs to say goodnight to the man that Daniel now thinks of as his father, Richard, who appears to be still asleep although restless, moving his arms from his side to his chest.

Not wanting to disturb him any more than necessary, Daniel kisses him on the forehead and whispers "sleep well Dad, we love you very much".

Getting no response, they say their farewells before making for the door. Just as Daniel reaches it, he hears Martin cough before saying in a half-drowsed state "did you take Bonny for her walk yet Dan."

Dan stands astonished, but before he can reply he sees that Martin has again relapsed into a deep sleep.

Ella is the last to go up to join her husband, needing to be with him as long as possible. Not bothering to undress she lies down next to him on the bed, soothing his tortured body as she runs her hands over his arms while whispering words of encouragement. She eventually begins to nod off, but just as she is at the point of sleep Martin mumbles something in his delirium.

Not hearing him properly she asks "What was that my love" to which she receives the reply "goodnight Princess".

When she wakes in the early hours of the morning, she can tell immediately that Martin, or Richard as she prefers to now think of him, has left her for the second and last time. She lies quietly embracing him for a while before gently kissing his brow, then going to tell her son that his father has died.

CHAPTER 42.

DANIEL'S DOCUMENTARY.

Chadlington Church is full to overflowing as friends, relatives, local villagers as well as many other people, who only knew of Martin as a famous artist, come to pay their last respects.

Many of them stand outside in the graveyard and listen to the service via a sound system that Daniel has had installed.

Daniel gives the eulogy lavishing praise, onto the person who the world thinks of is his father in law. He and Ella have discussed the situation with each other and agreed that it would be best at this stage not to say anything about Martin's true identity. The fuss and repercussions that would emanate from the revelation would be more than they could cope with emotionally. But they both agree that they will let it become public knowledge after a period, once things have settled down.

Ella forces herself to put on a brave face, knowing that Martin, or Richard would have wanted it that way. She has already arranged for him to be buried in a plot in the churchyard close to her parents, which has room for her to be with him when her time comes.

Three hymns are sung and as the service concludes Ella has arranged for "We'll meet again "to be played as the cortege leaves the church, a tribute to the times when Richard had left to go to fight for his country and which became a favourite for both of them.

* * *

On the sixth of June, forty-nine years after D-DAY, Ella, Daniel, Rachel and their families form a half circle round the television in the living room at The Manor House, anxiously waiting for Daniel's documentary on Second World War and the invasion of France in 1944 to be shown. Ella sits directly opposite the T.V., further back from those flanking her on either side.

As it is introduced Daniel is shown on screen saying "In the next hour I will be attempting to show you, from people who were there, just what it was like to have taken part in the landings on D-Day the sixth of June 1944 and beyond to the ultimate surrender of Germany in 1945".

"As you will hear from them in their own words, nothing about it was heroic or orderly in any way to that which was subsequently shown on reports at the time. In fact, all that was shown at the time were maps showing the progress that the forces were making. But their own experiences didn't reflect any of that, because all that they saw was from their own little bubble, which usually was chaotic and confusing, with comrades being slaughtered beside them.

Their main motivation was in fact fear, the alternative to not succeeding being too dreadful to contemplate".

Archival film is being shown of D-Day and other battles that happened during this period with Daniel's words voicing them over. Then one by one he introduces men who had been there, interviewing them individually so that they can tell their stories. As it progresses, Daniel's journalistic skills extract each individual's version of events from their own perspective, their fears and the close bonding with comrades that became so strong that when necessary they would make the ultimate sacrifice for each other.

This was so much more personal to people watching than the usual alternative, which was of the story being told by a historian who only describes the events in terms of the bigger picture, but to the men concerned there was no bigger picture, because to them it was all up close and personal. Viewers could relate more easily to Daniels version of events.

The documentary has by now been running for over forty minutes and it is at this point that Daniel comes on screen again saying "I would like now to introduce you to someone who may be familiar to many of you viewers, whose experiences of this period are worth including. He in fact didn't see all that much because he was severely burned and wounded on 10th August 1944 and took no further part in the hostilities. He is in fact the famous English artist Mr Martin Fleet".

"Before I go any further I have to confess my own interests here because Martin became my step-father last year when he married my mother, but seeing the results of the terrible incident in which he was involved and hearing his story made it essential for me to include it. As you will hear Martin did not recall anything about the incident because of the trauma he suffered. It was only when I found his war records at The National Archives that confirmed what he had been told after he was injured.

But enough of me let Martin tell you in his own words. I should warn you that his speech is slurred and difficult to understand at times, another result of his injuries"

The programme then shows Daniel's interview with Martin, at which point Ella sobs quietly into a handkerchief.

Once the interview is finished, Daniel tells the audience "There is one more fact that I can reveal about Martin who I came to know and love over the short period that I knew him. It happened like this; my curiosity about where and how my own father died had always been a mystery, both to my mother and me, so after I found Martin's war record, I began to look for my fathers, Richard Thornton".

"Once I had found them, what they had to tell me was quite frankly astonishing, because they revealed that my father was killed on the same day and at the same place as Martin was injured, just outside Falaise. Not only that, but as you have heard from Martin's interview, he was the only survivor on that fateful day. I thought that this was a coincidence of biblical proportions and felt that it needed more investigation; but where and how to look, I had no idea. That is until my mother began to notice things which made me even more suspicious. Like for example, why Martin had made the decision to move to Chadlington where my mother and father lived and I was brought up. She also noticed little things, like the way he and I used our hands when talking, flourishing them everywhere to illustrate a point.

Some of his oil paintings were of the area local to Chadlington, but amazingly a number of them were of the same views that my own father had painted in watercolour fifty years previously".

"None of these things on their own were conclusive and I am not suggesting for one second that Martin was aware that any of the things that he did gave us cause for suspicion, but they were enough when put together for me to try to find out more, so I took D.N.A samples from Martin without his knowledge I have to say, not wanting to cause stress unnecessarily to him.

I think that you can probably guess the rest, but I am going to tell you anyway because I think that it was without doubt the best moment of my life, (after marrying my wife of course), when I received the results which proved conclusively that Martin and Richard were one and the same person, my father and my mother's husband, although she married him twice in the process".

"Unfortunately, Martin died within a month or so of us finding out, although we were agreed that the shock of telling him would be too much for him. Sadly then, he died without knowing, but from things that he said, I think that subconsciously his memory would occasionally reveal things to him of his earlier life. It must have been like peering through a dense fog which suddenly clears for a brief moment and then almost immediately returns".

"But the rest of us had time to come to terms with it and although it was not long enough, we made the most of the short time that we all had together".

* * *

The television fades at this point and the credits begin to roll with the music of Vera Lynn singing "We'll meet again".

During the time that the documentary has been running Ella has been mentally reviewing and reliving her life or lives rather, with Richard. In her mind's eye she sees a series of fleeting images of various stages of their life together, dancing, locked together as they circle the floor intoxicated by the intimate smell and feel of each other, not needing to speak, just content at being in the moment. This is followed by a kaleidoscope of events, of them making their home together, first at the flat in Oxford and then afterwards at the cottage in the village; of the love and laughter they shared before Daniel was born, which was even more magical when he came into their lives. Next came the days out with Richard sketching and painting, while she and Daniel played games until he was finished, when they then ate the picnic that she had prepared.

As the threat of war approaches and then becomes reality, her visitations become extreme, fear on the one hand, mixed with a heightened sense of love and longing as Richard at first leaves to join the army and then returns each time relatively unscathed.

The images she experiences are so real that finally Richard is immediately standing in front of her, dressed just as he was on the very first night that they met. As she waits spellbound, almost in a vacuum, completely unaware of her surroundings, he beckons for her to join him, whispering "It's time now my princess" at which point she moves eagerly towards him.

* * *

As he turns the television off Daniel says "well the world knows who my father was now and what is more just how fine a man he was". Then addressing Ella "what do you think mum, did I do him justice"?

Getting no reply, he looks across only to see Ella with a serene peaceful look on her face apparently sleeping; but as he looks again, he becomes more concerned, so much so that he stands up and approaches her. He first shakes her and calls her name, hoping to wake her, but there is still no response.

By this time each and every one present are becoming concerned. Daniel attempts to take her pulse but after trying for several minutes he at last cries out in pain and desperation "will someone please call an ambulance as a matter of urgency" before breaking down completely and screaming in a voice of total loss "oh nooooooooooooooooo"!!!

EPILOGUE.

Ella is laid to rest at Chadlington Church two weeks later in the same plot as Martin, or Richard, as she came to think of him, the man she married twice.

Chadlington has turned out to pay their respects to one of its own, most of whose lives have been enriched by her in one way or another. Some of them sit in the church, while others who cannot get in stand outside and listen to the eulogy to her over the public address system that Daniel has rigged up.

In a broken voice filled with emotion Daniel summarises his mother's life, with its highs and lows, from her dancing which eventually led to her meeting Richard, to the shock of losing him after only a few short years. Then moving on he relates her successful career, while paying tribute to her sister Rachel's support and influence. He tells his audience of funny stories growing up, due inevitably to his mother's impish nature.

Finally, he pays tribute to her for her contribution as a grandmother to his children "times that they will cherish forever, for her laughter and never-ending love when they were young and later to her wise counsel as they grew older".

Both grandchildren take readings from the Scriptures and finally the service is finished, with the organ playing "we'll meet again" as Ella's coffin is carried out to her resting place in the graveyard.

Theresa comforts her distraught husband and children as they stand at the plot throwing earth down on Ella's coffin as the vicar relates "earth to earth, ashes to ashes, dust to dust": but she knows that Daniel is strong and in time will come to terms with his mother's death, understanding the inevitability and the natural order of life, while she wonders idly if he will want to move back to the village to live in The Manor House, which he now owns. She thinks that if this were to happen nothing could have pleased Ella more.

Manufactured by Amazon.ca
Bolton, ON